Gifts of the Wild

A Woman's Book of Adventure

From the editors of
Adventura Books

Illustrations by Clare Conrad

Seal Press

Seal Press
3131 Western Avenue, Suite 410
Seattle, WA 98121
sealprss@scn.org

Cover design and photograph by Trina Stahl
Text design and composition by Clare Conrad
Printed on recycled paper

Library of Congress Cataloging-in-Publication Data
Gifts of the wild: a woman's book of adventure / from the editors of Adventura books.
1. Outdoor recreation for women—Literary collections. 2. Wilderness survival—Literary collections. 3. American prose literature—Women authors. 4. Short stories, American—Women authors. 5. Outdoor life—Literary collections. 6. Adventure stories, American.
PS648.O88G54   1998   796.5'082—dc21   98-6000
ISBN 1-58005-006-9

Printed in the United States of America

10   9   8   7   6   5   4   3   2

Credits appear on page 338, which constitutes a continuation of the copyright page.

Distributed to the trade by Publishers Group West
In Canada: Publishers Group West Canada, Toronto, Ontario
In the U.K. and Europe: Airlift Book Company, Middlesex, England
In Australia: Banyan Tree Book Distributors, Kent Town, South Australia

Ichsc Clark

Contents

Foreword

When I backpack or climb a mountain, I believe each journey to be a lifetime in miniature. Like a masterful novel, each trip has a beginning, a motivation, conflict, hardship, struggle, growth and resolution. From character change comes revelation, sometimes subtle, sometimes grand. Such is the nature of the stories you hold in your hands. Reading this collection of diverse souls reacting to diverse situations is like befriending, risking with and having heart-to-heart talks with thirty-four different people. One is richer for it.

The wilderness and the flora and fauna encountered are as much the characters as any human—Patagonia, Ireland, Nepal, the Minnesota Boundary Waters, a camp in Rhode Island, the Siskyous of Oregon, the coast of British Columbia, roadsides in the Deep South, dark woods on a Washington island, intimate neighborhoods and even inner-city San Francisco. When I recognized my own sacred spaces, there was a gush of familiarity. Better yet, I encountered strange new lands or places beyond my own arbitrary limits. I did not breathe all the way through Susanna Levin's Rollerblade through downtown San Francisco nor skiing with Lucy Bledsoe down a high Sierra bowl alone in the backcountry—alongside an avalanche! One woman's fear is another's exhilaration.

I was pleasantly surprised to discover that the boundary-breaking struggles which "allowed" women into the most remote and challenging wilderness was almost complete. In an elegant nod toward one of the women who broke the barriers, Linda Lewis celebrates Ernestine Bayer, "rowing's matriarch," in "Etes-Vous Prêts?" Deborah Abbott helps break the barrier for handicapped women rowing whitewater rafts. Ann Linnea paddles around Lake Superior, becoming the first woman to circumnavigate that body of water by sea kayak. And judging by the number of flies whipping through this text, fly fishing and its pursuant camaraderie of fish camp, is wide open to women.

Age is no boundary at all. Betty Wetzel, nearing eighty, rides a horse through the Bob Marshall Wilderness in Montana, shocking her family by surviving—and enjoying—the sometimes grueling ten-day pack trip. At seventy-one, Ruth Jacobs swims illegally in luxury swimming pools or in laughing, wide open lakes and oceans. Jean Gould celebrates her fiftieth birthday on a trek through the Anapurna Mountain range of Nepal.

We are radically redefining age. Recently, on a hike through the North Cascades with eleven other people, I discovered that the youthful, strong women I befriended were all over fifty. In the nineteen-fifties, we thought that women were old by their late forties. If they had been Anasazi women, they would have been wise elders—had they lived to turn forty.

Young women no longer blink an eye about rock climbing with their male counterparts. I found Susan Fox Rogers's story of bouldering with her best male friend as teenagers absolutely enthralling. Sue Harrington is miserable, scared and cold as she climbs with her husband up Saint Exupery in Patagonia. The tension between the two differently skilled climbers builds, yet in the end, compromise and a glorious sunrise turns tension into romance. Through Kathleen Gasperini, we plunge again into that delight-terror of being out of the parental gaze and on one's own—while surfing with dolphins.

Women enter the wilderness both alone and with companions. Women *are* different from men in the manner in which they are embedded in family. A favorite theme of mine, the woman rediscovering her own identity after thirty years of child-raising, home-tending and husband-maintenance ripples through these writers: "In order to give my life meaning, I defined myself as both heart and anchor of my family. It was inconceivable to me then, that we—husband, wife, son, daughter—could break apart. But after many years, the inconceivable happened. . . ." (Nan Watkins, "Writing the Wind.") Soon we find her walking the wild cliffs of Ireland and Wales, sitting neck deep in rivers and creating her own, beautiful music.

The most breathtaking parenting of all explores the rocky, treacherous fjords and inlets of British Columbia in the form of M. Wylie Blanchet and five children on a small boat, the *Caprice*. She leads her children up precipitous slopes next to waterfalls, across bear trails, in front of a she-bear cave, and through dangerous tidal currents as if these were unremarkable activities.

The firm relationships which women weave in the wild are joyously celebrated by Lin Sutherland, who narrates her mother's summer ritual of packing her seven daughters in a DeSoto for a long drive from Austin to Charleston, camping and fishing along the way. Pam Houston casts her flies at two in the morning in a freezing north Michigan river with a "bunch of male poets"—and then guest-lectures to classes all the next day. Mary Ellis returns to the simplicity of childhood as she watches Jane, her sister and best friend, cast her fishing rod in the quiet fog of early morning.

Judith McDaniel broaches a powerful experience close to my own heart, yet one I never considered as subject-matter for a book: leading Girl Scouts into the wilderness. The character transformation of these adolescent girls is downright inspiring: "Out here the girls seem to me very independent and capable. They fix and eat dinner with no complaints and little direction from Sally and me. They are considerate of one another. . . . They all seem to be slowly sloughing off bits of that 'civilized' behavior I found so irritating back at camp." (Judith McDaniel, "Scouts on the Saranac.")

After a reading I gave from *Women in Wilderness*, coauthored with

Ann Zwinger, a person I had offended rushed forward to say, "You wouldn't ever find a book entitled *Men in Wilderness*, would you?!" I was taken aback: it was a good question. After centuries of being confined inside houses, tied to the kitchen fires and defined by men in certain cultures, women are discovering the joy and novelty of being alone in wild places, if only the woods seen out the kitchen window.

These essays buzz with the joy of solitude. With Gabrielle Daniels we wander solitarily through deep woods in the shoes of a black urban woman. Alice Evans climbs Mount Elijah solo, ticked off with her child and husband, then returns calm and reinvigorated. P. K. Price prepares her readers for the risks of going solo, warning, "There is danger in going alone. There is more danger in not going." Closest to home, Karen Monk meditates and prays turning the four directions on her Silva compass. Her companion, Abbey the German shepard, ". . . is a practitioner of some primal ecstatic religion." Callie, the cat, is a Buddhist, and Karen is the local Methodist minister.

Monk's essay opens this book of wisdoms with her own humorous nod toward diversity: "Ours is an interfaith household. . . ." This is an interfaith, interbelief, intercharacter, interphilosophy and inclusive collection of lives. And what could be more appropriate than women finding gifts in the wild? In wilderness, those positive character traits we have developed through years of evolution are intensified, leap forward in time-lapse motion. Through wild places, flora and fauna, and physical challenge, we befriend, learn, teach, laugh and love. We recreate ourselves in that masterful novel—our own story.

Susan Zwinger
Whidbey Island, Washington
December 1997

GIFTS OF THE WILD

Birch

December 24-January 20

Introduction

In 1925, Lady Clara Coulton Rogers Vyvyan and her friend Gwen Dorian Smith left the comforts of home and hearth in England to embark on a paddling trip on rivers leading from the Arctic Ocean into the Yukon basin of Alaska. Neither of them had any previous canoeing experience. At times accompanied by guides, at other times wholly on their own, the two women paddled through some of the most remote and spectacular terrain on earth. Their uncommon adventure, which Lady C. C. Vyvyan later wrote about in her travel memoir *Arctic Adventure*, is recounted in the anthology of women's canoeing stories, *Rivers Running Free*. Included in this collection is a passage which describes a moment of wonder and its personal reverberations for the author:

> *There are some feelings too deep for tears, some thoughts that may not endure the captivity of words, some memories that are set apart among life's enduring treasures. I can shut my eyes now, dismiss all that has happened in thirty-five years and recapture the silence of Loon Lake. We were two middle-aged women travelling for pleasure, disheveled and unwashed, with tired feet and tired bodies, but I think as we stood on the shores of the lake, gazing down at the reflected mountains, listening to the silence that was almost audible, we must have experienced what the Saints describe as ecstasy.*

Finding a moment of silent wonder in the outdoors amidst the hectic whirl of modern life can be a difficult endeavor. The hum of our daily routine is often too loud and insistent—phones ringing, children tugging, work beckoning—to allow us much pause. And yet pause we must, for it is in those moments when we connect with the wilderness that we begin to know ourselves in body and spirit.

Whether we push beyond our limits on a month-long rafting adventure or find revelation and clarity walking late at night beneath a starry sky, our lives can be immeasurably deepened with each encounter with the outdoor world.

Like a bountiful tree that bears fruit year after year, nature is endlessly generous. Its gifts often appear as revelations, quiet and slow or sudden and all-encompassing. In wilderness, away from the rote of the everyday, we are challenged by new experiences and open ourselves to other people and to our own emotions. We turn to the outdoors in search of many things—physical adventure and spiritual enlightenment, unencumbered freedom and deep-rooted connection.

It was with this in mind that we set out to publish a book that would capture on the page the many ways that the transformative power of wild places can inform us and sustain us, how we as women might find new meaning in our lives through nature's untamed and unshakeable rhythms. By presenting a selection of women's outdoor literature we hope to explore the myriad ways we can learn from our wilderness encounters—and turn such knowledge into guideposts for our everyday existence.

In this book we have collected literary works by thirty-four women who have been touched and transformed by their outdoor adventures—from trekking in Nepal to paddling Lake Superior—and who have written about them with insight and eloquence. All of the selections are taken from a series we have published at Seal Press, called Adventura Books, which specifically explores the outdoor experience from a woman's point of view. This series celebrates the substantial, but often invisible, tradition of outdoorswomen: women who embrace adventure and refuse to be relegated to the sidelines.

Encompassing anthologies as well as single-author works, the Adventura series has helped change the genre of outdoor writing—literary terrain once staked out and charted primarily by male authors.

These writings reward us with a wealth of women's insights and a rich variety of experiences—from high-flying adventure tales to passionate observations of wilderness glory.

We have organized the writings into a cycle of twelve themes which comprise important aspects of our lives as women. Each section contains several selections exploring a particular theme, a way in which our lives are enriched by wilderness. Some sections describe how our outdoor adventures prepare us for leading our lives in new ways, with greater joy or courage or independence, for example. Other sections focus on the ways we look to wilderness to feed body and soul, to give us solace or grace. Still others delineate how our relationships with those around us—whether friends, mothers, fathers, children, or animals—are enriched and illuminated in the outdoor arena. A section entitled "Protecting the Earth" reminds us of our responsibilities to this planet, of our role as stewards to a fragile home. A final section reflects on the wisdom, sometimes hard-earned, and joy of growing to be an older, vital woman, demonstrating that wilderness adventure is not solely the province of the young.

We chose twelve themes because of the deep connections of nature's cycles to women: As we move through the book's sections we are reminded of the moon's monthly passages, the progression of season to season through the course of one year. We have illustrated each section using the Celtic tree calendar, which designates a specific tree for each phase of the moon. We were drawn to this calendar because of its age-old, pre-Christian symbolism of nature's mystery and abundance, and because of our own abiding love for trees, which are a constant and cherished reminder of nature's grace. The natural cycles of trees—the shedding and regrowth of leaves and needles, branches and bark—like the rhythms found throughout the wilderness, remind us of our own need for periodic rebirth and offer both a model and symbol of life's remarkable capacity for renewal.

It is our hope that readers will find in the voices and perspectives of these women writers both entertainment and knowledge, something enduring and precious to carry along in life after the last page is turned. All of the writers presented here demonstrate a deep understanding of the power of wilderness. Though they seize their moments of pause in countless and sometimes unexpected ways, they share an eagerness to explore uncharted territory—both physical and personal.

We are greatly indebted to all those individuals who contributed to the books from which these writings have been drawn, and we honor their significant and lasting achievements. At the end of the book we have listed information on the Adventura series for further reading and enjoyment.

Lastly we salute and give thanks to the wilderness around us, to the wild places which shape our lives and destinies. To respect and preserve such places is the gift we must always give back.

Faith Conlon, Ingrid Emerick, Jennie Goode, editors
Seattle, Washington
December 1997

I

LIVING WITH GRACE

Gift of Serenity

Rowan

January 21-February 17

Karen A. Monk

Spirit Walk

Outside my study window a tufted titmouse enthusiastically sorts through the bin of the plexiglass feeder, splashing seed shells into the forsythia. The bird's energy is at once compelling and mesmerizing. I save the document on my computer screen and look over to see her finish her feeder dance, then take wing. I am left with the abandoned window to contemplate. The window is framed with shelves of books: Henry David Thoreau and Alice Walker, Lao Tzu and Margaret Atwood, all keeping odd company on the walnut shelves. For all their differences, these books are all witnesses to creation and its sacred source. Beyond the books, the window and the forsythia lie the sugar maples and hemlocks of the Catskill Mountains. To touch the heart of the mountains—to bury my face in the mossy earth—is to touch that sacred source that breathes under the words of all the poets and philosophers.

I make my home in a small town in these mountains. Besides the tufted titmouse and myself, the town is home to a couple hundred residents. The heart of the town consists of two small general stores, a firehouse, a post office (whose accessibility ramp is longer than the building is wide), a Methodist church, and an Odd Fellows and Rebekah's lodge. To complete the cast, there are our guardians and watchers buried in the hillside meadow of Tongore Cemetery.

I share my home in Tongore with an eighty-pound German shepherd, Abbey, and an assertive calico cat, Callie. Ours is an interfaith household: Abbey is a practitioner of some primal ecstatic religion, Callie is a Buddhist, and I'm the local Methodist minister. On this day, as the titmouse has returned to play in the feeder, Abbey patiently watches me. In her eyes, in the deep darkness of her open face, I see that she is praying to *Gitchi Manitou*, the Great Spirit. She is asking for divine intervention. She is waiting for those magic words to take shape in my thoughts: "Let's go for a walk."

Abbey's petition has been heard. She is fidgety with excitement, though she obediently sits as the leash is snapped into place. Still and detached, Callie watches us from the window. Then we're off—across Route 213, through the church parking lot and over the broken gate. I set Abbey free to dance and twirl and run ahead of me down the overgrown abandoned quarry railway that will lead us into the heart of the woods.

Here, Abbey will not heel, sit or stay. I won't ask it of her. We are both cut free from our domestic lives, and give over to the instinctual. As Abbey chases invisible trails of scent through the broken leaves, something is nurtured in her—something fiercely canine, carnivore and wild. Walking behind her, I am stripped by the earth, the stones and the trees. Entering this sacred and primeval space, all the illusions and pretensions of living with trappings of human community drop away. We are simply present to the "Great I Am."

In the village beyond these woods, I am clothed with expectations: a silk blouse for a woman, a quilted cloak for a neighbor, a damask stole—the "yoke of obedience"—for a priest. They are layered across my shoulders like garments of glory and protection. But they are also heavy and scratchy and ill fitting. And they are not a part of the original design of my creation from the dust and ash of the universe. With Abbey bounding and darting ahead of me, I drop these social roles, letting them bunch and gather at my feet, and emerge a naked soul bathed in *spiritus*, the wind, the breath of God.

The path into the woods is worn—originally from heavy carts carrying quarried stone that was built into a dam eighty years ago. A dozen villages were flooded to create a reservoir for New York City. Perhaps the exiled stone grieved upon leaving—a young friend of mine swears there is a sadness in the silent pit of the abandoned quarry. The path taken by the departing stone is used infrequently by neighbors on horseback or young men and their snowmobiles. The path begins in crushed stone, wades through blueberry bushes, then yields to a carpet of spongy green moss.

Abbey and I wander in the cool, moist passage beneath a canopy of hemlocks. We pass a tiny stream gurgling on our left and a giant fallen hardwood on our right. While the stream badgers the solemn hemlocks, I stop to touch the fallen tree. It is remarkably alive in its decomposing. I fancy I sense a pulse under my fingertips, as the tree gives its life over to new forms—moss and grub worms. The blond, damp splinters witness to surrender, to the yielding of life to life, and death to life. Receiving the gift of the tree, I bow and walk on.

As we walk, my breathing deepens, leaving my limbs tingling with the influx of oxygen. The breath opens me and shakes my dull senses until they are aroused. Every step I take echoes through my body like a drum cadence. My mind is awakening as the aroma of the evergreens floods in through my nostrils to fill the open spaces of my skull. It is as though the fragrance drives out before it all the clouds of the day's tasks.

Trotting ahead, Abbey has reached our destination, where she waits for me. She has come to the place where the hemlocks and mixed woods give way to sparse deciduous hardwoods. Among the roots of the hardwoods, patches of lichen-covered bluestone break open the earth, revealing its age. Above us the dancing leaves splash light on the rocks, the earth, and on Abbey's brown-and-black muzzle. This is a space alive with contrast and mystery.

The people who named these mountains *Onteora*—Land in Sky— brought their questions, existential and routine, to the sacred circle to seek its wisdom. In many cultures, the circle is the symbol for cycles of birth-death-rebirth. Having neither beginning nor end, the circle symbolizes eternity and unity. In counsel, the native peoples of this continent sat in a circle when decisions were made about the life of the community.

The sacred circle emerges wherever the power of the four directions converge, whether in human community or in the solitude of the forest. Particular places may focus and crystallize that power with unique clarity. The collective wisdom of native peoples tells us that each direction speaks with a particular voice, a particular viewpoint.

In these woods, Abbey and I have come to the perimeter of such a sacred circle. In this opening in the otherwise dense surroundings I have often been touched by great power. Here stands the great Teacher: this hemlock, this sheer rock face, these lichen.

Taking out my Silva compass, I walk into the clearing. In my hand, the needle bobs and twirls briefly in its casing. I know where north lies, but I need repeated confirmation. Stepping attentively, listening, I come at last to the right spot. Checking my compass, I find that, yes, there are four trees around me that mark precisely the four directions. As these four trees knit earth and sky, the circle is completed. I also note the presence of an altar of stone at the heart of this circle.

I have no special question for the circle today; I have only come to listen. Slipping the compass back into my pocket, I turn to face each direction. First the East, the place of the sunrise, of beginnings, of the spirit and of recurring epiphanies. Turning through the circle, the South speaks to the heart, to connections and boundaries within human community. Facing west, I see the sun has begun its imperceptible slide toward the horizon. The West, the place of fiery sunsets, is the place of magic and transformation. Finally, the North is the place of the mind and of cool clarity of thought. The points between the true directions nuance my experience, and the sky and earth orient this woman in the midst of the four directions.

Abbey leaves me and roams the perimeter of the clearing. Her instincts will prompt her to check on me from time to time, but she will not disturb my solitude without invitation.

Silently, I invoke the wisdom of the directions. Now comes the waiting. Taking a deep breath and exhaling slowly, I lie down on a large, flat stone nearest the western tree, my head pointing to the West. As I focus on my breathing and open my senses to the earth, wood, sky, stone, a mantra rises in my thoughts: "Not my will, but thine, Lord."

The circle speaks to me, sometimes in Christian language, sometimes Buddhist, sometimes Taoist. Often the circle speaks in a language of its own. Today the words are Christian—a prayer spoken by Jesus at a point of critical decision in his life.

My first response is to balk. After all, I am a feminist. And I am a survivor. I am a survivor of a Christian-fundamentalist journey in the Bible Belt South of my youth. I cringe at anything that reminds me of the call to obligatory, redemptive suffering as the way to the heart of God. It's not the words themselves that assault me. It is the layer of memory, the child who endured abuse because it would make her more like Christ. The child who had no will of her own because she was not allowed to set her own boundaries. The child who somehow survived and did find redemption in the face of suffering.

"Not my will, but thine, Lord." Jacob had his angel in the night from whom he wrestled a blessing. My accosting angel is this terribly orthodox whisper. I asked the circle, and she has spoken. In these sacred woods, I will wrest hope and meaning from these words, for they've come to me from the West, from the place where all is transformed. I begin repeating the prayer as a mantra, in rhythm with my breath.

As each breath moves in and out of me, the mantra takes root in my soul and the wisdom of the ancients blossoms. I realize that I cannot will myself to stop breathing. I am not in control of this life. I am not even in control of the simplest act of life, breathing. I need not try to be in control. I need only to let go and become a part of that which is pushing to flow through me. Let go into the stream. Let go.

Lying on this stone on state land, I understand. I do not control this life; I cannot control this earth. Nor can I possess it. Where I grew up, you could measure a person's worth by their assets, particularly by how much land they owned. This all seemed reasonable and natural to me. If you could fence the land and pay taxes on it, then of course it was yours. It wasn't until I was a graduate student living in New York City that I began to see the absurdity of thinking that one owned the land. In New York, I discovered that people could lease or buy airspace above a building or lot. Airspace?

But then, if it's ridiculous to think one can own airspace, is it not equally ridiculous to own the land? Lying here I realize that I don't possess the earth; yet she is mine to enjoy. I walk her moss-covered paths, breathe her sweet oxygenated concoctions and sweat and tumble with Abbey on her dusty breast. If anything, this earth owns me, for I have borrowed the matter from which I'm made from her sticks and grasses and clouds. Someday, she will reclaim this form, as she reclaims the fallen tree in the hemlock grove.

I know, too, all that is powerful and holy is here—breath and wind, stone and sky, trees and life. Here is God, the "Great I Am." If I flee this moment or fill it with fear and anxiety, I dishonor it, and miss a sweet touch of eternity. I will linger in this place for some timeless time, repeating the prayer, feeling the solid earth beneath my back and breathing the gentle incense of the woods.

The time comes for Abbey and me to return to our house and our feline housemate. Abbey leads the way, and I follow. The West has worked her magic; the earth has healed her creature. The prayer lingers with me, as each footfall repeats the even cadence over moss and stone: "not-my-will-but-thine-Lord-not-my-will-but-thine-Lord-not-my-will-but-thine. . . ."

We come to the broken gate in back of the church. The little pile of social expectations is lying right where I left them, at the threshold where the wild woods give way to the asphalt church parking lot with its rusty basketball hoop. I know that when I cross this threshold, they will clothe me again, that I may not appear naked in this post-Eden world. A soft cry floats above us. Looking up, I spot a red-tailed hawk, circling high above the church steeple, then drifting down over the post office. She does not have the manic joy of the titmouse; she is steady, and singular in focus.

I stand between the worlds in which each human must live, watching the minutest movements of her pinions, the occasional flap. It comes to me, as simple and unheralded as the breeze around us: This is the will of God—to sense the breath of the sun underneath you and to move in response to it. The witnesses on the bookshelf wait to confirm this revelation.

One more breath, one more prayer, and Abbey and I step across the nexus, her leash in place, her shoulder obediently by my knee.

Lorian Hemingway

Walk on Water for Me

I take fish personally, the way I have my life, like a sacrament. This is my body. Eat of it. This is my blood. Drink. I imagine this reverence is what they want of me. The alchemists made an eyewash (collyrium) of fish, believing it would bring omniscience. I've tried to envision the process: cooking the fish, as the alchemists instructed, until it "yellowed," mashing it into a crumbly pulp, mixing it with water and then filling the eyes with this paste so one might gaze with as much dimension as trout in a clear stream. But as with all things in alchemy it was the process that mattered, the final result never as important as the ritual preceding it.

Knowing fish is a process. I have been acquainting myself for forty years. To know fish you have to have been intimate, the way

the alchemists were. The first fish I ever caught was a baby bass net-
ted from a deep Mississippi ravine I lived near during summer. It was
my refuge, that ravine, a place of discovery, revealer of miracles, its
depth filled with a heavy current of reddish-brown water during the
spring floods, its clay bottom dried to a pockmarking of deep holes
by mid-July. I was tirelessly curious when I was young, bound inex-
tricably to all natural mysteries beyond four walls, nervous and
jumpy if made to sit too long indoors, recalcitrant once sprung. I'd
watched this particular fish for days, trapped in a pothole in the
ravine, swimming in a quick panic from one side to the other, instinctively seeking a tributary leading from its footwide prison. I
empathized, imagined myself locked in my room for days, dizzy and
breathless from ensuing claustrophobia, frantic enough to pull up the
flooring with my bare hands. I understood feeling trapped, my life
then nothing more than a crash course in how to escape.

After a few days the water in the pothole had diminished by half
and grew so thick with ravine mud that the fish hung motionless in
the ooze, its gills laboring for the oxygen it needed. On my knees I
stared into the hole, goldfish net in hand, thinking it was evil what I
was about to do, snatch a living creature from its habitat and bring
it, luckless, into my own. I remember the delicate, thin striping on
its flanks as I lifted it, unprotesting, from the muck, and how soft and
filmy the skin felt as I stroked a finger along his length. I remember,
too, how my heart raced as I dropped the fish into a jar, watched him
sink quickly and then just as quickly take his first breath in a new
world. Within moments he was moving through the jar as manically
as he had the pothole days before. I had given resurrection in a pint
of water, become God to a fish. Years later I would remember that
moment as one of grace.

Fish became my fascination, and began to appear in dreams, their shadows deep in dark water, cruising, fins breaking the surface from time to time, a teasing swirl of movement as I stood on shore with net or rod or hands poised to strike. In one dream I stood before a pool of monster fish with bare hands greedy, my fingertips singing the way a line does when it's pulled free from the spool. As I leaned forward, a shape would slide deliberately beneath my reach, and I would lunge into water that was dense and thick as oil, only to come up soaked and empty-handed.

I don't know now that the dreams had to do with catching fish, but rather with some unconscious, archetypal need. I have consulted Jung on this one for the obvious, loaded symbolism. I have even dreamt, in these later years, of Jung, standing atop the stone fortress of his tower at Bollingen, fly rod in hand, a wooden piscatorial carving dangling from his leader line. He smiles in the dream, proud of himself. He did say water is the unconscious and that fish are a Christ symbol. I deduce then, from these two boldly fitting pieces, that I am at times fishing for Jesus, or in some way, in recent dreams, dry-flying for Christ. I like the simplicity of it, the directness. I like that it speaks to Christian and Hedon alike.

But during those Mississippi summers I paid little attention to dreams, mesmerized then by a world filled with fish, snakes, turtles, toads and lizards, anything remotely amphibian. I progressed from netting bass to catfishing with a bobber and worm, frittering away entire days on the banks of muddy lakes, certain, always, that the fish lived dead center in the middle of the lake, assuming the notion that the truly elusive spend their time where we can never hope to reach them. To cast where they hid became my ambition, and once mastered I understood that fish went wherever they damned well pleased, unimpressed by my clumsy form hurling hooks into their midst, immune to my need to know them.

I had patience, the sort I suspect God has with people like me. It was nothing to be skunked for days on end. I lived in perpetual hope of seeing that wayward shimmy of the bobber, then the quick dip and tug that signaled I had made contact with aliens. At that time in my life this was my social interaction. I talked to the fish hidden deep in the ponds and streams I visited, trying to imagine what they saw beneath those mirrored surfaces and reasoned it was hunger and not stupidity that made them take bait so crudely hitched to an obvious weapon. Compassion surfaced. I pictured scores of starving fish grubbing for worms only to be duped into death by my slipshod cunning. When I'd reel them to shore I'd cry at what I'd done, at the sight of the hook swallowed to the hilt, at the flat, accusing eyes of the fish, and then I'd club them with a Coke bottle, the heavy green kind with the bottling company's name on the bottom. No one ever said there was another way to do it. In Mississippi, there was the hook, the worm and the bobber, a holy trinity on a hot day in August—low-maintenance fishing I call it now. My guilt was usually pushed aside by their quick death beneath the bottle, and eating what I had caught seemed to remove the shame considerably.

My favorite fishing hole—I look back on it now as Mississippi's version of Mecca—was a place that to this day I am certain only one other knew of, the landowner who'd barbwired it off and posted a huge, hand-painted sign along the fence—Warning: SNAKES. Roaming deep in a pine woods in rural Hinds County one summer afternoon, I came upon the pond, the edges of it rising in volcanic fashion from the otherwise flat land. I was accustomed only to ponds that were slipped like sinkholes into the surrounding pastureland, and as I made my way up the slight incline of earth, hands grasping the barbwire delicately, I beheld, not a rock quarry as I had expected, but instead a perfectly black pool of water, its dimensions no greater than those of an average swimming pool. At first I could not believe the color of the fish who were pushing to the surface, dozens of them, nosing one into another, their bodies as opalescent as pearls, and huge, their lengths dissolving into the shadow of the pond. I had never seen albino catfish, had never seen *any* white fish, and thought for a brief, illogical moment that they had been segregated from their darker mates simply because of their color. In Mississippi, then, it fit.

To have called this pond a fishing hole is misleading. I never actually fished its waters, too mesmerized by the cloudlike shapes that moved without sound through the deep pond, believing, beyond all fishing reason, that to catch them would bring the worst sort of luck. So I watched, alone in the woods with these mutants, some days prodding their lazy bodies with a hickory stick, which they rubbed against curiously, and on others merely counting the number of laps they made around the pond in an afternoon, hypnotized by the rhythm they made tracing one circle upon another.

The fish were as truly alien as my finest imaginings, and I became convinced they were telepathic, reading my thoughts with such ease I had no need to speak to them. I called these sojourns "visiting the fish gods," my treks to that mysterious water that had no business existing in dry woods, and took into adulthood the memory of them, as if they were a talisman, granting me privileges and luck in the fishing world others could only dream of.

As I grew older I began to think of fish as mine. I'd been in close touch with them long enough to develop something that I believed went beyond rapport and came, in time, to border on feudalism. Fishing became far more than sport or communion. It began to develop the distinct earmarkings of a life's goal. No longer content to watch and prod, no longer in command of patience, I lived to fish, becoming, in my own mind, a fishing czarina, my luck with rod, reel and bait phenomenal.

Holding true to my fundamentalist, country fishing ways, I began to gain a reputation for being the only person certain, on an outing, to catch fish. An attitude surfaced as rapidly as fish to my bait. Men were forced to regard me now, but warily, as I moved within their circles, trying always to outdo them. Gone was the solitary fishing of my childhood, the secret visits with fish gods. I had become competitive.

I cannot place the exact time when my fishing innocence turned streetwalker tough, when imagined power over the waters of childhood turned to a calculating game, but I suspect it was when I discovered that good-old-boy fishing and beer went hand-in-hand.

For several years I was flat-out on the gonzo stage of fishing, where any method of felling fish was acceptable. I never batted an eye at ten-pound teasers rigged to the transoms of forty-foot sportsfishermen. The anchor-sized saltwater reels looked normal to me, and fifty-pound test, what the hell. I had lost sight of that first delicate intimacy, the tiny bass swimming clearly in my see-through jar of river water. I no longer practiced communion, but sacrilege. My life, as well as my fishing, had turned brutal.

I prefer the confessional to the cross, figuring if I own to enough treachery I will be spared in a moment of mercy, like that bass in the ravine. When I quit drinking—finally—after an eight-year period of uncommon buoyancy on sea as well as land, my liver shot, my eyes as yellowed as the fish the alchemists sought for insight—I quit the gonzo lifestyle. "Blind drunk" is not a phrase without meaning, and to me it came to mean that I had been blind, almost irrevocably, not only to the damage leveled in my own life, but to the life beneath those waters that came so frequently in dreams.

Dead cold sober now, I took up fly fishing. Not on the same day, certainly, because the shakes wrack you for a while and all you're really good for is mixing paint. I'd held a fly rod only once during my fish killing days, off the coast of Islamorada during tarpon season, while fishing with legendary guide Jimmie Allbright. In the saltwater fishing world, *guides* and *anglers* are legendary, never the fish who serve them. After meeting enough of the old masters, I came to the conclusion that to become legendary all one needed was to catch oversized fish and not die from sunstroke or lip cancer, tie a few exotic-looking flies, cast phenomenal distances against the wind and remain steadfastly laconic when a novice is on board. What I remember most of the first fly fishing experience is a lot of yeps and nopes directed at my questions, the fly line cinched tightly around my ankles after a bad cast, and a sunburn that bubbled the skin on the tops of my ears. It was a waste of energy, I figured. I didn't get the point. All that whipping and hauling and peering into the distance just reminded me of bad Westerns.

But something happens when you get purified, take the cure, lob your body onto another plane of perception. Without a beer in hand fly fishing seemed far more appealing to me than it had when I'd been trolling with bait big enough to eat. Back then I'd called it effete, elitist, prissy, egg-sucking. I figured the entire state of Montana was crawling with seven million people who looked exactly like Robert Redford, all of them hefting custom fly rods. Now in a completely altered state of mind, I began to notice the grace involved in a simple cast, how the arm of a good angler was merely an extension of the fly rod. I studied the art a little, secretly, not yet ready to be labeled a wimp.

Somewhere around my fortieth birthday my husband Jeff had given me a new rod and reel, complete with weight-forward line, and I took to the business of learning to cast as earnestly as I take to anything, which means if I don't master it on the second or third try, I quit, stick out my lower lip and glare.

I had achieved mid-beginner status (capable of placing the fly on the water by wadding the line in my fist and heaving it) when Jeff and I took a trip to the Salmon River in Idaho. I had taken fish there years before, six-pack in hand, spinning gear in the other, dragging the rocks—twenty-four trout in half a day, my finest hour, but drunk when I did it so maybe the count's off by half. I wanted to return to make amends, to take a trout clean and easy without the heavy artillery.

The Salmon is a beautiful stretch of water, clear, relatively shallow and fast, unlike the slow, clay-weighted waters of Mississippi. When I first moved to the Northwest I was amazed you could see so deeply into the water and would sit for hours on a river shore staring at the rocks beneath. Jeff, on the other hand, grew up with this purity, which may explain why it seems to be in his blood to fish these waters, and fish them well, in fact better than anyone has a right to. He has the sort of luck with a fly rod that I used to have with bait, a fact that has compelled me to accuse him of actually robbing me of fish-luck, a high crime in our marriage.

Our first day on the river I'd waded in bare-legged and was fishing generally the same area of water as Jeff, but politely upstream so the fish would get to me first, when his luck (he calls it skill) kicked in. He'd released six fish before I'd even gotten my fly damp. Normally I handled such flagrant displays with stoicism, wanting to keep my image as a good sport intact, but this day was different. I'd returned to waters that had blessed me once with uncanny luck, to waters that had kindly not swallowed me whole as I'd staggered through them, and all I wanted was that brief, immortal contact with aliens, the way I'd known it when I was a kid, new and simple. I was obsessed that day with taking a fish on fly. I'd read A.J. and Norman. I'd gone to the outdoor shows. Nothing seemed more perfect or vital than the feel of a trout on the end of that nerve-sensitive line. I'd felt how mere water current could electrify the line, transforming it to a buzzing high-voltage wire, and I wanted some of that magic.

"Yee—ha!" Jeff yelled from down river as he released another perfect form into the water.

I false cast and hooked my chin.

I could feel them all around me, the sense of them, fish moving the current in swirls around my bare ankles, fish swimming between my thighs. I inched my way in Jeff's direction, watching his fly line thread out before him and then drop like a whisper onto the water.

I got within twenty feet of the man and flung my line in an awkward sidecast right where I'd seen his last fish surface. I waited. I prayed. I watched. I peered. Nothing.

My husband is someone who takes athletic grace for granted, figuring it's something we all can achieve in time.

"Your presentation's wrong," he told me.

Had I read about this? I searched my memory.

"My what," I said, coming up blank.

"The way you're putting the fly down. It's wrong."

Well, what the hell. It was enough, I thought, to get the fly in the water. Who could resist after that. And when did fish get so picky, worrying about presentation, the particular color of a hackle. With worms there had been no guesswork. Eat this tasty sucker, you cretin, I was thinking as I fingered a rubber worm I'd stashed in my vest pocket.

"Fish are color-blind," I said with some authority, apropos of nothing.

"So," he said in that way he has that tells me he's already written a book about it.

To illustrate presentation, Jeff whipped off another perfect cast. A trout rose to his fly, and bingo, the water around us was alive. I hated him.

"Maybe it's my fly," I said.

I waded over to him and switched rods, thinking, Okay you, give me that magic wand, we'll see who catches fish.

"Yours casts so easily," he said as he set the line in motion.

Wham. I swear to God that fish hit the fly in mid-air.

"Nothing's wrong with your fly," he told me as he released the biggest trout of the day.

"That's it," I said, stomping toward shore as gracefully as possible in four feet of water. I'd snatched my rod from him and threw it on the bank when I emerged, soaked and cold, as pissed as I'd ever been.

"I thought you were a good sport," I heard him calling from the river.

There, I'd blown it. Years of cultivating an image, gone.

"Go to hell," I yelled. "Go straight to hell, you and your stupid fly rod, you jinx. Jinx! Ever since I've fished with you I've caught nothing. Not a goddamned thing. You took all my luck, and now you rub my nose in it. I'll never fish with you again. I swear to God."

I sat down on the bank and literally stomped my feet, hands clenched into fists at my sides, my heartbeat clearly audible in my temples. I'd heard about people like me. Poor sports. Whiners. Lunatics.

"It's just your technique." The wind carried his words so that "technique" seemed to be underlined, and I shouted back, "Eat your technique. Eat it, you hear!"—a response I thought fair at the time.

It was then I saw the naked man in the raft drifting past, fly rod poised in mid-air. Ordinarily, naked would have been enough, but as I watched more closely I noticed he was throwing his rod tip up to twelve o'clock and then waiting for a beat before following through with the forward cast. During that beat the line straightened out behind him, unfurling slowly from the arc it made as he brought the rod forward. Again he cast, my own personal naked instructor, oblivious to me on the bank, and again with the same hesitation. Some technique, I thought, peering in Jeff's direction to see if he'd noticed the man. Nah. Naked women could have been skydiving into a bull's eye on his head and he'd have kept on casting. I watched the man cast another perfect length of line and discovered my arm moving involuntarily, following his motions. I watched his wrist. Hardly a bend in it as he pointed the rod arrow-straight in the direction of the unfurling line. At that moment something settled into place, the way it did that one time I bowled a strike, and I saw the whole process, not as frantic thrashing and whipping, but as one liquid motion, seamless and intact. It was the way, I thought, I should have always fished, naked, tethered to the water by a floating umbilicus, aware.

I spent the rest of the day practicing on a dirt back road, heaving that line at first as if it were a shotput. When it would drop in a dead puddle at the end of my rod I'd try again, remembering the vision of that man in the raft, his perfect rhythm, the way he seemed to notice nothing but his line as it spun out above the water. I kept trying against what I considered rather hefty odds until I had my line singing in the air and pulling out the slack around my feet as if it were ribbon shot from a rifle. I grew calm from the effort, a way I'd not remembered being for years. I looked at my hands, steady as rocks, as they rose above my head, left hand experimenting with a double haul. Hey, I thought, I might get good at this.

That evening at dusk I caught my first fish on a fly, a beauty I watched rise in a quick thrash, greedily, as if he'd been waiting all day for my one ratty fly, frayed and battered from the day's practice, but oddly noble. It's all I wanted, that one fish, electric on the end of my line, and, God, how I could feel him, his jumpy on-and-off current carrying all the way up my arm. How do you do, I felt like saying, it's been a long time. I wet my hand and cradled his girth in my palm. Such a nice feeling. Moist, alive, not slimy the way we're taught to think. I pulled some water through his gills and released the fly from his lip, delicately, no sweat, and watched as he fluttered and then dove in a quick zig zag, deep into the stream. For an instant I remembered the delicate feel of the baby bass as I slopped him into the jar of river water, then the fish gods, white and huge, circling the perimeter of the pond, aware, perhaps, of nothing more than the rhythm their movement created, and in that instant, I too, here in the clear water of an Idaho stream, understood rhythm, but as if it were the steady beat of childhood fascination returned.

M. Wylie Blanchet

Mike's Credo

The first time we met Mike must have been the very first time we anchored in Melanie Cove. It was blowing a heavy south-easter outside, so we had turned into Desolation Sound and run right up to the eastern end. There the chart showed some small coves called Prideaux Haven. The inner one, Melanie Cove, turned out to be wonderful shelter in any wind.

We anchored over against a long island with a shelving rock shore. The children tumbled into the dinghy and rowed ashore to collect wood for the evening bonfire, while I started the supper. Away in at the end of the cove we could see what appeared to be fruit trees of some kind, climbing up a side hill. It was in August, and our mouths started watering at the thought of green apple sauce and dumplings. There was no sign of a house of any kind, no smoke. It might even be a deserted orchard. After supper we would go in and reconnoitre.

We were just finishing our supper when a boat came out of the end of the cove with a man standing up rowing—facing the bow and pushing forward on the oars. He was dressed in the usual logger's outfit—heavy grey woolen undershirt above, heavy black trousers tucked into high leather boots. As I looked at him when he came closer, Don Quixote came to mind at once. High pointed forehead and mild blue eyes, a fine long nose that wandered down his face, and a regular Don Quixote moustache that drooped down at the ends. When he pulled alongside we would see the cruel scar that cut in a straight line from the bridge of his nose—down the nose inside the flare of the right nostril, and down to the lip.

"Well, well, well," said the old man—putting his open hand over his face just below the eyes, and drawing it down over his nose and mouth, closing it off the end of his chin—a gesture I got to know so well in the summers to come.

"One, two, three, four, five," he counted, looking at the children.

He wouldn't come aboard, but he asked us to come ashore after supper and pick some apples; there were lots of windfalls. We could move the boat farther into the cove, but not beyond the green copper stain on the cliff. Later, I tossed a couple of magazines in the dinghy and we rowed towards where we had seen him disappear. We identified the copper stain for future use, rounded a small sheltering island, and there, almost out of sight up the bank, stood a little cabin—covered with honeysuckle and surrounded by flowers and apple trees. We walked with him along the paths, underneath the overhanging apple-branches. He seemed to know just when each tree had been planted, and I gathered that it had been a slow process over the long years he had lived there.

Except for down at the far end, where the little trellis-covered bridge dripped with grapes, the land all sloped steeply from the sea and up the hillside to the forest. Near the cabin he had terraced it all—stone-walled, and flower-bordered. Old-fashioned flowers—mignonette and sweet-williams, bleeding-hearts and bachelor's buttons. These must have reached back into some past of long ago, of which at that time I knew nothing. But beauty, which had certainly been achieved, was not the first purpose of the terraces—the first purpose was apple trees.

He had made one terrace behind the house first—piled stones, carted seaweed and earth until he had enough soil for the first trees. From there, everything had just gradually grown. Down at the far end, where terraces were not necessary, the trees marched up the hillside in rows to where the eight-foot sapling fence surrounded the whole place. "The deer jump anything lower," said Mike, when I commented on the amount of time and work it must have taken. Then he added, "Time doesn't mean anything to me. I just work along with nature, and in time it is finished."

During the next couple of days I spent a lot of time talking to old Mike. The children were happy swimming in the warm water, eating apples, and picking boxes of windfalls for Mike to take over to the logging camp at Deep Bay.

In between admiring everything he showed me around the place—I gradually heard the story of some of his past, and how he first came to Melanie Cove. He had been born back in Michigan in the States. After very little schooling he had left school to go to work. When he was big enough he had worked in the Michigan woods as a logger—a hard, rough life. I don't know when, or how, he had happened to come to British Columbia. But here again, he had worked up the coast as a logger.

"We were a wild, bad crowd," mused Mike—looking back at his old life, a far-away look in his blue eyes. Then he told me of the fight he had had with another logger.

"He was out to get me. . . . I didn't have much of a chance."

The fellow had left him for dead, lying in a pool of his own blood. Mike wasn't sure how long he had lain there—out cold. But the blood-soaked mattress had been all fly-blown when he came to.

"So it must have been quite a few days."

He had dragged himself over to a pail of water in the corner of the shack and drunk the whole pailful . . . then lapsed back into unconsciousness. Lying there by himself—slowly recovering.

"I decided then," said Mike, "that if that was all there was to life, it wasn't worth living; and I was going off somewhere by myself to think it out."

So he had bought or probably pre-empted wild little Melanie Cove—isolated by 7,000-foot mountains to the north and east, and only accessible by boat. Well, he hadn't wanted neighbours, and everything else he needed was there. Some good alder bottom-land and a stream, and a sheltered harbour. And best of all to a logger, the south-east side of the cove rose steeply, to perhaps eight hundred feet, and was covered with virgin timber. So there, off Desolation Sound, Mike had built himself a cabin, hand-logged and sold his timber—and thought about life. . . .

He had been living there for over thirty years when we first blew into the cove. And we must have known him for seven or eight years before he died. He had started planting the apple trees years before—as soon as he had realized that neither the trees nor his strength would last forever. He had built the terraces, carted the earth, fed and hand-reared them. That one beside the cabin door—a man had come ashore from a boat with a pocket full of apples. Mike had liked the flavour, and heeled in his core beside the steps.

"Took a bit of nursing for a few years," said Mike. "Now, look at it. Almost crowding me out."

He took us up the mountain one day where he had cut some of the timber in the early days, and to show us the huge stumps. He explained how one man alone could saw the trees by rigging up what he called a "spring" to hold the other end of the saw against the cut. And how if done properly, the big tree would drop onto the smaller trees you had felled to serve as skids, and would slide down the slope at a speed that sent it shooting out into the cove. He could remember the length of some of them, and how they had been bought for the big drydock down in Vancouver.

I got to know what books he had in the cabin. Marcus Aurelius, Epictetus, Plato, Emerson, among many others. Somebody had talked to him, over the years, and sent him books to help him in his search. He didn't hold with religion, but he read and thought and argued with everything he read.

Mike's own Credo, as he called it, was simple. He had printed it in pencil on a piece of cardboard, and had it hanging on his wall. He had probably copied it word for word from some book—because it expressed for him how he had learnt to think and live. I put it down here exactly as he had it.

"Look well of to-day—for it is the Life of Life. In its brief course lie all the variations and realities of your life—the bliss of growth, the glory of action, the splendour of beauty. For yesterday is but a dream, and To-morrow a vision. But To-day well lived makes every Yesterday a dream of happiness, and every To-morrow a vision of hope. For Time is but a scene in the eternal drama. So, look well of to-day, and let that be your resolution as you awake each morning and salute the New Dawn. Each day is born by the recurring miracle of Dawn, and each night reveals the celestial harmony of the stars. Seek not death in error of your life, and pull not upon yourself destruction by the work of your hands."

That was just exactly how Mike lived—day by day, working with nature.

II

WILD PLEASURES

Gift of Joy

Ash

February 18–March 17

Susanna Levin

Night Skates

When you live in the city, it's easy to feel trapped: either you're indoors, or you're on the street. Stepping out of an apartment building onto dirty pavement isn't usually described as "going outdoors."

This is especially true if, like me, you're the kind of person who thrives on outdoor sports, and particularly the so-called action sports, like skiing and rock climbing, where your life depends on your ability to control your body through the dimensions of time and space. The thrill-seeking city dweller has to *go to* the outdoors by car or by plane. And so the outdoors becomes a distant abstraction, a temptation, a source of self-torment.

I recently discovered that it's foolish to make such a distinction between the wild outdoors and the urban outdoors. In the process, I discovered an action sport that was made for the urban environment, for *my* urban environment—San Francisco. Now, I get my outdoor ya-yas, risking my neck and overloading my senses, in the ozone-choked air of city streets. I do it on skates, after dark.

Taking to the streets at night with an eclectic assortment of people on in-line skates (also known as Rollerblades), I experience time slowing down. I have always associated this sensation with playing in the great outdoors—dropping into a chute on skis, for example, or descending single track on a mountain bike. My ears and eyes plug directly into my motor neurons and go on high-level alert.

The night is the crucial element in this transformation. For high-speed nocturnal navigation on skates, visual processing is secondary to kinesthetics and proprioception: you rely on your body's sense of where you are and where you're going; you continuously react to terrain and gravity in an effort to remain upright and under control. Where you are on earth is much less important than where you are in space.

Of course, on earth I am in a city, yes, but it's also the country's premier paved ski resort, with an endless supply of double black-diamond runs and near-perfect conditions year-round.

Night skating didn't always strike me as a great idea. When I first started skating, I stuck to the relative safety of Golden Gate Park and broad daylight. It seemed like a winning combination. I'd heard about the night skate, and it sounded scary. The thought of contending with cars, trucks and potholes, not to mention the hills, seemed far beyond me. Skating from Golden Gate Park to downtown was just absurd: not only was there a three-hundred-foot elevation loss between here and there, but downtown had buses and taxis and Muni tracks and lost tourists, faking left and then turning right across three lanes of traffic. All of this, in the dark of the night.

Then one Sunday, at a local skate race in the Park, I met Jenny, a night skater who turned out to be a friend of an old friend. Jenny was a better skater than I was, but she wasn't *that* much better. Maybe it was just stupid competitiveness, but I figured if she could do the night skate, it wasn't a total impossibility. Besides, I immediately liked and trusted Jenny. She was enthusiastic and reassuring; she made the night skate sound like something fun, not some keep-up-or-die hammerfest around the city. I agreed to come out the following Tuesday night.

Of course, one better offer for Tuesday night and I would have bagged in a minute. But no excuses arose, and at seven on Tuesday I turned up at "skate central" in Golden Gate Park. It was an uncharacteristically warm, bright spring evening in San Francisco; both the fog and the wind had the night off.

Skaters, on ice or pavement, are divided into only two categories: the balanced and the unbalanced. Either you are in control of your edges, and you glide with effortless, elegant grace, or you are at their mercy, prone to intermittent spastic contortions when they betray you. I was unbalanced. If I didn't try anything too tricky, I could pass, but in fact, I was too worried about looking like a dork to experiment and learn to skate backwards and do quick spin-stops. As with many sports, to gain control, you have to be willing to give it up.

Skaters slowly turned up. At seven-thirty, there were seven of us. I recognized most faces from around the park, but Jenny and a local racer named Mike were the only two I knew by name. Judging from the preponderance of racing skates and the sinewy legs that sprouted from them, it was a hardcore group.

The group convened. "Where should we go?" someone asked.

"Downtown," another replied.

Although this would not always be the case, on this night there was no dissent.

"Which way?"

"Let's go Golden Gate."

Helmets were adjusted (I was the only person wearing knee pads, but everyone had wrists guards and most had helmets) and a few of us turned on flashing red lights that were attached to our helmets. (I had one of these. In fact, I had every piece of protection except a condom.)

We skated out of the park and onto Fulton Street. The pack was immediately in the road and, since the sidewalk was rough and cracked, I soon joined them. As we snaked through the streets north of Fulton, I felt surprisingly safe. There were hardly any cars, and the heft of a seven-skater pack seems to justify occupying the road. Connect the dots, and we're big as a truck.

I was a little concerned that we were going *up*hill. There is no way to get from the Park to downtown San Francisco without descending at least one monstrous hill. Every additional foot of altitude we gained, we were going to have to lose. This, I supposed, was the whole point.

Within a couple of minutes, we were at the top of Golden Gate Avenue, on Lone Mountain near the University of San Francisco. From there, Golden Gate runs east, away from the park, toward the federal architecture of the Civic Center and downtown. As is so often the case on skates, I began to appreciate nuances of this city's topography that had eluded me before. Only the Golden Gate hill isn't really a nuance: it's a fucking ski jump, plummeting over three hundred feet.

As the group assembled at the crest of the first steep section of the street, I didn't really have time to think about whether or not this was a very good idea, or even possible. Had I been by myself, however, I never would have dreamed of attempting it.

Mike, a shy, somewhat awkward guy in his early twenties, had some words of advice for me. Mike looked like he wouldn't be caught dead on a dance floor, but with skates on, he was a regular Nureyev. It was the Zen master's blend of skill and brevity that made me hang on his every word. "The lights are timed," he told me. "When this next one turns red, count to ten and then go."

"All the way to the bottom?" I asked.

"All the way. But cut it loose or you won't make it."

Whatever you say, Mike. I'm putting my life in your hands. The light turned, and Mike bowed his head, giving a slow nod for each integer . . . nod eight, . . . nod nine, . . . "GO!" he yelled, and he went. Then I went, lemming-like. Mike got into a tuck and so did I. A guy named Chris shot past me, a light brown blur, but then no one else. Was everybody bombing this stretch, I suddenly wondered, or was I out front with the suicides while everybody else took the pro-life route?

The first light changed a few seconds before we reached it, just as Mike predicted. Just to be on the safe side, Chris let out an authentic-sounding police siren whoop as we entered the intersection. (That sound would become the clarion call of the night skate, and my first few times out he fooled me about half the time. Every time Chris shot through an intersection, I'd turn around to see where the cops were.)

All my weight was in my feet. I remember looking down to see my skates tracking straight, taking comfort in their solidity. We hit that light at full speed, and then the next, and the next—with two heart-beats of apprehension verging on panic before each light blinked from red to green.

Below Divisadero, the street turns into a three-lane one-way. Mike, Chris and I occupied the right lane leaving plenty of room in the two remaining lanes for cars. I was faintly surprised that no one honked at us, but traffic was light, and we were moving faster than they were anyway.

It wasn't quite dark as we buzzed through the projects near Buchanan Street: the air was still rich with the purple light that lingers in the San Francisco sky after sunset on a bright day. A certain part of my brain was assigned to vigilance: watching the lights, listening for cars, scanning the ground for those built-in reflective lane markers, which at that speed were like little tombstones. Most of my consciousness, however, was awash in something much more potent than adrenalin: I was having the kind of rush you only get when you're doing something really fun, really stupid and illegal.

A Beastie Boys song came into my head. It was the perfect soundtrack: adolescent. Aggro. While screaming downhill on in-line skates at thirty miles an hour may not be an obvious time for insight, I was struck by my pleasure at behaving like an insubordinate thirteen-year-old. It was a Peter Pan thing, and I *was* flying.

We crossed six lanes of traffic on Van Ness, just beating the light, and blew by Star's, where I drink scotch in another life. As we descended into the piss of the Tenderloin, screaming past the crack dealers and prostitutes, I recognized the practical advantages of speed.

The Golden Gate rollercoaster finally bottomed out at Market Street, in the heart of downtown.

It's a strange place to be at night—so strange, in fact, that nobody really seemed to notice a pack of skaters flying down the sidewalk and leaping over benches. Now and again someone would look at me through bleary eyes, and say, "Hey . . ." I had the distinct feeling that they were not completely convinced I was really there.

Mike and Nick were leading, and after a few blocks they pulled up at the entrance to the Montgomery station of BART, San Francisco's subway.

"Let's do it," Chris said. Augie, a lean guy with dark skin and thick black hair, who'd been smiling since we left the park, suddenly got serious. "I'm not going," he said.

The others started down the stairs into the subway, then stopped. "C'mon man, let's go," Mike said.

Augie just skated off, saying he'd meet us at the exit. I followed down the stairs—taking them skater style: walking backward, holding the rail. I was not particularly psyched about our imminent transgression. Skaters have been banned from the streets in a few cities around the country, and this kind of sortie seemed just the thing to make trouble in this town.

It was about nine, and the BART station was empty. It didn't take long for me to see why we were here. In these quarter-mile-long underground walkways, with their linoleum smooth as butter, there's no resistance to our urethane wheels. It's like the Bonneville Speedway of skating—surreal, like the Utah salt flats at Bonneville, and irresistible for speed freaks. With just a few strokes I was flying through the fluorescence, whipping by ads for shoes and shopping centers.

As we neared the end of the first section of tunnel, a disembodied voice buzzed over a loudspeaker. "No skating in the station. Exit the station immediately. There is no skating in the station." The voice faded as we rolled down the next section of walkway, whizzing under a city block in about seven seconds. At the end of that stretch, a second loudspeaker hissed at us, this one a little more insistent: "No skates allowed in the station. Take off your skates or get out of the station."

There was something comical about blowing by these fingerwavers in their little booths, one after another, but I was relieved when we hopped on the escalator and headed out of the station. I didn't mind being bad, I realized, but I didn't want to get called on it.

I was trying to figure out whether skating in a BART station was a misdemeanor or not, when I understood why Augie stayed above ground. He was probably not an American citizen. Getting busted, even for a misdemeanor, could be catastrophic for him. When the rest of the group descended the stairs to skate another stretch in the next BART station, I skated the street above with Augie.

The pack emerged from the underground back at the Civic Center; from there, it's a long, steady climb on Market to Church Street, in the Castro district. The lead skaters formed a paceline, tucked in tightly one behind the other. Like cyclists, skaters can work together to cut the wind and increase their speed this way, but I hung back, unsure of my ability to stroke in synchrony.

At Church, we turned right and started zig-zagging through the streets of the Lower Haight, past the slacker cafes and night spots. The terrain suddenly got much steeper; again, we were on streets that I travel every day but had never imagined skating. On a particularly steep stretch of Steiner Street, Augie skated up behind me and pushed me up the hill. My ego, which sometimes overvalues self-sufficiency, was tweaked, but my legs told me to be grateful.

When we turned left again, Page Street loomed monstrously between us and home. It was steep and five times the length of the stretch I'd just struggled up. All of a sudden, it felt way past my bedtime. Halfway up the first of three blocks of serious climbing, I realized how ill-suited the tools were to the purpose. When it's steep, you don't skate so much as run up the hill, in short choppy steps. In the space of three blocks, Chris and Mike had picked up about two-hundred yards on me; Jenny and Augie were not far behind them.

By the time we zigged back onto the relative flatness of upper Haight Street, I was sucking wind big time. I chased the other four through Haight-Ashbury in overdrive, never quite getting my breath back. Once at the park, the group dispersed quickly; I hardly had time to say good-bye, and thanks. I skated the short distance home by myself.

When I arrived at my house, I was still breathing hard from the chase up Haight. It was after eleven, and tired as I was, sleep was out of the question. All the brain chemicals that had me pumped up like that were a long way from quieting down. But this wasn't the kind of feeling I have after a good long run in the park or even a bike ride on Mount Tam. This was a complete release. I felt like I had been to another planet, and maybe the night is another world, as different from daytime as country is from city.

In the months that followed, I became a regular on the night skate.

I started seeing the city differently. I began to know where it is quiet at night and where it hums; where it is cool and where the warm air lingers. Parts of town that I once avoided because they were congested or boring became my favorites because there's a hill that's just the right grade or fresh pavement or timed lights.

After I started skating the streets at night, I noticed I could go for weeks without feeling that desperate urge to escape the city. And when ski season rolled around, I noticed an extraordinary change in myself. When I went to the mountains to ski, I didn't feel the old streak of longing, the sense that every day I spent back in the city I was missing out on the best life had to offer.

This is a good thing, because for now I am where I am. And for now, I'll find the thrill of the outdoors where urethane meets pavement.

Gretchen Legler

Mushrooms

People ask me where to find them, and they think that I am playing games with them when I say, "I'm not sure." I only know two things: look under and around dead elms with the bark still on them, and don't look in swamps. It's not a game that has a lot of rules. It's not a sure thing. You find them where you look, when you have learned how to look.

When I first started looking for morel mushrooms, when I first went into the woods with Craig, I didn't know how to see. He had to teach me. He had to point them out to me, even the ones right under my nose. Now when I go looking, I see them where others don't. "You stepped on one back here," I will say to a friend who has gone thrashing on ahead.

You look by strolling, walking through the woods, crawling maybe, ducking and bending, going slowly and looking out, away from your feet. When you look out you can see fuzzy gray-brown baby rabbits shivering in fear of you, even though you mean them no harm. When you look out you can see a fawn folded into the grass, eyes big and black as stones. When you look out you can see a still-as-death mother grouse on a nest, barely visible with her mottled brown and cream feathers. When you look out you can see bloodroot and new small purple violets, scarlet tanagers and the jawbones of deer. You can see the flattened and winter-hardened red skin of a dead fox, the skulls of skunks, the mouse-nibbled antlers dropped last fall by some buck.

You can find as many things living as dead. Going across fields newly planted to corn, to get to the line of elms on the other side, you step along the tiny green rows just coming up, and you can run into a barn cat, all whiskers and legs. And you can stop on the other side of the field in the woods and gather dandelion greens for salad.

When you find them, the mushrooms, poking up like tiny hay-stacks under the grass, or all crowded around each other, nubby like stones nudged into an embankment, it is always a surprise. To find morel mushrooms in the spring woods is like getting something for nothing: some marvelous thing free. Even as you pick them, you can taste them. They are barky and buttery and sweet like iron. When you come upon them, a lot of them, so many that if you squat in their midst with your penknife and your bag you can reach around you for half an hour, not having to get up and step away, then you feel ter-rific and nothing is wrong in the world.

Sometimes it is hot and dry and you walk across the corn fields into the next woods in dusty boots and a long-sleeved shirt to keep your arms from being scratched. You wear old blue jeans that already have been nicked by barbed wire, and you rub your neck when it gets sweaty. You hear in the distance the sound of tractors starting up, the sound of insects coming into spring, cows mooing, a horse whinnying. Sometimes there is rain pouring down and you slip and slide and get muddy all over.

Once, while Craig and I hunted mushrooms on a rainy day, he went on ahead and I stood in the rain and watched the water sliding down the smooth dark side of a long-dead elm, the bark layered at its feet, the rain slicking down, bright and flashing. I stood there, wondering at so simple and nice a thing.

When you get the mushrooms home, you lay them all out on a table and sort out the choicest ones for stuffing and baking. These can be as large as your fist, and their flesh is thick, ridged like bark, the color of caramel, and their cone-shaped heads will hold half a cup of wild rice and onions and nuts. You eat those first. Then you sort the broken ones. You eat those second on pasta or layered in thin pastry dough, or folded into omelets. Then there are the rest, which you set on screens on the porch and they dry to half their size, getting better, darker, denser, barkier. When you want to eat these, you put them by handfuls into water or white wine, and let them come back into themselves. They taste like the forest.

Heather Trexler Remoff

What Makes Grace Run?

I suppose the more accurate question is, What *made* Grace run? I mean, after all, she is dead, has been dead for ten years now. But accuracy is hard to come by. This is an emotional issue for me, not one that's easily sorted out with facts. The fact is, I never knew Grace. So why do I feel so close to her?

Grace Andrews was killed by a hit-and-run driver shortly before Christmas of 1985. She was sixty-eight. He was drunk. She was out with her dog, going for her nightly loop around the lake that is the heart of this mountaintop community we call home. One of her daughters tells me that she tried to persuade her not to run that evening. "Let me go get the paper for you, Mom." Part of the daily ritual in Eagles Mere, Pennsylvania (population 123), is to walk or, in Grace's case, run over to Enza Laurenson's to pick up a copy of the local paper. Grace wouldn't hear of letting her daughter take over this errand. "Oh no, I *need* to run."

It would be nice if I could tell you that that statement was the start of the peculiar intimacy I share with a dead woman, but I've only recently had this mother/daughter exchange played back for me. So it wasn't the start of my identification with her but merely affirmation of something I already knew. I understand what it's like to *need* to run. This is something Grace and I have discussed, mostly when I'm out running when I shouldn't be, when I have cracked ribs, or a swollen knee or have just had a chemotherapy treatment. I started running in the late seventies, about the same time Grace did. I didn't live in Eagles Mere then, but was a New Jersey graduate student going through an unhappy divorce. I was almost forty. Grace was sixty when she started to run. Her marriage was a long one, and I've heard rumors about it. But any union that produces fourteen children has to have had its moments of accord. However, the accord was pretty much over when Grace started running. Dene, a victim of Parkinson's disease, was moved to the nursing home where he would, within a few years, die. And Grace began to run.

What makes Grace run? She had no history of athleticism, except, in her words, "years of chasing after fourteen kids." When pushed as to her reasons, she gave the answer that is word for word the same explanation I've provided curious friends. "It's just something I always wanted to do."

There were other things Grace always wanted to do. Going to college was one of them. And so, in 1982, when she was sixty-five, she enrolled at the College of Misericordia in Dallas, Pennsylvania, a good hour's commute over hilly rural roads that are often covered with snow and ice. She liked English, psychology and Russian history.

What makes Grace run? Spirit has something to do with it. In 1965 the Andrewses' house burned, leaving the family temporarily homeless. One of the summer people, knowing of my love of running, asked me if I had known Grace. I confessed that I had not. "Oh, she was a character. You knew her house burned down, didn't you?" I nodded. "Well, do you know the Dillons?" I had to admit that although I knew *of* them (everyone knew *of* them), I didn't know them personally. "Well, you're new here." My informant glossed over my obvious lack of social standing. "You know where their house is. The family has been coming up here for generations. Now old Mrs. Dillon was especially fond of Grace. Grace worked for her, you know, helped out with running the house. Well, after the fire, Mrs. Dillon went down to see Grace." Anticipating the punch line to her own story, my newfound historian began to laugh. "That Grace was such a character. Anyway, Mrs. Dillon said to her, 'Oh, Grace dear, be sure and let me know if there is anything I can do.' And would you believe it? Grace handed her a laundry basket full of dirty clothes. Here was Mrs. Dillon, who'd never washed out so much as a pair of silk stockings, suddenly being asked to do the laundry for fourteen children!"

Many of Grace's sons and daughters and grandchildren are also runners. The year following her death, they held a race in Eagles Mere in her memory and honor: Grace's Run. It has been held every year since then and has become a race associated with the triumph of spirit. Because Grace started running late in life, it is a race that puts special emphasis on the athletic ability of women over fifty. Although there are prizes in all gender and age groups, the large Grace Andrews Memorial Trophy is awarded to the first woman over the age of fifty to cross the finish line. I had just turned fifty when my second husband and I moved to Eagles Mere. That year I amazed myself by winning the Grace Andrews Trophy. Her progeny rejoiced with me.

I felt they were all really happy to see someone from Grace's hometown capture the honor. It was around that time that I began talking to Grace.

What makes Grace run? That year I told myself it was her competitive spirit. After all, Grace, like me, had not been content simply to run, but started entering races shortly after she'd developed the conditioning to run more than just a mile or two. It was the same with me. The first race I entered was a 10K. Within six months, I'd completed a marathon.

That was seventeen years ago now. My mother was still alive, alive but not really well. She was in her seventies and seriously afflicted with emphysema. Mother had always been a shy person who kept her deepest feelings to herself. I thought of her as sedentary, conservative, not given to display. Her one act of rebellion had been to take up smoking when my sisters and I were all still in elementary school. From almost that time on, my memories of her are played against the background accompaniment of a hacking cough. She had her first nervous breakdown when I was in college. Misdiagnosed for thirty years as schizophrenic, the category of drugs the learned doctors administered aggravated her physical condition and did precious little for her mental one. She was in and out of hospitals. It was only in her eightieth year, the last year of her life, that she was correctly diagnosed as delusionally depressed. Lithium gave me my mother back. I try really hard not to be angry at the loss of all those years.

What makes Grace run? Maybe it's the same thing that made my mother run. Now, there's a surprise, this quiet, sedentary woman a runner? I didn't know this about her. I told you she didn't reveal too much about herself. She thought it was wrong to brag, to draw attention to herself in any way. But that year, the year I ran my first marathon, she pulled me aside and shyly admitted, "I used to love to run."

"You did?" I asked in amazement. "When was that?"

"When I was a little girl. It was before my mother died so I couldn't have been more than seven. Sometimes she would send me on an errand, and I never walked. I always ran. I didn't run because I was in a hurry. I ran just because I was so happy. I had a nickname then. All the neighbors called me Legs Almighty."

I ran my second marathon in Philadelphia, the city where I'd grown up and where my parents still lived. By then I'd shared Mother's story with my father. Daddy drove her down to Boathouse Row to watch me cross the finish line. She laughed, looked a little embarrassed, but was mostly pleased when I ran past her wearing the tee shirt my father had had specially made just for the event. Large letters proudly emblazoned across my chest identified me as Legs Almighty.

What makes Grace run? I began to answer the question with more certainty around the time I moved beyond talking *to* Grace. We were talking *with* each other now. I can't really pinpoint the moment when Grace began talking back to me. It was probably sometime after I had run a few more times in her race. There were years there when I just couldn't nail that trophy down. Someone was always faster. It was then that Grace and I decided that running wasn't about winning but about being in the game. And what a game it was.

Anyone lucky enough to run in Eagles Mere soon comes to understand the profound beauty sketched by the natural world. A runner's high takes on a whole new meaning when the transcendence occurs beside a mountain lake surrounded by deep woods. In addition to Grace, I have an *actual* running partner. Carol is six years younger than I am and shares with me a deep appreciation for all the wildness here. We, like Grace, both run with our dogs. Two laps around the lake, five mornings a week for almost eight years now and each run has been different from all the others. We've never seen the same sunrise twice. Every silvered shade of peach is lifted from a slightly different palette than the one of the day before. I really mean it when I call out, "Oh, look! I've never seen that deep a red in the morning sky." Sometimes deer will cross in front of us, drawing the dogs quickly to attention, but they are both good boys and won't give chase. In the spring, tiny spotted fawns teeter on their spindly, little, bent-kneed legs. Once we had to stop and wait while a huge black bear finished calmly scratching behind his ear and finally cleared the road so we could continue on.

We thrill to piliated woodpeckers and great blue herons flapping slowly over our heads, their long legs stretched out behind them. Every season brings a migration of a different sort. We run in rain. We run in snow. We run with cleats strapped over our running shoes on those mornings when ice storms transform our world into a glittering, crystal wonderland. We run in fog so thick that only the memory of the road embedded in our feet guides us confidently on our way. We watch night turn into day. We see the stars and moon fade. We watch them move with the seasons, changing their positions in the sky. We glory in blue-sky mornings. We see wind send branches crashing down. We run in cold so fierce our breath crystallizes and coats our hair with frost. We watch the lake freeze. We hear it thaw, tiny little shards of ice rubbing against each other and filling the air with tinkling melodies. We run when we are tired. We run when we are sick. But we always run. What makes Grace run? Beauty has a lot to do with it.

The year I was doing battle with an advanced stage of ovarian cancer, I ran because I was still alive. Grace understood that. She was a frequent companion that year. I talked to her even when I wasn't running. In hindsight, I see that I didn't listen much. I talked over her, pushing too hard to achieve, to win this one. Seized with a panicked determination to vanquish death, I forgot that Grace's conversations with me were themselves proof that life/death isn't win/lose, black/white. Life and death aren't opposite ends of a continuum but parts of the same whole, a beautiful spinning orb where each is immutably fused with the other.

I didn't think I'd be able to enter Grace's Run that year. The hospital had me scheduled for a seriously mean chemotherapy treatment the week before the race. I knew from experience that my blood counts would be so low as to rule out any hope of racing. But, for a change, a low white count worked in my favor. It was too low for me to receive the promised chemo, and I lined up at the start with visions of being once again the first-place woman over fifty. My husband, Gene, worried about my trying to race, insisted on running with me. I agreed but was secretly certain I would leave him and all the other old gray heads before the first mile was over. My prediction was partly right. By the time we passed the mile mark, I couldn't see another older woman anywhere. In fact, I couldn't see another competitor of any description, not because they were all behind me, but because they were all far ahead of me!

It wasn't until we hit the wooded, far side of the lake that I finally quit fighting the inevitability of my dismal showing in the event and relaxed and found the grace, so to speak, to just enjoy the experience. Grace's Run is scheduled in October of each year. The weather is almost always perfect. Grace's grandchildren give her and God credit for the fair skies, and who am I, with my reputation for imaginary conversations with dead women, to argue with that? On this particular day, I finally listened to what it was that Grace had been trying to tell me. "Beauty," she whispered, yet again, in my ear. And, of course, she was right. We ran through falling swirls of golden beech leaves. The sugar maple burned red and orange against the counterpoint of midnight-green banks of hemlock. Dancing water, mirrored light, the surface of the lake was too brilliant for the unshielded eye. My lungs were washed with air so clean I felt that I could drink it. The rest of the race was as glorious as any I have ever run.

Gene and I finished hand in hand, a deliberate tie for last, far behind the rest of the pack. I chilled easily in that cancer year, and so I hurried past the crowds that cheered us on and dashed home to take a shower. As I was pulling on dry clothes, I heard Gene banging on the bathroom door. "Hurry up," he told me. "You won the Grace Andrews Memorial Trophy." Unlikely though it seemed, I had been the *only* woman over fifty in that year's race. As I stood there accepting my award, I was certain I heard Grace giggle. "You imp," I thought to myself and to her. "How in the world did you ever manage to persuade all those other older women to stay home this year?"

The illness is behind me now. I think the doctors were the only ones who were surprised by my recovery. My runs no longer feel like calls to battle. I bring a different spirit to the activity. Therefore, I guess I should not have been caught off guard by what happened in this year's race. It was another glorious fall day, and I was moving lightly and effortlessly around the course. I was very much in the pack, passing women in my age group, even occasionally pulling ahead of a man or an insufficiently conditioned teenager. We had just a little over a mile to go. I'd pushed hard going up the hill to the Crestmont Drive and was ready for the lovely free-fall down the other side. This is my favorite stretch of road, a gentle welcome downhill where gravity does all the work. I felt that I was flying.

∽

What makes Grace run? I have the answer now. For suddenly, while caught in the sweetness of that downhill, I feel a gentle tugging on my left hand. I turn and don't recognize Grace at first for I have never seen her as a child. Her hair is auburn, cut in a tomboy bob with bangs to frame that laughing face. Her long legs are bare, flashing out beneath a simple muslin shift with each quick stride. This happy, running child can be none other than Grace Smeltzer, little Grace, not yet Andrews, more than a half-century away from formal entry in her first race. Realizing that Grace and I are galloping along shoulder to shoulder, I check and discover that I have moved back in time fifty years. I'm wearing brown laced oxfords, the kind I always hated, but I must admit they stay on my feet in a way that the Mary Janes favored by my friends would not. Grace and I are dashing along, having a giggling schoolgirl time!

But there is more to come. *Three* of us tumble down this hill, for on my other side, keeping pace, running right abreast with Grace and me is Legs Almighty. "Legs!" Adorable, grinning Legs, with her hair held back in a large satin bow, a bow so lovingly tied that only a mother could have put it there. Isn't it a wonder? How can the mind do this, just collapse the decades between us? We can't be more than seven, not one of us, not one of these three little girls running, laughing, calling back and forth like birds, caught up in joy, brimming with the sweet magic of this moment in our lives. What makes Grace run? The answer has been there all along, so plain I couldn't see it. What makes Grace run? It is joy, nothing more. But what *could be* more than this swelling, lifting joy?

III

TRANSCENDING FEAR

Gift of Courage

Alder

March 18-April 14

Janet Roddan

April Fools on Polar Circus

$\mathcal{T}$ he dance with fear fascinates me. Learning to accept fear, to take it in without letting it take over is one of the challenges of climbing ice. Climbing leads me into myself, through my hidden doors, into corners and attics. The doorway through fear always appears ominous, locked shut, insurmountable, impossible. Fear talks to me, whispers my weakness; it speaks of conditions, of my own mortality—it whispers "hubris." Fear sharpens my senses. It dances through my body. It tunes me. It wraps its fingers around my heart and squeezes gently. I learn to welcome fear and the edge it brings me, the whispered warnings, the adrenaline. The tango with fear makes me wise.

Two fireflies glimmer in the darkness. The tiny puffs of light float slowly upward and burn deeper into a maze of ice, snow and rock.

Snatches of our conversation drift up. We are on a quest, in search of ice. A note of opera breaks the white silence. We are singing as we approach the climb.

I learn the language; I articulate the right series of moves, body positions, ice axe and crampon placements to dance with a frozen tongue of ice. To talk with the mountain is strong medicine. Ice climbing allows me the privilege of witnessing the world. The *couloir* leads us into the mountain, up there to wild, silent places that wait, unconcerned with whether we view them or not.

An initial pitch of ice, steep enough to burn our calves, increases the intensity with which we communicate with this frozen world. This pitch is followed by a long, rambling walk, past the Pencil, a once free-standing pillar of ice that now lies broken and crushed in a heap. Then on up to the knoll, where we look out from the dark, claustrophobic *couloir* to see sun on the peaks. We continue to snake along a snowfield and arrive at last at the base of the route proper, six long pitches of undulating ice . . . varied, interesting, alpine.

Kafka said, "The words of literature are an ice axe to break the sea frozen inside us." We use our ice axes to shatter our frozen worlds into crystals of ice and fear. One of the strong pulls of ice climbing is the tremendous range of feelings one is forced to endure—tingling, shivering pain . . . bubbling, shining elation. We hold on, struggling to control the fear that pounds through our veins and capillaries. But just as fear begins to steal into the soul, a good axe placement thunks into the ice. This solid, physical connection to the world causes the fear to recede . . . first from the arms, then from the mind . . . then even more gradually fear's fingers release the heart, which eventually slows and quiets. The intensity is replaced with warm, smooth, flowing beats. The rhythm takes hold, and the dance begins again.

The last two pitches of the climb cascade out of the notch like an enormous wedding gown. Today's brides approach slowly, touched by the mystery and majesty of the place. We are filled with our fear and our audacity. We encourage each other; we push each other. Our vows are strong, but it is April, late in the season for ice climbing. The ice is rotten; the climb is falling down. Time melts and falls away along with great chunks of ice as I rail and pound against it. The dance becomes a struggle.

The entire world shrinks to a section of frozen water in front of my face. The ice is dripping wet and soggy. The rhythm has been broken. I force myself to breathe, to generate my own flow, to create my own beat. But nothing feels right. A chasm fifteen feet wide opens up between Barb, my partner, and me. Impossible to return. I fight. I hit hard to get good placements. A big block of ice disengages itself; my tool is embedded in it. Time stops, and in slow motion I swing onto my other ice axe. I "barndoor" open and the block of ice topples over my shoulder. I look down to see the ice explode beside Barb, who suddenly looks tiny and hunched in her small belay stance.

"I don't know about this, Barb," I shout down, hoping she will offer an easy way out. I reason to come down. But she calls back, "It depends on how much you want it." Indeed. How much do I want it? Doubt slides in with spaghetti arms and little shivers that evaporate my courage.

But desire, commitment and an incredible dislike for down climbing drive me. Up. One move at a time. Filled with solemn focus, I proceed. The final veil is gently torn away. The great Goddess reveals her face of frozen water. I witness her dark, foreboding pinnacles, her places of silent, quiet peace, her vistas too vast to contain in a single glance. Tingling, shivering, we arrive at the summit notch at 4 P.M., a happy marriage of fear, sweat, intelligent strength and smiles.

The vast mystery that spreads before us causes us to stop and look and take it in for heartbeats of silence. Endless jagged peaks. The silent contract, the ceremony is almost complete. We rappel down the climb. The ropes pull, snagging a few times just to remind us that it's not over yet. A climb is never over until you are back at the car. And even then, the journey that we are all on keeps going. As we descend, night overtakes us. We turn on our headlamps, tiny pins of light in a blanket of darkness.

The April fools, married with fear and laughter on Polar Circus, return to the car, smiling in the darkness, two tiny fireflies humming and buzzing softly.

Ann Linnea

Superior Spirit

When I stand on the shore of Lake Superior, I feel her power. In summer the invitation is gentle. Meld with the lake. When the azure-blue sky reflects itself in a mirror this massive, the effect is infinite calmness. The calmness embraces me, cleanses out the storms of my life, fills my soul with peace. I am in awe of the clarity. I can see into my own life as clearly as into the plunging greenness before me. Ten feet, twenty feet, sometimes fifty feet down into the depths of mysterious canyons and ridges. I lower my toes into the water and am shocked back into the reality of my separateness. The lake is cold. Not cool, but cold. Temperatures are seldom in the swimming pool range except in shallow bays during stretches of warm, calm weather. And so, I feel the peace, the serenity, but I remain perched safely on shore.

During fall and spring storms, the invitation is to wildness. Ten-foot, twelve-foot, sometimes twenty-foot waves pound mercilessly against the shore, cavort with thousand-foot freighters as if they were bathtub toys. I am drawn to stand next to the lake. Drawn there like many would be to the scene of a fire or an accident. Drawn to witness something spectacular. But unlike the fire or accident, I become more than a spectator. I am soaked by the wind-driven spray. My body becomes imbued with the ecstasy, the terror of that much power. I feel safe standing on the shore, but I am not safe from the energy. I become realigned inside. Empowered in a way I do not understand. I have been touched by the wand of belief in my own vastness.

In winter the invitation is to venture out of the cave of hibernation and into the unknown. Ice is not as safe as the shore. It is always changing, especially on Lake Superior who has refused the bondage of being frozen solid every winter except one in the last one hundred years. But to know her in winter you must venture out, beyond the safety of the shore. I walk toward the open water, but not too far off shore because I'm scared. I lie down, put my ear onto the breast of this gigantic being and hear her breathe, pushing against the cloak she does not want. I hear the deep sounds she sends up from the molten core of the earth. I am connected, grounded to something much larger than the fragility of my own life.

On a quiet snow-melting spring day, the invitation is to change with the lake. The shore I stand on is encased in ice. But I can see water. The lake does not submit to the demands of winter as do her sister northern lakes. They remain frozen. She Who Is the Biggest is white only around the edges. On a sunny April day, I can see huge sections of this perimeter ice floating before me. Hundred-foot strands. Two-hundred-foot strands. Broken loose by a lady eager to regain the total freedom of movement, of summer, of warmth. I feel that same eagerness to shed the constrictions and restraints around the perimeter of my life. I want to let go of the ways winter has held me in bondage. I watch a piece of the old hole-riddled ice break free of the shore and float out into the aliveness and movement, the fluidity of the wholeness. Something inside of me releases, dissolves, transforms. The hopefulness of spring vibrates within, and I can do nothing to stop it.

Big. Big beyond seeing across. Big beyond knowing what's on the other side. Lake Superior is about the size of the entire state of Maine. To paddle around it is the equivalent of hiking the full length of the Appalachian Trail. Because it is over a thousand feet deep in some of its trenches, it contains more water than the other four Great Lakes combined. Lake Baikal in Russia contains more fresh water because it's deeper, but in terms of sheer size Lake Superior is well named.

It was not until the first white explorers arrived in the 1600s and reported that the Ojibway people called the lake "Gitchee Gumee," or "Great Lake," that a name was recorded. Explorer Etienne Brule added his own name: "The Northern Sweetwater Sea." Shortly thereafter the French called it "Lac Superieur."

At age forty-three, I set out in my seventeen-foot sea kayak to paddle around this inland sea. I left behind my husband, my two children and all the trappings of my middle-class life in search of answers to some of the tough questions that had accumulated in the cargo hold of my life. For twelve years I had lived by Lake Superior. Allowed her to play with my children, to hold the ashes of a loved one, to comfort and inspire me. But in the summer of 1992, I changed the contract. Let go of control. I asked She Who Is the Biggest to set the rules, boundaries and challenges of our friendship. I gave her permission to become my teacher. I gave myself nine weeks to be her student. I had no idea that I would never again return to the safety of the shore of my life as I'd known it.

I remember the first time I sat in a sea kayak. It was a warm August day at a camp in Wisconsin. The instructor cautioned me about the boat's balance, but my slim, canoe-wise body slid easily into the narrow hold. It was like pulling on my favorite pair of pants. Comfortable. Snug. Close to the water. My hands moved back and forth along the shaft of the double-bladed paddle. Smooth, long and lean, it curved to fit the cup between my curled fingers and palm. I found my arms and shoulders rotating automatically to the dance rhythm of the paddle. Forward with one blade. Pull. Forward with the other blade. Pull. I was delighted by how quickly the boat slid across the smooth skin of water. Naked hull caressing its partner. Slipping into line and moving, moving to the rhythm of body and paddle.

For me, who had grown up in Minnesota, swam and boated since I was tiny, this was the boat of my dreams. I had always paddled canoes. A kayak is quite different from a canoe. In a canoe you get into your boat. In a kayak you put on your boat. In a kayak you are one step above swimming. You become a creature with license to explore beyond the realms of ordinary earth-bound existence. A creature that is capable of moving into small places with very little water or over immense waves on endless water.

Sea kayaking came into my life when I needed it. In the first eight years of my marriage to Dave we lived in the West. To Dave, a biologist in search of a Ph.D., the lecture hall and field trips were a source of truth and meaning. To me, a school teacher and Forest Service naturalist, time outside held truth and meaning. The more time outside, the wilder the place, the deeper the truth. The dichotomy in our approaches to life was obvious in the way we expanded on our undergraduate biology degrees. Dave kept studying things. I kept exploring them. He used his knowledge to develop his intellectual understanding of the world. I used my knowledge to become part of the world. And that brought me to sea kayaking.

We moved to Duluth, Minnesota, in 1979 for Dave's job as a university professor and adopted a Korean son and daughter within the first few years of being there. Young children gave me a whole new avenue for connecting to the magic and wonder of the natural world. They taught me, the marathon runner and mountain climber, how to saunter. But young children also put a cramp on my passion for physically challenging wilderness exploration. Sea kayaking was a perfect solution. I didn't need a partner, didn't have to coordinate with anyone else's schedule. And I was living on the shore of the largest, most dangerous lake on the planet. One early morning paddle in raging surf while children were still sleeping in the comfort of their beds could salve my desire for wildness for weeks. And so, with the introduction of kayaking into my life, I began to reclaim some of the fierceness and independence of my pre-children life.

It took me five years to get my 5'9", 125-pound frame strong and skilled enough to tackle a trip of the magnitude of circumnavigating Lake Superior. It was five years of taking short trips, of paddling in all seasons, of studying the weather. During that time, I lost my best friend to cancer, turned forty, watched my children enter adolescence and embarked upon a new career. By the time my friend and colleague Paul and I set our boats into the seven-foot surf of Lake Superior on the morning of June 17, 1992, I was ready to become the lake's student. What I didn't realize is that I was but a kindergartner in this school where I was going to discover my next life.

◠

Wednesday, ten in the morning, June 17, 1992. Park Point Beach in Duluth. Low clouds and fog. Strong winds. Four- to seven-foot surf breaking on the sandy beach. I knelt by my boat making last minute adjustments to her load. I moved the food bag forward to make sure the load was balanced. These little rituals were designed to convince me of my own readiness. Finally, I abandoned them in favor of hugs, kisses and goodbyes to the couple dozen friends and family members that joined us on the beach. Last minute whispers from the safety of land. From the life I was leaving behind.

"Are you ready, Mom?" asked twelve-year-old Brian. I had asked if he would help launch me. He was pleased to be asked, eager to help. I finished securing the spray skirt to my cockpit, picked up my paddle and nodded. He and Paul's son, Galen, grabbed the back of my boat and slowly slid me forward on the sand into the shallow water.

"Hold my bow steady," I said. "It's really important that I take off with my bow straight into the waves." Knee deep, then thigh deep, the boys waded into the thirty-six-degree water and pushed the bow within reach of the surf. Three large waves crashed in, one behind the other. The boys struggled to hold the boat straight. Three small waves. Three large waves. The boys still held me steady. The next wave was small, that was it, time to go.

"OK, let go!" I yelled above the roar of the surf.

"Be careful," I heard Brian's voice in my ear. My son. Letting go of me. Trusting me to return. With one strong stroke of the paddle, I was in the lake's power. Beyond the help of anyone on land.

The first wave crashed innocuously on my bow. I wasn't yet out to the big ones. This was the window of calm I needed and the boat was hardly moving. Stroke, Ann. Pull. Got to get out of here before that next big set of waves comes in. My boat felt like a barge. Of course, it was fully loaded! I leaned into each stroke of the paddle.

Pulled the sixty-five-pound boat and its eighty pounds of gear with every muscle in my body.

The next wave broke over my spray skirt. The next hit me in the face. Cold, shocking slap. No time to recover. Just keep paddling forward. Moving to get beyond the breaking surf. Can't look back to see how far out I am. Just keep stroking. Yes, I'm getting there. One more big one to get through.

WHAM—a wall of cold water hit me, engulfed me in stunned blackness. Terror. But as quickly as it hit, it was gone and there was light . . . and another wave coming. Paddle. Quickly up the slope of the wave. Don't let it break over your head. Yes, yes, I'm going to make it. WHAM—my boat slammed down the back side of the wave with a noise so loud I was afraid it would split. But that was all! No more breaking surf. I was free! I had made it beyond the surf, out into the rolling clutches of the open lake. "YAHOO!"

Carefully I turned my boat to face the beach so I could watch Paul come out through the surf.

Shore was so far away. When I rode a wave down into the trough, I could not see land. Up on the crest of a wave I could see dark little stick figures on the beach and Paul's boat resting on the edge of the surf. Brian's pink sweatshirt stood out next to the back of Paul's boat. It seemed forever before he got out to me. During that forever, I kept paddling and maneuvering my boat out of the reach of errant side waves that kept taunting me, trying to tip me over. But I wasn't going to tip. There was only one thing on my mind. I was waiting for my friend, my companion. I did not want to be alone out there.

Paul got to within earshot and let out a war whoop. I yelled back, and we turned our boats in tandem toward the north shore of the lake. We were partners out here, and we were going to be fine.

We held our boats in a position called "quartering." It's a bit like trying to walk along a precipitous mountain ridge when the wind is blowing forty miles per hour from the side, constantly threatening to blow you off balance. But I felt calm, skilled, and was warm inside my wetsuit cocoon, though I dared not divert my attention from the waves and look toward shore.

Gone. We were gone. Into our new lives. The sun emerged and lit up the city of Duluth to our west or left side. A benediction. One last look.

Betsy Aldrich Garland

Learning the Ropes

I never intended to go all the way.

It was not in my nature to take that much risk, to compromise so much, to push myself to the limits. I was a "good" girl who played it safe, hiked with my feet on the ground, considered what people might think and seldom tested the boundaries. Now here I was being strapped into a seat harness and choosing a helmet. If the group had its way with me, they would cajole me high into the trees where I would find myself grasping a thin wire for dear life.

A child of protective middle-aged parents, I was raised more timid than gutsy. I took school work seriously enough to become a good— though not great—student. It never occurred to me to sign up for sports, and I looked forward to trips to the Cape with my mother for nothing more strenuous than shopping and beaching. It was not until my college years that I realized I was missing something: When I let my father and brother go mountain climbing without me, I did not know that backpacks and blisters have their own rewards.

Reading was my passion, and stories about nurses had shaped my decision to become a nurse. Although my application was accepted at both a local Ivy League school and a state university, I chose the latter. Not only did the less prestigious program offer a chance to live on campus and a more science-oriented bachelor's program, it also felt less overwhelming and threatening. Once, in freshman gym class, I was dribbling the ball down the field, heading right for the goal. I was out ahead and my team was cheering me on. At the last minute, I passed the ball. I was not ready for challenges and risks.

Nevertheless, for the first time I excelled academically and graduated first in my nursing class. At the completion of the five-year program, I moved back home with my parents and worked as a public health nurse in the agency in which I had been serving as a student intern. A year later, just as I turned twenty-four, I married. All of my friends were married; it was the expected thing to do. I would not have wanted to be "always a bridesmaid, never a bride."

On our honeymoon at my family's romantic cottage on a little island in New Hampshire's lakes region, my new husband spent all of his time on the beach, working on the property. I was assigned the role of watching from the cottage steps. Building a stone wall took precedence over building our relationship.

Because ours was not a particularly fulfilling marriage, I soon began to volunteer in the community in order to stretch my wings, find some support and add meaning to my life. Out of the house, I had a chance to grow. By the time I began to think about taking legal action, the atmosphere was so bad that, one night at dinner, my perceptive three-year-old daughter leaned over in her highchair, put her sticky little hand on my arm and said, "I know Daddy doesn't love you, Mommy, but I love you." Nevertheless, I struggled along, for better or worse, for twelve years.

When I finally divorced my husband in 1975, I felt free at last—but free to cry tears of exhaustion instead of tears of rage. With total responsibility for two young children, I needed a place to live, a job, child care and a schedule that would mesh with my work (if and when I found some) and their schooling.

That first summer, I worked in a small nursing home, nights, 11:00 P.M. to 7:00 A.M. The director gave me permission to bring my children to work with me, and they slept in the lounge while I made the rounds from room to room. We were so poor that I didn't have change for the laundromat, so if the patients were quiet, I also did our family laundry in the home's machine. And I longed for someone to bring me flowers.

My friends worried about me. A breakthrough came when one of them called and urged me to apply for a position as executive director of a small nonprofit agency. I did, and based on my years of experience as a volunteer, I was hired.

Although I was well suited to provide leadership to the agency, I had no office experience. It was a mysterious place. Buttons on the telephone took on a life of their own and cut people off. Cabinets—if one found the magic button to unlock them—swallowed file folders between the hanging files. The compensation, for both the board that had hired me and for myself, was that the paid work was surprisingly similar to the volunteer work I had been orchestrating from my kitchen table. I learned quickly. At first, the weekly newspaper column I wrote as part of my job took a full day, but after a year or so, only an hour. Gradually, I learned new skills and gained self-confidence. In a few years, I was a busy executive with a budget to balance, reports to write, a staff to supervise. The trophy I earned was a house in the suburbs, maple trees and a lawn to mow. On Saturdays, the children, golden retriever and I went hiking. We were settled in—in every way.

It was to this predictable life that the summons came almost a decade later. Counseling church camp for a week in western Rhode Island was not my choice. But I was on the camp board, and my friend, the director, was short a few volunteers. She talked me into it—just to be there, to supervise the younger counselors, to add a little oversight, to share my wisdom and experience. Little did I suspect that what I would undertake there would change my life.

All week, we were preparing the campers for the high ropes. We spent a morning on group initiatives, spotting each other as we crossed the wobble log, learning to work together to solve problems, using the groups' resources to get everyone over a beam lashed high between two trees. Even though I was old enough to be their mother, I was handed up and over in an explosion of group excitement. With so many hands reaching out for me, I felt weightless and free from ordinary constraints.

Each evening was the day's reward. After hours of physical exertion, we trudged back to our campsite in the woods, hot, happy and tired—a family unit of sorts. And although we weren't through, we had only to gather wood, haul water and make supper over a campfire before we could rest. We all lingered in the firelight, reflecting on the adventures of the day, and tried to get some perspective on the serious business of being teenagers in a confusing world. As night deepened and the whippoorwills began to call and the owls to hunt, we made ourselves as comfortable as we could in hammocks slung between two trees—all under the guise of building community, learning to trust, forming healthy relationships.

Late in the week, we were scheduled for the biggest challenge of them all: high ropes. Since I had a proposal to write and needed to spend several hours at my desk in the city, I planned an escape. There was nothing I could do to facilitate the afternoon's agenda. The trained ropes-staff would be there for the teenage campers. I slipped out of camp.

Returning several hours later, I wandered up to the ropes course to see how my campers were managing. We were in a lovely pine grove, fragrant with evergreen and carpeted with needles. Forty feet above us was the Postman's Walk: two cables, one above the other, strung between trees ten feet apart. Those who mastered that could take on the Burma Bridge, a loose rope concourse with rope "rails." The way down was the zip line—or a return back over the full course.

A few of the campers already had completed the ropes. Others were in the trees. One girl was sitting on a branch, crying, waiting for the courage to go on. The boys were trying to act macho, but their pale faces broadcast their fear. Everyone, at the very least, was expected to try the ropes, to test themselves in extreme conditions— although how far one went was a matter of personal decision.

"OK, Betsy, you're next," someone called. Thinking he was joking, I laughed. "There's no way I can climb that ladder!"

"Sure you can." The bigger boys were feeling empowered and insisted with missionary-like zeal, "We'll hold the ladder steady for you, Betsy." Caution was my birthright, and reluctance, my middle name. I thought that I would take a few steps, and they would see that I was too old, too physically out of shape for this.

"How dangerous is this, really? I'm not very strong." I saw that Jack, the ropes director, belayed each climber. The rope on my seat harness went up through a pulley on the topmost cable and back down to the ground through Jack's harness.

"No problem!" he said. "If you fall, I just pull up on the line to catch you and then lower you to the ground."

Right, I thought, if Jack is paying attention. I had missed the dangling-in-mid-air, there's-nothing-to-worry-about demonstration while I was back at the office.

It was hot in the grove. OK, I decided, I'll fake it. I put one uncertain foot up on the first rung.

The boys showed me how to wrap my arms around the ladder, to hold on from behind, keeping the ladder close to my body. I inched up another couple of rungs. "That's the way, Betsy, keep it up," they said.

I didn't have a good excuse not to keep going, at least not one that would not have demoralized my campers. I climbed, sliding my arms up with each step.

Never expecting to go that far, I hadn't considered what I would do when I reached the top. The cables intersected with the ladder, one above my head about a foot or so; the other, near my feet.

"Now step out on the cable to your right," ordered Jack-the-Roper. Silent prayers winged their way to heaven. "Where do I hold on?"

"Reach up and take hold of the cable above your head."

Slowly, with my heart pounding, I did as I was told. I moved off the ladder and onto the cables.

"That's it," Jack said helpfully from below. He stood alert, head up, legs braced, more confident of my safety than I, hands on the line connecting us. "Now turn around."

I was suspended forty feet in the air. The cable under my feet cut into my sneakers.

Jack called up, "Lean forward a little and pull on the cable above your head; that will help you to stop shaking."

With perspiration running down the back of my scalp, along my jaw line and dripping off my chin in a steady stream, I wondered if anyone noticed it was raining on the ground. My God, now what?

"Now walk along the cable to the tree."

The tree was a long way off. I tentatively moved my left foot an inch or two and then pulled my right one up beside it. Like a crab, I inched sideways, one baby step, then another, trailing my rope like an umbilical cord.

"You're lookin' good, Betsy—keep it up!" my campers encouraged.

Persistence pays off. After a very long time, I made it to the tree where I was welcomed by a staff person who invited me to step up on her knee so that I could throw my leg over the waiting branch. She hooked me into the tree safety system and freed the rope for the next climber. "Rest for a few minutes," she offered graciously. I leaned my head against the trunk and breathed. Now I knew why this was called the most-hugged tree on the grounds.

What was I doing here, high in this pine with its rough bark against my cheek and its beads of pitch gumming my hands? Having made it this far was more a surprise than an accomplishment. Was this a bad dream or a cruel trick? Had I, in a moment of being a good sport, allowed myself to be manipulated into this situation? Or had I myself chosen this high adventure?

Now it was beginning to get crowded in the air. Someone else was nearing the tree; I needed to move on to make room. The staffer hooked me into the bridge system, a new terror to be confronted and overcome. I took a step onto the ropes and sank about two feet.

"Push out on the rails," I was told.

To my surprise, doing so made the bridge firmer. I pushed my arms along, afraid to let go to advance my hands. The skin began to peel off the inside of my forearms, a small price to pay for life itself.

My concentration began to wane. Although I was getting tired, I had made it this far and the end of the course was in sight. I noticed that my cheering squad had disappeared; those who had been so encouraging of my ascent had abandoned me for others who were starting to climb. I was alone, high above everyone, stripped bare, vulnerable. Time stood still. There was neither past nor future, only sky and wind and texture, and the moment to which I held on with every nerve and muscle. I was there forever.

The sound of voices, familiar voices, brought me back to my plight. Visiting church leaders had wandered up to watch the day's activities on the high ropes. "What is Betsy doing up there?" I heard one woman ask another. Good question, I thought, not knowing whether to be proud or embarrassed. High ropes are for campers, not for middle-aged women.

A new staffer hooked me into the tree system at the end of the course. There was a board nailed into the crotch of the tree where campers could sit. The only challenge left was to reach out, grasp the zip line and push off into space.

"Go whenever you're ready." Campers were waiting at the bottom to slow my one-hundred-fifty-foot slide to the ground.

After what I had just been through, this seemed easy. Nevertheless, I decided that, just like waiting on the end of the board to dive into cold water, I had better not think about it too long. I took a deep breath and a firm hold on the rope above my head, propelled myself out of the tree, spun around, and began my free-fall to solid ground. I had done it!

I was soaked with sweat and dizzy with excitement. My throat was dry, my knees weak. Someone took my picture. Someone else unhooked me and helped me off with my helmet. The ordeal—and I— were finished. Expecting, at my advanced age, that I would be allowed at least several hours to recover, I went and sat on the ground, until I realized I was needed to coax the boy behind me out of the tree. One by one, the campers were working their way through the system.

I sifted pine needles through my fingers. I had just had one of the most intense physical experiences of my lifetime. Only giving birth to my two children had demanded the same utter concentration, stamina and emotional control—before ropes. Now that my body was grounded, my spirit began to soar. I was, as my campers would say, "psyched!"

Because of that experience, I have learned to push against the limits. I have chosen, again and again, to discover what I can do, to expand my horizons, to achieve beyond my wildest imagination.

In mastering the high ropes, I knew, perhaps for the first time, that I could do whatever I needed to do to be true to my deepest self. Perhaps I had strayed outside the norm by being one of the first clergy wives to file for divorce, but I had not understood the significance of what I had done then. I could buy flowers for myself, whenever I wanted them.

I learned then that I have a deep well of personal strength from which I can draw living water when needed. A year later, while working full-time, I enrolled in graduate school to earn the classical education I had missed in my nursing program. During my first semester on campus, I met a woman in the courtyard. "Aren't you Betsy Garland?" she asked. "I was a visitor to the camp on the day you climbed the high ropes." I remembered the people in the clearing. "You can do anything," she said. I knew it was true.

Life, in all its fullness, has tested me many times since.

But over the years, I have learned to do what needs to be done, to focus on where I am going, to drink deeply. My experience in the air has helped me to become grounded, knowing how and when to hold on tightly, take one step at a time, trust the people around me, stay alert, do my best.

I am ready for almost anything. I have learned the ropes.

IV

ANIMAL KIN

Gift of Wild Creatures

Willow

April 15-May 12

Jessica Maxwell

Monarchs and Manatees

*C*all me a retro-nerd. Call me a gonzo naturalist. But when it comes to being impressed by genius, the Wild Kingdom wins over the Silicon Valley every time. Would computer wizard Steve Wozniak keep his teeth in his stomach, and his stomach in his head? Or replace a lost eye with a nose? The Maine lobster does. If a large gator attacked microchip genie Bill Gates, could Gates cast off his leg, then grow back another? The starfish can. This alone is reason enough for technobrats to remember to take a field trip every once in a while.

It's early winter. The monarchs are clustering in Santa Barbara. O excellent creatures, fragile and fair. How worms and ants do pale beside your royal markings of mandarin and black. I'm on the next plane south to California.

Christopher Nagano works in the entomology section of the Natural History Museum in Los Angeles County. Officially he's a research associate, but he spends a lot of his time educating the public about the plight of the migrating monarch, a hundred million of which fly hundreds, even thousands, of miles each fall to the coastline of California or the high mountains of central Mexico, where they wait out the freezing temperatures farther north.

Monarchs east of the continental divide head for Mexico. Those west of it fly to California, weaving their way through the passes and valleys of the Rocky Mountains, then across the deserts of California. "They have to stop to fuel up with flower nectar and water on the way," Nagano says, "but the most they travel in a day is eighty miles." Like hawks, they like to ride the thermal currents because they can glide without having to flap their wings. They don't migrate in flocks, Nagano explains; they fly solo, though mountain passes often funnel them together. "They start arriving in California in September, most of them show up in October, and they begin to leave in January. By mid-March they're gone." Every year these elegant black-and-orange lepidopterans return to the same trees. Like salmon and wild geese and whales, monarchs are living metaphors for what Native Americans call the Sacred Circle, representing a worldview that respects the ongoing cyclical nature of life and is opposed to interrupting or destroying those cycles. And as usual, we're wiping them out.

"Approximately one dozen colonies in California have been destroyed or heavily damaged in the last few years because of urban or agricultural development," reports *DANAUS*, a newsletter about California monarchs named after the monarch's Latin name, *Danaus plexippus*, and edited by Nagano and colleagues Walter H. Sakai and Gary Wolfe. Recently the International Union for the Conservation of Nature and Natural Resources made the protection of wintering monarch colonies a "top priority." The monarch is the only insect listed in the Convention for the Conservation of Migratory Species of Wild Animals—or "Bonn Convention"—an international treaty protecting many animals. And during his tenure as California governor, George Deukmejian signed into law a bill that officially recognizes wintering monarchs as a special California phenomenon. "It's the first time the state of California has admitted the environmental importance of an insect in a positive way," Nagano says.

He asks me to meet him at the Ellwood Colony at 10:00 A.M. It's a bright winter day, and following his map, I park at the dead end of a modest residential street, then venture into an adjacent grove of eucalyptus trees. It's another universe. The air is cool, perfumed with the mint and medicine breath of the gum trees. Colors are transcendent—mottled lavender and peach and jade. The ground is a crinkly mop of leaves and shredded bark that makes you want to kick at it, regardless of your age. Nagano said he'd be "in the wash with the monarchs," but everything looks the same, and I don't have the faintest idea which way to turn. I'm lost. Then, with that same bewildering otherness that imbues the whole place, a monarch butterfly appears out of nowhere and flies right past my nose like a guide manifest. I follow.

We make a sudden left-hand turn, and there is Nagano, sitting cross-legged beneath a tree with a long-handled butterfly net on his lap, writing in a notebook. A monarch is walking slowly up his sleeve. I'm stunned. The tree looks like it's strung with red Santa Fe chilies. No, I realize, it's covered with butterflies, and the butterflies are moving! This is a bona fide butterfly tree. The constant fanning of all their wings sounds like a light rain.

"There are about three thousand monarch butterflies here today,"

Nagano says, clearly enjoying my awe. "They are also known by the name milkweed butterfly because that's all they eat." It turns out that a chemical in milkweed both nourishes the monarchs and makes them toxic to most birds. "A bird eats a monarch once and never tries again," says Nagano. With a chuckle he adds, "Lincoln Brower, distinguished professor of zoology at the University of Florida in Gainesville, won an Esquire Dubious Achievement Award for determining how many monarchs it takes to make a blue jay vomit.

"You want to tag a monarch?" he asks. We hold the kicking butterflies in one hand, while with the other we carefully rub a bald spot in the powdery microscopic scales on the upper edges of both sides of one wing. Then we gently pinch on a rather unremarkable-looking small white sticky label printed with the words MAIL TO NAT. HIST. MUSEUM, LA, CA 90007, followed by a number like MP-L 38465. Nagano records the tag number in his notebook, then we let the butterflies go. The tag doesn't affect their ability to fly. Nagano says they don't even know the tag is there. Once they die, with luck someone mails them to the museum and says where the insect was found. By checking the tag number, researchers know where it was tagged and how far it got. "One that was tagged in Toronto showed up in Mexico," Nagano says proudly.

Scientists know just about everything there is to know about the manatees—from their evolutionary development, sexual behavior and physiology to their communication skills and feeding habits. These ancient, big, sweet, slow, vegetarian mammals, sometimes called sea cows, belong to the order Sirenia. Forty-five-million-year-old sirenian fossils have been found in Florida. Biologists believe that sirenians evolved from four-footed land mammals more than sixty million years ago, citing their undeveloped pelvic bones as evidence of terrestrial ancestors. Manatee bones also have been found in pre-Columbian refuse mounds in southeastern Florida.

There's no creature in the United States even remotely as strange looking as the manatee, which reminds one of a cross between the Blob and a vacuum cleaner. The manatee is almost hairless, except for stiff, cactuslike whiskers around the face and sparse, fine hairs on the body. Thrown in to complete the absurd look: a beaver tail and flippers with three or four nails at the tip. Just under the finely wrinkled skin is a layer of fat deposits. A bulbous face and small, wide-set eyes give the manatee a sort of lost walrus look.

Found in freshwater, brackish and marine habitats, they're usually about 10 feet long and weigh from 800 to 2,000 pounds, though some grow to a whopping 12.7 feet and weigh in at 3,500 pounds. This makes sense, since the manatee's nearest living relative is the elephant. Though nobody knows for sure, it's thought that if left alone, manatees can live up to sixty years. The oldest one in captivity is twenty-nine.

Manatees have a prehensile mouth that folds in and out much the way an elephant's trunk does. In the wild, manatees put away up to 100 pounds of abrasive water plants a day, which explains their bizarre ability to wear away and grow back one set of teeth after another. This factor, biologists say, allowed the manatees to survive in the New World and replace the dugongs, their relatives in the Pacific. At any given time, new teeth are sprouting in the back jaw of a manatee's mouth. The new teeth move toward the front as the old teeth fall out. It's like an ongoing dental parade that lasts a lifetime. Even a dying manatee often has a new set of molars.

The social behavior of manatees fascinates biologists. They have no natural enemies besides man, no social hierarchy, no daily set routines. Many of them will swim right up to divers to be petted. When manatees are together in groups, one manatee does not dominate the herd, although a manatee often initiates playtime. Manatees love to play. Between somersaults, head stands, tail stands and barrel rolls, they bodysurf, kiss, nuzzle, bump and chase one another. And eat. Manatees spend about five to eight hours a day feeding. The Flying Karamazov Brothers of the animal kingdom, what we're doing to them with our speedboats is unforgivable.

Of the 1,200 manatees left in the United States today, 900 are officially identified by their boat prop scars. "There's one huge cow whose tail is just spaghetti," says Cheryl Buckingham, a graduate student working with the United States Fish and Wildlife Service. During the summer months, Buckingham comes to the Gulf Coast town of Homosassa Springs, some eighty miles north of Tampa, to study the effects of boaters and divers on the 160 or so manatees that make the nearby Crystal River National Wildlife Refuge their winter home. The Fish and Wildlife Service staff—project leader Patrick Hagan, law enforcement officer Frank Brauszewski and biologist Larry Hartis—manage five refuges, covering eighty miles of Florida's central west coast.

"You probably won't see a manatee today," Hagan cautions. "It's late in the season, and they're pretty much dispersed." In summer manatees roam all over Florida's coastal waters, estuaries, bays and rivers. During the winter, cold temperatures drive the manatees to warm water discharges at power plants and natural warm water areas like the Crystal River refuge. But we take the boat out anyway and tour the nine islands and 33.12 acres of the refuge. Yellow-finned mullet leap out of the water all around us. We pass magnolia trees, red cedars and pickerelweed with their purple floral spears. There are pines, oaks, banana trees, sweet gums, cabbage palms and palmettos. And everywhere, just under the surface of the water, lies the spongy green countenance of hydrilla. Buckingham reaches in and grabs a handful.

"This is the manatees' favorite food," she says. "And this is where they like to stay when it gets cold. There are six hundred million gallons of water in the whole system and more than one hundred springs. This one stays seventy-two degrees year-round—it's the biggest one."

We pull into a little half-moon bay marked by signs that read MANATEE SANCTUARY and IDLE SPEED. Ospreys, eagles, cormorants, pelicans, major league gators and countless jump-for-joy mullet—but no manatees. "You can always see them over at Nature World," Hagan offers kindly.

Nature World is just a short drive from the manatee refuge center in Homosassa Springs. It's a tourist attraction with the usual snack bar and tackola gift shop setup. But the main part is built over a natural spring, and it's really quite pretty. I meet Betsy Dearth. She works full-time at Nature World, "doing just about everything." We're standing in the underwater observation room while the dozen or so resident manatees float eerily above our heads. "Rosie circles a lot—she has an equilibrium problem," says Dearth. With a sad smile, she adds, "They really ask for nothing. They don't kill anything. They just want to float along—and eat." Nature World manatees consume fifty pounds of carrots, five cases of lettuce and three cases of cabbage every day.

I ask if I can feed them by hand. Despite the fact that state law forbids the public to feed protected species, Dearth agrees to bend the rules and leads me to a little clearing on the shoreline. Several large manatees come over—Hugh, Magoo, Amanda. I hold out a carrot, and Rosie surfaces, working her lips like gates in a pinball machine. Her breath smells powerfully of cabbage. "Their mouths are like a hand," Dearth says. Rosie takes the carrot, nudging my hand sweetly in the process.

Her touch disorients me. Forty-five million years, I think, compared to our meager 250,000. They were here with the first whales and the saber-toothed cats. When the mountains came barreling out of the seas, they were here. When glaciers took the land like a cold cancer, they were here. What are the pyramids held against the cellular memories of manatees? What is a Corinthian column? Even, I wonder, what is the Pythagorean theorem? And, certainly, what is a 5000 Scarab Meteor powerboat with a Triple 420-horsepower Merc V8 cutting twenty-foot rooster tails across what's left of the natural habitats of these ancient beasts?

The natural properties—the sun, the trees, the bays and rivers— that have supported life so luxuriantly for millions and millions of years on this long green peninsula are the very same ones that make Florida so attractive to Homo sapiens. Every day 1,000 people move to the state. Every month they launch 1,500 new pleasure boats. Only 1,200 manatees are left in Florida—the odds aren't good. At least for now the animals are still there, and there's a strong movement in the state to keep it that way.

If you ever find yourself discontented about our age, thinking that technology's homogenization has bankrupted the planet of its original eccentricities; that the presence of McDonald's in Beijing and of Whitney Houston T-shirts in Borneo has rendered the earth, once again, quite flat; then it is helpful to recall that from Mexico to California, monarch butterflies prepare for their return trips north and gentle manatees float in Florida's waterways. For just beyond the roar of Mercs and Evinrudes, just beneath the dispassionate skins of Congoleum and Astroturf, that old natural magic is still going strong—and you don't have to float down the Amazon to find it. It's right here, snorting, flapping, wallowing and burrowing in America's own backyard.

Sherry Simpson

Where Bears Walk

*I*n the dream, I cower amidst tall grass, or beneath bushes, or behind trees. The place where I hide changes, but the terror never does. I hear the bear slavering and growling, its footsteps drumming the earth. It is looking for me. It sniffs the air, and I know it smells my fear. It will find me. Then it will tear me apart and eat me.

In the moment of discovery, as the bear rears high before descending on me, I always wake, my heart leaping against my chest as if it could abandon the rest of my leaden body to the kill. Sometimes, when at last I sleep again, the bear resumes stalking me through the night.

For years I could not enter the woods of Southeast Alaska without my heart flailing about like a crippled thrush, without dread persuading me that somewhere among the green twilight of trees, the great hunter hunted me. And yet, even though I have lived in Juneau since I was seven, never have I encountered a bear as more than a shadow fading away at the edges of some forest or beach. I have roamed through tidal flats and rainforest, alpine meadow and creekside brush, all the places where bears roam, and I have never been threatened by a bear. It is simply enough to know they are there, enlarged by lore every Alaskan cultivates.

I am a good student of such bear gossip. I could tell you about the hunter dragged off and partially eaten by a brown bear drawn to the sound of the man's deer call. I remember the neighbor boy chased down West Glacier trail by a black bear. There was the solitary camper missing in Glacier Bay, his death revealed by frames in his camera that captured the bear entering his camp. To believe in these tales of blood and flesh and teeth, to imagine them well, I had only to meet a man blinded by a brown bear he encountered as a seventeen-year-old hunter on a local creek. I saw the whole story in his face, a face rearranged into a topography of scars, and I wondered what he remembered of bears in his personal and enduring darkness.

Among shadows, things appear larger than they really are. I did not overcome my fear of bears until I smelled the dark, wild smell of bears on my hands, until I felt the slow wave of blood washing through a bear's veins, until I walked where bears walk.

LaVern Beier is not afraid of bears. The Alaska Department of Fish and Game calls him a technician for his proficiency in finding, trapping and tranquilizing mountain goats, wolves, wolverines and all manner of creatures that do not wish to be found, including the drugged brown bear slumped on the patch of stale snow before us. Vern is not just a technician, though. Something in Vern Beier makes me imagine he is part-bear himself, the offspring of one of those mythic matings between bear and woman that never led to any good for the bear. (As for the woman, who can say?) Perhaps it is Vern's wiry hair, the shagginess of his black beard, the economy and purpose in his stocky frame that make me think such things. More likely it is the steady brown eyes that see more than he ever says. But I detect the resemblance also in the rough but loving way he runs his hands through the thin spring pelt of this half-conscious bear, as if he knows her. Pretty bony, is all he says. Must have been a hard winter.

I am not looking at the bear's coffee-colored fur. I am looking at her teeth. My, what big teeth she has. Slobber webs canines the shade of scrimshaw and the size of a man's thumb. This bear galloped for more than ten minutes from the pursuing helicopter, her legs moving like pistons over ridges and up slopes, driving her across the alpine reaches of Admiralty Island. She did not hide; she ran. Even after Vern leaned through the copter's open door and sighted his rifle on her bounding rump, darting her twice with a tranquilizer potent enough to down an elephant, she ran and ran until the drug slammed into her and she did not get up. I make a promise to myself when I see that. I promise never again to fool myself into thinking a human can run from a bear.

Because I am in no danger at the moment, my sympathies lie entirely with the bear, though as a newspaper reporter writing an article about bear research, my job is to take notes, not to sympathize with anybody or anything. I understand the scientific rationale that volunteered this bear to be chased, prodded, poked, tagged, plucked, measured and collared with a radio transmitter that by a steady beep will describe her movements but never convey the true power of her motion. I have no trouble reconciling a personal fear of bears with a distant appreciation of them. But I don't tell anybody the real reason I asked for this story: so I can touch with my own hands what frightens me most.

Vern and his partner, wildlife biologist Kim Titus, are here on this mountaintop on an early July evening because they need data. It is not enough to know that a silver mine on Admiralty Island or too much clear-cut logging on neighboring Chichagof Island, means nothing good for bears. You must say it in a tangled dialect of science and bureaucracy, the way Kim says it in his cramped office at the Department of Fish and Game: "In theory the model will predict the capability of the habitat to support some given population of brown bears or some reduced population of bears, given certain developmental impacts." Out here under the naked sky, in the world of fish and game, he says it this way: "We're documenting the demise of the bears."

I have never been this close to a living bear. Her eyes flicker under half-closed lids. Does she see me? Does she dream of being scented out by strange and roaring creatures? Does her heart lunge in her chest? With each shuddering breath, she groans deeply, a sound laced with menace to my ear. "Is she snoring or growling?" I ask Vern, hoping my voice reveals nothing of the dizzy way blood spins through me.

"Probably both," he says without concern. Three times he has killed a charging bear in self-defense. He never sets his short-handled rifle with the custom stock out of reach. He is not afraid of bears, but he is not stupid.

Vern rearranges the bear, stretching out her legs and tilting her head so she can breathe more easily. He estimates her age at about six years old, a teenager in bear years, and her weight at about 280 pounds. "They come a lot bigger than this," he remarks. "They come a lot smaller than this. But she's big enough to kill you." Perhaps by the way I circle the sedated bear, leaning close, but not too close, he senses my nervous thrill. "Ever held a bear's leg before?" he asks. I'm not sure if he's provoking me or soothing me. He moves to her haunches and shifts a hind leg into my hands. I struggle to heft it as he draws blood from the tender groin. Each dark hair is ticked with white; skin shines palely through the sparse fur.

"Feel how warm her paws are," Vern says, laying the blood-filled syringe in the snow. I press my palm against the leathery pad. The curving ebony claws stretch longer than my little finger. Heat radiates into my skin. When I was eight, one of the fathers in our neighborhood killed a bear and stripped away its hide. His son showed me a naked bear paw that looked like a human hand with its bluish veins and knobby fingers. No wonder so many people regard the bear as a savage relation. The Inuit thought of bears as ancestors. The Lapps called the bear "old man with the fur garment." The Finns named him "golden friend." A Tlingit Indian who encountered a brown bear always spoke to it as if it were a person, addressing it in kinship terms. If a bear killed a Tlingit, the clan followed the social law of a life for a life; the Tlingit's family sent a hunting party to kill one of the bear's family.

Under my hands, this bear is a furnace, burning with life. Vern watches me, and when he sees the look on my face, he smiles a little.

When the helicopter lofts itself from the plain, the bear lifts her groggy head for a moment and peers after us. She looks clownish with a yellow and a white tag punched into each ear and a white leather radio collar circling her neck. We have stolen something from her.

In the helicopter, we soar around peaks still dappled with snow, dip into valleys, coast over alpine meadows. The evening sun drifts toward the horizon, where soon it will snag on the Chilkat Mountains. The slanting rays illuminate tufts of grass, beds of heather, purple lupine drooping with tight blooms. Beyond Admiralty Island, golden light spills across the rumpled waters of Chatham Strait. There is something not quite real, something dreamlike, in the way we float through this stained-glass light.

Admiralty Island is the Manhattan of bears, populated with one brown bear for each of the island's seventeen hundred square miles. In the Alaskan interior, where people call brown bears "grizzlies," though they are all of the same tribe, you will find, on average, a single bear in every fifteen square miles or so. There are more bears on this island than in the entire continental United States. The Tlingit Indians call Admiralty by the name *Kootznoowoo*, which means "Fortress of the Bears."

But Admiralty is not a haven, just a holdout. Trophy hunting, clear-cut logging and the constant press of civilization threaten bears even here. You can kill bears quickly, by shooting them, or slowly, by moving in with them. When the American West was bored through by railroads and pocked with towns, it took just fifty years to eliminate nearly all grizzly bears in those parts. Today, people fight with each other in places like Idaho over whether or not bears should be reintroduced to their former haunts, but I see little point in planting bears where they are not wanted. People will insist on seeing bears always as prey or predator. Life for a bear is more complex than that.

Flying high, swooping low, we spot several bears rummaging around the valleys and crowns of Mansfield Peninsula at the northern crook of Admiralty Island. Some escape with little more than a fright, for Kim and Vern seek females, especially sows with cubs. They want to know if Greens Creek Silver Mine pushes bear families into new ranges, rather like city families abandoning the neighborhood to a freeway. If the bears do strike out for more peaceful territory, who will they elbow out of the way? Or will they simply birth fewer young?

What angers the biologists most is clear-cut logging, especially in places like northeast Chichagof Island, where large tracts of old-growth timber are systematically shaved from Tongass National Forest and private lands. Bears rely on all kinds of terrain in their wandering lives, but a clearcut is not one of them. The problem is not only that logging squeezes bears into shrinking habitats. Logging roads lead hunters easily into the dense forests; garbage dumps lure bears into villages and logging camps where they are sometimes shot for their bad habits.

Officially, most of Admiralty is considered a national wilderness area, as if words were ever enough to create such a thing. But even here, bear hunting is legal on most of the island. Native corporations log their private lands as any other business would. Greens Creek Mine, though praised by environmentalists for its sensitivity, nevertheless has claimed a valley with a salmon stream and watershed. "The frontier is ending," Kim says. And Vern adds bitterly, "It stopped when they built the pipeline. We're not making brown bear habitat anymore. I don't know of any place where we're making it."

We descend into a wide bowl glimmering with a lake of melted snow. Six black-tailed deer, dainty as fairies, graze in a line along the ridge. Two bears shamble through this basin, one breaking into a half-hearted trot around the lake when it hears the helicopter whining.

Vern darts the other bear, the larger of the two, thinking it is a female. When it shows no sign of slowing, Vern aims through the open helicopter door and shoots it again with a particularly effective drug called M99. One drop will kill a human, but it takes several cc's to down a bear.

With the tufted darts dangling from its hindquarters, the bear starts up a bluff knitted with twisted spruce and blueberry bushes. "All I can say is, you guys are going to have fun in there," the pilot says over the intercom.

"Yeah, it'll be great," Kim replies, peering out the window. "She can roll a long way in there." He's worried that the bear will pass out and fall before it reaches the top. The helicopter rises about twenty feet from the bluff as the bear steadily climbs, its passage revealed only by trembling brush. Suddenly the animal lunges from an opening below the helicopter and swipes at the skids, so close that the pilot jerks the craft away to avoid the bear's reach. "Did you see that!" Kim exclaims, and we all look at each other, laughing nervously. But really, it seems only slightly amusing to reflect that if rescuers were to find our crumpled helicopter at the bluff's foot, they would never know a bear had clawed it from the sky.

The bear does indeed fall senseless ten feet below the cliff-top, but the brush holds it fast. The pilot lands the copter on the plateau so Kim and Vern can hoist rifles and a cargo net over their shoulders and scramble down to the animal. The pilot maneuvers a hook over the net and hauls the limp bear out. A scale on the net weighs the animal at 480 pounds.

It turns out to be a male, but Kim and Vern work him over anyway. Kim straddles the bear with his long legs, then lies with his face buried in fur as he stretches a measuring tape around its girth. I resist making bear-hug jokes. A hunter sizing up the pelt would call this an eight-foot bear. Vern estimates the animal at about thirteen years old. A brown bear can live twenty years or more in the wild, if it avoids disease, starvation, bigger bears, men with guns and unexpected tumbles down cliffs.

Vern asks me to hold the bear's head while he uses pliers to yank a small premolar tooth that will reveal the bear's age as surely as my driver's license reports mine. I grasp the rounded ears and pull, straining to lift the massive skull and to ignore the half-open, reddened eyes. The snout is scarred, gnarly with ridges and bumps. "Love bites," Vern calls them. You hear that bears smell terrible—people who have survived being mauled remark on the awful stench—but this early in the season, these bears smell no stronger than my dogs.

When Vern finishes, I lower the bear's head and then sit close, stroking the muzzle, admiring the nearness and smallness of my hand next to the range of yellowed teeth. It is these teeth I dream about, when I dream about bears. Teeth, and blood. Some part of me connects the dreams to the dark passage from childhood to adulthood, through rites of blood and sex and love and loss, beyond that youthful time when we're attracted to dying because we don't believe in death. When I was a teenager, I found both independence and discovery outdoors, in the places where my friends and I hiked and camped. It was a way to escape adult scrutiny, to go where we wanted to go. It was how we stretched our new bodies as we walked and walked among enormous Sitka spruce and hemlock trees or scouted along the high-tide line of rocky beaches for the proper place to build fires and make camp.

There always came a time of night when we told bear stories to scare ourselves, and then we told sex stories, to scare ourselves. But I was always the first to hear the bear's hoarse breath, to smell the rank presence, to imagine what waited in the dark. I was the one who worried that bears could smell us bleeding as only women bleed. I was the one who lay awake all night trembling, trying not to breathe, waiting to be rended, waiting to surrender.

I pass my hand over the bear's head, across thick, coarse fur. I can't help myself; I ask if a sedated bear has ever suddenly come to life. Vern tells about the time a biologist was nearly unmanned when a bear abruptly swung its head around and snapped. Everybody laughs, even me.

I smooth the black pelt, then ruffle it again. I'm taking liberties I haven't earned. I know that. Near the shoulder rests a tiny feather, creamy with tan stripes—from a grouse, I suppose. I lift it with my little finger and poke it into the coin pocket of my jeans.

As Vern and Kim finish collaring the boar, they notice a trio of bears rambling across a slope on the opposite curve of the basin. Through binoculars Vern sees a sow trailed by two tiny cubs—"cubs of the year," they're called. This is just the sort of family the researchers covet most for their mine study. Vern decides not to administer the antidote that would bring the drugged bear to its feet in minutes. The male was probably loitering in the basin with the darkest of intentions. Male bears are cannibalistic and will eat cubs, a fine reason for mothers to be so fierce. We leave the bear slumbering on the tundra and climb into the helicopter to hop across the valley.

As the copter begins tracking the sow, the cubs struggle to keep up, tumbling and falling, tripping over themselves. The mother slows to wait for them, then bursts into a gallop again. The cubs churn their short legs as fast as they can. I clench my teeth together when I see the way they glance blindly at the sky, not sure what they're running from. We circle, looping, twisting, hovering overhead. The bears slide down a gully. Vern hangs out the door, hair blowing wildly, takes aim, darts the mother in the rump. In a few minutes, as she begins mounting a rocky chute, she sags and then falls, hind legs splayed behind her.

The helicopter lands behind a ridge, and we creep over to the bears, whispering so we don't frighten the young. The cubs cling to their mother and watch our approach; only as we draw close do they retreat, turning back to look at us every few steps. They bawl in curious, wrenching croaks. A hundred feet away they clamber onto a rocky shelf and peer over the edge at us, and I try not to stare too hard back at them.

The men work quickly so the cubs do not wander off. Vern has a hard time finding a blood vein on the inside of the sow's hind leg, so when he does feel it, he asks me to mark the pulse with my finger while he readies the needle. Her blood surges in hesitant throbs against my skin. I think of the bear in her winter den, this faint beat offering comfort to the cubs while they, still barely formed, burrowed against her fur. Aristotle believed the mother bear licked her cubs into being, shaped them for the world.

The clean air chills. It's nearly ten at night, and the sun fades in a painterly way, coloring the sky in shades of salmon. The nearness of the honey-colored bear, the occasional squall of her cubs, the panorama that draws the eye beyond this green basin, across the straits— I try to saturate my memory with these details. A sense of beauty and loss pierces me as I struggle to tell myself something important, something lasting about this night, about how I have glimpsed the way bears live here, high above the world, and yet not nearly far enough away from roads, chainsaws, guns, helicopters. If this mountaintop is wilderness, then it is wilderness that rubs so close to civilization that I can feel it fraying beneath my feet.

It is one of the oldest stories in the world, how the woman married the bear and gave him half-human, half-bear young. In the Haida version, her brothers killed her bear lover, of course, but the offspring lived to teach the people, to help them hunt, before returning to the bear world. It's been said that we kill what we both revere and dread. That is what myths do, turn something greater than ourselves into something human. I'm doing it right now.

It's a hard thing to know, that our weakness is that we hate what is stronger than us. And yet, without bears roaming through forests, climbing down from mountains, frightening us, what will we respect on this earth? What is left to remind us that while we stand in a world shadowed by myth, wilderness, death, we cannot master it, nor can we deny it?

When Vern finishes collaring the bear, he injects her with an antidote so she will rouse quickly and gather her cubs. He stands for a moment, looking down at the sow. She should be stirring. Kim gestures to me, and we pick our way back to the helicopter. I look back just once, to fix the still bear and those cubs in my mind. A few minutes later, Vern climbs into his seat. He doesn't say anything. I want to ask him about the bear, but I'm afraid to know. Sometimes, not often, but sometimes, things go wrong. Sometimes the drugs kill them, or hypothermia, or other bears. I'm afraid to know what could happen to the sow and her cubs. This is my weakness, that I'm afraid to know.

Sky translates itself into night as we fly homeward, across the peaks. We land on a mountain slope to recover the passenger door removed earlier so Vern could lean into the wind and track bears. Kim leads me to a nearby ridge and pauses at the edge of a trail. After a moment, I see what he wants me to see. Deep into the tundra, hollows dimple the path where, for centuries, bears have placed their feet in the same spot with every step. They wear their passage into the earth as they come down from the mountains and then return, season after season. I realize that there's another way to see bears—that a bear has nothing to do with us at all, that it lives wholly for itself and its kind, without any obligation to teach us a thing. The trail rises from the valley and disappears into dusk above us, and I feel no urge to step onto that trail myself.

When we return to the helicopter for the last short hop to Juneau, Kim and I look across Mansfield Peninsula, the only part of Admiralty not set aside as official wilderness. "This is beautiful, isn't it?" Kim says, almost helplessly. A moment later, he adds, "This is all scheduled for timber harvest." He starts to say something else, but he stops. Some things words can't do.

At home, in the dark, I hold my hands to my face. The smell of bear clings to me, not a stench, but a wild, pungent scent that I breathe again and again, as if I could draw it into myself. Perhaps those who are half-human, half-bear, smell like this. Perhaps they look like everybody else, but they are cloaked by a feral spirit. Perhaps they see things they don't say.

The scent evaporates by morning. The scrap of feather I robbed from the bear's pelt disappears from my pocket. Anyway, it was so small. What remains is this: I still dream of bears, but in the dreams I watch. I don't run. I don't speak. The bears watch me, silent, waiting. I am not afraid of bears, I tell myself. I am not afraid.

Kathleen Gasperini

Princess of the Tides

she lives there,
among the kelp beds and starfish,
with the whales and dolphins.
the Princess of the tides makes her home
among the dead ships of men—
a beauty in the rusting beasts
left to her to play with forever . . .

There's a stretch of mountains and ocean along the northern coast of California that is rugged and undefined. It is a lonely place, where sailboats seldom cruise or people venture to picnic. Although the beaches look so near and tempting, they are difficult to reach. Trails that lead down the bluff are often hidden, rocky, switchbacking through coastal brush for fifteen hundred feet at a time. The cold, dark water, which attracts whales, white sharks, seals and dolphins, fends off timid tourists. Only a small community of surfers dare play in these waters. Disguised in black wet suits, they often look like seals from the bluff along the scenic highway. The sharks below the surface tend to agree and attack surfers, dragging them by the leg out to sea. Tourists who cruise along this highway every summer thrive on such tales but rarely stop long enough to see or understand any more than that it's not a place for them to swim.

One summer, for me, this area wasn't a shark-infested, lonely place. Rather, it was a place of independence—where hope was gained and the tides were turned during a time when I felt I wouldn't live to see the end of my student-loan payments. That would be the year 2000, far too distant when I could barely cope with every day. Generation X had been beaten into my head and the more I tried to shrug the label, the more I realized that maybe I was among the lost in a lost generation.

I came to Big Sur to find strength and maybe a bit of myself because after the last year, I couldn't hear myself anymore. Or maybe it had taken longer than a year? Even that I couldn't tell. Too much had happened: a divorce, pneumonia and being fired from a job I later realized I had hated anyway.

The bottom of my stomach had dropped out and I couldn't eat anymore. In the mornings I awoke from dreams filled with free falls off cliffs into the ocean. I'd had these dreams before. Only last time I was flying just before hitting the water. Now, I couldn't. The ocean had become a black hole—the very hole that was in my stomach— the hole I was falling into.

I came here to see if I could fly above the ocean again. In this same place, Robert Louis Stevenson had, as did Ansel Adams in his photographs, Henry Miller in his words and many other lesser-known artists, writers and philosophers in their various disciplines. It was a place, as Miller once put it, that defies comparison, " . . . a region where extremes meet, a region where one is always conscious of weather, of space, of grandeur, and of eloquent silence. It is the face of the earth as the Creator intended it to look." I'd have to agree—She knew what She was doing with this place.

The community of surfers here were naturalists—"Indians of the ocean," they called themselves—guarding their trails down to the beach, picking up litter, planting trees here and there and following the tides of the sea throughout the year. They were men in love with the land and ocean, moon and stars.

As for the women, most of us discovered the area as I had—through our surfer boyfriends. But I came back one day without him. I wanted to write and live the life of a bohemian in a place where books, natural ginseng root and pure honey would help fuel my independence. I thought the purer I could make my life—physically and mentally—the better I'd be able to deal with my emotions, which had somehow become far too ragged for a twenty-eight-year-old.

That summer, I grew to love bodyboarding, a sport that, like surfing, takes catching an ocean wave. Bodyboards look like big kickboards, yet they're big enough for your whole upper body to lay upon. A leash from the board attaches to your ankle, allowing you the freedom to duck under a wave, if necessary, without losing your board. But the best part about bodyboarding is the intimacy you achieve with a wave: unlike surfing, you don't stand. You lie on your board and skim the water, arcing on the rails (sides) of your board to turn, carving just inches above the surface. Some call it "a woman's sport" because it takes leg power rather than upper body strength to bodyboard a wave. And it's one of those sports (like rock climbing) that women can do as well or better than men because it has more to do with balance and finesse than strength and force.

Over the months, I had learned the sport well, and with my bodyboard, discovered a new activity at which I was actually fairly adept. In the past, everything athletic I had ever tried was with my husband: skiing, snowboarding, biking, camping. But not bodyboarding: it was my own.

For this reason, I loved it and went often with my new friends. They showed me their favorite break—a place where you had to know the swell intimately in order to avoid getting shredded on rocks and becoming yet another "shipwreck," as they called it, along the already-haunted shore. It was a rounder part of the wave break that was rarely ridden by surfers. Nicknames such as "Girls' Break" stuck because that's where most of us rode with bodyboards. It was more conducive to catching a wave and riding on a bodyboard: the swell produced big, high rollers that peaked slowly, then ran out long and smooth for a fast, powerful ride. Leg power and a pair of fins were all the muscle you needed to catch Girls'.

One afternoon in late summer, I became the mermaid in my poem which appears at the beginning of this essay. It was the last session of the day and my girlfriends had decided to boulder around the rocky beach in search of jade booty. I'm not sure why I stayed out, but the wave was so smooth and powerful, and I was feeling in such prime form that I figured I'd catch another set or two. While eight guys vied for rides far to my left, taking turns on a big swell that broke aggressively just before a splattering of jagged rocks, I bodyboarded alone along my smooth surf.

The solitude was soothing. I could hear my heart pumping and lungs stretching as they filled with oxygen as I ducked under another wave and popped up on the other side. I lay there on my board, kicking aimlessly as I waited for the next break and watched my friends, now far up the cliff, who were bending over and staring at the ground, picking up rocks here and there on their way to the car. From my perspective, the view looked like the 1-2-3 Jell-O I used to eat as a kid. A pale blue sky followed by green mountains made up the top layer. Frothy white water along the narrow, white-sand beach was the layer of whipped cream in-between, and the deep, blue-black ocean

I floated in quivered and rocked like the most flavorful part of the three-layered dessert.

So much had happened since the days of Mom's Jell-O: I had grown up, learned life was not always black and white and discovered myself along with nature. It always seemed that I learned more about myself the more I ventured into the forest or hiked along a beach or up a mountain. But for me, it was always the ocean that I found most attractive. Perhaps it's the enigma of waves that pull me to the sea whenever I feel lost. Unlike a mountain, they are a powerful force that's ever-changing—a piece of nature that defies analysis. And I was sick of being analyzed by a world of ancient beliefs.

Moving to the coast on my own was planned. But bodyboarding by myself was not. Yet, I quickly got over my discomfort at being a tiny thing in the huge sea and imagined myself the mermaid in my poem, swimming and communing with the waves and ocean kingdom below. As I turned to the horizon to look for the next set, I felt something rub against my legs and catch my fin. My heart leaped to my throat as I turned my board around, sure that a great white was about to have me for dinner, and my friends would find my board the next day washed ashore with a big shark bite in it, like the pictures we'd seen in the newspaper. Another brush against my left leg convinced me that I was now among a school of hungry sharks. Just as I was about to scream, "Jaws!" the head of a dolphin popped up three feet in front of my board. His shiny, metallic skin sparkled in the late afternoon sun. Then, just as suddenly, he disappeared. The relief made me howl with such laughter, I almost fell off my board. I looked up the beach and to my left and realized no one had heard my nervous laughter. The sounds drowned in the crashing waves. I was alone in that sound.

When a few more dolphins brushed against my legs, I reached out to touch them in return. And they let me. I stroked the underside of one with my hand and rubbed another with my leg. I dove under, knowing that my leash would keep my board from floating in, and watched the dolphins spin and perform back flips. With my legs together and arms overhead, I did the same, kicking my fins together and flipping over and over as they did. As my hair flowed behind and curved in a circle, one dolphin kept poking his head in my hair, playing with the tangles and circling with me.

It was an impressive show and I felt privileged to be part of their performance. I popped back up just in time to see yet another perfect wave coming my way. To stay or ride became my only concern and I chose the latter. With my upper body back on my board, I kicked hard with my fins and paddled with my arms until I caught the crest of the wave. As I steered left and rode down the falls, I caught the shadows of my dolphin friends catching the same wave. Three dolphins and I, riding a wave that had made its way from some unknown storm out in the Pacific, swelling right then, so perfectly, only for us to ride. We rode high, then dipped low, gaining speed in the trough, the dolphins alongside me, carving the same pattern.

With each wave came a greater sense of confidence. I was alone in human terms, but not in the ocean kingdom. I became a part of their family, like a sea creature, like a mermaid—more dolphin than human; more connected than solo. Only the parameters had changed and I wanted to stay here forever. I caught more waves, each one better than the next as the dolphins and I grew more comfortable with each other's styles, touching on occasion as we carved down the faces. At one point, I no longer had to paddle—I just reached out and grabbed hold of one of my friends' dorsal fins and was pulled into the wave's crest without the effort of my legs or fins. He gave me a ride that was bigger than the wave. Inside I was screaming with excitement, soaring along the water like a dream. The dolphins were teaching me to catch surf as they did (for the record: one powerful kick of the tail, head tucked, and glide with the current, dorsal fin for steering, barely slicing the surface). Feel the swell and hear the water crescendo rather than think about it, they seemed to say. I followed their lead, kicking with the momentum of the swell, and releasing down the face of each curl of blue-green water.

Girls' Break with its smooth curl and amiable ride was really Dolphins' Break and they let me in. I wasn't lost here. Or anywhere. I was home in the ocean, sharing waves and skimming across without wings. I was strong inside simply from being here in this special moment at this time, with these sea creatures. After all, what was it that I had overcome to find the independence to conquer a new sport, then ride a wave all the way from Bali, by myself, with dolphins? It was a moment of hope—a moment that made more moments like this seem possible.

If only the rides could last forever, I thought, but the sun was sinking and my friends were surely up at the road, waiting for me by the car. I rode through the white water and walked onto the beach, hoping that this wouldn't be my last and only ride with the dolphins. Maybe the tides would bring them back again. As I turned around, I saw the glimmer of a smooth head, curved like a question mark, as it popped up for a brief second as if to say good-bye. Then it disappeared back into the ocean.

I packed up my fins and towel in my backpack and with my board under my arm, headed up the rocky trail, switchbacking higher and higher under the light of a rising half-moon.

V

ON OUR OWN

Gift of Independence

Hawthorn

May 13-June 9

Candace Dempsey

Alone Again

I never went anywhere when I was a child, all because of a pig house my mother had burned down. She'd grown up on an Idaho homestead without running water or electricity, and her Italian mother had been too busy grinding pork for homemade sausages, plucking chickens and performing the million other tasks of the pioneer to keep an eye on her nine children. One day while playing with matches in a fit of boredom, my mother and her cousins burned down the pig house. This could have been a tragedy, fire spreading rapidly over the dry fields and wooden buildings of the farm. That didn't happen. Still, that red pig house, its long troughs filled with table scraps, shaped my whole childhood.

"We ran wild," my mother recalls with horror. "I made sure you kids

were *watched*." To this day she claims her greatest mistake was allowing me, third-oldest of seven children, to escape to Yellowstone Park
for a summer job. When I boarded that Greyhound bus I was seventeen, a skinny girl with a high-school diploma and plastic suitcase.
Never had I been more than thirty miles from the border towns of
Eastern Washington and Idaho.

"You'd be a different person today if you hadn't gone to Yellowstone," my mother claims. She means I'd be a household saint, not a
travel writer. But I believe wanderlust is in the blood, as natural to
certain people as water cascading over cliffs, the tumbling of tum-
bleweeds across desert sand.

Until this escape my life had been like a toy train stuck on a single
track. I grew up with three brothers and three sisters in a pretty pink
ranch house in Spokane, Washington, a landlocked city of stone and
pine on the edge of a vast lake country. After Sunday Mass we piled
the family into two cars and drove across the state line to the Idaho
farm where my mother grew up. Down the road on a lake was the
log cabin in which we lived every summer. We never went anywhere
else, because my mother saw no need. Our life was a closed circle of
family.

"You can go, but don't go too far," Italians tell their offspring,
whether they are toddlers or grown-ups with kids of their own. "Stay
near your folks. They are the only people you can trust."

In Italy these rules confine children to the range of the village bell.
In America we had to stay within range of my mother's police whistle.
In summer that gave us the run of the farm where the pig house burned
down; the nearby lake and the meadows above it; woods with make-
shift tepees and wild strawberries; fields of clover and wild peas. Not

to mention the joyful company of countless cousins.

In Spokane we felt our chains. The pine woods above our new housing development offered mysterious caves and tantalizing boulders to climb. Kim Momb, later to stand atop Mount Everest, trained on the black lava cliffs that rise from the river valley. But this paradise was forbidden to me.

"Those are *city* woods," my parents warned. City woods were overrun with perverts and hermits and vandals who pushed stolen cars off cliffs. The fact that nobody ever spotted these desperados did not bother my folks one bit.

So we children braked our bikes at the edge of the woods, trembling with fear and desire. The price of disobedience was high—what our parents called "a good licking." Although convinced they had radar that could track our every move, we often defied them with mad dashes into the woods.

The odd thing was that the neighborhood kids, who found our old-fashioned clothes and copious rules bizarre, never ratted on us for following them into the forbidden realms. Forging ahead of us through the brush, they were bold adventurers braving untamed lands. What they took for granted, we found magical: fields of yellow bells and violets, breathless games of hide-and-seek, the mesmerizing scents of syringa and wild roses. We hunted blue-tailed lizards, fled from spiteful porcupines, waded barefoot across murky ponds floating with water lilies. We shot our Flexible Flyer sleds down snowy slopes we called "Suicide" and "Danger."

"Where have you been?" my mother asked whenever we failed to respond speedily to the police whistle. "I've been calling and calling."

"Just riding our bikes."

Somehow she managed not to see the pine needles in our hair. Once I convinced her that the wood tick she had to remove from my scalp had fallen from a maple tree at school. My best excuse, although I was afraid to use it often, was that I *had* to go into the woods to retrieve our Brittany spaniel—a spotted rebel named Penny who hated girls and wouldn't come when I called.

The few lickings we got for our forest explorations made us philosophical about crime. "Damn it, it was fun," we said once the pain wore off, vowing to do it again and again.

While my mother kept us home, Dad fed our wanderlust. I've always suspected he would have been a rolling stone if he hadn't gotten hitched. At bedtime he dazzled us with stories about his days in the Merchant Marines. He knew how rain fell in the South Seas, what Shanghai looked like before "the Commies" took over. He filled our house with adventure books, detective stories, sci-fi thrillers. He read us everything from *The Iliad* and *The Odyssey* to *Tom Sawyer* and *The Jungle Tales of Tarzan*. We believed, boys and girls alike, that we could stride the world in seven-league boots, ride magic carpets and climb beanstalks to castles in the sky.

These dreams eventually took me places my father did not wish me to go. Yet he himself came from a restless clan, German and Irish. His German grandmother had a pass on the Chicago–Milwaukee Railroad—courtesy of her husband, who worked there—and she rode the rails all her life. Sometimes she took her kids, other times she boarded them out with family members. Although based in Spokane, she spoke casually of St. Louis, Minneapolis and Chicago—golden cities glittering out of my reach like names on a movie marquee. I never saw a jet rise over Tower Mountain nor heard the whistle of a west-bound freight, hell-bent for the coast, without imagining myself aboard.

"How could she!" my mother complained about that vagabond grandma. "How could she dump her children on her relatives and gallivant around the country that way?"

How could she not? Alone, my great-grandmother could reinvent herself. I liked to think she went by a different name on the train—something daring like Carlotta Delmonico—and changed her age and hair color and said she'd gone to finishing school in Paris. How I longed to possess that train pass, that life. They were as beguiling to me as the silver passenger trains that still roll across the dusty flatlands, high deserts and blue mountains of the West.

Like that German grandmother, I am famous for mad dashes, for suddenly deciding I must breathe the air in another state or country. I believe in following these impulses even when they're dangerous. When I was twenty-six and two weeks shy of getting married, I boarded a dented Chevy Nova and hightailed it from my parents' home in Spokane all the way to Eugene, Oregon, some thousand miles round trip. My excuse for fleeing was that I'd left belongings in Eugene, where I'd just wrapped up graduate school. But the truth was I feared that brief journey down the aisle, the sudden loss of freedom. Afterward, my new husband and I planned to live on the East Coast for several years. I wanted to be alone when I said good-bye to the West, which I had loved longer than any lover.

Listening to my mother's travel advice—"You must get a good start!"—for the first and last time, I left Spokane hideously early that spring morning and shot south. Crossing wheat fields and deserts and lava outpourings, I caught I-84 and turned west. This road, following the Columbia River along the Washington–Oregon border, is famed for its high cliffs, deep gorge and bold, blue water. It unfolds like a book of postcards, the same beauty mile after mile. Quickly, I got bored. I should have known I was in trouble when I began simultaneously driving and reading a road map. Sunlight drifted into the car, wrapping around me like a soft blanket. I slipped luxuriously into sleep.

Then something jolted me awake. The Nova was on the gravel shoulder, headed straight for the ditch. Slamming on the brakes, I threw it into a tailspin. Round and round the car spun on that broad highway. The spinning took forever. I thought: *This is it. I'm going to die.* I saw flashes of my life—cramming for finals, pulling my wedding together, flying east into uncertainty. Life was nothing but struggle. It was a relief to let go.

Then the car stopped spinning. I grabbed the wheel. I steered to the roadside and stopped. When a highway patrolman knocked on the car window, I thought I was hallucinating. He told me he'd been parked at a rest stop. "I was sure you were going to flip," he said, as though that would have grieved him. "You know how lucky you were that nobody else was on the road?"

I tried to pour black coffee from my plaid thermos, but my hands shook. I couldn't look that patrolman in the eyes. I felt so lost.

Like a wrangler getting back on a horse after a spill, I rode the Nova all the way to Eugene, a lovely red-brick college town of greenery and mist. For two blissful years I had studied writing there while carrying on a long-distance romance with Mark, a law student in Spokane. I kept my two lives so separate that nobody in Eugene knew Mark and I were about to tie the knot. But that night I bunked with a grad-school friend named Jill and over a bottle of wine managed to spill my secret. She said she understood. "Sometimes it's hard to talk about the things that mean the most to us."

The next afternoon I followed the McKenzie River east out of

Eugene and cut across Three Sisters Wilderness and its haunting stretch of snow-draped volcanoes. Then I swept into the high desert of central Oregon, a land of lava spires, dry washes and fossil beds. Shying away from I-84, the highway of my near crash, I drove the back roads all day and into the night. I was determined not to think. With no one to talk to and a busted radio, there was nothing to hear but the wind blowing across the desert and the occasional clatter of a passing truck. There was nothing but the grip of the wheel, the earth rushing by, the sweet scent of the blueberries bought for my mother at a roadside stand.

A half-moon dangled over the darkened town of Milton–Freewater as I tried to cross the border into Washington. By this time I had been on the road more than six hours. A highway patrolman turned on his siren and stopped me in a whirl of red light. He said he'd clocked the Nova at 104 miles per hour. I hadn't felt that speed. I tried to tell him about my long journey and the bewitching names on the Oregon map that had spurred me on: Three-Fingered Jack, Bear Wallow Creek, Crooked River Gorge. I had been in perpetual motion, the Nova a rocket ship flying through space.

The patrolman smiled. I had the feeling he was a long-distance addict himself, an explorer of the back roads. He said lots of people speed up near the border without realizing it, because their minds tell them they're almost home.

"Not me. I always slow down when I'm near home."

He laughed. "Well, I have to write you a ticket, but I'm going to say you were doing eighty. That way it won't cost you so much."

The second he took off, I felt my weariness. It was all I could do to limp across the state line into Walla Walla, where I had friends. Major travelers themselves, Glen and Janice were unfazed when I showed up on their doorstep in the dark, almost unable to talk. All night long I lay in the upper bedroom of their half-furnished Victorian, wheels churning in my head.

The next day I kept putting off my departure, expressing a sudden desire to see Whitman College, the site of the Whitman Massacre and even the state penitentiary. It was dinner time before I saddled up, thinking that the last 160 miles would be a snap. A ribbon of highway spun north across the rolling hills of the Palouse, one of the world's richest wheat lands, and into Spokane. The problem was that the Palouse, like the Columbia Gorge, has a monotonous beauty. Three years of college in nearby Pullman had been enough for me. Now I veered northwest toward the farming town of Lind. A woman from up there had told me the place was so tiny that I could write "Meredith. Lind, Washington" on a postcard and she'd get it.

I cruised for hours on automatic pilot, choosing well-marked back roads that skirted lush wheat farms and rolled over neat little bridges. Then the sun started to dip. The land turned dry. Somehow I slipped onto an unmarked road, then another. Coming over a ridge I dropped into a flatland so desolate that it made me stop the car.

All around me was untracked desert. A low horizon over dark earth. No trees or rivers or fences or power poles. I was lost on the moon. Checking the gas gauge I figured I had enough for maybe thirty miles. But which way was north? How far back was the nearest town? I couldn't remember.

I got out, shaky on my feet after riding the range for so long. Beams of light broke through the gloom, tracing silver veins on the dull sand. I breathed in the familiar scents of warm rocks and musky plants. Never had I been anywhere so quiet, so beautifully still. There was no one to say, *How could you have been so stupid? What the hell were you thinking?*

I heard a roaring in my ears. Suddenly my mind cleared for the first time in weeks. It was simple. The road only went two ways and I wasn't about to turn back. That didn't suit my personality. Gripping the car keys, I promised myself that if I drove over the next ridge and the land was just as desolate, I would stop the car and scream. I'd scream and scream. Then I would keep driving.

Over the next ridge was another trackless flatland. But on the far horizon I saw a glow. I followed that glow for maybe twenty miles until the lights of a town sparkled ahead. Ritzville, about sixty miles from home. "A pit stop on the interstate," I would have called it a few days before. But that windy spring night I was enchanted by Ritzville's brightly lit gas stations and burger stands, curtained houses and boxy taverns with flashing beer signs.

Pulling into a station, I filled up the tank. Then I stopped at a painted shack for a double burger and French fries. Dipping into the greasy paper sack, which gave off an intoxicating fragrance, I hungered for the road. Even though I'd been gone only a few days, I felt wiser and more joyful than before. I knew now that I was capable of getting myself into terrible jams, but also of wangling my way out of them. Nothing could stop me from roaming, not even a gold wedding band.

All these years later I still love to climb into a car for no reason and drive hundreds of miles.

"What are you looking for?" asks my husband, Mark, who grew up in New York, where nobody calls driving thirty miles for Marlboros "just a hop, skip and jump." Like many vagabonds, I married a person who never wants to leave town.

"I'm not looking for anything," I tell him. "I just want to go."

Depending always on the kindness of strangers, I've been everywhere I dreamed of when I was a landlocked little girl—and I've only begun to wander. I've seen the sun set on Mount Kilimanjaro in Africa, hopped a plane to Jordan after the Gulf War, watched the moon rise over the olive groves of Calabria where my grandparents once tilled the rocky land. Like my father, I've seen Asia. I've seen how rain falls like the wrath of God on the South Seas, then stops as suddenly as it begins. Blue skies reappear over the coral lagoons of Bora Bora, coloring the water, and white boats ride the waves once more.

Even though I'm a grown woman with a child of my own, my mother still frets every time I step out the door.

"Something might happen," she says.

"That's the whole idea."

"Can't you go with someone?"

"No."

"At least take your husband."

"No."

I'd rather set off on my own, even when I feel scared and lonely. Something might happen: I might meet a stranger, jump ship, climb an unnamed mountain, lose myself on a winding trail. I might forget who I am and where I came from.

Who knows? I might even run away from home.

Alice Evans

At My Own Speed

*H*ow many times had I set out to climb a mountain with my husband, only to find myself climbing the mountain alone?

The truth is, that suited me just fine. We had such different ideas about why we were climbing the mountain. He always wanted, or needed, to get to the top as fast as he could. The peak was not only goal, but necessity.

Usually, I didn't care if I reached the top. I liked to get there, but I didn't have to. I wanted, or needed, to stop along the way and look at rocks. Flowers. Gnarled junipers. Darting rodents. Glacial lakes. Clouds. I wanted, or needed, to stop and take out a book of poetry. Snap photographs. Jot notes in my journal.

Sometimes, perhaps often, I felt judgmental toward my husband

and his abandonment. Always the forced march, never the act of discovery. His wildness was expressed through fast, hard movement. I couldn't keep up with him. His heart-lung capacity far exceeded my own.

And so I didn't try to hold him back, past a certain point. He would wait for me, periodically. We would speak for a few moments. Maybe share a snack. Then he would move on ahead. And I would climb alone, at my own speed.

Such was the existential state of our marriage. Each of us climbing the same mountain, traveling the same path, but going it alone.

Then came a day when we began climbing different mountains. Separately. Perhaps the change had something to do with raising a child, a child who would often climb with us, but who would just as often refuse to go along.

We had gone to the Oregon Caves National Monument for Labor-Day weekend, a journey that was becoming a tradition. South on the Interstate to Grants Pass, then southwest on the Redwood Highway, then southeast on the long, steep road that led us deep into the Siskyou Mountains. At the head of the steep valley, where the road ended, stood a six-story lodge planked with enormous slabs of cedar. A dozen yards from the lodge door, a bear-sized crack in the marble cliff opened into miles of cave.

The morning after our arrival we left our warm nest in the wood-lined lodge and toured the cave. Our daughter, Ursula, stayed right with the guide as he called out low bridges, pointed out favorite formations and warned us not to touch the marble walls, lest we leave destructive body grease.

After the half-mile hike underground, I was ready to hike through the complex ecosystem of the Siskyous, one of the continent's oldest mountain ranges. Ten-year-old Ursula refused. "Well, maybe after a good lunch," I coaxed. "Well, maybe," she conceded.

Into the coffee shop. Fir counters. Mirror-lined walls. Revolving seats. Order up milkshake. Chili. Saltines and pickles. Hamburgers. Fries. Candy bars. Now, are we ready?

Ursula refused to climb the mountain.

OK, negotiation. I haven't busted free all summer, while you, Jon, have taken any number of weekend hikes up Cascade peaks. It's my turn. You stay with Ursula. I'll climb the mountain alone. Be back in time for supper, before six, before the coffee shop closes. Too expensive to eat in the dining room a second night. Too much food.

I climbed up to our fourth-floor room, collected my backpack and packed in three bottles of water. Packed in Barry Lopez's new collection of short stories, *Field Notes*, which I was reviewing for a local arts weekly.

Good-bye. I'm on my way up Mount Elijah. Mad as hell but on my way. Nobody wants to go with me. I'll go alone. Damned if I'll spend all day sitting by the pool watching trout. Damned if I'll spend my whole summer serving other people at the bookstore while no one serves me. Huh! Who serves *me*? Now, here I am in the woods, and no one to walk with. Well, isn't that usually the way it is? Haven't I usually gone alone into wilderness, when it comes right down to it? Nobody's taking these steps for me. Nobody's making these butt muscles move. Nobody but me.

I'm heading up Mount Elijah. I'm going so fast I can't even see the plants except as flashes of color, variegated leaves, nodding stems. I acknowledge the dark humus of rotting logs, the heart-shaped fungus, trees like spectators lining the path, cheering me on as I charge up the mountain. Jon couldn't climb this fast if he wanted to. Ursula, that little sass who dances by me fast as feathers, faster than Jon even, she couldn't keep up with this pace. No way. I'm on my mountain. I'm going up my mountain. Haven't I always loved the Siskyous? Haven't I always said the Siskyous remind me of the Appalachians, the mountains of my childhood? Haven't I always said I take power from these mountains, they feed me?

All right, I'm at the Big Tree. One-point-eight miles and I'm already here. Thirty minutes, at five thousand feet. I must be in shape. Usually I'd be gasping for breath. I'm not even breathing hard. I'll stop here and put my arms around the largest Douglas fir in Oregon and kiss its thick bark. Tree big as a redwood. Old as a redwood. Maybe fifteen hundred years. Big Tree says, *Move, move on up the mountain, you can do it, you can be big.*

I'm a-going, Big Tree. I'm passing two men, panic flashing through my body. I'm always afraid to meet men deep in the woods, all alone. *Breeze on by them,* Big Tree says. Be friendly but don't stop. Keep on going, go by so fast they don't have a chance to realize you're alone, and by the time they do, you're way on by, they'll never catch you, not the way you're moving. Moving faster than the clouds, you are, faster than the earth, with Big Tree pushing you. Moving on up, one more mile, two more miles, past the boundaries of the National Monument, into the Siskyou National Forest. Nobody's going to be coming up here, not today. Just you, honey. All alone.

The theme for the park this year is biodiversity, Big Tree. Big Tree, do you hear me? Are you still with me? Last night the ranger was talking about how old the area is, how unusually complex the interconnections between plants and animals. Rare plants, here. The last stand for some. I'm so glad they're preaching this at last. Twenty years ago, when I studied ecology, hardly anyone spoke this language. Now, the visitors to the park are being educated. Maybe there's hope, Big Tree.

Keep on going. Up the mountain. Maybe there's hope.

What about the book review I planned to work on this weekend? Time to stop. Read another story. I love the words of Barry Lopez. This one, called "The Runner," is about a brother who suddenly wants to reconnect with his sister. She turns out to have a special relationship with Grand Canyon, deeply spiritual, magical even. She discovers lost Anasazi trails and caves that contain their pottery. She runs the pathways of the deer and the Anasazi, and leaps the Colorado River at will.

Well, I am off again, the book in my backpack, the words in my mind, Big Tree behind me, pushing me on. Good-bye, Big Tree, good-bye.

I'm not running, but I am moving, hard and fast, up to the top of the ridge, then along it, then again along the steep section of path that begins the ascent up Mount Elijah. I have already decided I will turn back at 4:00. Otherwise, we'll end up eating in the dining room again. But I've come this far. It's what, another twenty minutes to the top? Make it thirty. Forty-five? I'll do it in fifteen. Something's behind me. Something's urging me to move.

Moving this hard, I'm sweating hard, too. But I don't want to stop. I've broken out into the sunlight. I'm free of the trees. I'm starting to get a clear view of mountains. And clear cuts. Mountains. And clouds. Clouds, and clear cuts. I take the pack from my back as I move. I unzip the pack as I move. I take out the flask as I move. I unscrew the cap as I move. I drink the water as I move, hard and fast, hard and fast, up the mountain.

What is that pounding in the distance? I thought I had this mountain all to myself. What is that pounding? Drumming. Voices. Chanting. A group of people, already there, on Mount Elijah, drumming and chanting. It's 4:25. It's taken me three hours to climb, what?—

five miles up this mountain. I'm five minutes from the top, and if I go up there, if I sit and rest and take it all in, I'll have an hour and twenty minutes, maybe, to get to the bottom of the mountain before the coffee shop closes.

And what's up ahead there? Who's that drumming? I feel something pulling me now, when all along I thought I was being pushed. Now, a pulling. I'm moving these last few hundred yards, over ancient stone. Lichen-colored stone. Past gnarly madrone, toward the people who are drumming, chanting, on top of Mount Elijah.

I see them. They see me. A white-haired man, hair spilling over his shoulders, beard dragging across the top of his drum. A woman dressed in animal skins. Two small children, in animal skins. Another man, younger, with dark hair spilling to his waist, likewise dressed in animal skins. Lord be. They see me. I see them. We behold one another. The man stops drumming. He wraps the drum in a leather bag. The others move toward me.

They are leaving the mountain. We are changing places. They are giving me the mountain. They have held the mountain long enough, and now it's my turn. The young man asks me to name the mountains we can see around us. "Mount Shasta, to the South." He knows that already. "The Trinity Alps." He knows that too. "The Marble Mountains?" Yes, he nods. "Over there, the Kalmiopsis Wilderness." "No, that's over there," he says. Why is he asking? He knows more than I do. "Yes," he says. "It's one hundred, maybe two hundred miles south to the next major road." I nod. He walks away.

The children are thirsty. They ask their mother for something to drink. "We have nothing," she says. I take out one of my two remaining flasks and hand it to her. "Take this," I say. "I have plenty." "Thank you," she says. The children smile. I walk toward the absolute peak.

The older man has finished putting away his drum. He points to two black forms moving through the clearing on a distant slope. "We thought they might be bears," he says. "Or range cattle. But we think they're bears." "Yes," I say. "I think you're right. They're bears." He smiles and picks up his drum. He moves on down the mountain.

I have forgotten about time. I sit where he was sitting. I watch the bears. I peruse the distant peaks. Mt. Shasta shining in the sunlight. The Trinity Alps have lost their snow, so late in the year. The Marble Mountains, no snow now. And all around me, near me, the peaks of the Siskyous, their ancient stones, their soft covering of rare plants. Clear cuts abrading their slopes. I have forgotten about time. There is only now on this mountain. The sun dropping toward the not-so-distant sea. The drumming, still in my mind, my heart, beating, beating. Big Tree. Big Tree. A woman, running the trails of the deer and Anasazi, leaping the Colorado River. I could live here. This could be my place.

The wind blows across my face, the scent of kinnikinnick. The wind blows in my ears, I have been here forever. The wind blows through my hair, a woman alone in the wilderness. The wind blows hard against my back and I am running, down the mountain, the urge to move throbbing in my blood. I am released. The mountain says *Go now, go, the day is late, you have been here forever and now you must go.*

And so I run, stepping lightly over rocks. I run, now like a deer, now like a bear. I am running, running down the slopes of Mt. Elijah. This is where I almost turned back, I am running. This is where I stopped to pee, I am running. This is where I thought a mountain lion was watching me, I am running. This is where the trail leaves the ridge top and enters the National Monument. I am running, running past the spot where I stopped to read "The Runner." I am running, approaching the fallen fir. I am running, scrambling over the top. I am running, being pushed, being pulled, a cord of light passing through me and connecting me to the top and bottom of the mountain. I am running, like Carlos Casteneda and Don Juan, those radiant beings. I am running, from one place to another, the forms and smells and colors flashing by. I am running, through the clearing where I watched the hawk. I am running, down the slopes of Mount Elijah and I can hear the voices of people at the lodge, I can hear the drumming on the mountain, I can hear the beating of my heart. And I am running past the cave entrance, past the pool of trout and into the coffee shop where the clock reads 5:55. And Jon and Ursula are sitting at the counter, waiting to order, and I am running into time.

P. K. Price

Navigational Information for Solo Flights in the Desert

I am a solitary desert-goer, a solo river-watcher, a woman who walks the forest without companion. I first went to the desert thinking I knew the name of God. But once there, I realized I knew only parts of a name: golden marmot, red-tailed hawk, mule deer, river ouzel, merganser, owl, red-shafted flicker, slick rock, river swallows, trout, sage, alders, lupine, juniper. I return to the desert to gather more parts of the name whispered by the voices. There is danger in going there alone. There is more danger in not going.

I have spent seasons in the wild: autumn in the slick rock, spring near Kennebec Pass, summer on the Dolores River, winter in the snow shadow of Taos Mountain. Each journey is unique. In solitude, I add or shed layers, either lose myself or find myself or do both and not know the difference. I have learned to follow the path of personal reality. Openings appear: doors into the desert's heart, real and illusory. To walk through requires courage. I might not return unchanged. I might not return at all. Bones in the desert testify to this. It does not seem important any longer. An opening in the wilderness is a challenge and an invitation: to shed layers, to gain strength and savvy, to dance unencumbered under a desert moon, to lie on a boulder like a lizard, to bathe in the intimacy of constellations. To learn my name and my true transit. To hear my voice echoed from the silence of the Persiad Showers.

Solitude is not for the unprepared. And only for those who will not plan. I offer a bit of navigational information, a few traveling tips, for women. For I travel and breathe and live the desert as a woman and the desert has taken me in that way. Neither these tips nor any navigational information I offer constitute a map, just an image upon the soul. You will make your own list.

1. About Getting Away

When you first go to the wilderness alone, it is best to have a purpose. This will be both a knife and a defense for the first challenges that you will encounter: family, friends and interior inertial reluctances. Our culture acknowledges, understands and respects "the purpose," "the task," "the goal." Unless you have one of these, a reason, it will be difficult to leave: expect this and you will probably actually succeed in getting away. You may choose any reasonable purpose that you feel you can sell to your family, your friends and yourself. It is best to choose a solitary activity. If you are a painter, writer, botanist, this is good. For example, if you are a painter, you can say: "See here, I must do several landscapes, numerous botanical sketches, various bird drawings and I need to complete at least twenty-five to thirty of these as a collection for my next show. I'll have to go alone to get that much work done." You have just fooled them and yourself: you seem to have defined a goal. This makes your journey appear logical. The task, tangible.

A writer can do the same thing. "See here, I must finish the last 267 pages of my novel and write the six to seven magazine articles that I've outlined and sent to publishers." Easy sell.

Set the goal at such a level that you will clearly be working very hard to achieve it. This discourages those who might want to come along. They know that they might quickly become bored.

This goal will be very useful to you for structuring your travel, choosing your destination and leaving everyone behind with a comfortable conviction that you are a person with a purpose. This purpose will also be the knife that you will use to cut the weeds that have grown up around your ankles and rooted your boots to the ground. It will be your defense against comments from yourself and others questioning your sanity.

2. About Tents and Setting Up Camp

For the first few days you are out there, your goal will be an anchor, a map, your name, the image of yourself in the water and the reflection of your shadow cast off the underbelly of the moon. You will need this structure. Your first few days alone, you will encounter high winds, fear, rains that will sweep you off the ground, panic, the breathing of rivers, the blindness of no-moon, new neighbors: lion, bear, otter, eagle, deer, coyote, fox, regiments of ground squirrels in full parade dress. They will ask your name and your purpose. You will know it. This will seem as it should be for a while.

At first you will think that setting up your tent is part of the process of being out there. It will be another skin. That will seem good.

Comforting. A boundary in a limitless space. A place where you can separate yourself from the line of the horizon that stretches so far that only the curvature of earth can stop the distances from running away from you. The curvature is a visual reminder of the protection of the circle if you worry about getting lost. If you walk the circumference, being careful not to deviate even a fraction of degree in latitude or longitude, eventually you will return to the point of origin. If you are like me, you will take a side step to look at a copper-green rock, a flicker feather beneath a wild gourd. You will be off course. Your plans are now altered. You will spiral instead of circumscribe.

It is important to start within a circle. Set camp there. In an enclosure of boulders, of junipers, of sage. There are many places like this in the desert. They are pre-prepared, set-aside places to be used when you are alone. They protect the desert from you and you from the desert. *Even if you believe this, stay alert.* You will find that it seems as if you are not actually alone in these places. As if there are people you cannot see—pack rat, prairie dog, raven—who guard these places. Set camp carefully. Your camp is your *kiva* and in the center, if you stay long enough with the proper intent, you will eventually find the *sipapu:* your place of emergence into the next, upper world.

3. About Getting Lost

Be prepared for the turn you take on a walk up the side canyon that leads you to the ancient juniper. You will sit down to rest. The sun will seduce you. You might get drowsy. You might sleep. A few minutes later you will open your eyes and realize that your water bottle is gone. While you have drifted, a crow has snatched your notebook, the desert breeze has taken your name, a ground squirrel has carried off your pen, paper and your maps. You will turn around again and again in circles, looking for your boot tracks in the sand: north to east to south to west. You will not be able to tell from which direction you came.

You will be alone. You will be immediately tempted to search for your sketchbook, driven to find your notebook and pen, frantic to find your comforting USGS topographical maps. Your throat will be suddenly parched. The pain of attempting to speak words into the silence through cracked, dry lips will be too much. You cannot cry out for help. You cannot run for shelter. You are alone.

Be still.

I started to panic when this happened to me. I ran. I clawed my way up a talus slope trying to reach higher ground where I could see. Instead, my boot turned under me in the scree, my fingernails broke off grasping for handholds. I rolled and slid down the side of the canyon wall, scraping and cutting my arms, legs and face on slick rock and boulders. I lay on the canyon floor for a long time. I bled. The sun dried my blood into a red patina, then darker until my body resembled the slick rock: skin painted by streaks of desert varnish. I realized a crushing sense of vulnerability. The stirring of a feeling that this desert is alive. That it might drive me away. That I must be careful. I was as close and as far from the desert's heart then as I ever would be again.

This is why I say: be still. Though I know you will try to run also. Perhaps you will not fall. Not be painted by the desert with your own blood. Perhaps you will reach the top of the mesa. It will not matter. The sun will be in mid-sky. It will not reveal direction to you. You will still be lost. You will still be alone.

If you have run or wandered, return to the place where you first dozed off and sit down again. This time: wait. It is helpful at this point to listen. It is also useful to look around. You might find it comforting to count the pebbles under your right boot. Notice their colors. Do not put them in your pocket or you will never find your way back to your tent. The pebbles will grow into boulders and you will not be able to move.

This is how you listen: slow your breathing down until the desert wind enters your lungs and like a bellows, takes in air and expels it for you. This way your breathing will not be so loud that you cannot hear the dry melody of rice grass all around you. Soon the juniper will begin to sigh. Counterpoint and slightly syncopated and percussive will be the scraping of branches against each other even when there is no wind. This is desert music.

You may not have noticed, but look now. The delicate heart-shaped leaves of the squaw bush have begun to turn persimmon and plum colors. The sky has collected snow-mist from a distant mountain range and has marbleized them into streamers of pearl-white swirling across the azurine blue above you. Look down again. Small buds cover the tips of the sage. Female sage surrounds you. Breathe in the fragrance of their pungent leaves. Look over there to your left, you will see a male plant of epiphedra, Mormon tea. Behind the boulder where you sit, you will see the female plant: stalks and nodules so different in form and nature that you will know the female plant in a moment. These things are subtle. Some people try but can never discern which plant is female and which is male. You will know. Even with your eyes closed. Run your hands gently over each plant and touch it in greeting. If you begin to relax, prop yourself up against the boulder and close your eyes. The wind will breathe for you while you rest. The rice grass and sage music will continue.

When you awake, your water bottle will be next to you. Drink deeply. Your map, sketchbook, paper and pen will be there also. You will see your boot tracks. You can follow them out now. The sun has slipped over your shoulder like a silk dress, leaving you bare and vulnerable. Drink deeply. It is time to return to your camp and await the night.

4. Night, Moon and Rain

It is best to plan to enter the desert so that you will pass your first night at new moon. Go into the night without light. Go blindly. It is the only way you will learn to walk carefully. To see without glasses. To sleep without getting dizzy as the constellations turn soundlessly above your tent.

I will tell you that it will not be easy at first. One night this happened to me.

It was not many hours before dawn. I awoke startled by the sound of small animals skittering outside my tent. Thousands of them, judging by the hoopla and noise they created. Rain fell on the tent in a continuous downpour. I suspected sleet as the sound was loud and the night cold. What animals would be so active at night in a sleet storm? I asked into the darkness. In the tempestuous cold wind, my tent flapped and sighed and tried to pull itself out of its stakes. I did not move. Cold, my body rigid, I listened for hours until I saw the gray of dawn from the East. Though the animals continued their scurry and the sleet continued to fall, I hesitantly looked out the front flap of my tent.

There were no animals. No rain. No sleet. Instead, the cottonwoods under which I had set my camp were dropping their leaves. The brittle, dry, gold leaves filled the air. Falling on my tent, on the ground, falling down against themselves in the trees, falling through branches, rustling and crowding against each other, piling and swirling in the eddies of the cold morning wind. I slipped on my jeans and sweater and walked in cottonwood leaves up to my ankles.

In my journal that morning I recorded the following phenological report: "October 27, 1987. 35° this morning. clear sky. windy. received 4" of cottonwood rain last night."

Make a place in your journal for your list of possibilities. Add cottonwood rainstorms. Leave many pages open. Your list will grow as the desert gets to know you.

One of the things I added to my list was moon thievery. The moon has one perfect night in her cycle. She is a planet. Being much smaller and of much less importance, I have decided that I too will expect no more than one night of fullness each cycle. Thus I can wax and wane without whining and wait for those few hours when I can illuminate the darkness for my own pleasure.

I say this because I learned it in the desert. I entered the desert at new moon and watched each night as the moon gathered more light each day. I ran with her in apogee and circled close in perigee. I watched her illumine herself, casting herself in the lead night role by stealing what sun she could hold.

I decided to do the same. During the day I laid out on a boulder. Took off my boots, socks, clothing. Unencumbered, I let the sun touch my skin. I washed my hair and let the sun dry it. The wind whipped it into long, lazy curls. Each strand took on a bit more sun each day until my hair was patinaed with gold. My skin burnished. At night sitting beneath the waxing moon, my skin held the warmth of the sun for hours. This is how I learned to catch and carry sun on my body and in my hair.

At full moon, against the faint persimmon moonlight reflected off the slick rock, once again I took off my clothes. Light fell around me. The wind began to sway the juniper branches. The shadows of boulders reached out to stroke me. I broke off sprigs of sage, crumbled them in my hands and rubbed sage over my body. I broke off several sprigs of juniper and plaited them in my hair. From my leather pouch I chose several pheasant feathers and wove them in with the juniper sprigs. I scooped up a handful of sienna-red earth and drew on my body: sun above one breast, moon above the other. Zigzag lightning on my arms. Spirals on my belly. I let the wind lead and I danced until moon-set. Slowly each day thereafter, I let my skin fade until at new moon, it was time again to begin catching sun.

5. *Rivers*

There will come to you a time when you must find water in the desert. You will wander. Pick up the trail of mule deer and follow it. You may walk for hours. If night catches you on the trail, look for the place where deer slept the night before. Curl up in deer-nest but do not sleep. First imagine that your skin is deer hide covered in tawny, brown, taupe and white fur. This way you will stay warm throughout the night. Do not be alarmed if at midmoonrise, you awake and sleeping mule deer surround you. Wait until dawn when they rise. Then follow them to the river.

It is important to know that you must bathe when you reach the river. The water will be cold. Your heart will stop beating. This is necessary. Stay with the river. Swim. Roll on your side. Rest on the bank. Dig deeply into the riverbed with your toes. Immerse yourself completely. Wash your hair and your clothes. Dry yourself by lying on a boulder in the sun. Your heart will eventually start beating again. But your blood will run slowly. It will be riverine and smell faintly of seep willow. You will feel the paws of a lion on the bank upstream, drinking from the river at dusk. You can find mint and watercress in a side stream feeding into the river. Eat them. You might find one lone chokecherry bush in a copse of oak and alders. Crush the berries and rub them into your hair. Then sleep.

It usually takes at least one night to know whether you have bathed in a female river or a male river. Between midmoonrise and dawn you will awaken. There will be a sound coming from the river. It will be deafening and inaudible. It will resonate in your belly. It is the river. It begins at the headwaters and by the time you awake the entire river will be chanting. Over and over in the darkness you will hear the repetitive melody. Try to follow. Your lips and voice cannot do it. You must learn to river-chant with your body. Words may come. I thought I heard them. I do not know what they meant. It was an old, old song. It is by this song that the river will reveal itself: male or female, its history. The names of each animal, each bird, each desert-goer who has drunk from its waters, sat upon its banks, will be in the chant. Wait by the river night after night until you hear your name. Lie by the river quietly. Bathe each day and let the sun dry your skin and hair. One night you will hear your name in the river-chant. You can leave the following morning.

The river-chant is meant to be sung at night. It is the name of the river. To know the name of a river from its running-water chant is to know all that we can ever know about rivers. Such knowledge will seem significant. But it is very little. Leave a sprig of sage and a *paho* stick by the river when you go.

6. *How to Approach a Juniper Tree*

When you have been in the desert alone for several weeks, you will notice that your actions will begin to take on patterns: each done with attentive deliberation at a certain time and in a certain manner. You may have thought of yourself as considerate and courteous when you entered the desert. Think again of the meaning of mindfulness. There is more to learn. Desert ritual and ceremony will teach you how to walk, to breathe, to eat, to sleep. There is a proper way to do everything. The desert will teach you this: desert manners. Even the certain way in which to approach a juniper tree. There are variations. They depend upon the tree, the soil in which he or she has set its root-feet and the time of year.

This is what I learned. Walk toward the tree but get no closer than five or six feet. You will know when to stop.

Then, wait. Do not speak. Wait until you know that the juniper is willing to have you approach. This is the most difficult step. A juniper tree will always keep you waiting. This is a certainty. You will wait sometimes for hours. Once I sat all day and into the night until the moon rose over the mesa. It was only then that I felt juniper turning to face me, openly acknowledging my presence. I felt frightened for a moment. Silhouetted against the light of the moon, the tree transformed herself. She was the eldest in the company of her companions. She was in charge of receiving.

She was a singer. The wind carried her dry, dark green, pungent voice on its eddies. A sound light as owl feathers fell around me like gossamer.

She was a dancer. She stopped the wind at her command and began to move sensually. From her trunk through every branch, limb, sprig and leaf, she began a gentle stretching at first. Reaching outward in all directions and upwards to the Pleiades. She stretched for what seemed like hours. I waited. Then she began her dance on the windless, moon-glazed mesa. A slow, undulating meander. Rhythmic. The movement of circles and spirals on moonlit canvas. With countless juniper sprig brushes, she painted her dance upon the night and my eyes to remain like the memory of something unutterably lovely, someone's touch exquisitely tender on my face.

I drew in my breath. Hours passed. The moon set. Only then did she stop her dance and her whisper-song painting. She was still then and silent in the gray dawn. She waited for me. It was acceptable to approach. Acceptable to speak to her. She had spoken first, as is appropriate for an elder. She had seen me wait: desert manners.

I took two steps toward her. Sat down. So long had I waited. No audible words came. Yet with each breath I heard my body say: thank you.

7. About Going Home

Avoid going home at all costs. It is too dangerous. Stay out there. Stay with the desert wherever you go. Even if you must remove your body and cart it back to the city. Leave the river in your blood, the bloodstains from being lost on your legs, the copper sun of full moon on your skin, the reverence for juniper in your litany. Remember your manners.

You must be careful when you return to the city. There is no safety for womanness there. You will have to go about your way veiled in order to protect yourself. You will be stronger and more vulnerable than when you left.

It is best to remember not to speak of some things you have seen and done while alone in the desert. People will misunderstand what you say. It is difficult to explain. If you try, your listener will miss the point. Perhaps be inattentive or interrupt your story. This person and many others you thought you knew will not know about desert manners.

Remember each place where you put your foot down on the desert. Remember the feel of the river in your hair, sun on your bare skin. Walk freely and rhythmically. Walk sensually with the knowledge of juniper dance-paintings in your body. See your reflection against the underbelly of the moon. Never in a mirror. Return to the desert each night. To dream and dream.

VI

WOMEN TOGETHER

Gift of Friendship

Oak

June 10-July 7

Judith McDaniel

Scouts on the Saranac

Y ou're going to do what?" my friends asked when I announced my summer recreation. "With how many Girl Scouts?" And, "What do *you* know about canoeing?"

Not a lot, I had to admit. I hadn't been in a canoe for ten years when I went on the spring trial run with others who had also agreed to lead a short canoe trip on the Saranac River. I am more often behind a desk or at my typewriter, but my canoeing muscles hadn't been *too* out of shape, I remind myself as I stand looking at the piles of gear stacked around the first two girls to arrive. Another car pulls up and deposits two more girls. As Mary's mother gets back in the car, Mary pulls out a huge portable radio and starts to tune it in. I signal to her mother to wait and edge toward Mary.

"Gee, Mary, I don't think you'll have much time to listen to that. And we wouldn't want it to fall out of a canoe, would we, hmmm?" I maneuver her toward the car and she very reluctantly deposits the radio with her mother.

So does her friend Julie, to Mary's distress.

"Oh, Julie, why'd you have to tell them you have one?" Mary pouts. "You know I can't sleep without a radio on."

As I wave goodbye to the departing mother, I hear Beth's undertone, "Never mind. I brought mine with me and my mother is already gone." They all looked relieved. I file the information for later. At 10.00 A.M. our sixth canoer arrives and we heft our gear and set off down the path to the tents we will occupy for this one night before our outing. By 10.30 the girls are out in canoes on Hidden Lake, getting checked out by the resident canoe staff on how much they remember about their strokes and canoe safety from last year's lessons. I take half an hour to reconnoiter.

Checking through the gear, I realize that most of it is borrowed from the other volunteers. This is an all-volunteer camp, sponsored by the Adirondack Girl Scout Council. The staff has run the camp for three years now, more elaborate each time. This year the girls who were trained in camp last year are eligible for an out-of-camp canoe trip, which is why I'm here.

At noon the girls troop up to the boat house where I've laid out peanut butter and jelly for sandwiches. Mary tells me she doesn't eat peanut butter. I explain that it is all we will have for lunch for the trip, since it doesn't spoil. I'm irritated with her already because of the radio incident, because she seems so lethargic and whiney.

"What's for dinner, then?" she asks, looking with distaste at the sandwich counter.

"Barbeque chicken," I tell them enthusiastically, "won't that be good?" But Mary doesn't eat chicken either. "What do you eat?" I inquire with some rancor.

"Oh, steak," she replies languidly, then more animatedly, "and pizza." I grind my teeth. It is time for the food statement.

"Look," I tell the group as we sit on the dock for lunch, "the food for this trip was planned for nutrition and easy preparation over a campfire. There will always be plenty to eat. If you don't like some things, eat what you do like. The main thing is, I don't want to hear complaints. O.K.?" They say O.K. Mary eats two stale Girl Scout cookies in silence.

After a rest, I put them in the water for swim tests. They are all water rats. They love the water and undergo instant and complete personality changes when they're soaking wet. Mary and Beth want to learn the butterfly so they can try out for the swim team when they start ninth grade. Julie is a gymnast and takes her lithe young body through a marvelous series of contorted dives, then asks, "Can I do a cartwheel dive off the end of the dock?" I suggest it might be a little narrow and unsteady. She settles for a handstand backflip. I feel stiff just watching her.

Sally arrives late in the afternoon. She is the other adult who is going with us. The girls come up from the lake, tired, but less cranky, it seems to me. Sitting around a table in the kitchen area, I try to set a few rules for the next three days, just a few so we can all relax. Buddies all the time. No swimming without the lifeguard (that's me) present. Camp jobs get traded off—fire, cook, cleanup. When I get out the map, they begin to believe we are really going. I trace our path from the put-in at Second Pond, up the Saranac River to Oseetah Lake, then through the inlet to Kiawasa and the lean-to there.

It's dinner time and they cook. We all eat chicken, even Mary. After dinner I go through the gear each girl wants to take. We leave home

Mary's seven extra t-shirts, Elaine's five pairs of blue jeans and Beth's radio. She gives it up with good grace. I am looking forward to our trip.

The next morning we are up at six, packed and canoes loaded by eight. The girls sleep most of the drive north, but start to wake up as we drive by the Lake Placid Winter Olympics sites and are ready to go when we pull into the unloading ramp. I let the girls untie the canoes and start carrying them down to the water, while I worry to myself about how to pack and tie down our gear in each canoe, something I'd thought a lot about, but never done before. It seems to me to be common sense—a canoe trip's gear has to stay dry and with the canoe—but the practice makes me feel all thumbs and the end result was not the neat packaging I had imagined. Nonetheless, we stow all of our gear and shove off into Second Pond.

Sun is hot, humidity high as we paddle up Second Pond to the lily pads where we take a right and meander over to Cold Brook. One of the canoes is making a crisscross rather than a straight path, as Mary's stroke is so strong in the bow, Beth can't hold a course. It looks like they are canoeing twice as far as the rest of us! After lunch we canoe through Dead Tree Lake and down to the state locks, the highlight of Mary's day. The iron gates clang shut behind our four canoes and the floodgates in the front are open.

As the water pours out and our canoes begin to descend, Mary asks longingly, "Oh, wow, can we come back this way when we go home?"

"Why?" I ask. "Now you've already seen it?"

"I know, I know," she said, "but I want to go the other way. I want to know what it's like to be elevated." We all agree that may not be possible for Mary and paddle on laughing.

We come out of the locks into the marsh of Oseetah Lake, lily pads and purple-spiked flowers. The sun is even hotter than at noon and our heavily-loaded canoes move slowly around the point to the creek into Kiawasa. In midafternoon we reach the lean-to, find it uninhabited, and even, Sandy tells us all proudly, find a roll of toilet paper in the latrine. General rejoicing. I promise them a swim as soon as camp is set up. Tents spring up miraculously. I check the swim area with mask and snorkel and then we spend the next hour jumping and diving off a large rock.

Out here the girls seem to me very independent and capable. They fix and eat dinner with no complaints and little direction from Sally and me. They are considerate of one another. Although four of the more lively girls bond instantly, the other two are never left out, or teased, but given room to enter in as they wish. They all seem to be slowly sloughing off bits of that "civilized" behavior I found so irritating back at camp.

At dusk I sit writing in my journal, resting under the pines on this beautiful and silent lake. The girls are fixing popcorn around the fire up at the lean-to.

I wake at dawn to hear a single white-throated sparrow greet the first light and wake the other birds. I lie for a half-hour listening to each separate chorus enter the cacophony. The last of the night's rainfall drips on the tent fly.

Elaine and Sandy rise with the birds. I suggest that it *is* their one morning to sleep in, if they want. But Elaine is practicing with the hatchet, to her sister's disapproving, "Elaine, not now, go somewhere else, you're such a *twerp!*" from inside the tent. Sandy is washing out the pillowcase that got muddy when she used it in the canoe as a kneeling pad. She is the only girl on the trip I have not yet seen laugh.

After cold cereal and hot cocoa we head to Pine Pond. The morning is grey, but still. I am afraid of a storm, though it is more overcast than threatening.

We beach the canoes in marsh mud and walk into the woods carrying our paddles, lunches, raincoats and watermelon. Paddles are hidden behind a log and we quickly walk the half mile to the pond. As we come over a rise and look down at the water, we are all amazed. This incredibly pure and beautiful pond with a natural sand bottom and beach is breathtaking. The morning is still grey, and we are hungry after the canoeing, but we swim for nearly an hour before I insist on a lunch break. I feel totally relaxed, at ease, and sense the girls feeling a new freedom. After lunch we slice the watermelon and Sally starts a vigorous watermelon-pit spit. They are all easily roused, love the attention and the forbidden pleasure of spitting their watermelon seeds at one another.

I wake from a catnap on the beach to see Elaine covered with sand from her shoulders to her feet, the five other girls gravely smoothing the wet sand over her entire body, admonishing her not to breathe too hard or she'll cause an earthquake. They decide she will be Dolly Parton and I watch as they mold her enormous breasts, smoothing each fondly, placing a nipple on top, consulting about whether they are lopsided or not. "Can you see your toes, Elaine?" Beth asks, "'Cause if you can, they're not big enough yet." Sandy giggles with embarassment and glee behind her hand.

I go over and suggest Dolly needs a belly button, craft one carefully in the approriate zone, but Beth chides me, "Judith, Dolly Parton wouldn't have an inner belly button, hers is an outty," and she corrects by sculpture accordingly. Elaine decides she has to breathe and an earthquake finishes off Dolly.

I have to flog them out of Pine Pond. No one wants to leave, but it is late afternoon and the sun is gone again. I am afraid to take more of a chance with the weather. But it is too late. When we pull away from the cove, out past the protective point, a gusty wind hits our canoes broadside. An enormous thunderhead lowers in front of us, the wind is picking up even more, but I see no lightning, hear no thunder. I decide to head for home and turn to see how the girls are. They are paddling ferociously, putting their shoulders and backs into the effort as I have never seen them before, and I lead us out across the choppy lake toward our inlet. Virginia is in the bow of my canoe and in my anxiety I shout directions at her: "Pull right, Virginia, now left. Virginia, put your shoulders into it," screaming at her in frustration. "Feather your paddle, it will help me." As a gust of rain hits us, I catch a glimpse of her face. She is grinning with exhilaration.

The rain comes harder, but no one thinks of rain gear. We are all soaked and if we stopped we'd be blown clear back to Pine Pond. Still I hear no thunder. When we make the narrow channel a fisherman calls out to offer us shelter in his camp. We are only a half a mile from camp now, so we shout no and head for home. As we beach the canoes at our lean-to, the rain comes down in sheets and I hear the first thunder blowing across the lake.

"They all loved it," Sally says in amazement as we flop into our tent to dry off after drying off the girls and giving them hot chocolate. "They weren't scared. Just Mary. She kept asking me, what will Judith do if there's lightening?" She pauses, then turns to look at me. "What would you have done?"

"Put in," I answer emphatically. "We'd still be sitting in the rain on a shoreline somewhere waiting for this to pass. Were you scared?"

"Nervous," she allows.

"Me too," I confess, "me too."

The rain quits in the early evening while we make dinner and sit around the campfire toasting marshmallows. When it starts to pour again, we all go to bed. In the grey morning we cook french toast and start to break camp. I contemplate the peanut butter for the day's sandwiches, eye Mary, and ask, "Anyone prefer pizza for lunch to-day in Lake Placid Village?" Mary's whoop echoes in the trees and her enthusiasm carries us back down the trail, packs the canoes and sets us off again.

We vote to go back through the locks, retracing our steps, hoping to give Mary a real "elevation" like she'd asked for. As we start up the inlet, we all cheer to see the sun come out through the clouds, shining on just us. I know that when we get to the village Mary will start to whine and complain about her wet sleeping bag, she and Julie will point at every teenage boy we drive by, and Beth will spend fifteen minutes in the only ladies room at the pizza place combing her hair while five of us are waiting to go to the bathroom. But for now I let the girls lead the way out into the marsh, enjoying the sparkle of the water as it comes off their paddles, watching the reflection of their firm and strong strokes in the rippled water.

Lucy Jane Bledsoe

Solo

I stood on the rim of a huge, perfectly formed bowl, deep with snow. I'd just skied over a pass that, according to my map, was 9,200 feet high. The peaks surrounding me were banked with snowfields that looked blue in the late afternoon High-Sierra light. Massive clouds, the color of pearls, swarmed around the peaks. And I knew exactly what I was—this being on skis in the marrow of wilderness—a human body and nothing more. That was one thing Elizabeth and I agreed on, even in the last couple years—that the goal is to reach that stripped down state where your cells know everything there is to know, where your feelings go so deep they become one simple force, where sorrow and joy become the same thing.

How I missed Elizabeth.

I cut the metal edges of my skis into the ice-crusted snow for balance and then reached into my pocket for a few yogurt peanuts. We'd always saved the yogurt peanuts to eat at the tops of passes, and nowhere else. Next, I checked to make sure the batteries in my avalanche beacon still had juice. What a joke, carrying a beacon on a solo trip. Who would pick up its high-frequency beeps if an avalanche buried me? I guess it was just habit.

Then I looked down into that steep bowl below me. Its snow pack fed a long drainage that in the spring would fan out into half a dozen streams. My destination was the bottom of that drainage. I planned to camp at High Meadow tonight and then ski out tomorrow morning. I scanned the slope for a safe route down. I figured it was about a five-hundred-foot drop.

"Yahooooo!" Elizabeth's voice hollered in my head. I could see her spirit lean forward with that open-mouthed grin of hers that looked more like a shout than a smile. She shoved her ski poles into the snow and flew off the mountain. Elizabeth would have taken what she called the crow's route, straight down. Her tight telemark turns would have made a long, neat squiggle in the snow all the way to the bottom of the bowl. In the meadow below she would glide to a luxurious stop, then purposely fall in a heap, exhausted from her ecstasy.

"Oh, Elizabeth," I said, missing her foolhardiness with a pain as sharp as this bitter wind. How I longed to lecture her right then: "Listen, girl, we've had over a foot of fresh snow in the last week. Got it? The snow pack is *weak*. Add to that the fact that this is a leeward slope on a gusty day."

By now she would have quit listening. Her face would be turned toward the valley, and I'd know she was already flying, dead center in that rapture of hers.

And yet, I would go on with my lecture: "And look at that cornice!"

I'd point to the one about ten yards below me right now.

"What cornice?" she might ask, because it really was a small one and nothing subtle ever figured into Elizabeth's world.

"Elizabeth," I spoke out loud now. "This is a prime avalanche slope in prime avalanche conditions."

I think my voice was a mantra for her, the droning noise against which she took flight. My words of caution were her starting blocks. If she were here, this would have been her cue. Off she'd sail. I'd watch her back for a few moments and then realize that being stranded on a ridge top in the High Sierra in March, with a storm pending, was a greater risk than skiing an avalanche-prone slope. I'd be forced to follow.

The wind stormed over the pass, interrupting my thoughts and broadsiding me with so much force that I lost my balance and fell. I lay with my skis and legs tangled in the air above me, let my head fall back onto the snow and watched the clouds. They'd lost their luster and were becoming swarthy. The feeling of knowledge in my cells disappeared, and now I felt the opposite, as if I were all spirit, practically not here at all, like Elizabeth. How fast things changed at this elevation.

They found her car, of course. Who could miss it? Her bumper stickers were as loud as she was. This whole trip I'd been trying to imagine where her body might be. Deep in some crevasse. Buried in an avalanche. Or simply sitting in her camp somewhere, dead of exposure. I couldn't help wanting to believe that she had that shouting smile on her face, wherever she was, although even Elizabeth must have learned the meaning of fear in the moments before death. Or had she?

Elizabeth and I had been mountaineering partners, off and on, for almost twenty years. We began backpacking together when we were

fifteen. I was the crazy one then, wild and daring, wanting to go farther, deeper, longer, faster, later or earlier. But over the years there
was a shift. I grew more cautious and Elizabeth grew more reckless.
There were several years in there, when her recklessness had caught
up with but not yet overtaken mine, that we were perfect partners.
We could choose a campsite and make route decisions almost without talking. We shared the implicit understanding that courting the
mountains was our first commitment and working as a team got us
closer to those peaks.

I noticed her impatience for the first time on a hiking trip in the
Brooks Range of Alaska, just a few months after her mother died. She
wanted to take a short-cut and bushwhack some ten miles across a
spur where we could join our trail again and save thirty miles.

I pointed to the map. "Elizabeth, that's a cliff. And there aren't
enough landmarks to ensure we'd find the trail. What's the hurry,
anyway?"

"Don't use my name," she snapped.

"What?" I must have looked hurt.

"The way you use my name is patronizing. I can read the map. We
can scramble up those rocks."

"You mean that vertical cliff."

"Oh, geez," she said but gave in to me. We had several similar
encounters that trip, but I attributed her impatience to the recent
death of her mother, nothing more.

Back then I thought that if she would just slow down she could
discover what it was she so badly needed. Now I think that she
hungered only for this moment I faced. That in a strange, almost
ghoulish way, she got what she wanted—to see how far she could
take a risk.

My choice now, to ski this prime avalanche slope or to turn around and ski out the three-day route I'd skied in on, was almost exactly like the one that precipitated Elizabeth's and my first all-out fight. We were circumnavigating Mount Adams in the state of Washington in late spring. Near the end of the trip, we reached a torrential river gushing out of the foot of a glacier. We spent an entire day, on my insistence and to Elizabeth's disgust, searching for a safe crossing. We never found one.

"Our choice," Elizabeth finally pointed out, "is backtracking five days, being home late and not completing the circumnavigation, or jumping the river, being home in two days and completing the circumnavigation." Her gray eyes looked like nails right then.

"You missed one option," I added. "One of us jumps, lands in the river and is washed downstream. The other goes home to tell her family."

"Oh, shit." She looked up at Mount Adams as if appealing for understanding, and I felt very small, cut out. I was in her way, had come between her and the mountain. And that, I knew, was the one sacrilege she wouldn't tolerate.

"Look," she deigned to explain. "Basically, there are two approaches to life. You can mire yourself in precautions as you endlessly try to outwit fate. Or, you can let her fly. There's risk either way. In the first scenario, you might—probably *will*—miss all that is good in life. In the second scenario, you get what you want, but you might not get it for as long as you want. Your choice."

I watched the chalky white glacial water as she hammered out her opinion. On either side of the river, a reddish moraine had built up, bereft of life. I longed for a forest then, the thick comfort of living things. I felt very alone with my cautious, fearful self. I also felt angry, used. I felt like that moraine, a pile of debris pushed aside by her forging glacier.

We did jump the stream, adrenaline carrying me across a much broader distance than my body could normally go. But nothing was ever the same between me and Elizabeth.

Another blast of icy wind, stronger still than the last one, blew me off my feet. I slid to within one yard of the cornice, my legs and skis once again a tangle. "Elizabeth!" I shouted. "I know you're out there! Quit pushing me, you goddamn wild woman."

Then, surprising myself I added, even louder still, "I love you!" In spite of everything, Elizabeth was as good as these mountains, this wild, stormy sky. She was part of my wilderness. But that didn't mean I had to be crazy, now that she was dead, and go against all common sense and ski this slope.

I had an idea. I'd have to check the map, but I thought that if I backtracked just to the other side of this pass, I could go out the south fork drainage and still only lose a day. I could hitchhike to my car from there. It was a good plan. I'd always told my friends that my coming home late meant nothing more than I'd used good sense and changed my route. I had plenty of food and warm clothing.

I got to my feet, without sliding over the lip of the cornice, and skied back to the top of the ridge. The hard wind died down suddenly and now a gentle breeze brushed my face. I stopped at the top to take one last look at the bowl before retreating down the back, gentle side of the pass.

"Yahooooo!" Once again, I saw her spirit fly over the cornice and down the slope.

I remembered the night of our final fight, a year ago, when we were marooned in our tent. I was lying on my stomach, cooking freeze-dried honey-lime chicken on the stove just outside the tent door, my sleeping bag pulled up to my shoulders. Outside, the snow fell thickly in tiny flakes. We'd been stuck in this camp for twenty-four hours already. Elizabeth had a date the following night and wanted to ski out in the morning regardless of the weather. "It's only fifteen miles," she'd said.

"Fifteen miles in a white-out."

She shrugged, "We've skied this route before."

"You'd risk your life for a date?" I challenged.

"Yeah," she grinned, "if it's hot enough. And this one is. I mean, I'm not talking about O.K. sex, this is, oh, how can I even explain to you. . . . " She looked up to the ceiling of our tent, searching, as if the English language just didn't contain the words to make me understand.

"Elizabeth," I said calmly. "I know what hot sex is. And it's not worth dying in a blizzard for."

"Then," she said snatching off her wool cap. Her short, honey-colored hair was mashed against her head. "Then you *don't* know what hot sex is."

"Oh, fuck you!" I yelled. I was so tired of her constant mocking. "You're a goddamn lunatic!" I managed to pull on my boots and squeeze out of the tent without knocking over the pot of honey-lime chicken cooking on the stove. I stomped around outside in the blizzard for a few moments, fuming.

When I started shaking violently with cold, I returned. She had a novel propped on one knee and the last of our yogurt peanuts in a plastic bag between her legs. The honey-lime chicken bubbled away, most of the liquid boiled off. She wolfed down the yogurt peanuts one after another, munching loudly.

"What are you doing?" My voice was dry and accusing. "Those peanuts are for the pass tomorrow."

"I'm feeding the lunatic," she answered softly, faking innocence. "She's hungry." A bit of chewed up yogurt peanut spewed out of her mouth as she spoke. She held the bag out to me. "I think your lunatic may be hungry, too. Want some?"

"Oh, fuck you," I said again. And we were silent the rest of the evening. I lay awake all night reading short stories and looking forward to being rid of Elizabeth at the end of this journey.

By the next morning the sky had cleared and we skied out, Elizabeth happy to be heading back to the Bay Area in time for her hot date. Me, bitter. It was the last trip we took together. She called me occasionally after that, but neither of us suggested any trips. I went with other friends, she went alone. I dreaded the day when she would see our impasse as yet another unexplored territory she must venture into.

I did find some satisfaction in the fact that she didn't take another partner. Yet, in a way, I was even more jealous that she went solo, that she'd stretched to a place I didn't think I could stretch to.

When her brother called me two months ago to ask if I'd heard from Elizabeth, I knew instantly. He figured maybe an impromptu trip to L.A. Or that she was camped out at some new lover's apartment. "Nathan," I told him. "I don't think so." He waited silently for my explanation, and I could tell from his breathing that he knew too. I said, "She'd mentioned a trip in the Trinity Alps last time I talked to her."

"Who should I call?" Nathan asked dully. I hung up and went over to his apartment. We called the Forest Service, and they located her car within five hours. They gave up looking for her body after a week.

For a long time, all I could think was that I had been right and she had been wrong. She was dead, and still I wished I could continue our dispute, find some way of telling her, "I told you so." Now, as I turned my back on the bowl, deep with snow, preparing to retreat back down the safe side of the pass, I realized just how great my jealousy had been. She was right. My lunatic *was* hungry.

Suddenly, I turned around again and faced the steep bowl. A pillow of fog nestled in the trees far below. Somewhere beyond was my car.

I dug my poles into the snow. I pushed slowly at first and then shoved off hard. I sailed out, directly over the lip of that cornice and landed squarely on my skis several feet below. I shot downhill, taking the crow's route, straight down. I wasn't a particularly good downhill skier, I'd never learned telemark turns, so I skied a straight, seemingly vertical line, amazed that I didn't fall. My feet vibrated as they stroked the long slope. My legs felt like springs, supple and responsive. My head roared. Everything was a white blur. I'd never skied so fast in my life.

Then I heard it. A bellowing that drowned out the rush of wind in my ears. I felt the entire mountain thundering under my feet. In the next split second, I saw powder snow billowing up fifty feet in the air. So this was it, I thought, feeling a strange, dead center calm. No one skied faster than a slab avalanche. And yet, as if I could, I crouched down lower, held my poles close to my body, allowed my legs to be even more elastic, and concentrated on the width between my skis.

Then the avalanche overtook me, careening down the slope to my right, missing me by about ten yards. The roar was deafening and the cloud of snow blinded me, but still I skied.

Elizabeth, I thought, perverse in the coolness of my mind, never raced an avalanche down a slope.

I came crashing into the flats of the meadow below the bowl and plunged into the snow, face first. Sharp pain splintered up my nose, across my jaw. I rolled over on my side and gingerly wiped the snow off my face with a wet mitten, touching my cheekbone and forehead.

Nothing seemed to be broken, just mashed. I blinked hard to clear my eyes and finally saw the wreckage of the avalanche to my right; masses of snow that moments ago were as fluid as water were now as set as concrete. I could have been locked in that pile of snow, my beacon transmitting tiny beeps for some chance stranger to pick up. They would have had about thirty minutes, if I was lucky, to locate and dig me out. I stared and stared at that icy rubble as awed as if it were the remains of an ancient temple.

"Oh, God," I whispered.

My arms and legs felt paralyzed, but slowly I was able to move each limb, bending and straightening until it regained feeling. I rolled over in the snow and tried to get to my feet, but didn't yet have the strength.

I sensed Elizabeth nearby. "Did you see me?" I asked, still whispering.

Finally I wept, and as I did I thought I heard her laughing, that hard, wild-woman laughter of hers. Then I realized it was my own laughter, in concert with my tears, shaking the very centers of my cells, wringing the sorrow out of my pores.

Mary Ellis

Casting in the Fog

*I*t is six-thirty in the morning. A foggy and gray Sunday in July in northern Wisconsin. My sister and I step outside our mother's house into an unusually cool mist. We're going fishing, and this is the kind of weather we've been hoping for—when the air is so heavy with water that it sets off an even sharper smell of swamp cedar and tamarack; when the fish seem more inclined to take the hook. We are both grateful for the overcast sky. It releases our eyes from the glare of the sun, allowing us to look comfortably at everything: green moss, pink ladyslippers, the loudmouth Canada jays, or whiskey jacks as they are more commonly called, perched in the tamarack branches above us.

We trudge through the swamp to the lake. My sister, Jane, walks ahead of me. I smile: She is still dressed in her blue flannel nightgown but has on the necessary green rubber boots and a baseball cap saturated with Muskol. She carries a Browning graphite rod with a Shimano quick-release reel and a carton full of worms. I carry my first-of-the-morning cup of coffee.

Despite the squishing of bog under our boots, we try to be as quiet as possible because of a pair of loons that live on the lake. We reach what could be called a dock: an old, slowly-rotting barn door sunk into the vegetative bedding of the swamp. I park myself off to the side on a half-submerged log the swamp is also slowly reclaiming, and watch as my sister walks further down the bog shore. Jane moves far enough away so that she can cast comfortably without hooking me. It's a reality and an old family joke. I've either managed to move at just the wrong time, sat in just the wrong place or had the misfortune of being with Jane on a day when her arm was rusty. When we were children, it was my back that got it the most; now as an adult, it is usually an arm, and once it was a finger, a dazzling feat that sent our brother, Paul, who was paddler and navigator on a family fishing trip down the Chippewa River, into a laughing fit that nearly tipped the canoe. I had been pointing out a great blue heron when Jane, casting back, deftly managed to snag just that finger. Now she stands a good distance away from me, but still I keep a careful eye on her casting arm.

The fog drifts over the top of the water, so thick in places that I cannot see the opposite shore. The shoreline we own on this kettle lake has been in our family for almost thirty-five years, and we have never called it anything but "the lake" or "the lake by the house." I don't even know if it has an official name. It is this lake, almost a stone's throw from the farmhouse we lived in when we were very young, that my sister has probably fished and loved the most. It looks, especially now in the early morning, like photographs of Alaska's boreal lakes and forests. Except for an occasional party of crows and, if we are lucky, the loons, it is completely quiet. Sometimes a car or truck rumbling past on the gravel road by the house disrupts the peace, but most of the time, the lake seems to be part of our own private world. When we were little girls, innocent of our effect upon land and its effect upon us, we thought the lake belonged to us and we belonged to the lake. We could have fallen off the bog and drowned, and then we really would have belonged to the lake—our mother warned us about this possibility constantly. We only superficially believed her in our arrogant innocence. We believed we were a part of the lake and land— like an arm or leg—and therefore it would not hurt us. Besides, we reasoned, we had life jackets on, and we could swim.

We applied this same reasoning toward time. Like most children, and especially as rural children, we did not measure time in minutes, hours or days. If we felt it was "time" to go fishing at the lake, we went regardless of whether it was morning, afternoon or evening. We jumped out of bed as soon as the sun hit our faces, not because it was six in the morning. And we fell asleep when it got dark and we became tired. As much as we took our surroundings for granted, we were also in daily awe of them. We wondered why the sun was so bright, how caterpillars turned into butterflies, why the lake's surface looked like a mirror on windless days and what it looked like on the bottom. We were in awe of this lake even when we did not know about the tremendous force and power of glaciers (learned about in fourth or fifth grade) that carved out kettle lakes such as this one. And when we did learn about those natural forces, it only increased our love for the lake.

As I watch my sister, I realize that fishing brings her this feeling of time that cannot be measured by a contrived human clock.

Jane reaches into a carton of worms and pulls out a fair-sized night crawler.

"Sorry, wormie," she says, threading the squirming night crawler on her hook. When she is done, she wipes her hand on her night-gown and adjusts the yellow bobber.

"We're goin' for those big ones today!" she whispers and grins. I laugh into my cup. As deep as this lake is, it holds mostly pan fish: perch, bluegills, crappies and sunfish.

She draws the rod back and throws it forward, skillfully releasing the line so a tiny hum sings through the air. The line, bobber and worm-laden hook disappear momentarily into the fog until we hear the splash of contact. Then she slowly reels, pauses, slowly reels and pauses. She stands with her weight mostly on one leg and watches, almost stares, with Buddhist-like devotion at the very faint yellow outline of the bobber.

Except for being an adult, my sister still strongly resembles the child she used to be. She was a teddy-bear kind of kid, incredibly good-natured and cuddly, trusting and patient. She crawled out of bed this morning the same way she did when she was four—with that doey brown-eyed happiness that said *fishin'*. Her reddish-brown hair is very short and neatly caps her head. From a distance in a baseball cap, jeans and a sweatshirt, she might appear to be a teenage boy. But when you get closer, the tall and slender figure and sharply defined face become distinctly and elegantly female. It surprises many people to see her, a woman fishing alone. And that, to our family and friends that know her well, is the quintessential Jane.

Looking at her now, I am reminded of how the act of fishing and her experience of fishing are colored by her femaleness.

Absent is the Great White Hunter approach, the camaraderie of beer buddies in the boat, the male bonding of father to son, or the great sporting "wife" to a Hemingway-like figure. Nor is she a snob insisting on fishing with only the most expensive lures or the best rod and reel that money can buy or in an outfit straight from L. L. Bean or Eddie Bauer that would declare her the genteel and well-educated lady fisherman, a word combination that always causes me to smile cynically because of the contradiction in gender and implication of class.

There she is standing fifteen feet away from me, dressed in an old blue flannel nightgown, with sleeping sand in her eyes, and fishing with worms. Although she has and uses more sophisticated lures such as french spinners, rapalas or brightly-colored flies for fish such as trout, walleye, muskie and northern, she is just as happy with what other fisherpeople would consider less. Jane fishes, as she says, by "instinct," and if that means a long yellow cane pole such as the kind we used as kids, then so be it.

The bobber bobs and then goes under. Jane jerks the rod up and begins reeling. "I'll bet it's a bluegill," she whispers, and sure enough, it is a small but energetic bluegill. They're fun to catch because they are such little fighters. Jane reaches out to grab the line and carefully slides her hand along the bluegill's back to smooth down the dorsal fin so she won't get stuck. She gently pries the hook out of its mouth and, bending down, slides the bluegill back into the water. I see a flash of butter yellow from its side, and then it is gone, diving for safety underneath the floating bog shelf. Jane threads the hook with another night crawler and casts. I slap a mosquito on my cheek, and the sound seems to echo across the lake. I ask Jane if the mosquitoes are getting at her legs beneath her nightgown. She shakes her head and continues to stare at the bobber. I wish I had thought to bring the camera.

∿

We have several pictures of Jane fishing when she was three or four. Our family lived on a string-bean economy, what with seven children and basically one parent, but after borrowing a camera from her in-laws for years, our mother finally squeezed the money together to invest in a Kodak.

In a couple of these photographs, Jane is wearing a woman's one-piece orange swimsuit (minus those torpedo-like padded bra cups), the crotch of which is hanging around her ankles, the scooped neck-line framing her navel. Over this engaging outfit, she has on an orange life jacket (mandatory in our family if we were by the lake or the smaller pond close to the house), and in her hand, a fishing pole. She is standing ankle-deep in the pond, which is fed by a channel from the lake. In one picture her face holds that wide beam of baby teeth demanded by a mother wielding a camera ("C'mon now, Janie . . . smi-i-i-le"), and in another, she is staring at the pond surface with the seriousness that a possible ripple or break in the water requires.

Jane would sit on the bank of this pond and happily catch bullheads or whatever was biting for hours. If the fish were slow in responding, she would wedge the end of her fishing pole into the mud and prop it against one of the iron stakes supporting the bank. She would then get a long-handled net from the barn and spend the rest of the morning or afternoon wading in the water and netting pollywogs, frogs and minnows, stopping every so often to check her line. She was an easy child to watch—a fishing pole, worms and the pond enabled our mother, with a glance out the kitchen window, to keep track of her youngest daughter. It was considered cute and novel that a little girl loved to fish so much, and Jane drew patronizing smiles from visitors, relatives and the like. All the girls in our family were tomboys, that is, capable of doing "boy" things—shooting a gun, fishing, playing ball, climbing trees, fist fighting—as well as "girl" things—playing with dolls, playing house, learning to bake, wearing dresses when the occasion demanded it. But the unspoken assumption, as it was with Jane's fishing, was, *they'll grow out of it.*

Obviously she did not.

A loon appears through the fog. Jane quietly reels her line in and waits. Even from a distance, it is remarkable how big a loon is compared to most water birds. We watch it turn its head from side to side, gauging our position, maybe even our intent. The loon stays silent while it swims in our direction. "I wonder where its mate is," I whisper. Before Jane can answer, the loon suddenly gives a short, sharp cry. Minutes later my question is answered: The mate appears out of the gray sky and makes its long and magical landing, skipping across the surface and then, breast up, skiing into the water. We watch for a while hoping they will come closer, but they stay toward the middle of the lake.

It must be seven-thirty by now. Jane bends down to pull another night crawler from the carton. I watch her cast into the water in front of me, listen to the squish of her boots as she shifts position. She has caught several fish but kept none, disengaging the hook from their gills or mouths carefully before returning them to the water. Her fishing style is gentle, much like teasing a good friend but ultimately being respectful of her feelings.

Jane absent-mindedly hikes up her nightgown to scratch her knee. Her water-dwelling playmates, the bluegills and crappies, are not taking the worms as fiercely as they did an hour ago, and now the bobber registers nibbles, not fully engulfed bites. Jane reels once and lets the bobber sit in a new place. She sighs deeply. I can't tell whether the sigh signals contentment or sadness, but I think it's a mixture of both. The fog is slowly lifting, and with it goes some of the morning's mystery that touched us when we first got out of bed and headed for the lake. We are no longer little girls who sneaked out of the house in our nightgowns while our mother was asleep. And soon, we must return to our adult lives.

But the morning's stillness has given us the comfort just to sit, just to *be*, instead of going, going, going most of the time. It allows us to be sisters in the way we were years ago, when the blood connection between us was so strong we never had to think about it. Jane for years was my closest playmate. Her fishing was a variation of something *I did*, what *we did* together and what we learned and became in our private rural world.

"Are you getting tired?" Jane asks. I shake my head even though it's true—I am a little tired. The white blanket of fog over the water has thinned in places, and I can see the opposite shore rimmed with tamaracks. Jane grins at me and adjusts her cap before reaching down for another night crawler. The loons give off their peculiar laughing cry, and we listen as their voices trail off. Jane threads the worm on the hook. Then her right arm gracefully arches behind her, poised like a messenger bearing gifts of food. She swings it forward, and I watch as my sister casts into the fog.

VII

MEN IN OUR LIVES

Gift of Companionship

Holly
July 8–August 4

Pam Houston

The Company of Men

I can't remember the last time I envied a man, or, in fact, if I ever have. I have loved men, hated them, befriended them, taken care of them, and all too often compromised my sense of self for them, but I don't think I have ever looked at a man and actually coveted something his maleness gave him. And yet envy was at least one of the surprising things I felt last spring when I found myself standing armpit-deep in a freshwater stream at 2:00 A.M. near Interlochen, Michigan, fly casting for steelhead with a bunch of male poets.

Winters are long in northern Michigan, and dark and frozen. Spring is late and wet and full of spirit-breaking storms. The landscape is primarily forest and water and has not been tamed like most of the Midwest. Both the wildness and the hardship show on the faces of the people who choose to live there.

When a man named Jack Driscoll first calls and invites me to Interlochen, he tells me about the Academy, a place where talented high-school students from forty-one states and fifteen countries are given a lot of time to develop their art. Although he makes it clear that I will be expected to read from my fiction and talk to the students about craft, every other time we speak on the phone, all he really wants to talk about is fishing.

For all the time I spend outdoors, I am not much of a fisherman. And fly fishing, like all religions, is something I respect but don't particularly understand. If Jack bothers to ask me if I want to go fishing, I will say yes. I have always said yes, and as a result the shape of my life has been a long series of man-inspired adventures, and I have gone tripping along behind those men, full of strength and will and only a half-baked kind of competence, my goal being not to excel, but to simply keep up with them, to not become a problem, to be a good sport. It is a childhood thing (I was my father's only son), and I laugh at all the places this particular insecurity has taken me: sheep hunting in Alaska, helicopter skiing in Montana, cliff diving in the Bahamas, ice climbing in the Yukon territory. Mostly, I have outgrown the need to impress men in this fashion; in the adventures I take these days, I make the rules. But, as my trip to Michigan draws nearer, I feel a familiar and demented excitement to be back at the mercy of a bunch of lunatic outdoorsmen, a stubborn novice with something intangible to prove.

I fly up to Traverse City on what the woman at the United Express counter calls the "big" plane, a twin-engine that bumps between thunderstorms and patches of dense fog for an hour before skidding to a stop on a bleak and rainy runway surrounded by a leafless April woods.

I am greeted by what looks like a small committee of fit and weathered middle-aged men. Their names are Jack Driscoll, Mike Delp, Nick Bozanic and Doug Stanton. Their books are titled after the landscape that dominates their lives, collections of poetry called *Under the Influence of Water*, *The Long Drive Home* and *Over the Graves of Horses*, and Jack's award-winning collection of stories titled *Wanting Only to Be Heard*. They fight over my luggage, hand me snacks and sodas and beers, and all but carry me to the car on the wave of their enthusiasm.

"Weather's been good," Mike says, by way of a greeting. "The lake ice is breaking."

"It's a real late run for the steelhead," Doug says. "You're just in time."

"Any minute now, any minute now," Jack says, his mind full of the long, dark bodies of fish in the river, and then, "You've got a reading in forty-five minutes, then a dinner that should be over by ten, the president of the local community college wants to meet you. At midnight, we fish."

By 12:25 A.M. I am dressed in my long underwear, Jack's camouflage sweat clothes, Mike's neoprene liners, Doug's waders and Nick's hat. I look like the Michelin tire man, the waders so big and stiff I can barely put one foot in front of the other. We pile into Mike's Montero, rods and reels jangling in the back. Jack and Mike and Doug and I. Nick, each man has told me (privately, in a quiet, apprehensive voice), is recovering from bursitis and a divorce, and for one or the other of these reasons, he will not fish this year.

No one asks me if I'm tired, nor do I ask them. These men have had nine months of winter to catch up on their sleep, cabin fever reflecting in their eyes like exclamations. The steelhead will start running soon, maybe tonight, and there is no question about where they should be.

It takes almost an hour to get to the river with what I quickly understand is an obligatory stop at the Sunoco in the tiny town called Honor for day-old doughnuts and Coca-Cola and banter with the cashier. Along the way we listen to what Mike and Jack say is their latest road tape, three Greg Brown songs recorded over and over to fill a ninety-minute drive. "Gonna meet you after midnight," say the lyrics repeatedly, "at the Dream Cafe."

The rotating sign on the Honor State Bank says 1:51 a.m. and twenty-two degrees. The men have bet on what the temperature will be. They have also bet on how many cars we will pass on the two-lane highway, how many deer we will see in the woods between Mike's house and the bridge, if it will snow or rain and, if so, how hard (hardness gauged by comparison with other nights' fishing). Doug wins the temperature bet, closest without going over, at twenty-one degrees.

The betting is all part of a long, conversational rap among them, a rap that moves from Mike's last fish to Jack's latest fiction to concern for Nick and his lost house to the girl at the Sunoco to an in-unison sing-along to their favorite Greg Brown lyrics. The whole conversation is less like speaking, really, and more like singing, a song they've spent years and years of these cold spring nights together learning, nights anybody anywhere else in the world would call winter, nights filled with an expectation that can only be called boyish and shadowed by too much of the grown-up knowledge that can ultimately defeat men.

Sometimes they remember I am there, sometimes they forget I am a woman.

I feel, in those moments, like I've gone undercover, like I've been granted security clearance to a rare and private work of art. And though I have always believed that women bond faster, tighter, deeper than men could ever dream of, there is something simple and pure between these men, a connection so thick and dense and timeless that I am fascinated, and jealous, and humbled, all at the same time.

"Shit," Jack says, "Look at 'em all." We have come finally out of the woods and to a bridge no longer than the width of the two-lane roadway. As impossible as it is for me to believe, at 2:00 A.M. the gravel areas on both sides of the bridge are lined with pickups, a counterculture of night stalkers, two and three trucks deep.

I can see by the posture of the men who line the bridge and look gloomily over the edge that they do not teach poetry at Interlochen Arts Academy. One of them staggers toward the truck, reeling drunk. A boy of nine or ten, dressed all in camouflage, tries to steady him from behind.

"They ain't here yet," the old man says, an edge in his voice like desperation. "It may be they just aren't coming."

"They'll be here," Jack says, easing himself out of the Montero and steering the man away from the broken piece of bridge railing. "It's been a long winter for everybody," Jack says, almost cooing, and the old man drunkenly, solemnly, nods.

Mike pulls me out of the truck and hands me a flashlight. We creep to the edge of the bridge and peer over. "Just on for a second and off," he whispers. Even to me it is unmistakable; the flashlight illuminates a long, dark shape already half under the pylon. "Don't say anything," Mike mouths to me soundlessly. Jack leaves the old-timer to sleep in his car and joins us. Mike holds up one finger, and Jack nods. "We'll go downstream," Jack says, after some consideration. "Nobody's gonna do any good here."

We drive downriver while Mike points out all the sights as if we can see them—a place called the toilet hole, where Doug and Nick got lucky, the place Mike got his car stuck so bad four-wheel drive couldn't help him, the place Jack caught last year's biggest fish. We can see the headlights of people who are smelt-dipping out where the river empties into the lake, and a red and white channel marker lit up and looming in the darkness, its base still caked with lake ice and snow.

We drop Doug off at his favorite hole near the mouth of the river, drive back upstream a few hundred yards, park the Montero and step out into the night.

"It's a little bit of a walk from here," Mike says, "and the mud's pretty deep." It is impossible for me to imagine how I will move my stiff and padded legs through deep mud, how, at twenty-two degrees, I will step into that swift and icy river, much less stand in it for a couple of hours. I can't imagine how, with all these clothes and pitch dark around me, I'll be able to cast my fly with anything resembling grace.

Two steps away from the truck and already I feel the suction. The mud we are walking in ranges from mid-calf to mid-thigh deep. I'm following Jack like a puppy, trying to walk where he walks, step where he steps. I get warm with the effort, and a little careless, and suddenly there's nothing beneath me and I'm in watery mud up to my waist. Mike and Jack, each on one arm, pull me out of the hole so fast it seems like part of the choreography.

"Let's try to cross the river," says Jack, and before I can even brace for the cold, we are in it, thigh . . . hip . . . waist . . . deep, and I feel the rush of the current tug me toward Lake Michigan. "One foot in front of the other," Jack says. "The hole's right in front of you; when you're ready, go ahead and cast."

I lift the rod uneasily into the night, close my eyes and try to remember how they did it in *A River Runs Through It*, and then bring it down too fast and too hard with an ungraceful splat. "Let out a little more line," Jack says, so gently it's as if he is talking to himself. A few more splats, a little more line, and I am making casts that aren't embarrassing. Jack moves without speaking to help Mike with a snarl in his line. "This is your night, Delp," Jack says, his shadowy form floating away from me, a dark and legless ghost.

What in the world are you doing here? a voice giggles up from inside me, and the answers sweep past me, too fast to catch: because I can't turn down a challenge, because my father wanted a boy, because touching this wildness is the best way I know to undermine sadness, because of the thin shimmery line I am seeing between the dark river and the even darker sky.

Soon I stop thinking about being washed to Lake Michigan. I marvel at how warm I am in the waders, so warm and buoyant that I forget myself from time to time and dip some unprotected part of me, my hand or my elbow, into the icy water. A deer crackles sticks in the forest across the river; an angry beaver slaps his tail. In whispers we take turns identifying planets and constellations—Ursa Major, Draco, Cassiopeia, Mars and Jupiter—and murmur at the infrequent but lovely falling stars.

When we are quiet I can hear a faint crashing—constant, reverberant—sounding in the dark for all the world like the heartbeat of the earth. "Lake Michigan coming over the breakwater," Jack says to my unasked question. "There must be a big wind on the other side."

My fishing is steadily improving: every fifth or seventh cast hangs a long time in the air and falls lightly, almost without sound.

"You know," Jack says, "there aren't too many people who could come out here like this and not hook themselves or me or the shoreline . . . isn't that right, Delp?" Mike murmurs in agreement, and my head swells with ridiculously disproportionate pride.

The constellations disappear, and a light snow begins falling. "God, I love the weather," Mike says, his voice a mixture of sarcasm and sincerity, and for a while there is only the whisper of the line and the flies.

"Fish!" Jack shouts suddenly. "Fish on the line!" I am startled almost out of my footing, as if I've forgotten what we've come for, as if the silence and the night and the rhythm of the flies hitting the water have become reason enough. We reel in our lines and watch Jack land his fish. It is long and thin, and its speckled belly gleams silver as it thrashes in the tiny beam of the flashlight. Jack looks at us helplessly, delighted by his luck and skill and yet wishing, simultaneously, that it had been me who caught the fish, wishing even harder, I can see, that it had been Mike.

We fish a little longer, but now there's no need to stay. The spell has been broken; the first steelhead has been caught in its journey up the Platte.

"Let's wade downriver a little," Jack says, when we've reeled in our lines, "to try and avoid the mud." I take short rapid breaths as we move through the water. "This part is deep," Jack says. "Take it slow."

The water creeps up my chest and into my armpits; I'm walking, weightless, through a dark and watery dream. For a moment there is nothing but my forward momentum and the lift of water under the soles of my boots that keep me from going under. Then I feel the bank rise suddenly beneath my feet.

"No problem," I say, just before my foot slips and I do go under, head and all into the icy current. I thrash my arms toward shore, and Jack grabs me. "Better get you home," he says, as the cold I've ignored for hours moves through my body with logarithmic speed. "You've gotta meet students in a couple hours." Back at the truck Doug is curled under a blanket like a dog.

The next day Jack sleeps while Mike makes sure I meet my classes. The students are bright, skeptical, interested. My head buzzes with the heat of the all-nighter, a darkness, like the river dark, threatening to close in. Mike and I drink bad machine coffee in one of the tunnels that connects the English department to the other school buildings, tunnels to keep the students from getting lost in the storms that bring the blowing snow.

"It's hard to explain how much I love these guys," Mike says suddenly, as if I've asked him. "I don't know what I'd do without what we have."

The cement walls of this poor excuse for a lounge move in on us like the weather, and this poet who more resembles a wrestler looks for a moment as if he might cry.

It is late in the evening. I have met three classes, talked to at least thirty students, given another reading, signed books in Traverse City, and as part of an orgy of a potluck, cooked elk steaks, rare, on the grill. Mike, in his other favorite role of DJ, plays one moody song after another on the stereo: John Prine, John Gorka and early Bonnie Raitt. We are all a little high from the good food and tequila. Mike's ten-year-old daughter Jaime and Jack dance cheek to cheek in their socks on the living room floor.

"So are we gonna do it?" Jack says when the song ends, a sparkle in his eyes that says the river is always in him, whether he's standing in it or not. This fish and fiction marathon is in its thirty-eighth hour, and I am beyond tired now to some new level of consciousness.

I have spent too much of my life proving I can be one of the guys, never saying uncle, never admitting I'm tired, or hurting or cold. Tonight I am all three, but the thing that makes me nod my head and say yes I want to go back again and stand in that icy river has nothing, for a change, to do with my father, or my childhood, or all the things in the world that I need to prove. It is the potent and honest feeling between these men that I covet, that I can't miss an opportunity to be close to. I have stumbled, somehow, onto this rare pack of animals who know I am there and have decided, anyway, to let me watch them at their dance. I want to memorize their movements. I want to take these river nights home with me for the times when the darkness is even heavier than it is in this Michigan sky.

A flurry of rubber and neoprene, and we're back inside the Montero. Greg Brown is singing the song about the laughing river. "This is your night, Delp," Jack says, "I can feel it." Around the next bend will be Honor's scattered lights.

Holly Morris

Homewaters of the Mind

*I*t is five o'clock on a dark and damp Northwest morning. What I thought was a brilliant idea only six hours ago now seems lunatic. As I will the coffee maker to brew more quickly, I remind myself that the invigoration of a predawn angling adventure outweighs the unpleasant exhaustion of the moment. Last night when going through my dusty, stiff gear, choosing a collection of nymphs, caddis and stone flies, and reframing my mind, I realized that being an armchair angler had become far too comfortable. This morning it felt just comfortable enough as I huddled under my blankets. But my father is coming to town next week, and I need to prepare.

Fishing has long been an escape for me, and of course, escape is complicated. Escape is good when it means freeing oneself from the weight of an obscure father or the constant grating of a mind embattled by memory. Escape is bad when it means ignoring the kinds of memories powerful enough to turn a life into a fortress, a being into stone. Few images of lessons fondly passed from father to daughter linger in my memory. I never fly fished with my father. We spun no stories together. No line connected us in silence. No metronome. He never knew the meter of his own life, or mine. But he inhabits my fishing life. His image rises like a rainbow to disappear elusively or be hooked and tangled with.

The day after my eighth birthday marked the first of many flights. I was in the back room playing with my new Zebco fishing rod and reel that my grandparents had given me. From the living room came a thunderous "Gaaahd Dammit!" Not the usual I've-added-this-column-sixteen-times or where's-my-other-shoe-goddammit, but the clinched-jaw profanity that was a prelude to the real rage to come. I stiffened. I knew the glint in his eyes. Although my father governed through intimidation, the threat of violence was always lurking, ready to ignite. I began to tick through the things I'd done wrong, but before I got very far he was in the doorway and starting toward me. My mother appeared, and tried to put herself between us and hold him back. Her interference signaled that a line had been crossed. She sensed violence. I grabbed her cue, my pole, and ran like hell.

After a quarter-mile barefoot sprint, I walked on the hot, cracked pavement steadying my emotions, testing the pain on my feet and concentrating on the fish that I would catch. The pond was a mile from our house, and I doubted he knew it even existed. I made my way down a winding trail and nestled in among the swaying grasses at the water's edge. In many ways the place was unremarkable: a midwestern pond filled with bluegill and bass, surrounded by tall grasses and few trees. On other days, I would discover the pond rough and alive, gun-metal gray like a pre-tornado sky. But on that day the water was blue and still and heavy as the humid summer air. I threaded a freshly dug worm on my hook, cast my line and rested my mind on the tip of the pole, waiting for a nibble from the darkness to tell me what to do next. The thick air wrapped around me like a security blanket and at that moment, fishing became my refuge.

Twenty years later, I am driving the hour to North Bend, the launching point for a simple day of fishing the Snoqualmie River. Six-thirty in the morning and the reason for this day comes back to me. I feel lighter, happy with anticipation. Caffeine helps. A wet fog blankets the evergreens that spread up hillsides from the shoulder of the four-lane highway. The spaces between the mountains invite my eyes: rich valleys multiply and offer something beautiful and new with each one I look into, and beyond.

A dirt road leads from the highway down to where I leave my car next to the river. I know this stretch of water, but it can still surprise me. I slide into my brown neoprenes and the place that fly fishing takes me. The comfort of ritual and the draw of another world: cold and shadow, wonder and fear, currents that offer both danger and movement. Fishing offers me new ways to look at a sunrise, a small feather or a fork in the river. The rhythm of the casts and the power of place untangle the knots of my emotions. Problems get loose and wet, slide apart, become just a part of the landscape of my life, no longer the line that binds it.

I check my tippet and leader and fumble a clinch knot twice before successfully tying on a #12 nymph. Then I choose my line, that is, the line I'll travel when I enter the river. The holes and currents will frame my movement. I feel exhilarated by the strength of the river and by the cold that I think will never reach me.

My first casts are about as gracious as the Tin Man's movements upon Dorothy's arrival. Cast number five wraps around me. (Must be the breeze that has picked up.) I hook a tree branch. (Where did that come from?) Sometime around cast number twenty-two things start to go right. I begin to relax, forget about mechanics, and start to think about placement, and place.

Gray moss-covered boulders scatter the water's edge. Brown and green bushes mask the trunks of the tall evergreens that secure the banks. The fog lifts from the Cascades revealing crisp, snow-covered peaks and soppy-looking brown and green foothills. The beauty makes me realize I've noticed little beyond the confines of my mind for a very long time, and I feel arrogant and small. Rivers and mountain trails have always led me to places where truth means less and there exists a simple clarity. I come here to know my own life and transform it. To revive my senses, to smell, to see, to hear. To turn everyday politics and responsibility into distant phantoms and to put the dissonance of pain into its proper place. The pull of the land, the texture of its body, the slow rhythms of growth and death—these things teach me grace.

In Montana, strip farming dehydrates the soil and intensifies its saline content. Toxic concentrations of salt enter the ground water only to resurface elsewhere in the form of salt deposits. Saline seep. When I fish, decades-old secrets and feelings bubble to the surface, and my foundation of carefully constructed logic washes away in a current of uncertainty. Emotional seep. Much of the time I choose to avoid these feelings, but, in truth they carry the ability to erode pain and leave me resensitized, feeling, able to see possibility beyond this bend, that boulder.

The last time I saw my father he seemed slight, not the towering man from my youth, not the powerful figure that occupies my memory. Was it his age or my own growth that reduced him to mortal? For the first time there emerged a vulnerable person whose navigation of life left a trail of both blunder and accomplishment, and portions of love that were by turns cloaked and confused. I saw myself as a little girl trailing behind him pausing at these strewn obstacles; hoisting them on my back to be carried along or deeming them too heavy and foreign, leaving them behind. His parting grip was gentle and his eyes seemed soaked with decades of unspoken emotion. The scar tissue that embalmed his own wounds of youth parted and he whispered, "I love you." When we said goodbye that day, I packed away that new, incongruous image of my father. But that image comes to me now.

My father's world is silent and dark and has been as much a wonder to me as the primeval world of forests and fish. The latter anchors my soul and offers mysteries with depths to be plumbed; but I've let the former become a counterweight that, in some ways, still guides my movement, or prevents it.

Rousing myself from the haze of emotional seep, I move to catch a fish. I change to a Royal Wulff #10 and cast in earnest. My pulse picks up as I anticipate the unique elation that comes with the take. In spite of the preparation and forethought fishing requires, in a strange way, I never expect to catch a fish and am always surprised, and slightly panicked, when it happens. The moment of the take is a mix of chaos and elation and a connection that never ceases to catch me off-guard. Like Spalding Gray's sought-after "perfect moment." You never see them coming and they are best had alone. They give closure and tell you when it's time to go home. A sixteen-inch rainbow bearing down on a #14 Zug Bug. That's a perfect moment.

Eight-thirty and still no action. I crouch and cast and feel that the morning's slight breeze has calmed. A good sign. Behind a boulder a roiling hole beckons. Was that a rise? Two false casts and the first lay falls short. My second cast is close, but the fly immediately hooks a passing twig. On the third try, it lands right on the sweet spot. At the same instant of my tiny celebration about the perfect lay, the water explodes; I see the flash right before I feel the strike. *The line sings.* I play the fish and try to imagine her size in between the cracks of my panic that I'll lose her. Twice she takes line and heads into deep, mid-river current. Twice I bring her back in slowly, cautiously. After ten minutes she's next to me, twelve inches long, exhausted and beautiful. A rainbow of color courses down each side melting into her sleek belly. I hold on to the moment, the meeting of our worlds for as long as possible, but know it must be fleeting. I gently remove the hook from her lip and revive her. She fins for a few seconds, then darts back to another side.

After the rainbow is gone, I glide through the water easily, my casts are satisfying, no longer stilted by tension. My brother's words come back to me. "He's changed. He's really trying. Come on, always making him the bad guy is the easy way out." My brother's opinions, which have lingered in the recesses of my mind for the past year, seem almost plausible. I dare, tentatively, to imagine what it would be like to have a dad.

As I take off up-river to fish and think for a few more hours, I wonder . . . perhaps I'll ask my father if he'd like me to teach him to fly fish.

Sue Harrington

Saint Exupery

I woke up with a start, my right hip and arm numb, my back pressed into a sharp rock, and my feet hanging off the edge. Shifting my position, I noticed that Alan, sound asleep, hoarded most of our tiny bivy ledge. I shoved him over, feeling not the least bit guilty. "Hey, what did ya do that for?" he moaned. I ignored him, and tried to fall back to sleep, content that I wasn't the only one awake. Misery loves company.

As I lay there, eight pitches up on the North Face of Saint Exupery, I thought about my husband's (Alan Kearney) and my decision to climb together in Patagonia, mulling over some friends' comments on climbing with their significant others. Debbie once told me, "Because of Andy's and my different experience levels, I get worried that we can't complete long difficult climbs. I want to retreat too soon." Peter admitted to Alan that he fretted when his wife Rachel was leading: "I'm afraid she'll get hurt." Rachel's comment was that if she didn't do her share of the leading she didn't feel as satisfied with the climb.

Alan and I have shared similar experiences while climbing together. On a few climbs I have had to remind Alan, a much more experienced climber than I, that he was not climbing with one of the boys. We have had to retreat because I wasn't willing to be pulled up a route. Nevertheless, climbing together has remained a high priority. The chance for us to do a route in an exotic place such as Patagonia didn't seem to require a second thought. However, I began to realize just how much work it took to make an expedition with one's spouse successful. Certainly, one did not go on a climb like this for romance.

Our trip had been inspired by a desire to do a new route on Saint Exupery, a lesser-known yet striking twin-summitted spire of clean granite in the Argentine Patagonia. It had only seen four ascents, all by the East Ridge. Alan had been to the area on two other trips, and was intrigued with Exupery's unclimbed west face. When I asked him to climb the west face of Exupery with me, he agreed without pause.

Upon arriving in Fitz Roy Park, however, our plans were uprooted— Exupery had recently been climbed twice by new routes, once via the west face. Alan immediately lost interest. I was disappointed by Alan's change of heart, but after a lengthy discussion we decided on an alternative, Exupery's neighboring peak Torre Innominata. It had been climbed only once by a British team in 1974.

After three false starts due to stormy weather, our climb of Innominata went smoothly except for a long offwidth that poor route finding forced us into. We made the summit on a beautiful, clear day.

From there, our view of the steep north face of Exupery revealed a perfect-looking ramp, rekindling our desire to climb the mountain— providing the weather held.

We returned to base camp exhausted. It had been easy to agree to climb Exupery while feeling the high of success on top of Innominata. But now I didn't want to move. I liked the peaceful forest, and was ready to spend a week there, reading, baking bread, washing clothes and getting my head together for the next climb. Secretly, I hoped for a real whopper of a storm.

On our third morning at base camp, when we went out to gaze at the mountains, Alan cheerfully announced, "Looks like the day for our next trip up the glacier." I could have killed him! It was bad enough to have my dreams of numerous naps and lavish eating smashed, but his enthusiasm was too much. I tried to convince him that the thin layer of clouds overhead was an ominous sign—to no avail. He insisted that we had to take advantage of the good weather, something that comes in rare spells in Patagonia.

I was beginning to see that Alan's drive and mine were much different. He was energized by the unknown, whereas I liked the predictable. I was finding it difficult to match his rising level of enthusiasm for climbing a new route on Exupery when a week before Alan had no interest in the mountain. But I knew he was right about the weather. So with dread and suppressed anger, I repacked, and began plodding toward high camp with heavy feet. Intuition told me this would be another false start.

That night I couldn't sleep. I was dreading the next day and not entirely sure why. Fatigue? Stress? A partner whose undying enthusiasm for this place was beginning to wear me down? I came here enthused to climb so I couldn't understand this change. I let anxiety rob me of sleep.

The next morning dawned beautiful. The surrounding peaks glowed orange in the morning light, but my mind was still a dark cloud. I tried to tell Alan how I was feeling but he didn't want to listen. Our spouse/climbing partner relationship was weakening. We were experiencing a conflict in roles. I wanted Alan to be a consoling spouse, not a driven climber, and he wanted the reverse of me. We were having difficulty balancing these competing needs.

I had decided long ago that I wasn't about to stay home in the kitchen while my husband gamboled about the world climbing, so here I was. And like it or not, it was a perfect day to climb. I told myself I would feel better once I started moving.

Three hours of scrambling over talus, up a snow couloir, and up steep loose slabs delivered us to the base of the wall. Alan led the first pitch, leaving me with the pack, which wasn't light (we had planned at least one bivy on the peak). He climbed over a bulge and into a steep, shallow chimney dripping with snowmelt. I followed, free climbing as far as the protrusion, where the pack threw me off balance. I thought, "Don't worry, you can always jumar," a task easier said than done. I struggled, I swore, I struggled some more, and I still couldn't get over the bulge. Finally, the tension from the past two days was too much—I cried.

I pictured myself hanging dead on the rope because I couldn't move. I hated Alan for taking me to this place and "making me" climb. I swore I would never climb again, provided we made it down. I felt utterly alone.

"What the hell are you doing down there?" questioned Alan, tearing me from my tension-induced fog and inspiring me with anger. I was determined to get up this pitch just so I could give him a piece of my mind. With profuse cursing and animal grunts I was over the swell, through the chimney and finally into a crack where the going was easier. But when I reached Alan I was too short of breath to chew him out.

By now it was late afternoon and clouds were boiling over Cerro Torre to the west. Alan asked if I wanted the next lead. "No way," I barked. "I am tired, scared, sick of climbing and I don't like the looks of the weather." In a disapproving tone Alan said, "Guess we better go down then." I was flooded with both relief and guilt as we began rappelling.

Snug in our sleeping bags once again at high camp, we exchanged few words. I think Alan was afraid to say anything to me. I fretted over his silence for awhile, but finally I realized that what was really bothering me was me. I had let both myself and Alan down. It had been so easy for me to blame Alan for my problems on the climb. I rarely lost my temper with other climbing partners, and I didn't expect them to instinctively know how I was feeling. That was a large burden to place on one's partner and Alan was taking it surprisingly well. But he was becoming short with me. Maybe all this was why some couples prefer not to climb together. It dawned on me that I had been relying on Alan to keep the momentum going. Somehow I was going to have to rekindle the spirit that first inspired me to climb in Patagonia.

That night it stormed. The wind picked up, and the rain came down in sheets. No longer was high camp snug. We awoke to water dripping from the rock onto our faces. However, the sound of the rain and wind was reassuring to me. In my half-awake state I imagined it was a sign that we were not supposed to be on the mountain that night; maybe my reluctance to climb was due to an intuitive sense rather than to being a failure. With that thought, I pulled my bivy sack over my head and fell back to sleep.

By morning, the weather had not improved and it was obviously time to return to base camp. We had a difficult decision to make. Did we pack everything, or did we leave our high camp intact for another attempt? Alan left it up to me, encouraging me to do whatever I felt was best for me, and saying he would accept that decision without question. He knew that to push me would only create resentment. I thought that I really could climb the mountain if I didn't have to struggle with such a big pack. I suggested to Alan that we reduce the load and with a smile he said, "I'm sure we can take care of that." Leaving our gear behind, we headed back to the peaceful forest.

The skies soon cleared. With machine-like monotony we re-packed, and although I was more optimistic this time, I hoped this would be our last trip up the trail. My knees screamed with the thought of all the boulders and uneven terrain we would have to cross again. Even Alan, who normally chatters away, was silent. We made it to high camp in five hours and cooked a quick meal of instant potatoes before bed.

Beep-beep-beep-beep! I tried to pretend I didn't hear it, but Alan did. Up he popped, as chipper as ever, to start the stove.

Awfully optimistic, I thought; he hadn't even looked at the weather. Having drawn the cramped side of the boulder, I couldn't see out, so I rolled over and waited until the water was boiling. It was 4:30 A.M.

After a hot breakfast Alan looked outside, then swore at seeing a bank of storm clouds. As I saw it there was nothing to do but go back to sleep. Six hours later the clouds dissipated and after a brief discussion we decided to go for it, regardless of a late start. We reached the base of the wall at 2:00 P.M.

I wasn't sure how I'd feel climbing. As I looked up and saw the ice-filled chimney on the second pitch I quickly grabbed the first lead. Gritting my teeth I tackled the pitch, feeling like I'd never climbed before. My feet rattled, my hands wouldn't grip, and I couldn't get in the proper pro. Why did I want to do this? I made it to the belay, letting out a big sigh of relief. Alan arrived, oblivious to my chattering teeth. He stopped just long enough to hand off the pack. I could see that leading was where it was at.

After two hundred feet of chimney climbing we hit a series of clean, parallel finger and hand cracks that led to the ramp we had spotted from Innominata. Every time it was my turn to lead I felt nauseous, but to overcome my illness all I had to do was look at the pack. Slowly, I began to regain my courage, and the climbing became more enjoyable with every pitch.

By dusk we had climbed two pitches up the ramp. Failing to find the perfect bivouac site, we ended up on a tiny ledge eight pitches up, where sleep was hard to come by. I pondered the wisdom of climbing with my husband. Our relationship had been strained, but it was far from severed. By feeling free to yell and express some fears I had been able to work through things that bothered me. I wasn't holding grudges against Alan for "making" me be here any more. I was pulling my weight as a climbing partner, and Alan was being supportive. We were working as a team.

Morning came after an eternity, but the clear skies of the day before were replaced by somber gray clouds. Trying to be enthusiastic, I pointed out that there was no wind. Alan pointed out that there also was no sun. We lingered in our cramped one-person bivy sack and hid beneath its thin layer of warmth. Finally, we wriggled out of the sack and stomped our aching feet back into stiff, cold rock shoes. Doubts began to resurface, but I quickly squelched them, focusing on moving instead.

I again drew the first lead of the day, starting off cold and shaky. But I warmed up quickly. As my confidence grew I became more talkative, and Alan responded with an improved mood. We climbed easily together and swapped leads with little fuss. The seven-pitch ramp yielded enjoyable 5.7 and 5.8 climbing—more my speed. At the end of the ramp a short wall with flaring shallow cracks led up to the East Ridge. We dropped our plans to continue up the north face with the onset of light rain. The top of the East Ridge route was circuitous, made more so by our stubborn desire to free climb the route.

After nineteen pitches, we arrived on top, elated. But clouds and rain already obscured the tops of Poincenot and Fitz Roy to the north, so we quickly began an endless succession of rappels. Finally, we dropped into the snow gully after seventeen rappels. It was 11:00 P.M. and I could barely see Alan in front of me. We were thankful that the threatening storm never fully developed. Unfortunately, we didn't make it back to high camp that night. Totally exhausted, we opted to spend the night out above the gully.

The next morning we awoke—if one really wakes up from not sleeping—to a brilliant sunrise. Sitting on our ledge and looking across at Cerro Torre glowing pink in the distance, my feelings gelled—this *was* romantic! What better person to be with than your spouse in such a magnificent place? We had worked hard to overcome some unforeseen stresses which climbing placed on our relationship. We would share this experience forever. It was with a stronger bond that we packed up our gear and headed off toward camp.

VIII

MATERNAL LOVE

Gift of Mothering

Hazel

August 5-September 1

Lin Sutherland

Catfishing with Mama

My mother was a fishing fanatic despite her Charleston, South Carolina, blue-blood upbringing. When she was twenty she graduated *magna cum laude* from the College of Charleston and left that city of history and suffocating social rules forever. With the twenty-dollar gold piece she got for the Math Prize, she bought a railroad ticket for as far west as it would get her. Austin, Texas, was $19.02 away.

There she met my father, a poet and horseman, and proceeded to have seven children—all girls. She also took up fishing, and by the time I was born, she had enough tackle, lawn chairs and fishing hats to fill a steamer trunk. To my father's horror, her favorite lure was blood bait. Bass and catfish were her prey.

Every summer it was my mother's custom to pack the seven of us girls into the DeSoto and drive from Austin to Charleston to visit our grandparents. We camped and fished the whole way.

Mama's preparations for the fifteen-hundred-mile trip consisted of packing the car with seven army cots, a basket of Stonewall peaches and sixteen gallons of live bait, with her tackle box and assorted rods and reels thrown in. Her idea of successful traveling was to get us all in the car without one of us sitting on the blood bait or being left at a gas station. Once she'd done a head count and ascertained the security of the bait, she'd drive like A. J. Foyt until it was too dark to go any farther. This meant we were usually tired, hungry and lost on some back road in the middle of Louisiana or Mississippi when we stopped to camp.

"Stopping to camp" in our case meant suddenly swerving off the road when my mother spied a river or lake that stirred her sporting blood. She never once planned our stops like normal people do, timing themselves to arrive at a campsite or park around dusk. But this was the 1950s, when people still slept with the screen door unlocked and left the keys in the car. We felt perfectly safe at any roadside area, and we were.

The trip that brought us face to face with history was the one we took in the summer of 1958 when I was ten. It started normally enough. We had driven all day from Austin, into the dark and the Deep South. From the back seat, groggy and weary from the hours of travel, my sisters and I felt our mother wheel the car onto the shoulder and turn off the motor.

In the dim glow of our flashlights, we pulled out the army cots, set them up and sucked on leftover peach pits. We wanted to drop into a dead sleep, but as far as Mama was concerned, this was a perfect time to go fishing.

The problem was, Mama never seemed to notice that she was the only one who ever caught anything bigger than a deck of cards. She also failed to recognize that she had borne seven girls, not seven Captain Ahabs. She lived under the illusion that everyone had the same enthusiasm as she did for sitting on rocks at waterside and waiting hours for something to steal the bait. Which of course never happened to her.

While we slouched around the camp making unintelligible grumbling noises, she unloaded the gallons of blood bait and her tackle box and got to work.

"Look at that big dark pool just under those cypress knees, honey," she said. "You just *know* there's a ten-pound bass waiting for me in there! I hope it's a stupid one." She whistled a snatch of "High Noon" as she explored her stock of lures, jigs and spoons.

Mama was very Zen about her fishing, giving it her complete concentration and ritualized observation. She examined each item in the tackle box with pleasure, murmuring to herself. She emerged from this reverie only when she decided on the right lure to use.

This night she announced, "I think I'll use my Good Luck Lure Number 242 on this baby." She glanced in my direction to see if I was watching and abruptly emitted a theatrical, diabolical laugh.

"He'll never escape my Magic Lucky Lure!" she went on. "We have ways of making fish welcome here at our little fish camp . . . no, Herr Lucky Lure?" Then, adjusting her fishing hat, she addressed the water in a tough-guy voice: "Prepare to meet your Maker, Lord Bass-ship."

And she cast perfectly into the heart of the cypress-root pool.

For her children, the enthusiasm and high drama my mother created around fishing was more intriguing than the activity itself. She was ceaselessly energetic and entertaining, and when she went up against a largemouth bass with a brain the size and density of a dust mote, it was no contest.

Fifteen minutes later she was addressing the bass in person as she cleaned it.

"I regret to inform you, Lord Bass-ship, that the inscrutable order of the universe has destined you to serve in the dual role of Main Guest and Dish at this evening's festivities. You have my deepest sympathy. On the other hand, the jig's up for everybody at one time or another, Bud. Fire up the logs, girls. Dinner just arrived."

Our second day on the road we passed trees dripping with Spanish moss, stately old homes and vast fields of cotton and snap beans. We sang and talked and Mama told fish stories. And finally, in the pitch black somewhere deep into Mississippi, she stopped the car.

"I hear running water," she announced.

We bailed out of the DeSoto and traipsed down from the road until we found a place where the ground got gravelly. We figured we were far enough from the road so we wouldn't be run over in the middle of the night, and we set up our cots in the usual manner: jammed against each other in line, so that if, during the night, one of us flopped an arm or leg out, the warm body of a sister would be felt. Sitting cross-legged on the cots, we munched Vienna sausage and Wonderbread sandwiches and watched Mama fish in the fast-running creek next to us. Then we fell asleep, exhausted.

As the dawn light began to come up, something like a gentle lapping at my side awoke me. I slowly let a foot slide over the edge of my cot. It fell into two feet of cold water. I bolted upright and saw that seven sisters and their mother were about to float away.

My mother had camped us in a creekbed. The water had risen during the night from rains upstream and had us surrounded. We practically had to swim to the car, pulling our cots behind us.

The third night found us somewhere in the mountains of Kentucky. I was never quite sure where we were at any given point on these trips, since I knew only one landmark—the tree-lined road to my grandparents' house—the finish line. But again, we had driven for hours into the night futilely looking for water. When we finally pulled off the road, the hills around us were black as midnight under a skillet. Then a slice of a quarter moon slid out from behind a cloud and delicately illuminated a rock gate in front of us.

"Oh, look!" Mama cried, "a national park."

There was an audible sigh of relief from the back seat. "Let's camp here, Mama!" we clamored urgently.

Since she had been slapping her cheeks for the last hour to stay awake, she agreed.

We cruised down a black dirt road into the parking area. Nestled nearby was the outline of a log cabin. Beyond that, the glint of water.

"See that!" Mama said excitedly. "A sleeping cabin. By some kind of lake. This is paradise."

We parked and unloaded the car, dragging our stuff into the log cabin.

It was open and empty. We could see it was very old and rudimentary, but it had a bathroom with running water. For us it was luxury quarters. We bathed and ate our dinner of kipper snacks and soda crackers, with Moon Pies for dessert. Then we snuggled into the cots that we'd fixed up in the one bare room.

Mama set off with long strides toward the water, gear in hand. The faint murmur of her voice as she conversed with her tackle box drifted through the open windows. With that and a cozy roof overhead, my sisters curled up and fell to sleep like a litter of puppies.

I picked up my rod and reel and, still in my pajamas, slipped quietly out the door. Across the damp grass I could see my mother's silhouette making casting motions. For a moment I felt the thrill of anticipation inherent in fishing: there was a fat catfish with my name on it waiting out there, I just knew it.

I joined my mother and we fished together. Just us, the water and the quarter moon. It was one of those moments that form a permanent part in the book of parent-child memories, though it was destined to be brief. Mama could practically conjure fish up to her, and sure enough, within half an hour she got a strike and brought in a fourteen-pound cat. Probably *my* Fat-Cat, I thought irritably.

"Look," she said, bending around me, her hands grasping mine as I held my rod. "Let me show you . . ." She made a deft flicking motion and suddenly my line shot across the water. The light of the moon made it look like the trail of a shooting star. It fell silently on the dark water and disappeared. "Right *there*," she said lowly. "Hold tight to it."

She turned away and began cleaning her fish. I gripped the rod until my knuckles were white. I had a feeling for what was coming. Suddenly, the line lurched tight and my arms shot forward. I almost flew into the black water of the lake.

"It's a big one, Mama!" I yelled. "I don't think I can hold it." My feet were slipping down the bank, and the mud had oozed up to my ankles. "Mama, quick!"

She grasped me around the waist and yanked me back up the bank. The pull on the line lessened. "Now! Bring it in now!" she shouted. I reeled in as hard as I could. Suddenly the fish was right there below me, lying in shallow water. It was a big one, all right. Almost as big as Mama's.

"Good work," she said, leaning over and carefully pulling the catfish onto the bank. It slapped the wet grass angrily. I was exhausted. We took our fish back to the cabin and fell into a deep sleep.

It seemed only minutes later that sleep was penetrated by voices. Lots of voices. Suddenly, the door of the cabin burst open and sunlight and a large group of people led by a woman in a uniform flowed into the room. The uniformed person was in the middle of a speech. "And here we have the boyhood home of President Abraham Lincoln—Aagghhhh!!"

We all screamed at once. My mother, protective in her own quixotic way, leapt off the cot, her chenille bathrobe flapping, and shouted at the intruders, "Who do you think you are, bursting in on a sleeping family like this?"

The guide was struck speechless. She gathered herself with visible effort. "Ma'am, I don't know who *you* are, but this is Abraham Lincoln's Birthplace National Historic Park," she reported tersely. Her eyes quickly shifted sideways to take in two huge catfish lying on the floor. Though she tried to conceal it, her lips pursed with disgust. I knew right off she wasn't a fisherman.

"And his log cabin," she continued, "is *not* an overnight stopover for fishing expeditions. This is a restricted area with guided tours beginning at 7:00 A.M. and . . ."

"Oh my God, we overslept!" Mama shouted. "Pack the car, girls. We've got to get on the road!"

We lurched into a flurry of experienced cot-folding and were out the door in seconds.

"But, ma'am," the guide called at my mother's disappearing back, "You weren't supposed to sleep in here. This is Lincoln's Log Cabin. *It's a National Treasure!*"

"We treasure our night here," my mother shouted back, as she gunned the car around. "Abe wouldn't have minded."

With that we roared off in the direction of South Carolina. I saw a sign as we left: "Leaving Hodgenville, Kentucky, Abraham Lincoln's

Birthplace. Ya'll Come Back."

"Not likely," my mother laughed. "A good fishing spot, but I hate to do anything twice, don't you?"

And that's how it happened that, during the summer I was ten, the course of history was changed. Unofficially, to be sure, but if there'd been a historical marker by that lake, it would now have to read ABE LINCOLN FISHED HERE . . . AND SO DID I.

Barbara Beckwith

Nature Buddies

When my grandson was born, I gave his parents a gift. I would baby-sit for Daniel each Sunday while they took yoga classes. I was sure that grandparenting would come naturally to me.

I was wrong. Daniel wanted only milk or motion. I didn't have milk-filled breasts to offer, so I used my arms to jiggle him as we speed-walked around the apartment. The moment I stopped, he'd cry. After a month of Sundays, I started weight-lifting classes to strengthen my baby-sitting arm.

But I still didn't get it right. "Daniel's diaper needs changing!" my son declared on returning from his first yoga class. "But I kept checking! It was dry," I said in my defense. "These are nineties diapers, Mom," he explained. "They're maxi-absorbent. The top layer wicks liquid away. You have to check how heavy his diaper feels."

I had failed my first grandparenting test. I panicked. I could lose my baby-sitting privileges. Humbled, I asked my son and daughter-in-law: how do you change him, carry him, amuse him, put him to sleep, wake him up? I no longer felt like an all-wise grandma. I was a bumbling Mommy-Daddy substitute. The special bond that Daniel and I were meant to have, just us two, was fraying.

I myself never had a grandparent. At least, not the lap-sitting kind. One grandparent lived far away and two others died before I was born. The grandparent I did see frequently was more interested in entertaining his grandchildren than in getting to know them. He'd line us up and scramble our names to make us laugh. He didn't know or seem to care that I climbed trees better than anyone, was a champion at mumblety-peg and wrote poetry and stories.

I was determined to be the warm and wonderful grandparent that I'd never had myself.

Daniel was born in winter. For months, we were stuck indoors. I occasionally tried stroller and carry-pack outings, but the stroller wheel skidded on the ice and the Snuggli-pack straps stumped me. They'd loosen after a block or two, and I'd be left carrying my grandson's chilled body in my arms.

Finally, spring came. Daniel was now four months old. He could see yards ahead instead of only inches away. One Sunday in April, his father said that I could take Daniel to the city pond nearby. He warned me, however, not to get Daniel sunburned. He draped a blanket over the stroller and pinned it tight: "to keep the sun out," he said. To keep the *world* out, I grumbled to myself.

Off we went, they to their yogic Salutes to the Sun and Daniel and I to the shady pondside path. On arrival, I removed the blanket. Now Daniel could see the natural world. He turned his head to watch the trees above him. Their shapes entertained him as I pushed the stroller around the pond.

When we came to a clearing under a canopy of maples, I lifted him out of the stroller. I whisked off his socks, and set his feet—maybe for the first time—on Mother Earth. His toes explored the grass, a tree stump, a granite boulder. He wiggled and bounced on the bumpy grains of mica, quartz and feldspar—ooh, nice feel!

I knew, right then, what we'd do together, Daniel and I. We'd be nature buddies.

I'd show him what I loved as a child: salamanders, Indian pipe, pine trees, red shale, gooey marsh and trees to climb. Daniel may be a city kid, but still, we'd "do nature" together. We would explore his neighborhood's natural spots, one by one. We'd feel inchworms, catch ladybugs, collect pine cones, skip pebbles, make maple "noseys," blow dandelion seeds and kiss soft moss.

Later, I told his parents about our nature adventure. They were not pleased. "His feet are dirty!" my son remarked, as he grabbed a Handi-wipe. "I see a cut on his foot."

I remembered my own country-toughened feet as a child. I showed off their calluses—proof of a summer of barefoot play. But I did not argue with my son. Instead, I promised that I'd be more careful next time.

The next week, my son and daughter-in-law brought Daniel to my house. Off they went to twist their limbs into unnatural positions, as I resumed my quest for a natural place in Daniel's life.

Daniel and I went out to look at trees that he'd seen from afar on our pond walk. I held Daniel in my now-muscular arms and stood on our porch where tree branches dangled across the railing. He grabbed a leaf and held tight. I flapped the branch up and down to show him how it moves. He got the idea and jostled his limb. His leaf soon ripped; he grabbed another. He burst out with a belly laugh. I did, too. We stripped the branch of leaves, but we didn't care.

His parents liked my story of Daniel's leafy fun, but they were alarmed as well. "He could have fallen off the porch!" my son said sternly, and then: "What about the squirrels? They crawl on those branches and they could leave droppings." He reached once more for his Handi-wipes.

As a child, my son was golden-haired and sweet, but not the outdoor type. We brought him on camping trips. There, he swatted the mosquitoes and refused to eat the campfire-blackened hot dogs. He was a city boy. He wanted his stickball and Legos, his comics and TV. It wasn't until he married a woman raised in the Sierras that he came to love woods and wilderness, for himself, if not for Daniel.

One recent Sunday, Daniel and I explored his parents' back yard. We left the plastic toys inside; I took out a twist of paper bag as a plaything. I threw aside the blanket his parents usually kept between him and the earth. I sneaked off his socks and let him feel the grass. He pulled and babbled. I got down on my belly to see what he saw. I liked the view. We rolled on the ground, grabbing whatever we could reach.

I heard the bumblebee's drone before I saw its huge and fuzzy body. It hovered over us like a helicopter and then dove straight toward my grandson. I threw the blanket over Daniel's bare legs. He yelped with surprise. I clasped his body to me. *Can a bee sting through blankets? What if he's allergic? Where's the nearest hospital?* I had no idea.

The intruder circled us twice, as if gauging our sweetness. Then it zoomed off to the next yard. Minutes passed. I slowly lifted the blanket. Daniel blinked, his fists still clutching tufts of grass.

The beast was gone, but the yard was transformed in my eyes. Underneath the grass we had played on, bugs crawled. Black ants, red ants, beetles, sowbugs, centipedes—and a spider-like insect I couldn't even identify. *What if it burrowed in Daniel's clothes and bit him in the middle of the night?*

I saw that spears of grass were sticking to Daniel's hands and I worried: *what if he puts his fist in his mouth? He could choke on a single spear! And the paper bag twist—could the Bruegger's Bagels label on it be printed with an ink that's bad for babies?* I snatched away the bag and shoved it into my pocket.

Daniel had now rolled onto his back. He was cooing at the trees overhead. I rushed to turn him back onto his stomach—what if he looked at the sun and went *blind?*

When my son and daughter-in-law returned, they were glad that Daniel had been playing outside. "But he didn't eat dirt, did he?" my daughter-in-law asked. "Because it's got toxic lead in it." She's a soil scientist; she knows these things. "No," I said, but I felt chilled. I had never considered the dangers of back-yard dirt.

Driving home, I remembered from my own childhood: the snakes in the lake, the splinters and sprains and poison ivy, the sea surf knocking me down, my howls when I fell off my bike into mud: "I'm blind!"—but I wasn't.

More soothing memories rose up: my mother examining daddy longlegs and worms and beetles with me so I wouldn't fear them. My father standing at the window to marvel with me at the flashes of lightning as my mother retreated to her room so I wouldn't catch her fear.

I knew then that my son would discover—as all parents do—that his son is tough. And I knew that my grandson would climb rocks, skate on ice, pick up snakes, take a dive and show off his callused feet.

Last week, I took Daniel to a park where a miniature Old Faithful shoots water up from a stone circle. At his first sight of the spurting water, he cried. That's O.K. Next time he may reach out and feel the gushing water. Later, he may jump and splash in it. One day, he will play in it till he's soaked. He may fall and scrape a knee. Or swallow water and have to cough it up. But he'll go back for more.

M. Wylie Blanchet

The Curve of Time

On board our boat one summer we had a book by Maurice Maeterlinck called *The Fourth Dimension*, the fourth dimension being Time—which, according to Dunne, doesn't exist in itself, but is always relative to the person who has the idea of Time. Maeterlinck used a curve to illustrate Dunne's theory. Standing in the Present, on the highest point of the curve, you can look back and see the Past, or forward and see the Future, all in the same instant. Or, if you stand off to one side of this curve, as I am doing, your eye wanders from one to the other without any distinction.

In dreams, the mind wanders in and out of the Present, through the Past and Future, unable to distinguish between what has not yet happened and what has already befallen. Maeterlinck said that if you kept track of your dreams, writing them down as soon as you woke, you would find that a certain number were of things that had already happened; others would be connected with the present; but a certain number would be about things that had not yet happened. This was supposed to prove that Time is just a dimension of Space, and that there is no difference between the two, except that our conciousness roves along this Curve of Time.

In my mind, I always think of that summer as the Maeterlinck summer—the year we wrote down our dreams. The children always called it—the Year of the Bears.

Towards the end of June, or it might have been July, we headed up Jervis Inlet. This inlet cuts through the Coast Range of British Columbia and extends by winding reaches in a northerly direction for about sixty miles. Originally perhaps a fault in the earth's crust, and later scoured by a glacier, since retreated, it is roughly a mile wide, and completely hemmed in on all sides by stupendous mountains, rising from almost perpendicular shores to heights of from five to eight thousand feet. All the soundings on the chart are marked one hundred fathoms with the no-bottom mark . . . right up to the cliffs. Stunted pines struggle up some of the ravines, but their hold on life is short. Sooner or later, a winter storm or spring avalanche sweeps them out and away; and next summer there will be a new cascade in their place.

Once you get through Agamemnon Channel into the main inlet, you just have to keep going—there is no shelter, no place to anchor. In summer-time the wind blows up the inlet in the morning, down the inlet from five o'clock on. In winter, I am told, the wind blows down the inlet most of the time—so strong and with such heavy williwaws that no boat can make against it. I know that up at the head of the inlet most trappers' cabins are braced with heavy poles towards the north.

For some reason that I have forgotten, probably the hope of trout for supper, we decided to anchor in Vancouver Bay for lunch. Vancouver Bay is about half-way up Jervis, and only makes a very temporary anchorage good for a couple of hours on a perfectly calm day. It is a deep bay between very high mountains, with a valley and three trout-streams. You can drop your hook on a narrow mud bank, but under your stern it falls away to nothing.

After lunch I left the youngsters playing on the beach, and taking a light fishing line I worked my way back for perhaps half a mile. The underbrush was heavy and most uncomfortable on bare legs, and I had to make wide detours to avoid the devil's club. Then I had to force my way across to the stream, as my trail had been one of least resistance. It was a perfect trout-stream, the water running along swiftly on a stony bottom; but with deep pools beside the overhanging banks, cool shade under fallen tree trunks. The sunshine drifted through the alders and flickered on the surface of the running water. Somewhere deeper in the forest the shy thrushes were calling their single, abrupt liquid note. Later, when the sun went down, the single note would change to the ascending triplets. Except for the thrushes, there was not a sound—all was still.

I didn't have a rod—you can't cast in this kind of growth, there is no room. I didn't use worms, I used an unripe huckleberry. An unripe huckleberry is about the size and color of a salmon egg—and trout love salmon eggs. Almost at once I landed a fair-sized one on the mossy rocks. Another . . . and then another. I ran a stick through their gills and moved to another pool.

But suddenly I was seized with a kind of panic. . . . I simply had to get back to my children. I shouldn't be able to hear them from where I was, if they called. I listened desperately. . . . There was just no sense to this blind urge that I felt. Almost frantic, I fought my way back by the most direct route—through the salmonberry, salal, and patches of devil's club.

"Coming—coming!" I shouted. What was I going to rescue them from? I didn't know, but how desperately urgent it was!

I finally scrambled through to the beach—blood everywhere. Five wondering faces looked at me in horror. The two youngest burst into tears at the sight of this remnant of what had once been their Mummy.

"Are you all right?" I gasped—with a sudden seething mixture of anger and relief at finding them alive and unhurt.

After an interval, the three girls took my fish down to the sea to clean, the two little boys helping me wash off the blood as I sat with my feet in the stream. Devil's club spikes are very poisonous and I knew their scratches would give me trouble for days.

"There's a man along at the other end of the beach," volunteered Peter. "He's been watching us ."

"All day!" broke in John. "And he's all dressed in black." I glanced up—a tall figure was standing there, against the trees, up behind the drift-logs at the top of the beach. Just standing there, arms hanging down, too far away to be seen plainly. Peculiar place for a clergyman to be, I thought inanely; and went back to the more important business of washing off the blood. Then I put on the shoes I had washed.

"Mummy!" called Elizabeth. I glanced up. The three of them were looking towards the other end of the beach.

"The man is coming over," said Fran. "He's . . . !"

"Mummy!" shrieked Jan. It didn't take us two minutes to drag the dinghy into the water, pile in, and push off. The man was coming—but he was coming on all fours.

The bear ate the fish that the children had dropped. Then, as we pulled up the anchor, not thirty feet away, she looked at us crossly, swung her nose in the air to get our scent, and grumbled back along the beach to meet her two cubs. They had suddenly appeared from behind the logs and were coming along the beach in short runs. Between runs they would sit down—not quite sure what their mother was going to think about it. She didn't think it was a good idea at all. She cuffed them both, and they ran back whimpering to the logs. She followed, and then stood up again—tall, black, arms hanging loosely down, and idly watched us leave the bay.

"Mummy!" demanded the children, when they were quite sure they were safe. "That bad dream you had last night that woke us all up that you said you couldn't remember—was it about bears?"

"No . . . at least, I don't think so." But even as I spoke, I could remember how very urgent and terrifying something had been in that dream. I hesitated—and then I decided not to tell them about the strange, blind panic I had felt by the stream—I could have smelt the bear down-wind. But I knew that the panic and sense of urgency by the stream, and the feeling in my dream, had been one and the same.

An hour or so later we were at the entrance to little Princess Louisa Inlet. But the tide was still running a turbulent ten knots out of the narrow entrance—so we tied up to the cliff and ate our supper while we waited for slack water.

The inlet is about five miles long, a third of a mile wide, and the mountains that flank it on either side are over a mile high. From inside the entrance you can see right down to the far end where it takes the short L-turn to the left. At that distance you can see over the crest to where all the upper snowfields lie exposed, with their black peaks breaking through the snow. The scar of a landslide that runs diagonally for four thousand feet is plainly visible. At certain times of the day the whole inlet seems choked with mountains, and there is no apparent line where the cliffs enter the sea and where the reflections begin.

Three miles farther down the inlet, the high snowfields become obscured—the mountains are closing in. You turn the corner of the great precipice that slightly overhangs—which they say the Indians used to scale with rocks tied to their backs: the one who reached the top first was the bravest of the brave, and was made the chief. . . .

Then suddenly, dramatically, in a couple of boat lengths, the whole abrupt end of the inlet comes into sight—heavily wooded, green, but rising steeply. Your eye is caught first by a long white scar, up about two thousand feet, that slashes across . . . and disappears into the dark-green background. Again, another splash of white, but farther down. Now you can see that it has movement. It is moving down and down, in steep rapids. Disappearing . . . reappearing . . . and then in one magnificent leap plunging off the cliff and into the sea a hundred feet below. As your boat draws in closer, the roar and the mist comes out to meet you.

We always tie up at Trapper's Rock—well over to the left of the falls, but not too close to the mile-high, perfectly vertical cliff. It is a huge piece about twelve by twelve with a slight incline.

"Did this fall off that cliff too?" somebody asked, as they took the bow-line and jumped off the boat onto Trapper's Rock. I was busy trying to drape a stern anchor over a great sloping rock that lay just under water, ten feet astern, and avoided answering. Dark night was coming on rapidly and the cliffs were closing in. Night was a foolish time to answer unanswerable questions. I was glad we couldn't hear the waterfall too loudly at Trappers' Rock. That waterfall can laugh and talk, sing and lull you to sleep. But it can also moan and sob, fill you with awful apprehensions of you don't know what—all depending on your mood. . . . My crew soon settled down to sleep. On the other side of the falls I could see a light through the trees. The Man from California, who had started building a large log-cabin last year, must be there—in residence. I didn't want to think about him, for he would spoil much of our freedom in Louisa. . . . Then I started feeling the pressure of the mile-high cliffs, worrying about the two huge rocks we were moored between, and all the other monstrous rocks that filled the narrow strip behind us. As you stepped off Trapper's Rock onto the shore, you stepped into a sort of cave formed by an enormous slanting rock that spread out over your head. A little stream of ice-cold spring water ran on one side, and dropped pool by pool among the maiden-hair ferns down to the stony shore. A circle of blackened stones marked our cooking fires of other summers. The back and top of this prehistoric cave were covered with moss and ferns and small huckleberry bushes. All the slope behind was filled with enormous rocks. They were not boulders, worn and rounded by the old glacier. They had sharp angles and straight-cut facets; in size, anywhere from ten by ten to twenty by twenty—hard, smooth, granite, sometimes piled two or three deep—towering above us.

They were undoubtedly pieces that had fallen off the cliff, the cliff that shut off the world and pressed against me. The first night's question always was—was Trapper's Rock one of the first to break and fall, or was it one of the last, which fell and bounced over the others to where it now lay? In back of the rock, the masses are piled one on top of the other. There are deep crevices between them that you could fall into—no one knows how many feet. It would take rope-work to get on top of some of them. None of us is allowed to go in there alone.

The stars had filled up the long crack of sky above me. Brighter stars than you see anywhere else . . . bright . . . so bright . . . .

Somewhere in that uneasy night I dreamt that I was watching a small black animal on a snowfield, some distance away. I don't remember why I was so curious about it, but in my dreams it seemed most important for me to know what it was. Then I decided, and knew most certainly, that it was a black fox playing and sliding on the edge of the snowfield. Then moving closer to it, as you sometimes do in a dream's mysterious way, I saw that it wasn't a fox at all, but a small black pony. I remember that it looked more like a pony that a child had drawn—low slung and with a blocky head—sliding on a most unlikely snowfield.

In the wonderful bright morning the cliffs were all sitting down again—well back. All the fears and tensions gone. We had a swim in the lovely warm water. The sun wouldn't come over the mountain edge before ten, but a pot of hot porridge, toast and coffee kept everybody warm. I made the children laugh about my dream of a black fox that turned into an ugly black pony. Everyone decided that it must have been the man in black down in Vancouver Bay that turned into a bear. I couldn't think why it hadn't occurred to me before. It's just as well to have dreams like that in the Past.

Over on the other side of the falls we could see a big float held out from the shore by two long poles—new since last year. Somewhere in behind lay the log cabin and the intruder. His coming last year had changed many things. We used to be able to stay in the inlet a couple of weeks without seeing another boat. Last summer, when the cabin was being built by skilled axe-men, there were always a few boats there—coming and going with supplies. And the men who were building the cabin were there all the time. We had only just met the Man from California, and we had stayed for only two days.

On the other side of the inlet, on the right-hand cliff beyond the falls, which is not as perpendicular and is sparsely wooded with small pines, there is a great long scar. You can see where it started as a rockslide four thousand feet up. It had carried trees, scrub and loose stones in front of it—gradually getting wider as it scraped the rock clean.

In rainy weather a torrent races down tumbling noisily from pool to pool. But in summertime only a thin stream slides over the smooth granite, collecting in an endless series of deep and shallow pools. Heated by the sun on the rock, the water is lukewarm. We used to climb up perhaps half a mile, and then slide down the slippery granite from pool to pool like so many otters. We found it too hard on the seats of our bathing suits, and had got into the habit of parking them at the bottom. Now, with the coming of the log cabin, we had to post a guard or else tie our bathing suits around our neck.

Boat scrubbed and tidied, sleeping bags out in the sun—everybody had their jobs. Then we collected our clothes for washing, piled into the dinghy and rowed across the landslide. There was a green canoe turned over on the wharf; no sign of the owner. He probably didn't even know that anyone was in the inlet, for you can't hear a boat's engine on account of the falls.

The three lowest pools of the landslide were called Big Wash, Big Rinse, and Little Rinse. All snow-water, all lukewarm—so washing was easy. And we carry only one set of clothes, pajamas, so there is practically nothing to wash anyway. We scrubbed our clothes—we washed our hair—we washed ourselves. That, interspersed with sliding, took some time. Then, all clean and shining bright, we gathered up our things. The three girls said that they would swim on ahead. Peter wanted to go too, but he swims with only his nose above water, and it is hard to see if he is there or not. So I said that he could help John and me gather huckleberries first.

When we followed later in the dinghy, Peter with his snorkel up, swimming beside us, there were the three girls sitting on the wharf, talking to the Man from California. He said he hadn't had anyone to talk to for a month—except old Casper down at the entrance, and he always brought back a flea when he went to visit him. He asked us to come over and have supper with him that night and see the new log cabin. The children held their breath . . . waiting for me to say—yes.

After lunch, needing to stretch our legs, we started off to scramble up through the mighty chaos that lay behind Trapper's Rock. Peter carried a coil of light rope for rescue work, and John his bow-and-arrow, ready for you can never tell what. We had to be pulled and pushed up some of the biggest barriers. Devil's club made impenetrable blocks around which we had to detour. Then suddenly we found ourselves on a well-defined trail that skirted all the biggest rocks and always seemed to find the best way.

"Who do you suppose this nice person was?" asked John.

"Trapper, I should think," I said, very thankful for it.

Then it ended in a big hole between two great rocks that overhung our way. The youngsters were intrigued with the thought of a real cave and wanted to explore it. But there was a very strong smell coming from it.

"Just like foxes," someone says. "No, like mink," said somebody else.

Certainly it was something, and we decided to skip it. We had to go partly through the entrance to get past . . . and for some reason I could feel the hair standing up along my spine.

The trail led beyond as well. The huckleberries were ripe and the cave forgotten. Then we could hear the roar of the river ahead, so we left the trail and cut down towards the sea. We soon wished we hadn't, for the going was heavy and we were very vulnerable in bathing suits. Finally we broke through to the shore close to the falls; and there being no other way, we had to swim and wade back to our rock. I waded, with John sitting on my shoulders, up to my neck at times. The sun was off the rock, but the cliffs hold the heat so long that we didn't miss it. Later, each of us dressed up in his one set of clothes, we rowed leisurely across the float, probably as glad to have some-one to talk to as the Man from California.

The cabin was lovely. The whole thing, inside and out, was made of peeled cedar-logs—fifteen and twenty inches in diameter. There was one big room, about forty by twenty feet, with a great granite fireplace. A stairway led up to a balcony off which there were two bedrooms and a bathroom. A kitchen and another bedroom and bath-room led off the living room. Doors, bookcases, everything was made of the peeled cedar-logs—even the chesterfield in front of the fire-place, and the big trestle table. A bookcase full of books. . . . A lot of thought and good taste, and superb axe-manship, had gone into the construction.

After supper, sitting in front of a blazing log fire, the children were telling him of our climb back into the beyond.

"And there was a cave, and it smelt of foxes," Peter burst out.

"Dead foxes," added John.

I asked if there were any foxes around here.

"What on earth made you think of foxes?" the man asked. "There are no foxes in country like this."

Then he asked questions as to just how far back we had been, and just where. Then he told us—a she-bear and her cub had been around all spring. One of the loggers who were building the cabin had fol-lowed her trail, and it crossed the river on a log some distance above the falls. He had found the den in the cave. Although he had a gun with him, he had not shot the mother on account of the cub.

Then, of course, the children had to tell about my dream of the fox that had turned out to be a black pony . . . shaped much more like a bear than a pony, I now realized. It all more or less fitted in. But what about the man down at Vancouver Bay who had turned out to be a bear? Maeterlinck was beginning to spoil our summer—if the dreams were going to work both ways we would soon be afraid to get off the boat.

The Man from California, who hardly knew us, was full of the perils of the surrounding terrain. We were perfectly willing to say we wouldn't go near the bear's den again—we knew as well as he did that bears with cubs are dangerous. But we forbore to tell him that we were going to climb up four thousand feet the next day to get some black huckleberries we knew of at the edge of the tree-line. After all, *he* was the intruder—probably attracted the bears. Black bears like hanging around the edge of civilization. And this man and his log cabin made the first thin wedge of civilization that had been driven into our favorite inlet.

Judging by the enormous stumps, at one time there had been a stand of huge cedars in the narrow steep valley. Just behind the new log cabin there is an old skid-road—small logs laid crossways to make a road to skid the big logs down to the sea, with a donkey-engine and cables. The skid-road goes up to about six hundred feet—back the way the old glacier had retreated. Cedar grows quickly, and in this moist valley, with heat and rotting ferns, the growth would be rapid.

Six hundred feet high doesn't mean that you get there by walking six hundred feet. It must have been two miles back to the little trapper's cabin at the end of the skid-road. The road slanted at quite an incline, and every muscle screamed with the punishment before we got there. We had to stop to get our breath every hundred feet or so—all except John and Peter who ran around in circles. At the cabin we dropped exhausted . . . then drank and bathed our faces in the ice-cold stream.

The skid-road ends there, and we had to follow a trapline marked by axe-blazes on the trees. The traplines are only used when the snow is on the ground, so there is no path to follow—just the blazed or white scars on the trees. We rested often, as the going was really hard—soft earth, moss and rolling stones. We had to walk sideways to get any kind of foothold. Then we came to the cliff. The boys thought it was the end of everything. But the blazes led off to the right, to the bottom of a chimney with small junipers for hand-holds. John went up directly in front of me. If he were going to slip, I would rather be at the beginning of it, before he gathered momentum. It had its disadvantages though; for he filled me up with earth and stones which trickled down inside my shirt and out my shorts.

At last—on the edge of a flat near the end of the tree-line—we reached the huckleberry bushes. Wonderful bushes! Waist high and loaded with berries twice the size of black currants. Growing where they did, in the sun with the cliffs behind to hold the heat, and all the streams to water them—they are sweet and juicy. In no time we had our pails full—you just milked them off the bushes. And then we just sat and ate and ate and ate—and our tongues got bluer and bluer.

It was Peter who started sniffing, swinging his head in a semi-circle to pick up the direction. . . . "I smell foxes—no, I mean bears," he said. I had smelt them some time ago—bears like huckleberries too. But I hadn't climbed four thousand feet to be frightened by a bear. Also, I was getting tired of Maeterlinck conjuring up bears in our life. By now, everybody was sniffing.

"Bang your lids against your tins," I suggested. "That will frighten them away."

So we all banged and banged. Then, as our tins and ourselves were full, I eased everybody down the trail—just in case. As was perfectly natural, everybody had dreamt of bears the night before. Well— Maeterlinck may have some kind of a plausible Time theory, but the children are not sure how he manages about the bears. If they are going to climb onto both ends of the Curve it will be a little too much.

Going down a mountain is easier on the wind, but much harder on the legs. The back muscles of your calves, which get stretched going up, seem to tie themselves in knots going down—trying to take up the slack.

We tried to sneak past the cabin to our dinghy at the float, but the Man from California was lying down there in the sun.

"Where have you been all day?" he asked. "I've been worried about you."

"We smelt bears," offered John. "And we banged our tins at them, and they were all as afraid as anything."

The man groaned . . . his paradise spoiled, I suppose. But what about ours? I hastily showed him the huckleberries and asked him to come over and eat huckleberry pie with us on Trapper's Rock—two hours after the sun went over the top.

The we rowed home and fell into the sea to soak our aches and pains and mud away—around the rock, out of sight. We couldn't wear our bathing suits, for now our only clothes were dirty again, and we had to keep our bathing suits for supper.

We made a big fire on top of the rock to sit by; and cooked our supper on the little campfire in the prehistoric cave. A big corned-beef hash with tomatoes and onions—our biggest pot full of huckleberry dumplings—and coffee. I had warned the children not to mention bears again, so beyond a few groans when he heard where we had got the berries, we had a pleasant evening.

Clothes had to be washed again—the mountain climb had certainly ravaged them. So we spent the morning away up the landslide while our clothes dried. The man had paddled off in his canoe early, to get mail and provisions that some boat was to leave for him at Casper's—so we had the inlet to ourselves.

I had snubbed everybody at breakfast-time who tried to report a bear-dream—and felt that I had things back on a sane basis again. I had dreamt of climbing all night—my legs were probably aching. It wouldn't do for me to write mine down when I had been snubbing the children for even talking about theirs. By breakfast-time the only thing I could remember about it at all was hanging on to a bush for dear life, while something—water I think—flowed or slid past. . . . It had been terrifying, I know.

Later in the day we climbed up beside the falls. The stream above was very turbulent—you would certainly be battered to death on the big boulders if you fell in. And if you escaped that, there were falls below to finish you off. Quite a long way farther back there was a large tree across the stream which made a bridge to the other side. We crawled across on our hands and knees—no fooling allowed. I brought up the rear, holding John's belt in my teeth. . . . The others were across and had gone on ahead before John and I got safely over. . . . I swear that either the tree or the shore shook with the force of that raging water.

The others were out of sight and I called to them to wait. When we caught up, we started to follow them over a steep slope of heavy moss. They were romping across, clutching onto the moss and completely ignoring the torrent sixty feet below at the bottom of the slope. Suddenly I was sure I felt the sheet of moss under my feet slip— as moss will on granite. I shouted to the children not to move, and worked my way up a crack of bare granite, pushing John ahead of me—then anchored myself to a bush. I made the children crawl up, one by one, to where there were some bushes to hang onto. From there they worked up to a tree.

Elizabeth had to come to our help. Holding onto a firm bush, she lowered herself down until John could catch hold of her feet and pull himself up and past her. Then holding onto Elizabeth's feet, I put one foot on the moss and sprang forward, clutched a bush and then somebody's hand. . . . The youngsters were all safely anchored to a tree and I to a bush—and we sat there watching in horror as the big sheet of moss, to which I had just given the final push, gathered momentum and slid down and over the edge.

"I want to go home," wailed John.

"So do I," echoed Peter, his superior years forgotten.

"Don't be sillies!" I said sharply, recovering my breath.

"How . . . ?" they all moaned.

"How what?" I snapped.

"Get home . . . ?" they meekly sniffed.

Well, I wasn't quite sure at that stage. Besides, I was shaken. As soon as the moss slid, I had recognized the bush I was hanging on to—it was the bush in my dream.

Straight up seemed to be the only way we could go. Tree by tree all linked together, we finally got onto quite a wide ledge. And there on the ledge was a distinct trail.

"Why, it's that old she-bear's track again!" cried somebody.

"And that must have been her bridge!" said somebody else.

"Well, she certainly knows how to choose a good safe path," I said—wishing I knew which way she and her cub might come strolling.

I certainly didn't want to go over the trembling bridge again—so we followed the trail the other way. Going by the logger's tale, it should lead us to the old skid-road and then down to the cabin.

"Isn't she a nice old bear to make this nice path," said John hopefully—tightly clutching my hand.

"Silly!" said Peter, clutching onto my belt behind.

"Let's sing," I suggested.

So, all singing loudly, we followed the nice bear's trail. . . . A *nice* bear—whom I fervently hoped didn't care for singing.

IX

THE SENSUAL SELF

Gift of the Body

Vine
September 2–September 29

Gretchen Legler

Gabimichigami

*I*t is morning. I wake up to a confusion of diffused yellow light sinking down on me through the bright tent dome. I am in a canoe camp Craig and I have made on a cliff at Gabimichigami. We are in the Boundary Waters Canoe Area Wilderness, three days' paddle from our car at Sea Gull Lake.

I start to dress. Craig has been up for an hour and has lit the stove. There will have to be breakfast, then dishes, then packing the canoe and paddling the canoe, then hauling the canoe over portages to another camp, then on to another, and then back to the city. I have no desire to leave; no desire to move, to go forward into the day. Reluctantly, I start pulling a blue shirt over my bare body. I start to button it, then stop.

She doesn't want clothes.

She undresses, lets the shirt fall. Her boots are set outside the tent door, laces in the dirt, damp from the water in the air. She ignores them.

She doesn't want shoes.

She wants her feet to be bare.

She does not pretend that she is dressed. She knows she is naked. But she walks outside without any shyness, with the same confidence of movement she would have if she were covered in bluejeans and a red wool jacket and her green hat.

Craig sits by the lake drinking coffee. She walks into the woods, away from him. He turns his head and sees her. She has never done this before. She wonders if he will think she is strange. She wonders if he will follow her, and is glad when he does not. He says nothing.

The sky is gray and the big lake is duller and darker than the sky. In this dull light every color is accentuated, especially her skin. Her skin is white. The whiteness of her skin is like a thick, pale candle with a flame deep inside of it. In this light, the trees radiate greenness. In this light, blue veins glow through her skin.

She grabs the arm of a spruce and it springs back. She reaches for it again and puts it onto her shoulder and rubs it around there. She picks up a long pine needle from the ground and puts one end of it in her mouth. She is chewing on it. She puts her back against the thin bark of a birch tree.

Her shoulders and her hips and her thighs are softer than anything else: softer than pinecones or small chips of greenstone scattered around. She is the softest thing in the forest and the smoothest.

She is walking around trees and bushes and ducking under branches, naked. Some water is falling on her back. Her feet curve around rocks and moss and twigs. Wet leaves stick to her heels. She isn't cold. The air is still and as warm as she is. It is August.

She thinks her body is fine, out here.

Fine.

She wants to stay in the forest for a longer time.

But Craig calls to me.

"Come here and listen."

I walk to him, past the tent, where I reach in and grab shorts and my blue shirt. He is still sitting by the lake. I smell his coffee. I sit down by him on a rock. I imagine her bare skin against this rock. He says, very softly, "Listen."

I ask, "What for?"

"For nothing," he says. "There is no sound."

Susan Fox Rogers

One of the Boys

"Ty, you can't go unless there's another girl along."

I sighed. We'd been through this before, my mother and I. In the past, I'd won, but it always took so much talking, persuading, convincing.

"Fine. Fine, there'll be another girl."

My mother turned to me, her eyebrows raised, her dark eyes set, staring into mine. Truth, she seemed to demand silently. She knew there weren't any other girls around who climbed. I looked away, but not with any guilt. After all, why should I be deprived of climbing just because there weren't other girls to join me? My mother, however, didn't seem to think she was depriving me of anything. She was protecting me. "Sixteen-year-old girls simply do not sleep alone in the woods with boys."

Tonight I didn't feel like doing battle, so I walked to the phone and dialed John.

"I can go," I said.

"Psych."

"You have to bring your little sister," I said.

"My little sister? I don't have a little sister."

"That's great. I can lend her some shoes. She has a sleeping bag, right?"

"Is your mom enforcing the 'another girl' rule?"

"You got it. Pick me up at seven. I want to climb all day."

"Seven-thirty." And John hung up.

I walked past my mom who was standing in the kitchen near enough to listen.

"I didn't know John had a sister."

"She's only seven."

"Isn't that awfully young?"

I shrugged. "She's a girl."

I was ready and standing in front of my house at six-forty-five the next morning. The air was cool and moist, early spring when everything smells green and brown and my body aches to move, to pull, to lunge. To climb.

I pushed against the large oak tree in our front yard and felt the muscles in the back of my legs slowly loosen. Then I propped one foot against the tree and leaned over it, stretching further. I hoped John would arrive before my mother woke up. She would appear in her blue bathrobe at the door to ask me if I'd had breakfast, or she'd peer out the window and see there really was no girl along. I thought it was such a silly rule. What would another girl do: ask me to stop making out or to stop having sex? How far did my mother imagine I went? I wasn't interested in any of that, so I really didn't feel bad about lying. I just didn't want to get caught.

John and I had been climbing partners for two years and were best friends. We met at lunch in the cafeteria and again after school to builder, that is, climb on the walls of buildings. We spent our weekends together climbing at the local crags. I never thought of us as a couple, though I bet most of our twelfth-grade class did. I knew I trusted and loved John but in that push-and-pull way you love a brother. There was nothing close to romantic about our hugs after a climb, or even when we huddled up next to each other in our sleeping bags. We were family, part of the climbing family that came and went and had random reunions at the Gunks in the fall or Joshua Tree in the winter. We shared meals and stories and tents, and sometimes the climbing blood seemed richer and thicker than family blood. So I wasn't interested in sleeping with John. Or any guy for that matter. I liked being one of the boys. I just wanted to climb.

I heard the purr of John's truck, and as it approached I could see someone sitting in the passenger seat. I threw my pack and sleeping bag into the back and then squeezed into the cab. I made the stranger sit in the middle. I would have offered to be the sardine, but as the smallest, or maybe because I was the only girl, I was always chosen (and sometimes I offered) to sit in the middle. This morning I decided I'd sat there too many times, my butt going numb and John knocking my knees every time he shifted.

"Tim this is Ty, Ty, Tim. I met Tim down at the wall yesterday. He's at Penn State."

"Where from?"

"New Hampshire."

I nodded.

"We're going to take a road trip to New Hampshire this spring."

"I've never been there," I said.

"Best climbing on the East Coast," Tim said.

"No, the Gunks is."

"Depends on what you're looking for."

"The Gunks has everything."

"Wait till you see New Hampshire. Routes ten pitches long." He turned to me and smiled. "You'll love it," he said. "I promise."

John slipped in an Emmylou Harris tape. We always listened to country to get us ready for our future lives out West. We were both saving our money to go the minute we graduated, and we'd spent the winter dreaming and planning: Eldorado Canyon, the Wind Rivers, Vedauwoo, Tuolumne, Yosemite—we were going to go everywhere.

"I'm going to stop for coffee," John said.

John was a caffeine fiend. He always drank too much then ended up shaking on the rock.

"Get me a donut," I said.

"Did you guys eat breakfast?" Tim asked. "I'm starving. Let's stop for breakfast."

I was hungry, too, but I didn't have the patience to stop and eat. "I want to get to the rock. Let's get something to go."

"Fine with me," John said. Everything was usually fine with John.

We stopped at Jim's Deli on the west side of town and each got an egg on a roll and a large coffee to go. The truck smelled of eggs and coffee. John was juggling, trying to eat, shift, steer and drink at the same time. Usually when we drove and ate, I shifted for him while he clutched. We had it pretty well coordinated, and I'd only once thrown us back into first instead of third.

"These things aren't bad," Tim said holding up his egg sandwich.

He was right, but I didn't want to agree with him.

We went to Hunter Rocks, a bouldering paradise on a piece of private hunting land. John and I were the only ones who climbed there a lot, and so we had put up most of the routes. We'd work through the boulders in a set order each time: first the warm-up rocks and then the test pieces we threw ourselves at. We'd push each other, fall off, and try again all afternoon. Today, John started with one of our warm-up climbs that used to be a test piece until we figured out the secret hold.

I was going to suggest we let Tim try it first, but John was already on the gritty sandstone, his feet smeared onto the first holds.

"There's nothing when you start, except this." John grabbed a large hold with his right hand. He moved his feet up, smearing and crouching low. "Watch," he said. His body extended completely off of the big hold as he reached, half lunging, for our secret hold out left. We'd worked for months to find that hold and when we did we laughed and laughed. And then we'd done the problem a dozen times as a victory dance. When John walked around to the front of the boulder, Tim was already on it, moving his feet up to crouch and reach.

"That's it," John said.

In one motion Tim had the hold and was moving up the rest of the boulder. He made it look casual, easy.

"Great," John said. He turned to me. He looked happy, his eyes shining, his mouth curved into a soft smile.

I smiled back. "I'm going to head up to the slabs. I'll meet you guys there later."

"Wait for me to try the Super," John said.

I jogged up the hill to a set of rocks that formed a perfect circle. The sides of the rocks are smooth, dotted with sharp, thin holds. This was my favorite section of the rock. "If you like this, you'll like Tuolumne," John had promised. "It's like this for days." I already liked Tuolumne—the name rolled out of my mouth, and it felt magic and strong.

I sat down to put on my shoes. The ground was still damp and cool. It felt good to breath deeply, to be quiet and alone.

Once I touched the rock and started to move, I felt great. My muscles tightened and relaxed, and I stepped high for holds that felt sharp and cut into my fingers with a secure bite. I did the five problems I knew, and they all felt good and solid. Then I turned to the Super Slab. It was the highest boulder, and the hardest moves were at the top. John and I always jumped off, half trying the last moves. At one point we decided the last move wouldn't go; it was a problem we just couldn't do. But we both still tried it each time we were at Hunter. We didn't want to give up.

I had the first moves wired and did them quickly and smoothly. I hadn't felt this secure in a long time, and when I got to the top I suddenly saw how it should go. It meant standing up on a nothing of a hold, using a pebble to move up left and then smearing on a slight indent to reach for the top. Maybe I'd seen all of this before, but it had never seemed possible.

I didn't hesitate, because I knew I could psych myself out of any move. Everything hit right, and my hand slapped, then stuck to the top. As I pulled myself up, I heard John and Tim whistle and clap.

I stood up, turned around and smiled.

They were sitting in the sun, perched on a nearby boulder.

"Thanks for the spot," I said. Though I knew if anyone had been there, standing behind me, I wouldn't have made it.

"I tried," John said. "Tim wouldn't let me."

"I didn't need it," I said.

"That was obvious," Tim said. He turned to John. "She's good."

"Don't tell me," John said.

Tim sat down and then stretched out on the rock. His body was laced by the sun that filtered through the new green leaves. "This place is great," he said.

John and I smiled at each other.

John sat down beside Tim, taking in the warmth of the sun.

I walked over to join them, and as I approached I almost expected to see them holding hands, their bodies connecting in some way. They looked happy together, resting, exposed in the woods. They both had their eyes closed, and Tim's face was smooth and relaxed as if he were asleep. But I could tell his eyes were moving under his lids. He had deep brown eyes, the color of rich Pennsylvania soil, and they were always moving, searching. The slow afternoon sun reflected off the gold in his dirty blond hair.

John opened one eye and looked at me. "Show me how you did it?"

"I'll tell you," I said. I'd done this in the past: tried to repeat a difficult move I'd just done, only to fail. Then the success becomes a fluke, and the happiness of that moment of inspiration vanishes. I'd try it another day, but I knew I couldn't do it again today.

John stood up and walked down to the slab.

"You looked good," he said.

"I feel good."

"Tim's all right," John said. "He likes you."

"What's that supposed to mean?"

John shrugged and winked, then turned to the slab. He moved up the first section quickly and then hesitated.

"See that sliver of nothing? You have to stand on it. Reach left, there's a pebble you can use to balance."

John stood, shifting his weight on the small holds; then little by little he moved his weight onto the wrinkle. Each time his foot began to slip, he returned to his more solid holds.

"You can't do it slowly," I said. "Move through it. Move upward. Do you see how it goes?"

"Yeah, but you made it look so easy."

I laughed.

John concentrated, breathing steadily, preparing himself. I stood with my arms in the air, spotting him if he fell, and shielding my eyes from the sun. I watched his calf muscles flexing and tensing, as if they were thinking, breathing, contemplating what they had to do. Everything was still, and I was almost holding my breath waiting for John to move when, in the silence, I felt something near me. I turned to see Tim leaning against the rock directly behind me. I hadn't heard him approach, and it surprised me to see him there, so still and calm, standing as if he'd been there for a while. He smiled, his face wrinkling into a grin. I turned back to John.

Soon John came sliding down the rock and landed heavily on the ground. I caught him under the arms as his body tilted backward.

"I can't do it," John said. He stood up and shook himself out. "You really stood on that?" he asked.

I nodded. "You have to believe."

"No, you have to invent."

"You did it because you're a girl," John teased. He imitated our friend Ron's voice: "Girls have amazing footwork." Ron categorically believed women had better footwork and so should be better climbers. It was only our own personal failings that held us back from being genius climbers.

I punched John on the shoulder. "And you can't do it because you're a boy."

"No, it's because I'm out of shape."

"When will you be in shape?"

"1997. Or thereabouts."

John and I were playing in our usual way, ignoring Tim. I turned to him. "Want to try it?"

Tim looked at the wall and shook his head. "Maybe in 1997."

We spent the afternoon climbing, alone and together. I got used to Tim, but he treated me differently than John did. He'd go back and get my shoes for me, or chalk up a hold to show me where to put my foot.

This is too easy, I thought. This is easy to accept. And then easy to expect.

When Tim caught me when I fell, he helped me up, holding me under the arms. He'd squeeze me quickly. Small tight hugs.

At three-thirty we were all burnt. We lay in the sun for a while, each on our own rock, resting and warming.

"Let's go for a swim," John said.

"Where?" Tim asked.

"There's a swimming hole off 45. It means driving back toward town a few miles."

"The water will be cold," I said.

We stopped at Edson's country store for a root beer and vanilla ice cream. An older lady served us our sodas in glass bottles, and we finished drinking before she managed to scoop out the cold, hard ice cream.

Back in the truck, Tim turned up Emmylou real loud. I sat in the middle, and we all rocked against each other, our shoulders touching as we licked our ice cream cones.

John was the first to jump out of the truck. He took off for the pond, running in long strides. Tim and I walked side by side, carrying towels over our shoulders.

"This place is beautiful," Tim said.

I nodded, but I didn't feel like talking.

We walked past the no trespassing signs onto the narrow path. I walked in front of Tim. He walked close behind me; I could feel his eyes peering into my back, into the nape of my neck. I felt as if he was trying to look through me.

I spotted John flying through the air on the rope swing. He let out an ape-man yell as he let go of the rope and arced into the water, his naked limbs flapping in the air. Tim and I laughed.

I stepped back from the edge of the pond and watched as Tim pulled his T-shirt over his head. His back was smooth and glowed with a layer of sweat. He dropped his shorts and stood naked. The blond hair that ran down his legs started off as soft wisps on his buttocks. I stared at his long legs and firm, round bottom. I knew he knew I was staring at him, and that was fine.

John popped out of the water and climbed up next to Tim. John was breathing heavily from his swim.

"Try it," he said. "The water's freezing." He turned to me and smiled. "What's the matter with you?"

I shrugged. "Nothing." I never wore a bathing suit when it was just me and John, but suddenly I wished I'd brought one.

John grabbed the rope and swung out letting out his tremendous call one more time. He dropped into the water and for a brief moment it was silent as he swam underwater.

Tim turned back to look at me. Just his upper torso turned. He had half a smile on his face. For a moment I thought he was going to step completely around and walk toward me. But he turned, reached for the rope and arced into the air before dropping into the water. I watched him disappear for a few moments then surface, gasping, not for air, but from cold. I laughed as I quickly pulled off my shirt and slipped out of my shorts. Then I ran for the rope and swung out high over the water.

Deborah Abbott

Stones All Around, An Abundance of Water, of Bushes, of Birds

for Chris Adams, who brought me back to the water

I am lying naked, warm and drowsy in my sleeping bag, half caught in a dream, when I am startled awake by a small bird that alights on the back of my head. For an instant I am still, and the bird is still and then, even before there is an urge to breathe, the bird has flown noisily into the thicket in which I am ensconced.

I open my eyes. It is just light. The river has fallen in the hours I have been sleeping so that it is close, but not so close as when I curled up beside it, under the expanse of night sky, and let its waters murmur in my ears. I draw my body out of the bag, gasp at the chill, and walk gingerly across the sand. I squat and pee. The warm stream washes over my vulva and, with a rush of pleasure, I shiver.

I look at my body, tawny from these days on the river, at my arms, thick and achy from hours of handling the enormous wooden oars, at my blistered palms, at my breasts, clustered against my chest, at my soft belly. Finally I look at my legs: the left one supporting me as I squat, and the right one, frail as the twigs around me, sagging under the weight of the birds.

I look out at the water and see myself rising up from my haunches, running the few yards to the riverbank, scrambling up the large stone that lies below and diving into the still space of its eddy. Like the bird on my head, my mind is startled by this image, takes sudden flight. I cannot run. I will not run, ever, except fleetingly, in dreams.

My mind settles itself quickly onto that which can be done, which must be done. I consider the plan for the day. I am responsible for building the fire this morning, for organizing breakfast and for securing a massive load of gear onto my raft. Before I leave this place to take on these tasks, I reach for a small, cool stone. I draw it back, fling it outward. The strength of my arm propels it faster than any legs could run. It lights on the water once, twice, skipping, then sinks with a plop near the farthest shore.

I return to my sleeping site, rummage through my pack and find my clothes. I pull on my bathing suit, still damp, and my soft khaki shorts. I smile, knowing Kate, my lover back in Santa Cruz, would be pleased to see me now, so casually buttoning my shorts. It was she who managed, with her tender insistence, to get me into shorts for the first time in twenty years.

I lace up the boot on my left foot. As I'm ripping at the velcro on my brace, ready to slip my right leg in, I am struck by the sound of the tearing. I think: torn. This is how I am. My body is able. My body is not. I touch down like the bird, and then I am away. For a moment I am the rock nestled among others on the riverbank. Then I am hurled to the opposite shore. I occupy both places. I belong in neither place.

Last evening I hiked to the farthest point on the beach, so my walk to the kitchen site is long. I gather twigs for the fire and a rusty can, bottle caps, a bit of shredded webbing. My thoughts are like litter, cluttering my mind's landscape. I realize that the hardest part of this trip is not in the physical strength, endurance, nor skill required in rafting, but in finding a place for myself, a place to make camp. The company for which I am volunteering organizes trips for people with different needs. On this particular trip there are five rafts. Five guides: four able-bodied guides and myself. Four attendants and five participants: two paraplegics, one quadriplegic, a deaf woman named T. J. and a girl with cerebral palsy. I am both disabled and a guide.

The day spreads before me. I make the fire. T. J. joins me, gathers more sticks to feed the flame. We haul water up from the river, signing with our free hands and giggling because, with my limp, I slosh half of the bucket onto my feet. Back at the fire I boil the water, brew coffee. I set the griddle out over the flame and cook french toast. The attendants have dressed the other participants, tended to bladders and bowels, and brought the wheelchair users, with a great deal of effort and humor, to the kitchen area. Marta, the quad, and I greet each other. I sit beside her on an overturned bailing bucket, give her sips of coffee, bits of french toast dripping with syrup. She makes faces, tells me my coffee tastes like river sludge, that I'm making a mess of her new Patagonia jacket. We laugh. In that moment of laughter, like the bird, I land. We are two disabled women enjoying the morning.

An instant later, I take wing. I am down on the boats with the other guides, loading gear, fastening purple ribbons of webbing around Marta's chair, my brace, our supplies. I am scrambling over the load, cinching the tether with the full weight of my body. In these moments and all morning as I negotiate rapids, row through the calm stretches, I am indistinguishable from the other guides. I fit into the able-bodied world more than the disabled.

I go back and forth between worlds all day. I think that the hawk crisscrossing the gorge above me, hour after hour, is looking for more than food. It is searching for a place to come down, for a nest.

Marta calls to me. I look for the nearest large rock and pull hard on the oars, pivoting into its downstream eddy. Marta's body is slipping. I lift her into my arms and settle her into a more stable position. I return to the oars. By bracing my legs and pulling with the combined strength of my arms and belly, I break through the turbulent eddy fence back into the current.

An hour later, our party is stopping to scout a rapid, which involves walking through thigh-high water, climbing a steep bank and walking a half mile downstream along a narrow, rocky path. From there, there will be a sort of aerial view of the tricky whitewater we are approaching. The four other guides make a bridge for me to walk along since my one strong leg and one weak one cannot hold me up in water this swift and deep. When we reach the shore, one of the guides carries me piggyback up the bank. At the top, another gives me her arm. We walk behind until finally I tell her to go on without me. Even with her support, my leg has given out.

I sit in the hot sun, watching the guide disappear around the bend. I look down at Marta, the other disabled participants and their helpers. Marta catches my eye and nods her head, which is her way of waving. I wave back, raising my arm and wagging my hand. T. J. signs, "Stuck there?" I make a stab at my throat with two fingers, then a fist which I shake up and down. "Stuck. Yes. Stuck here."

Then I draw my knees up to my chin, put my face down and cry. It is a relief to be crying; my body has been holding these tears all day. At first I am crying out of anger, anger at my body for its limitations. Then I am crying out of sheer loneliness. I am the hawk weary of its solitary circling, wanting company, a place to claim as home.

I am neither in the boats, nor at the lookout with the other guides. I am somewhere in between. Amphibian: the one who passes between water and land. The one who occupies the border. I am on the faultline looking into the abyss. I am the fence-sitter. The bridge. I am the woman who straddles the gap. Like the light-skinned black who can "pass." The lesbian who can slip in and out of the closet. I am the disabled woman with access to able-bodied privileges but without inclusion in either world in any predictable, solid way. I live on the outskirts, the fringes, the edge.

I sit on the embankment for a long time. After a while, there are no tears left to cry. I hear something stirring beside me. I lift my head. A young rattlesnake crosses the path with a lopsided motion, as though it has not yet learned to glide. It reminds me of myself moving unevenly yet gracefully through space.

I smile. There are stones all around, an abundance of water, of bushes, of birds. In this moment, my solitude dissolves. I am part of this place, peaceful and content. My kinship is here, with the snake. My community is here, with the population of stones. I have no need of any other.

The guide who led me up the path is the first to reappear around the bend. She has brought a sprig of wild mint, which she presents to me as a bouquet. I put my nose into its center and breathe in. She squats beside me, clears a space on the ground and draws a map of the rapid I will be navigating. We discuss the various routes, the risks involved in each. I am distracted by the sharp, good smell of her body, by the two sturdy legs on which she leans. When she finishes, I have memorized my course down the rapid, the curve of her strong right thigh. She rises, gives me her hand and pulls me to my feet. We walk toward the boats, toward Marta, T. J. and the others, arm in arm.

Linda Lewis

Etes-Vous Prêts?

*E*arly on a brisk December morning in 1984, nine women took a borrowed shell from Philadelphia's Vesper Boat Club for a short row on the Schuylkill River. The women had all been inducted into rowing's hall of fame the night before in an emotion-filled ceremony. The chill of the morning air and the mist rising from the still waters of the river provided a delicious contrast with the heat and excitement of the previous evening. The moment just before the row began was particularly sharp and poignant for the woman sitting in the number two seat of the shell. This woman did not look like the others in the boat. She was smaller and considerably older, by about fifty years. The other eight women—the coxswain and the seven rowers—were Olympic gold medalists, having swept with power and precision to that honor just four months earlier. The white-haired woman had never rowed in an Olympic event or even in any kind of elite national competition. Yet, the eight gold medalists felt that they owed what they had accomplished in rowing to her. They had impulsively invited her to row with them the night before when they were all celebrating how far women had come in a sport that was closed to them for so long. The eight Olympic gold medalists had used all the words they knew to thank this white-haired woman for insisting, nearly fifty years earlier, on women's right to row competitively. Now they wanted her to feel with her body what a force she had unleashed. The Olympic eight wanted to perform exquisitely, to show the woman in the number two seat the level of athletic accomplishment that she had made possible. There was some hesitation, though, out of deference to the woman's age. The eight wondered how much a display of speed and strength they could put on without pushing her too hard. After all, they were in their twenties and thirties, the best rowers in the world. She was seventy-five and primarily a recreational rower. If they took the stroke rate up too high, would they turn what was meant to be a triumph into a disaster?

As the coxswain considered what cadence to call after the warm-up, the woman in the number two seat yelled out: "Let's do a start and a ten."

She was asking to feel the boat's explosiveness off the starting line. A start is five rapid strokes designed to get sixty feet of shell and 1,500 pounds of bodies moving. The ten strokes after the start are full power strokes at the high rate set in motion by the start.

The coxswain stopped the boat and got the rowers ready for a start. All eight moved forward on their sliding seats, planted their blades in the water and breathed deeply, preparing for the quick burst that would get the boat going. The coxswain gave the traditional French starting sequence: *"Etes-vous prêts?" (Are you ready?)* Every body was at the same angle, knees bent, back forward, arms extended, compressed, poised to release maximum power.

"Partez." (Go.)

All eight oars pulled as one. The shell heaved through the water as the rowers rammed their legs down and pulled through on the oars to pry the boat forward. All eight brought the oars out of the water together and slid forward on their seats together to begin the next stroke. After the tenth power stroke, the coxswain told the rowers to "weigh enough" (stop) and let the boat glide.

For a moment there was only the rush of water and the sound of hard breathing. All nine women floated in a cocoon of suspended time. Then from the number two seat again came the call: "Let's take a start and a ten."

The other women in the boat came fully awake. They understood immediately what the tone of that request implied. The honored guest in the number two seat was saying to them, "Come on, you gold medalists, show me how it *really* feels." She was challenging them to row as hard and as fast as they could. That first start and ten had not been at full pressure. The Olympians had held something back. They had been quick and graceful but had not turned on the explosive power. The woman in the number two seat had kept her part of the bargain, staying right with them. Now she wanted to see what more they could do.

The second five-stroke start and ten high on that December morning was charged. All eight rowers moved up their slides into the starting position determined to hold nothing back. They buried their blades in the water and shook the tension out of their shoulders. They were coiled and ready to explode when the starting command came. *"Partez."* The boat flew, slicing through the placid waters of the

Schuylkill. With every stroke, the rowers translated their muscle into motion. They took every stroke as one flawless unit, achieving a power that transcended their individual efforts and lifted the boat over the water. When the rowers stopped and feathered their oars so the boat could glide, Ernestine Bayer, in the number two seat, wept.

Ernestine Bayer is rowing's matriarch. Her efforts to establish a competitive rowing program for women led directly to the high point of women's rowing in the United States—the eight's winning of the gold medal in the 1984 Olympics. Her continuing involvement in the sport is an inspiration. She is in her late eighties, and she still competes in certain regattas. People point and exclaim when they spot that cap of white hair and that sharp, intense profile out on the water, gracefully rowing her single to the starting line.

Ernestine Bayer began working for women's right to row in 1938 when she founded the Philadelphia Girls Rowing Club (PGRC), which marked the beginning of the modern women's competitive rowing movement. From the PGRC's boathouse on the Schuylkill River, she taught hundreds of young women how to row in the forties, fifties and sixties. She rowed in the first women's race on the Schuylkill in 1938. In 1967, she took the first American women's eight to compete in Europe, where they proved they had the skills to go up against international crews. And she served on the first United States Women's Olympic Rowing Committee, which sent rowers to the Montreal games in 1976.

Ernestine Bayer now lives with her husband and daughter in Stratham, New Hampshire, in a spacious house on nine acres along the Squamscott River. She likes to imagine rowing from the dock in her back yard all the way to France. Such an adventure is possible, for the Squamscott flows into Great Bay, which leads to the Atlantic. Rowing has taken Ernestine Bayer to Europe already, but that was the plodding, plotting organizational side of the sport, not the pure, undiluted movement that she has sought all her life. All that Ernestine Bayer ever wanted to do was to race a rowing shell against other women. But to perform that simple act, she had to create an entire structure. She had to start from less than zero, faced with a firmly entrenched bias against women's participation in the sport. To get what she wanted, she had to sit in stuffy meeting rooms instead of concentrating on the timing of her oars' entry into the water. She never considered herself very good at politics. It was not her "dish of tea," as she puts it. Yet she managed to become proficient enough on the organizational side of rowing to stage the kind of races that she craved. The sad irony is that by the time women's events in regattas became accepted, Ernestine Bayer was too old to compete at an elite level.

Had Ernestine Bayer been born fifty years later, she could have stepped into a ready-made rowing program as a youngster and gone as far with the sport as her talent and will would have taken her. As it is, she takes satisfaction from knowing that young women now have the opportunities she longed for because of efforts she made. And she still has the pleasure of rowing itself, the hypnotic rhythm of it, the constant motion her body craves: "I like to keep my body moving. What better way than to be in a boat on the water that you love. It's a beautiful sport. You don't have to have quickness and power. But rhythm you have to have. You can row as easy as you want to. You can row along and look around. I don't know why everybody doesn't row."

Every spring, as soon as the ice melts from the Squamscott and flows in chunks out to sea, she is on the river in her single stroking the water.

X

NATURE'S HEALING

Gift of Solace

Ivy

September 30-October 27

Wuanda Walls

Doves

Spiritual Affinity. It is wrong to think that love comes from long companionship and persevering courtship. Love is the offspring of spiritual affinity and unless that affinity is created in a moment, it will not be created in years or even generations.

—*Kahlil Gibran*

*I*t all seems so logical in retrospect. Nevertheless, I'm still mystified whenever my devoted doves appear, always calm and peaceful.

In 1977, I moved into my paternal grandparents' homestead. Both were deceased but their home stood solid and stark. Green and white, the two-story wood-frame house possessed a coal furnace, pantry cellar, an inviting, sunlit, airy kitchen and a well-used front porch facing the village's quaint post office.

According to family lore, my parents met by way of the porch. When my mother's family moved from rural Maryland to rural Pennsylvania, the mail fetcher's task was given to her. My mother's future mother-in-law, Helen, was a friendly, generous, sweet-humored woman who immediately saw the young maiden as the perfect match for one of her two sons. Often she invited her in for chitchat and her legendary cinnamon rolls. Eventually, the porch became the "in" place, providing a diversion from farm chores for Mother, which suited Helen just fine. She delighted in introducing the newcomer to her neighbors, church members, professors and students from the nearby college and a few flibbertigibbets.

Two months after I moved into the house my father died at age fifty-four from a massive heart attack, just two years after his mother's death. No one was prepared for the challenge of grief, the void and finality. It was a shock that pulled everyone from the mundane. Although as Catholics, we (my mother, sister, brother-in-law and two nieces) had our faith, which was comforting, it was the unceremonious, intimate presence of friends and family, their kind words, deeds and love, that helped to strengthen and console.

For me, living in my father's parents' home, which was located next to his grandparents' property, was providential. Everything I touched and saw took on a new, more historic and spiritual meaning: the changing seasons, the sounds of crickets, buttercups in bloom, my great-grandfather's cradle and Mom's Mom's cookbooks and china. Surrounded by cherished keepsakes that evoked heartwarming memories of my ancestors, I felt connected to something primordial, mythical, wise and loving.

One day while reflecting and sorting through things in the attic, I discovered my father's Boy Scout manual and a colorful, handmade Saint Valentine's card made for his mother. Touched, I called my mother, and we both rejoiced. Over the years she had kept all of his cards, and asked me to save my prize if I didn't want it. Admittedly, I felt a tinge of selfishness, but realized the joy was my discovery. Without hesitation I wrapped it in vintage newspaper and sent it with love.

My parents had a special love affair crowned with harmony and romance. There was no room for competition. A quiet, devoted family man, Dad was endowed with an understanding heart and humanitarian spirit. He adored his wife and daughters. Their happiness was his happiness. A breed apart, many called him a saint, shaped by the morals and genteel nature of his ancestors.

One of my fondest memories of my parents is when they had their new convertible, which was forever in motion, heading nowhere special or for uncharted territory. They liked to drive along the super highway as carefree as birds, basking in the glory of it all, the beauty of life. They led a charmed life, wholesome, and uncomplicated. Their closeness intrigued and delighted many while others may have kept an envious eye camouflaged.

Spring was near, budding pussy willows, crocuses and forsythia teased anxious hearts. During this period I made it a matter of intent to appear cheerful, free from anger, sadness and resentment. These feelings, related to my grief, had a tendency to creep up when I questioned my father's death. My conversations with God were spirited, at times amusing and always forthright. I tried to keep my mind working at a breathless pace, focusing on my studies, research and writing. Nevertheless, I did allow myself to feel pain. In fact, frequently I invited it by looking at family photographs, those of us ice skating on the village pond, and the treasured one of my father and me taken the day I was christened.

Much later, when my mind was filled with images both felt and observed, due to a series of ill-timed events I was compelled to meditate out-of-doors on one of those humid, enervating summer days. The perfumed air blending honeysuckle, roses and bee balm vivified my soul as I walked near the pond. Then, without warning, a flock of birds landed directly at my feet. Startled, I stayed motionless, struck by their delicate beauty, boldness and serenity. My pulse quickened coupled with an intensely peaceful sensation which overtook me; thus, the birds transmitted their energy to me. The air resounded with their musical whistling as they flew away.

During the next years I lived in Europe and the Caribbean. My life changed a little but for the most part I was studying languages, writing and traveling. I didn't see the birds. However, I often thought about them while living in Spain because almost every household kept some type of bird. Besides, the fact that Spain was such a Catholic country heightened my curiosity about how I was raised. I was prompted to begin studying the history of the Catholic Church.

After spending days in the archives in Seville, I came away disillusioned. My discovery revealed horrors encompassing corruption, sexism, racism, violence, the Inquisition and more. Notwithstanding, the lives of several saints captivated me along with the symbolism of birds, mainly doves, and certain rituals and pilgrimages. Eventually after a time I was able to put the horrors into their proper perspectives. To my delight, from time to time, I saw white doves, those painted by Picasso, and contemplated their divinity.

Back in the states, several years later, trying to find a place for myself, I decided to visit a close friend in Texas before moving to Colorado. My life consisted of coming back from one place, only to seek a new one. This decision was not easy and my friend, being the sensitive, loving person she is, invited me to spend time with her family before claiming my new home. On day two, I refused to stay immured in an air-conditioned haven. Instead I opted to inhale the suffocating, warm air as I walked to find shade. Upon returning, my thoughts were sober, bordering on melancholy. Was the Southwest the place for me now? Then I heard them: their unmistakable cooing. At once, my eyes scanned the dry field catching a glimpse of their etched, white tail feathers. Somewhat befuddled, I couldn't help thinking their appearance was a good presage related to my new home. Quite unexpectedly, smiling images of my father gratified my soul. I remained in the field for some time hoping they would reappear.

When I told my friend about the incident she said she believed I was connected to the birds in some deeper dimension. I agreed, knowing that over the years following my dad's death I had begun to understand how everything in nature is connected. In addition, I embraced meditation, Native American spirituality, and communicated with my ancestors on a daily basis. These things, plus the acceptance of certain metaphysical tenets, undoubtedly made me more receptive to supernatural phenomenon. I relinquished both my attachment and disenchantment with the Catholic Church and found strength and guidance in nature.

That evening, as I sat in the middle of the bed, I remembered stories about birds associated with peace and good omens. In the Holy Scriptures there are four instances when the Holy Spirit appeared, once as a dove at Jesus' baptism. As the stories kept coming, I remembered one about an eagle and eagle feathers used by Native Americans in their prayer markers, tobacco pouches tied with string taken into sweat lodges. The eagle is revered because he flies high, close to the sky realm of the Great Spirit. Then I had a flashback of a conversation I overheard my parents having about death. Half-jokingly, my father told my mother that if he died first, he wanted to visit her in the form of a bird. This really amused me because our religion did not believe in reincarnation.

The beauty of Colorado enthralled me. Walking, biking and hiking became my favorite activities. My consciousness relating to health, the environment and endangered species expanded. My penchant for certain material things diminished. The breathtaking beauty of the majestic Rockies satisfied needs on many levels. My vision waxed clearer. I evolved into a minimalist.

More settled one year later, I moved into another house in the same Denver neighborhood. When I met my neighbor, Mary, I knew we were kindred spirits. Her backyard reminded me of my grandfather's garden. Irises, roses, violets, lilacs, peonies, mint and the state flower, the columbine (the Latin word is columba, "dove") enchanted my senses. We connected instantly with no thought to race (I being an eighth-generation African-American and she of French-German ancestry) or age (she being my grandmother's age). Having a nimble mind, enamored with universal pleasures encompassing history, music, nature and the arts, Mary became my confidante.

On a lovely, clear spring day while lying in my hammock, I spotted two birds perched on Mary's slanted roof. I moved cautiously as I approached her back door, hoping to find her in the kitchen humming to the music coming from the radio. When she noticed me, she smiled kindly and said, "Isn't this a glorious day!" I whispered, asking her to come and identify the birds. Her blue eyes lit up when our voices disturbed them and they flew away. She quickly exclaimed, "Oh, they are mourning doves. They visit me every spring."

When I heard the word mourning I repeated it and commented that I never heard of morning doves. Mary off-handedly spelled out the name. I was taken aback, as the word mourning conjured up images of gloom. Momentarily, I sensed some significant break-through; however, it was nebulous. I was unsettled. I felt movement toward some incredible revelation that would connect me with the spiritual world and I opened myself to receive.

For some reason, I didn't share my mystical experience with Mary but went instead to the library to research the bird. The first book I picked up proved useless, but the second one amazed me. Here were the mourning doves depicted in a lovely color illustration, their countenance as delicate and beguiling as in reality. I discovered that the birds mate for life, and if one mate dies the other mourns forever. Both are protective, doting parents. The beautiful mournful cooing gives the bird its name, and it is a protected songbird in some states. Suddenly, I understood their connection. My father possessed those same traits. At that moment, his spirit seemed to embrace me tenderly. My heart rejoiced.

A few weeks later while walking, I decided to explore an unfamiliar neighborhood. Cottonwood, aspen and poplar trees graced the wide street. Immersed in the glory of the season, I was in my own world until one small dove landed directly in front of me. This time I greeted the bird and blessed it with a prayer. As I entered the food market I heard a customer ask the clerk for the date. She replied, "May the first." Literally, my heart skipped a beat as I breathed deeply, realizing it was my father's birthday.

The sky was calm and clear, and the air lulled me like a philter as I made my way home, secure in a newfound knowledge, wearing comfort, peace and serenity.

Laura Waterman

Climbing With Margaret

A Story

She stopped moving upward. Time spun itself out so that tasks she knew took only a second, such as placing an ice ax, took hours. Stalled, she leaned out on her tools and looked up at the sky, dark and scabbed with hard stars. Her eyes moved to the soft void on her right, blank and without sound.

She let her arms hang out in her wrist loops, dropped her head forward to touch the ice. She wasn't using the rope, but it was in her pack. Her head repeated: *partners belay partners belay partners* with such tedium it made her gag.

A voice! It nearly tipped her backward and she felt wild from the adrenalin as she caught herself. Where am I? That voice sounded so high and weak. It made her laugh! She rested her head again on the

raw flank of the mountain until her brow went numb. She made herself kick in her left crampon and the ice cracked like brittle bone.
"Damn you, Margaret," she said.

She had arrived in Talkeetna first, as they had planned, and began repacking the food. She expected Margaret in two days. But she
wasn't on the passenger van that arrived from Anchorage. She called
the university where Margaret taught and someone with a voice like
crushed ice told her, "Didn't you hear? Professor Simon was in an
accident last night on her way to the airport. A tractor-trailer jumped
the median. It took out several cars."

No, she hadn't heard. Was she. . . ? "Not dead," the voice said.
"Professor Simon is in a coma. Her spine is broken. They fear brain
damage."

She returned to the building where she had left their gear and
walked around, touching things, bending to pick up fragments of
herself. Ropes, snow pickets, carabiners, ice screws, webbing, rock
gear, the stoves, pots, fuel, their tent, their sleeping bags—ready for
climbing. Her eyes felt parched.

She had had herself flown in anyway. After all, it was to be their
fiftieth-birthday climb.

Time slid back to normal and she continued climbing. After a while
she knew Margaret had reached the alcove and was waiting there. Or
perhaps she wouldn't wait, but would keep just ahead, hedged behind
the dark. She heard the soft thunk, thunk of Margaret's tools, and
imagined Margaret's hands gripping the shafts, relaxed in the wrist
loops. She felt the power of Margaret's surging swing vibrate down

her own arm.

The alcove: where the avalanche caught them last time. Not a direct hit, just a sideswipe when the snow slope slid. She was belaying under a skimpy rock overhang and had a gallery seat when a Niagara-like rush of snow and ice spewed in front of her nose and out onto the glacier, creating a mound the size of a New England hill. "Margaret! Margaret!" "Fay! Fay!" Their cries rang in the turbulent air dense with snow dust. She had fully expected the rope to go slack and was surprised not to see Margaret whirl by, a cartwheel of arms and legs and ice chunks. "Heck, Fay, it missed me by fifty feet, easy. Just noisy, that's all. I was more concerned about you. It was big!"

The avalanche creamed their route, removing all their anchors and fixed ropes, which they discovered when they began rappelling. Not an ice screw remained. They were two-thirds of the way up the mountain.

They had lost too much to improvise with scanty gear, and after that, they had to admit they were too undone to go on.

Her eye caught the headlight of a star skidding toward her, and she clenched her tools, in a panic over being nudged into nothingness. She saw the tractor-trailer, lit up for night travel, blasting the median. She clawed to her left, crampons screeching. Her tongue turned to sawdust in her mouth, and she smelled her own bitter sweat. Cars were upturned, scattered like jackstraws. The New England hill hardened into a concrete burial mound.

"The Alaska Range is not for sissies. That's what some climber told me, Fay, after my slide show. Oh God!" Margaret laughed. "The Alaska Range makes me go weak in the knees faster than I can sink an ice screw."

They had hooted their way up a whole summer of routes with this line. Mouths caked dry down into their throats. Hands sweating inside gloves, feet freezing in damp socks, minds riding high on animal instinct. How they both loved it. How she still loved it.

The stars dimmed. She paused and pushed her cuff back to check the time. The liver spots on the back of her hand glowed faint as phosphorus.

She looked up. It was light enough now to see the outline of the overhang. Her heart caught. Its form had lived in her nighttime thoughts for so long. The way the rock tunneled into the snow slope, making a cave-like space tall enough to stand in if you were short, then sloping to a crawlspace at the back. Exactly the same.

She scrambled up, her crampons biting into the firm snow under the overhang. She had stood right *here* to belay Margaret. The crack she'd slotted a chock into was—she fell to her knees and crawled to the back of the alcove, reached to rub rime off the rock—here. She tore off her glove and ran her bare fingers into the rough crack. It had been five years.

"But I can stop right here," she said aloud, on her knees before the crack. The rock dug into her fingers. Margaret was ahead, on the upper snow slopes. It was getting light now.

"After all, Fay," she heard Margaret's voice, "we're perfect. You teach writing with all that woolgathering and horsing around of imagination, and I keep us solid with math and logic."

She, Fay, was an Easterner; precisely, a New Englander who taught in a college town of white clapboard buildings set on a village green. Joe taught there too. Fay arranged her classes in order to be home when her children came home. She could be counted on to make pies for church suppers. But she could see that the folks she ran into at the post office felt uncomfortable with her peeling nose and raw brow. *Rash* was the word she picked up on the supermarket line. It made her smile at her weather-browned hands.

Margaret had spent four years in a New England college, which was where they had met and first climbed together. Then she had returned to Berkeley.

"You're more rooted than I am," Fay told Margaret, "and if we didn't climb together every summer that would be the end of us." She watched Margaret's hands in the Cascades, the Alps, once in the Andes, one holding the pot steady, the other stirring the dinner, the skin taut and fine-lined as an etching. Hairline thin, white scars.

The two of them had gone climbing even when her children were small, even when Joe said two weeks was his limit. Then he changed his mind. "We love canned spaghetti, Fay. Take three."

Margaret never had kids. She hardly had a husband. "Oh, Richard?" Fay heard impatience and saw Margaret's eyes clench whenever his name came up around others. Then she'd laugh. "Gave him up for climbing." Margaret let go of nonessentials, going through her climbing pack in the Purcell Range, tossing out a sweater, a fistful of rock gear, half her gorp. "Hasn't been used in the last three days. Gets dumped. Too burdensome." Yet on that trip Margaret pulled out dry mittens when Fay soaked hers.

Margaret, fitting her fingers into narrow cracks, slotting chocks as precisely as a surgeon, climbing the hard bits fast, placing her left foot, then the right, one time only. If Margaret could lead the pitch, Fay knew she could follow. They were the same size.

She hadn't called Joe after she found out. He wouldn't have asked her to come home, but just hearing his ordinary voice would have put an end to it.

Back in Talkeetna when the notion not to go through with the climb struggled to surface, she had squashed it down. Stomped on it, as her kids would say. Because if she had paused to consider her options, like a rational human, she would have given the whole thing up. Now wasn't the time to come to grips with what had happened to Margaret. So, all she had to do was keep on track, like a lioness out for a night's hunt, keeping to the scent, not letting in details that didn't pertain. She had never done anything like this. She wasn't a solo climber. But, that was the thing: she didn't consider this a solo ascent.

She crawled back from the crack and pushed up. Her knees had stiffened from kneeling too long. She stood in the alcove, took off her pack and stowed her headlamp, which she had never turned on. "That was a damn fool thing, to climb without your light, Fay." Margaret's mother-hen tone. Fay saw Margaret's fingers rake off her hat and push through tangled black hair, through that central plume of snowy-egret white.

Her right elbow ached and she pumped her arm once or twice, feeling the tendon resist. Below, a shadow welled, but far out on the earth's rim heaved countless mountains, frosted peaks in pale pink rows.

She yawned in the cloudless dawn and shut her eyes, weary but strong after a night of climbing. She stretched, arms raised, standing at the mouth of the alcove. "I'm still good at this," she said aloud to Margaret.

After the avalanche they had backed off to the Wind Rivers, the Tetons, blaming their retreat on cranky knees, stiff wrists, reluctant elbows and shoulders. But this Alaskan mountain adhered to their minds like ice to rock.

She hunched on her pack and felt the crushing weight of the rope. Separately they had run their East- and West-Coast hills with packs of rocks, training for the fiftieth-birthday climb. Spent hours on the phone.

As she moved to the lip of the alcove she spotted the sling looped over a horn of rime-crusted rock. She knelt again and removed her pack. Bleached to dull rust, the sling was frayed and stiff and tore away lichen when she peeled it off. She held it in her gloved hands and time spun out again. Margaret was bending to sling the rock, rigging the rappel with her largest red sling, after the avalanche, when they were together again. Fay stuffed the sling in her pack. It smelled so cold here, like the inside of a meat locker. Her knees groaned when she pushed up with her palms.

Then she backed out of the alcove. Moved onto the snow slope, and adjusted her tools for climbing. She stood a moment on her front points, looking up, scanning the high slopes for safety, for a dark speck moving. The summer was dry, the snow well consolidated. The sun bounced off the snow's surface, blocking her vision. *Thunk, thunk.* Margaret was ahead, moving for the summit. And she was following.

Margaret wasn't on the summit. She searched the sheltered side of the boulders. Margaret wasn't sprawled on the snow with the gorp bag open, hat askew, sweat beads like jewels on her upper lip, tan hand offering the canteen. "Drink, Fay, to another strong mountain!"

She let the wind push and tug and rattle her clothing. Her ungloved hand sprang out to ridges, vanishing into farther ridges, kaleidoscopic changes in the glittering light. She had never felt so alive.

Margaret must be behind, still on the route. In the darkness it was easy to pass her by. "That's logical, Fay." Margaret's soothing voice in the wind steadied her.

Her eyes smarted and she bit her knuckles. Her teeth chattered even though she was soaked in sunlight. That summer in the Cascades when every summit had been in clouds, Margaret had said, "What the hell, Fay, who said we climb for just the views?"

They had planned to rappel and downclimb the route anyway. She couldn't possibly miss that snowy-egret crest on the way down. She would have to guard against knocking off loose rocks, chunks of snow and ice, with Margaret below her now.

On the sixth rappel—she counted to keep her mind alert—the 'biner gate the rope passed through wavered. She watched it open and shut, open and shut, from the tension, like a wagging finger. She had forgotten to lock it. She hated rappelling.

She watched the rope slide around in the curve of the 'biner, gaining on the gate, backing off. She felt a white heat in her head that made the 'biner glisten a foot tall, remembering when Margaret fell down that snow slope in the Selkirks with nothing in. An easy slope. Fay had been taking in the view, paying out rope in a dreamy way. Then, out of the edge of her eye, she had caught Margaret shooting by, like a sack of laundry. She had dug in her boots and braced herself, more as a way to pass the time than anything else. Her anchor hadn't been up to this. Then her vision had cleared and she could distinguish each snow crystal on her gloves as she let run a deliberate length of rope. Slowly, she clamped down the belay. "You hauled me out of the rinse/spin cycle," Margaret had hooted, safe, back in their tent, their thin voices shrill and high, six candles blazing.

The high, bright light dimmed. The glacier was in shadow when her feet touched it and there was a cold wind. The last light flicked over the summit. By now the wind up there had blown away her footprints.

She started walking toward the tent, feeling cold. Her jacket smelled of wet, metallic cold. She could see—yes!—a hand waving out of the tent door, jerking like red flagging in the bitter glacial wind.

Climbing! "As close as we'll come to flying," Margaret said after every climb. "Just like you New Englanders say every fall, 'I've never seen the foliage *this* beautiful!'"

"We mean it, always," Fay said.

"So do I," Margaret answered. They were in the tent on a mountain, drinking tea with sugar, cold fingers wrapped around warm cups and grinning like kids on Saturday.

A great darkness welled up, obscuring the glacier, ensnaring her feet. She was closer now, and saw steam from the cook pot wafting out the tent door.

Professor Simon is in a coma, the crushed-ice voice had said. Coma: a dark, hard land where move after move is at the limit of ability. Then an endless drop.

She was worn now. The ache in her knees made her stop in her tracks, and she pressed gloved hands to the sides of her face. She felt her eyes swell, then a stream was moving down her cheeks, over her chin, soaking her gloves. She was safe, but a panic rode in her throat. She began to run, smearing tears with her wet gloves, blinking back darkness, lurching toward the flapping tent.

Nan Watkins

Writing the Wind

for Ellen

As long as I can remember, I have been attracted to windy places and have been excited about taking a trip, no matter how small. A passion for the journey is what led me to walk the streets of Casablanca, to camp on the North Rim of Grand Canyon, to watch the sun rise over the Himalayas high above the Kathmandu Valley. I remember the excitement of the windy places of my girlhood vacations on the beaches of Barnegat Bay and Nantucket, and the thrill of raising a homemade American flag on the windy edge of the Rhone Glacier on the Fourth of July. This passion also led me, at sixteen, to cross the Atlantic on an old student ship, standing for hours on the deck in the wind.

Now I was setting out on another trip, this time to Ireland and

Wales. My affinity for Celtic civilizations was calling me again, and I was off to explore the west coast of Ireland and to return to Wales, the land of my ancestors. I wanted to find people still living in simplicity from the land and the sea. And I wanted to pursue my lifelong affair with the wind.

For someone who loves wind, Ireland and Wales are the right places to be. Situated on islands in the North Atlantic, they receive the brunt of the winds coming across the whole expanse of ocean. In both countries I was attracted to the coastlines where the winds howled along the beaches and cliffs, and I stood wrapped in a zipped-up coat, with scarf flying and cap snug on my head against the June and July weather.

When I landed at the airport in Dublin, I was greeted by the cheerful smile of Joan O'Flynn. Joan, whose blond hair shone above her lavender jacket, was an Irish friend I had come to know back home in North Carolina. I arrived on a "soft day," she told me, humid with a gray drizzle in the air.

In the next days, I made my way to the west coast of County Mayo along the freezing stormy North Atlantic. There I found refuge with an old couple who lived snug and sheltered from the wind in their small cottage on "The Hill" in Corraun, a community of a few houses overlooking the incredibly beautiful Clew Bay. I joined them in the kitchen around a slow-burning peat fire for a midday meal and a mug of hot tea. Then that afternoon I set out alone to walk the beach.

Of course there was wind. It was a rare, brilliant day of sun, showing off the deep colors of the Irish coast at its best. Across the cobalt-blue water of Clew Bay I could see Croagh Patrick crowned with its halo of clouds. I sat on the edge of a high dune and watched the myriad facets of sunlight sparkling on the water. I tried to collect my thoughts. It was difficult to center down; my body had been in motion so much of the time. My senses had been assaulted, though pleasantly, with so many new experiences, and it was hard to concentrate with that infernal wind roaring in my ears, coming at me from behind. What I need is a quiet place out of the wind, I thought. I moved forward and stepped down under the grassy ridge of the dune onto the warm sand. By sliding down a little further, I discovered that the wind shot over my head, providing me with a haven of warmth and stillness on the leeward side of the shore. I lay back and relaxed, watching singular clouds change shape as they moved by overhead. In these clouds I saw my life parading across the sky: first a child, then a wife-mother, then a woman walking on her own.

If too many men, I said to myself, spend their lives fighting battles for turf and dominion over rival clans, too many women spend too much of their lives defining themselves in relation to others. In my case, I lived my childhood in my passion for music. I played the piano four hours a day and raced across windy beaches. Looking back, that's what I remember. Then I burst out of my first family into the world, defining myself as musician, adventurer. When I married, I slipped into the family I would help create and became wife and mother for nearly thirty years. But I could feel a shift even as I was making my vows on my wedding day. When the veil was lifted, I felt I had lost my liberty. My attempt to maintain my individual freedom within family life became a daily struggle. Like so many wives and mothers before me, I gradually sacrificed my own will for what I thought was the good of the family. I knew something was wrong, but I couldn't grasp how to right it.

In order to give my life meaning, I defined myself as both heart and anchor of my family. It was inconceivable to me then, that we— husband, wife, son, daughter—could break apart. But after many years, the inconceivable happened, not once, but twice. In the black of a winter night, the phone woke us from sleep. It was a stranger calling to tell us our son was dead of cardiac arrhythmia. He had been lying on a sofa watching the eleven o'clock news with a friend, when his heart, inexplicably, stopped beating. Peter was just twenty-two, standing tall and handsome on the crest of his manhood, and now a strange doctor was saying he did not exist. Never, never, have I felt so helpless, so useless. And, oh, I had not been there to comfort him in his dying as I had been present to hold him in my arms at his birth. For a long time I was drawn into the darkness of that black night. My body grew so exhausted from the strain of the loss that I felt I was a hundred years old. Every minute I was afraid my daughter would die, and I lost all desire to live myself. Then gradually, but also rather quickly, the rest of the family I had worked so hard to build fell apart. The cord that once had bound my husband and me together grew taut, then snapped. Our daughter, stunned and confused, went her own, tentative way.

Abruptly I found myself living alone in a little white house with a porch, overlooking a long, grassy lawn and the Smoky Mountains beyond. My moments of peace came when I drank my tea each afternoon on the porch, pouring it from a china teapot which my mother had given me just before she died. I sat out on that porch in all kinds of weather, taking the necessary and long-overdue moments for myself in contemplation of where I had been, and gathering strength to move on.

During that time, I took control of my life. It seems second nature to me now. I am no longer married but live in a no-less-holy alliance. I live with a sovereign man and enjoy my own sovereignty as a woman—finally.

The solitary and hypnotic clouds passing by overhead in the

midday sky had become a bank of gray mist. Turning my head, I saw a yellow wildflower bobbing in the wind. It made me think of Joseph Campbell, how he held up a daisy, and with a broad smile, asked, "Meaning? People want life to have meaning? Does this flower ask, 'What is the meaning of life?' No! It just blooms. It just *is!*" And that's the way I see my life now. Just being; no questions asked about the meaning.

When my Welsh friends Wil and Rosemary Rees greeted me at the Fishguard Dock, they were all smiles. We picked up our conversation of two years before as easily as if it had been yesterday.

We headed back home to Laugharne, the seaside town nestled in a valley out of the west wind, on the south coast of Wales. It is famous for its Norman castle and the Boat House that served as the last home of Dylan Thomas. This place is so much like home to me that each time I leave it, I feel as if I am ripping my own roots out of the soil. I first came to Laugharne when I was twenty, with my sister, to see for myself where the legendary Welsh poet had lived. Then I returned two years ago to visit the land of my ancestors and live with Wil and Rosemary in their bungalow for six weeks. Now I had come back again, attracted by the simple way of life in the Welsh town that lives side by side with the rhythm of the tidal river Taf. Every six hours the waters of the Celtic Sea and Carmarthen Bay pour into the riverbed of the Taf, flooding its banks, and every other six hours the waters recede and flow back out to sea. This whole miracle is accomplished by the moon, that sphere of silver light, that muse, which rises and sets to the music of its own rhythm, over both river and town.

I love taking walks with Rosemary. She is a fifth-generation native of Laugharne and knows the town and its long history by heart. Everywhere we go, she tells me stories from her childhood about the local people, the "Larnies," as she calls them. She remembers Dylan and Caitlan Thomas when they lived with their three children in the Boat House. She tells me stories of her grandfather and uncle who were sea captains, how her grandfather lost his left arm in an accident at sea. She takes me over stiles, across potato fields and on dirt paths through woods to a hidden little church in Llandawke. When we push the church door open, we hear the hum of a thousand bees buzzing against dusty cobwebbed windowpanes. To the left of the simple altar she shows me the marble coffin of Margaret de Brian, who died in the thirteenth century. She was sister to the lord of the great castle in Laugharne, and somehow ended up here in this forgotten church.

We are headed out to cross the river Taf, walking down our steep driveway, down Gosport Street and across the Grist Square. We walk the cinder path below the castle and continue on the red rocks that serve as foundation for the Boat House and the old Ferry House next door. Because of the strength of its tidal currents, no one swims in the Taf these days. Rosemary remembers seeing her best friend, age ten, sucked into the current off the jetty where they were swimming as children, and drown. So she has deep respect for the power of the river.

We slip out of our sandals and begin walking over the damp sand and mounds of seaweed drying in the sun. It is low tide, and what had been underwater last evening is now sandy river bottom exposed to the sun. The wind picks up as we walk along the shore, next to the deepest channel of the river that always contains fresh water, flowing down from its source in the hills. Rosemary leads me out onto a plateau of warm sand that we walk over until we come to the river at its shallowest point. There, we cross fresh warm water, feeling the tug of the current on our legs. We walk across slippery black mud, and Rosemary tells me its story: it is called "slime" and is a mixture of river mud and coal dust from the freighters that used to come up the river to deliver coal. The Larnies would gather the slime in baskets, mold it into balls and let it dry briefly, before poking a hole through it with a stick. These slime balls were excellent slow-burning fuel for the fires. They would glow hot all night long so that the women would still have a fire to start cooking breakfast when they woke in the morning.

As we walk on, I gather cockle and mussel and razorfish shells. We walk past the Scar, a point thrusting out into the river where it makes a turn to the left around the base of Sir John's Hill. Rosemary says the Scar is always covered with seaweed and looks the same today as it did when she was a child. We stop to look at the sand that harbors the cockle beds, where air bubbles come to the surface, then walk on to a line of fishermen's stakes, standing upright in the sand. Across the river channel is the Ginst, a windy stretch of strand where thousands of rabbits inhabit the grassy dunes, yet another place where Rosemary ran as a child. We stand and survey the huge expanse of open sand, the riverbed, marveling at how broad it actually is. We look across to the medieval town and see it from a completely different perspective. Then, watching the placement of the sun, Rose says we had better turn back, so we'll have plenty of time to cross the river before the tide comes in. We turn around and walk back closer along the river channel. Finally, we reach the crossing point, and legs tired, we fall into the warm water, letting it wash over us, clothes and all. We can't help laughing; it feels so much like being children again. Rose tells me she hasn't taken this walk in years, and that it is bringing back all sorts of memories for her.

We sit in our own spots in the rushing water, sinking into the sandy bottom as the force of the wind and water pushes against our backs. While Rose becomes lost in the memories of her childhood, I am thinking that the river is like a feminine force, flowing softly, yet firmly, around me. I can easily identify with the flowing motion, always moving on, yet definable in its own right. It is constantly in a state of change. Motion is its very essence. I love liquid and swimming and water. I think of the river Liffey carrying the woman's name Anna, and wonder if the Taf has a feminine first name, too.

In a time when it is not always popular to praise the feminine, I can say I love being a woman. I think of coming into my own, belatedly, but nonetheless vibrantly: of being myself, and doing what I desire to do. I think of the sheer thrill, now, of composing my own music, performing and recording it. "Windblown Watkins," the reviewer said of the photo on the cover of my first solo album. That photo was taken right here: in the sands by the river Taf.

I consider the women I have known in my life. I think of Gail who used to say, "I have to get out of the house. I can't stand being alone with my own thoughts." I never feel like that. I love my own thoughts. I think of Mona and Shanti, two beautiful sisters I visited in Nepal, how they lead their lives of grace as wives and mothers in an ancient country where women are trying to find a place for themselves in the modern world. I think of Rani living in Lagos, Nigeria. She's caught in a corrupt society where nothing works, and bribery and brutality are the order of the day. "I'm so tired of the fight, of the constant haggling," she says. I think of Les who is struggling with the nightmare of Parkinson's disease. "I have to dance with it or I'll go mad," she tells me. "I am dying." "We are all dying," I say. And that makes me think of Renate, so beautiful, talented, sensitive, kind. The deepest conversations I have ever had with a woman were with her. But

Renate was dying of leukemia in Germany while I was innocently writing her cheerful letters from North Carolina. When I received the black-bordered card in the mail announcing her death, I couldn't believe it. I hadn't even had the chance to say good-bye, to wish her farewell, to tell her I loved her.

I was sinking deep into the sandy river bottom now. The water was approaching my neck. I looked over at Rosemary, and she was getting up out of the water. We shook ourselves off, like dogs after a cool bath, and laughed at the sight we would make walking back through town. We returned to the red rocks and dry seaweed beneath the Boat House. As we sat down to clean our feet and put our sandals back on, I heard the sound of waves forming in the river channel. It was the tide coming in. "We're just in time," Rose said. The salt water from the sea was meeting the fresh water from the hills and trying to overpower it. Of course it was succeeding, and each minute it progressed a little further up the channel. The sea was flowing into the river and making it overflow its banks. We stood awhile and watched. The wind and the sun were slowly drying our clothes. When we reached home, we looked back toward the river. The broad sands we had walked were once again covered with water.

That evening, my last in Wales, as I walked alone by the river in the slow-setting sunlight, I could hear the sound of the water birds' cries punctuating the steady drone of the wind. Nature's music, I thought, and I remembered the "singing fence" on the Isle of Skye from a previous trip I had taken to Scotland. It was a fence of metal pipes at the edge of a cliff high above the sea, and when the wild wind blew through the pipes, it produced a music as haunting as the pipes of Pan. For a moment, my heart leaped, knowing that on this journey my body, too, like that magic metal fence, had become an instrument of the wind.

~

I'm back home now in North Carolina at the old farmhouse with the tin roof that has stood more than a century on these sixty acres. It is raining softly. A soft day, as Joan O'Flynn would say. Sitting outside on the porch, I listen to the whir of the hummingbirds' wings as they fly in for their early-morning feed. It is my son's birthday today. He would have been twenty-nine if he had lived. I'll go to my local Saint David's Church and play his favorite Bach on the organ, the way I used to bake him his favorite angel food cake. The music will fill the old wooden church, and the sound will flow out the tall, open windows and be carried by the wind of the Southern Appalachians toward heaven, just as the wind carries Buddhist prayers written on colored silk flags up over the Himalayas to God. The wind is my winged messenger to all those I have loved, and to those who have left this earth before me.

For a lifetime, I have carried on a magnificent affair with the wind. Everywhere I have gone and been, the wind has greeted and dismissed me, pushing me ahead to new places and people, to new vistas and plateaus, like those reached inside, where the wind fills my spirit like a sail.

XI

PROTECTING THE EARTH

Gift of Wild Places

Reed

October 28-November 24

Gretchen Legler

Plum Tree

Our backyard garden in St. Paul is probably built on a trash heap. Craig and I deduced this as we dug during the first spring, and the second and the third. The winter freezing and thawing pushed up more bits of glass and pieces of twisted metal and coins and curled blue plastic. Under where we put the cabbage, Craig thinks, is an old driveway that was at one time slicked over with oil.

Outside the back door of our house, across the falling-down chain-link fence in the neighbor's yard, is a plum tree. This spring it is full of white blossoms, and it fills our kitchen with a sweet, clean smell.

I am working in the garden today, looking over the flats of tiny cabbages and tomatoes I started on the dining-room table in the house in March. The starts are out here in the part-sun underneath the plum tree, hardening off, getting plum-blossom petals dropped upon them, getting squirrel toothmarks and footprints on them, getting used to the real world.

While I am looking over the tiny peppers and cabbages and tomatoes, the neighbor comes over with a saw. He is a burly, big-bellied man with a kind face. He is out in the yard a lot, cleaning up, spreading grass seed, picking up trash, thrashing at weeds along the edges of his lawn with an electric grass-trimmer. His yard is clean. There is little in it but grass—a few teenage rose bushes in front, trying to get the hang of it, but that's all, except for this plum tree, and a black walnut tree on the other side of the yard.

I ask him what he's up to and he says he plans to cut the plum tree down. I laugh, thinking that it has to be a joke. I notice for the first time that there is another tree, or was, right beside the plum tree and that it has been cut away, so that there is just a stump. I also notice for the first time that on his side of the fence the plum tree has no branches—they've all been trimmed there, so the tree grows crook-edly, all the branches reaching out over our side of the fence, into our yard, like some wind-blown pine on a mountaintop.

I ask him not to cut it down. Just wait, I say. Wait until the plums come out. Wait at least until the fall, and let me get the plums, then you can go ahead. He tells me that the tree has been here a long time and that half the time it never has any fruit and when it does nothing eats it, not even the birds.

He tells me that he doesn't like trees in his yard. They shade the grass, for one thing. In fact, he's been thinking of taking down the huge black walnut tree that has grown next to the fence on the other side of his yard. Why, I want to know. He asks me if I've ever been hit on the head by a black walnut. The tree drops them all the time, he says. He's been hit on the head one too many times. I laugh again.

Whoever heard of such a thing? Cutting down a tree for dropping a walnut once in a while.

He agrees to postpone the cutting down of the plum tree and returns to his garage with his saw. It occurs to me that he was just looking for something to keep him busy today.

The little girl next door, the granddaughter of the would-be tree-cutter, tells me that everyone loves our garden. "How do they see it?" I ask her. They come over into her grandpa's yard and just peek over the fence, she says.

At first we had only two raised "French intensive" beds, twenty feet long and three feet wide. The next year we added three small beds which we turned into an herb bed, a pea bed and a bed for carrots and spinach and lettuce. The next year, we dug another twenty-foot-long bed. Year by year we ran out of room, so we started planting cabbages and tomatoes and herbs along the side of the house and even in the front yard.

The summer we first put cabbages in the front yard for lack of space, someone told me that there was still an ordinance in the city of St. Paul prohibiting residents from growing vegetables in view of the street. The person who passed this along to me thought the law was meant to discourage know-nothing immigrants from planting rutabagas in the medians.

I draw garden maps every year and put them in a three-ring binder, along with lists of seeds ordered, when the seeds were planted inside, when they sprouted and how well, when they were put out to harden off, and when I put them in the ground. On my maps I draw rhubarb and cucumbers and zinnias along the garage. One short bed bordering the gravel driveway I map out for tulips and daffodils in the spring, and daisies, purple coneflowers and mums in the summer and fall. Along with the peonies that hug one fence, I draw in horseradish. In the other beds I carefully draw in tomatoes (one whole twenty-foot bed), peppers, zucchini, broccoli, beans, and their companion herbs and flowers—petunias for the beans, nasturtiums and marigolds, sage, oregano, and summer savory for the other plants. The herbs and flowers planted alongside the vegetables help keep bugs away.

I only use two chemicals in this garden: Miracle-Gro to keep the tomatoes healthy, and Rotenone to get rid of cabbage worms and squash vine borers. But really, the best way to get rid of the cabbage worms and the vine borers is to pick them off the cabbage leaves every day and squish them, and to cut open the zucchini and yellow squash vines and scoop out the borers with a knife.

In every space in the yard we try to make room for something to grow. In the fall the little finches come and hang upside-down off the big sunflower heads to eat. The sunflower seeds that the birds drop we let go, so that they sprout up amid the broccoli. There are ferns in a shady spot by the side of the house where rain water flushes down. And there is a mint bed in another shady spot by the cracking, always wet foundation.

It is fall, and I am making notes for how to harvest the garden. I write:

> *What's Out There* (Do in this order):
> Carrots—pull: freeze 1/2, 1/2 in fridge (1/2 shreds, 1/2 sticks)
> Cauliflower—freeze
> Spinach—freeze
> Eggplant—1/2 frozen slices
> Zucchini—1/2 in shreds

Yellow squash—1/2 shreds

Cabbage (white)—soup and some in basement?

Tomatoes—sauce

Cabbage (red)—1/2 just freeze shreds, 1/2 in basement

Brussels sprouts—freeze

Jalapeños—dry, pickle

In addition to the above, I make sweet pickles, dill pickles, frozen, whole, hollowed-out green peppers, pickled beets, borscht, cabbage soup, sauerkraut, rhubarb pie, frozen rhubarb, gazpacho, ratatouille, frozen beans, bean soup, onions tied in a string, spinach soup, squash soup. The herbs—basil and oregano and four different kinds of thyme and marjoram and rosemary and sage and lemon balm—I cut and hang to dry in little bundles on the porch.

And then there are the plums.

It is late at night. I have been picking plums all day. I have no idea what I'm doing. I have never made plum jam or jelly. Craig brings in box after box of the plums and dumps them into the sink. They roll out of the box with a rumble; small, round, firm, orange-blushed plums pile up in the sink. I bend over the sink, putting my weight on one leg and, when that leg gets tired, switching to the other. I have on a white shirt, my gardening shirt, which is getting plum juice all over it. I wash the wild plums, then squeeze the pits out. I do this for hours and hours. Then I follow the directions in the cookbook. I make jelly (without skins) and jam (with skins). The hot jars start crowding the table, golden lids shining.

When the jam and jelly is all made I give a half-dozen jars to the neighbors. The would-be tree-cutter's wife, whom I catch in the back-yard in her dressing gown on a Sunday morning, seems confused. She is a thin, tired-looking woman. I can hear the years of cigarettes in her voice. "Okay," she says, taking the plum jam and jelly in her arms.

The next year, the man who wanted to cut down the plum tree plants corn and tomatoes along the fence and we see that when the plums come out, his grandkids, even though they have to reach way over to our side of the fence, are picking the small orange fruits and eating them.

.

Patricia C. McCairen

Looking for Glen Canyon

I take up the oars and row, enjoying the fluid sweep of the motion. Today I've decided to do eighteen miles. I'll pass up hikes at Buck Farm, Saddle and Little Nankoweap Canyons. If I had more time, I wouldn't need a schedule. If I had forty-five or sixty days, I might be able to cover the entire Grand Canyon. Then again, I might need a lifetime.

I come upon the talus from test holes that were dug into the Redwall at a proposed dam site. One of the great crimes against the earth, humanity and other living creatures would have been committed if David Brower of the Sierra Club had not taken full-page ads in the *New York Times* and *Washington Post* in June 1966, stating: "Only You Can Save the Grand Canyon from Being Flooded—for Profit."

Instead, the flood came in the form of protest from the public, resulting in a series of laws being enacted to save Grand Canyon from further development by dam builders.

Amen.

I hope. Although we live in an era of expanding environmental awareness, we also live at a time when a growing population has increased the demand for electricity and water. With particular irony, the Southwest, with little natural water available, has become a desirable place to live. It is dry, it is warm, it is sunny. One might think it is an ideal environment, and yet people coming from the eastern and midwestern cities to escape the snow and cold proceed to air-condition it to escape the heat. Or they come from California to get away from the crowds and pollution and debase the new area. Many desert dwellers waste water, because of ignorance, laziness or selfishness. Bright green lawns, deciduous trees and swimming pools abound, demanding water that is not naturally available. This extravagant use of water is shocking and the low cost encourages waste. As some communities have discovered, consumption can be drastically reduced by increasing the price of water, but few have taken this important step to conserve water.

The quickest answer to a shortage of water is to build a dam. This avoids the real issue of waste, and ignores the need for everyone to learn about conservation, an unpopular approach because it takes effort and sacrifice. Most often dams are pushed through by financiers and politicians who stand to increase their capital or enhance their influence by the inclusion of another dam in their territory. They are a dominant group of people who usually do not care about the damage incurred by their actions, and who frequently acquire public support by expounding upon the benefits, often imaginary, a dam will bring.

Behind most dams lies an irreplaceable wilderness, an area that can provide escape from the overcrowding, pollution, and frantic pace of the city. The greatest losses incurred when damming a river are often subtle: the simple pleasures of floating downstream, "the easy, natural way," as Huck Finn proclaimed; enjoying the serenity of throwing a fishing line into a quiet pool; picnicking next to the sound of water playing over rocks.

Although Grand Canyon has no dams within its environs at this time, it nevertheless shows the effects of having the giant plugs of Glen Canyon Dam at the upper end and Hoover Dam at the lower end. The Colorado River is no longer "too thin to plow, too thick to drink," as it was when Major John Wesley Powell ran it. Now, the river is a deep green color, apparently due in part to algae and in part to the elimination of the one hundred forty million tons of silt that once scoured the Canyon every year. Instead the silt settles out in Lake Powell, trapped there to extend the life of Hoover Dam, over three hundred miles downriver. One dam built to save another. Today the sediment in Grand Canyon has been reduced to an average of twenty million tons, not enough to replace beaches when a high water release washes them away.

Before the construction of Glen Canyon Dam, the river fluctuated with the seasons, frequently raging at one hundred thousand cubic feet per second in the spring with the snow melt from the Rockies, before dropping throughout the year to winter lows. Although it is commonly thought that dams enable river runners to have a longer season on the water, it is interesting to note that many of the old-timers ran the Colorado during the winter months, when water is traditionally at its lowest flow. In addition, the elimination of annual spring floods upsets the natural cleansing effect of high water. Tamarisk trees, native to the Middle East, take over, choking out the indigenous vegetation; rapids are able to grow in size and difficulty; and various human scars that mar beaches are left to remain as a painful reminder that nature has been checked by humans from doing her proper job.

Glen Canyon Dam has had another dramatic impact upon the canyon with the change in water temperature. Before the dam was built, the river ranged between temperatures of forty degrees in winter and eighty degrees during midsummer. With the water being drawn two hundred feet below the surface of Lake Powell, it never sees the sun and enters the river channel at a chilly forty-five degrees—all year long. This drop in temperature has caused the extirpation of some of the native fish and increased the danger of running the river for humans. Hypothermia is a serious, life-threatening condition; a long swim in forty-five-degree water can result in death.

Lake Powell, created by Glen Canyon Dam, is the second largest manmade lake in the United States. It is one hundred eighty miles long with nine trillion gallons of water and eighteen hundred miles of shoreline. It receives hundreds of thousands of visitors annually who contribute to the reservoir's pollution with heavy metals and human waste. Fuel from motors dumps the equivalent of the Exxon Valdez oil spill into the lake every four years. As popular as the lake is, I somehow doubt that if it disappeared today it would be as sorely missed as Glen Canyon, the exquisite place that Lake Powell drowned. The loss of Glen Canyon is real, felt by the people who never had a chance to visit it, along with those who were fortunate enough to spend time between its sandstone walls before it disappeared.

If the Environmental Protection Agency had been in existence in 1956, when Glen Canyon Dam was authorized by Congress, it is doubtful the dam would have been approved. The government misled people and only David Brower and a few environmentally focused people raised a cry of concern. Unfortunately, it wasn't enough to prevent the dam from being built.

Now, however, there is a glimmer of hope that the Colorado River can be restored to a natural state. In November 1996, the Sierra Club Board of Directors voted unanimously to support an effort to drain Lake Powell. This initiative is supported by the Glen Canyon Institute, Friends of the Earth, International Rivers Network and the Earth Island Institute. New studies show that Powell reservoir loses approximately one million acre feet of water every year to evaporation—enough water to meet the demands of cities the size of Phoenix or Salt Lake City. Removing Glen Canyon Dam would improve riparian life in Grand Canyon and farther downstream at the Sea of Cortez estuary. It could also help avert a potential catastrophe to Arizona, Nevada, Southern California and Mexico if the dam cracked due to poor engineering, flood, landslide, earthquake or human intent. The cost is insignificant when compared to the damage the dam inflicts on the environment. Dismantling Glen Canyon Dam and draining Lake Powell is an endeavor worthy of serious consideration.

I turn my back on Marble Canyon Dam Site and glide along on a river that hides all trace of my presence. The miles pass by quickly. The river meanders past Royal Arches, Tatahatso and Hansbrough Points, President Harding Rapid and Triple Alcoves; names applied to cliff forms and water currents by man, hoping to gain some connection to the infinite, or perhaps once again prove his mastery over nature.

Gabrielle Daniels

A City Girl Discovers the Forest

A walk in the woods

*I*t's usually early afternoon when I take a walk. Today I've been up since about eight. I've been writing since nine-thirty. I've eaten lunch. I want the meal to circulate in my body rather than lie like stones slowly melting in my stomach during a siesta. I slide into my don't-stop-green Sportos, take up the walking stick leaning near the door and head up the trail.

Actually, many trails wind around Hedgebrook Farm, a women writers' colony, my home for two months. Some are large enough for a little truck, some are simple footpaths. I am fascinated by the little heap of stones which appear here and there. I am unsure whether they are pointing out a new path, or how much farther on this path there is to go.

It's a semblance of wilderness here; there are six cottages and the farmhouse where we meet for dinner and other activities. Grasses and secondary growth encroach, seemingly waiting for their chance, then the woods begin. The nearer one gets to the property line, several long thin silvery wires broken at times simply by the weight of a bush, one hears cars a few hundred yards away on Washington's 525, and closer, the activity of neighbors, sawing, shouting, or even shooting on the next lot, as it is also deer hunting season. I have yet to see a deer, although some of the other writers have seen them. They have watched each other behind the barriers of wood and curiosity, glass and fear. It is safe here and there are no guns.

Right now, I feel like a deer. I can't believe that the quiet is so safe. Sunlight peers through the trees. I lean on my third leg, the piebald walking stick. Hearing tree frogs call to each other, I am startled. I strain my ears for an enemy that never appears. A yellowed leaf spirals and flutters to my feet like Mary Poppins' umbrella.

Spider webs flatten against my face like veils. I take off my glasses, dry wipe my face, dust my hair for creepy crawlies and brush my shoulders. But a dragonfly takes dead aim between my chest and lands, attracted by the vivid red in my pullover. It has been a long time since I've had this kind of attention; I frantically shoo it away. When I was a child, my boyfriends and I called them mosquito hawks, because they fed on mosquitoes, the carriers of disease. Diseases that existed long before we were born: such as yellow fever, *vomito*, the New Orleans scourge. Seeing a mosquito hawk is a pleasure; they have disappeared even from the open spaces in the suburbs, like the doodle bugs and ladybugs that we'd let crawl all over our hands. We watched caterpillars munching on poinsettias, sucking milk, green lizards and if we were lucky, small snakes. We wished for a real hurricane, so the levees would "bust" and we'd see the water moccasins and even a gator.

Only certain insects have survived in the cities. Flies. Ants. Moths. Cockroaches. The most hardy. Mostly scavengers. Pests.

The mosquito hawk gets the message. It has dropped down on some tetchy animal—me. It flies high, takes a ninety-degree turn toward the berry patch and disappears.

Mushrooms have sprouted everywhere since the rain arrived, in many sizes, shapes and colors. A gigantic white mushroom looms from under a bush. It must be a toadstool, but it is as big as a child's wagon wheel, with a thick stem. Enough for Holly, our house manager, to brew several bowls of soup, if it is not poisonous. Several mushroom patches are already turning brown, fading back into the dead soil, ready for another episode of rain. I think it is like playing hopscotch, studying the ground, self-consciously avoiding where they grow. Where I least expect, I nearly mash one growing defiantly purple and bumpy and alone in the middle of the trail.

There has been some logging and clearing for firewood for the cottage dwellers, with little caches curing, stacked in the open and covered with plastic. During the storms, some trees have blown down, or are on their way to the ground. They lean as if defying gravity, hoping that something like a nearby tree will break their fall. *Catch her, catch her.* Dead trees wear little orange ties about them as if dressed nattily for death, though their roots still cling tenaciously to the soil. Some look naked and sad, their stark boughs reaching out in the air, *why, why?* The stumps are another story: happy, teeming condominiums. If it isn't lichen spreading on the stump, it will be insects chewing through the bark, weeds choking the roots.

The trail, strewn with fading, wet leaves and fallen branches, crunches or slides under my feet. The sound scares off a blue heron, the first I've ever seen in the wild, which spreads its magnificent wings and alights on a nearby bough, watching me. I sit on a rock beside

Green Pond. Unlike the manmade waterfall and its pond, this pool doesn't drain off. It is very still and black as yin with a burgeoning coverlet of algae, leaves, pollen and some kind of bog clover. The heron gazes, disapprovingly I think, over his shoulder at me. He wants me to leave. This was his pond. I am his predator and I could hurt him at age six or thirty-six. He will not come down closer for me. He will groom himself and wait for me to leave. I watch the stillness of the pond, the reflection of the trees framing it. A snapshot will not do justice to this picture. The air is fresh; I breathe in and the trees breathe out; the lungs of the earth.

While driving from California on Highway 1, I remember encountering large-bed trucks, sometimes one behind the other, hauling sweet-smelling, fresh-cut timber to the mill like a funeral cortege. I imagined the sap still running like blood in my veins, shocked. Their cousins, other trees, lined the highway. *What did they think?* Pieces of bark and pine needles flew off by the wayside. Some thudded on my windshield, then caught in my wipers. Hawks above me flew from branch to branch as if fleeing from a sight.

Then, in Oregon I saw a timber graveyard. I was astounded. Like many photographs and documentaries I had seen of concentration camp victims, the logs were stacked. There were acres and acres of what was left of trees, denuded of leaves, branches, families of animals, the hum of wasps. Some appeared in various stages of rot. Bark had dropped off in places, exposing what I call the real skin of the wood; it looked speckled and discolored as if, separated from the soil, it had been poisoned. It is one thing to see a dead tree surrounded by its living cousins, and another to see a dead tree surrounded by its dead cousins. Men in their forklifts next to these poor giants resembled sinister Lilliputians. *Remember,* a random thought courses, *they need a job, too; they are just doing their job.* But I don't believe it. On the other side of the road, rising over more logs like a chapel presiding on a hill, lay mills, their relentless engines chuffing smoke into the sky.

And yet, in the little stove in Owl Cottage, I burn wood. Everyday, I haul logs up the small hill and, alternately, starter: newspaper or pine cones or small pieces of wood. This is the only heat in the cottage. And so I keep warm, feeding the flames. Making a fire, like writing, is an art, too. It's hard work to keep it stoked. I hate to waste kindling. Sometimes I let the kettle boil on the stove. Watching it, I thought it took about twenty minutes to bring it to a boil at two hundred degrees. The time was probably less. I live in a cottage framed in warm-colored wood. An owl sitting on a branch is carved above the hobbit windows. Sometimes I hear the beams and pillars creaking and settling and humming, and not just at night. The whole house is yet alive. The public radio announcer warns that much of the air pollution in Seattle and its environs is caused by wood-burning stoves. This morning, I open the stove door to find the sap from one of the logs is boiling, bubbling, popping. When I return from the bathhouse, the chimney puffs a greeting.

It is night

I've washed the empty lunch containers, placed them in the basket, folded the colorful paper tote in which I pack my breakfast when the after-dinner talk fades. The basket waits while I put on my coat, my Sportos if it has rained, then pick it up with the cottage key and the beam flashlight. I can't trust the good fortune of living in the country. How you can leave your cottage, your car unlocked, the windows wide open and challenging. I tried it once or twice until my thoughts hyperventilated. I worry because I have always lived in the city. I am a person who scratches her driver's license number on what little she possesses; who was robbed while a student; who leaves the lights blazing and the TV talking when I am gone at night. Whether I'm going into downtown Langley, or going to the farmhouse at night, I'll lock the door.

It is dark around four in the afternoon, as October has somersaulted into November as gently as scattering leaves. Less than a month to go at this writing retreat. A storm is buffeting the island, but it is mostly the wind; the rain hasn't yet arrived. The trees are swaying with a *whoom, whoom!* I sweep the flashlight in a protective arc every few paces. I chose it at the Price Club because the packaging promised that the flashlight would be seen from two miles away. I pass the avenue where the bathhouse, the pump room and the wood pile lie. H's cottage is illuminated, but her porch light is off. All my antennae are up, *he could be behind any bush, the next tree,* though every vestige of common sense insists, *there's no one there.* Everything is rustling, twisting and bowing. The wind parts my unbuttoned coat like a knee between my legs; it flaps. I look up. The darkness reveals not trees but boughs like shadowy, many-headed Hydras. They could fall on me, their fantastic weight crushing me flat, to death. I feel like running, but I think, *if I run, I'll panic, and if I panic . . .* I take a deep breath as the wind swallows my face, whips my hair.

Home in the Heart

In East San Jose, near Ocala Avenue and Berona Way, across the street from Reid-Hillview Airport, behind the public library, there once was an open field.

It encompassed an entire city block. The planners could have extended the subdivision, but apparently there were big plans for this open field, which did not develop until my junior year in high school.

Until then, the surrounding neighborhood took the field for

granted. Like the mountain range beyond, it turned green, high with weeds and other growth in the fall and winter, and with the spring and summer became golden brown and brittle. The grass was mowed in the summer, and against the cracked adobe-like soil, it resembled dry spaghetti. In the winter, school-age children took delighted short-cuts through the squishy muck. Adventurous mothers would *boot up*, bend over and forage for wild dandelion greens, poke salad and other greens and onions. The women pointed them out for those who ventured past and didn't know their uses, or who thought the women were crazy for bending over what looked like weeds as diligent as farm workers in such a wild-looking place.

Then, without warning, the field was roped off. The bulldozers arrived. The soil flew in all directions as they made little hills and valleys, and paved a new shortcut. Destroyed were that year's and all subsequent years' patches of dandelion greens and onions.

The open field is now Ocala Park. It was carpeted with rolls and rolls of new weedless lawn laid from up hill to down dale. Young trees were planted. In one corner, there is a baseball diamond for Little League. The bathrooms can be freshly painted one day, and within twelve hours, covered with graffiti. At another corner, there is a center named for a Chicano community leader, with teeter-totters, swings and a sandbox.

But some mothers won't allow their children to play in the grass, afraid they would come up with a needle stuck in their hands. Drug deals are sometimes made in Ocala Park under hills, down dales, at night. Such a wild-looking place, after all.

Sometimes, I think black people forget that we once were an agrarian people. That for seventy-five or eighty years, we lived mostly on the land. That our most vivid cultural memories, even from the time before slavery, spring from our connection to the land. That we celebrated the harvest and believed in our own hands. That we often joined with the other original people, the Native Americans, whose respect for the land mirrored our own. *Runago, runago.* That we have always fought for our claim to this land, through hunger and debt. That when we continued on the land, the spirits continued to live with and within us.

And yet we try in the cities. The Fillmore District, where I spent my first two years in California, is now in the last stages of "redevelopment" and is almost unrecognizable to me. There, at the age of seven, I fell in love with real quarter-pound burgers and the busy, jooking bars. I saw the Ice Capades at the Winterland before the hippies flocked to concerts there. Today, the remaining black citizens, mostly elderly, fight in vain to keep the community gardens in two colorful blocks, incongruous to the surrounding highrises and condos marching from Pacific Heights.

The forest as desire

The forest is only what we choose to see, out of our fears and myths. Most of the time, it is dim and unknown. We hear the keening of hawks and eagles, the buzzing of cicadas mating, and we think there is danger. We attack without reason. When it is chopped or scythed down, when it is finally prone and overcome and cleared, there is nothing left but rotting stumps, space and dead leaves scattering on the wind. Generations are cut off, heredity and possibility for difference and change stand still for the sake of control. And so, where was the monster, after all? Where does it reside? Did it ever live among these boughs, these leaves? And the axes are turned in yet another direction. There, and there, and there. The endlessness, the open-mouthed voraciousness of the chase to *subdue*. Between court orders, let them sneak in and cut and haul the beautiful ones away. Despite periodic complaints, let the train of tank cars full of chemicals fall into the river, choking the fish, turning the clear blue waters into a smoky green, which mocks us. When can we finally congratulate the prince for slaying the dragon?

The black woman as wilderness. Unlike Sojourner Truth, however, the forest is forcibly trained, like bad nappy hair processed into good straight hair, until one tree looks like another. Every tree, like every black woman, is different, full of an intimate magic. We dare to name ourselves. Cypress, redwood, sycamore, chestnut, yucca, willow. Eartha, Andrewnetta, Oletha, Syrtiller, Mattiwilda. Straightened, dreadlocks, permanents, fades, jheri curls, finger waves, French braid, Afros, dooky braids. My name for the overnight braids that stuck out of my head, making my brothers and sister laugh: *Medusa*, after the mythological woman who turned men into stone, whose beautiful hair was turned into one mass of hissing snakes. And yet in the morning, my hair rises out of my braids from the coaxing of the comb into my seventies natural hair: soft, thick and high.

XII

Passages

Gift of Age

Elder
November 25-December 22

Betty Wetzel

Near Eighty—
and Tall in the Saddle

*N*ow this," announced our outfitter, "is a horse."

The seven of us stood in a circle inside the corral at the Holland Lake trail head as trim, white-moustached Jack Hooker explained the basic mechanics of riding a horse. He was obviously a good hand. His quiet handling of the big appaloosa mare, already saddled and bridled and ready for the ascent into the twenty-four hundred square miles of Montana's Bob Marshall Wilderness, was reassuring.

I needed reassurance. After living for many years next to North America's largest roadless preserve but never venturing into it, I had made up my mind to experience "the Bob" before my fast-approaching eightieth birthday. My husband, four grown children and six teenage grandchildren all pleaded too busy or too far-flung (or too chicken?)

for the ten-day pack trip. So I signed up with the White Tail Ranch of Ovando, Montana, on my own.

Jack Hooker and Bret Clarke, a wrangler, boosted me into the saddle of a big brown gelding called Badger, and adjusted the stirrups. Badger and I would become well acquainted but now it seemed to me that I was much higher off the ground than I remembered being when I grew up on a ranch outside of Roundup, Montana.

Jack headed us out without ceremony—twelve riders and seven pack mules. The well-maintained trail along the shore of Holland Lake, past roaring Holland Lake Falls and Upper Holland Lake, was lush with ferns and greenery, but it was all uphill. Occasionally, Jack called a halt to let the horses breathe and us dismount. This proved a questionable relief when I found my legs would barely support me, and I faced the problem of remounting. It seemed hours before we stopped to eat the sandwiches from our saddlebags at the crest of the Swan Mountains and looked back on the Holland Lakes and distant Mission Mountains.

It was a perfect, cloudless July day; the trail was spangled with brilliant wildflowers—whole hillsides of Indian paintbrush, lavender salsify, magenta vetch, golden arrowroot and giant tufts of beargrass— but the afternoon was agony. I gasped at the splendor and the steepness of the trail, and from pain.

The pack string passed us, but I was too preoccupied to notice. It was late afternoon when we left the trail to follow Jack to a secluded meadow where, to our great joy, camp was set up. After a short walk to reactivate our legs, we claimed our duffel bags and spread air mattresses and sleeping bags in our tents. I stripped off my clothes, got into my sweat-suit night gear and washed up in an icy stream nearby. Supper (turkey, mashed potatoes and gravy, cranberry sauce, corn on the cob, tossed salad, olives, fresh peaches on angel food cake with whipped cream and coffee) was served at six o'clock.

We were a motley bunch as we became acquainted around the evening campfire: a couple from Ireland who had read about the Bob in National Geographic; a woman from Texas on her ninth Bob Marshall trip; a seasoned couple from North Carolina in their forties; a Seventh-day Adventist preacher from Lewistown, Montana; and I, the senior member. Still washing dishes was Karen, Jack's wife, who ramrodded the outfit as cook, business manager, nurse, friend and counselor.

Although it was not yet nine o'clock and still daylight, I left the campfire circle for my tent. I was exhausted. Everything hurt. Jack Hooker had just reported that we had ridden fourteen miles uphill from 4,031 feet at Holland Lake to our Lena Peak camp at 8,364 feet. It was obvious to me that he, knowing there is no painless method of equestrian conditioning, had elected to get it over with.

The morning commotion of horses and mules, the smell of wood smoke and coffee and the feeling of excrutiating pain woke me. It was humbling for one who fancied herself fit, if aged. It was some comfort, however, to hear groans coming from neighboring tents.

In the morning light everything from the chiseled mountains surrounding us to the miniature flowers just creeping out from receding snow banks was stunningly beautiful. The ground was carpeted with trillium, spring beauty, gentians, Alpine forget-me-nots, mountain heather, and glacier lilies. It was springtime in the Rockies.

After a breakfast of pancakes, bacon and eggs and much strong coffee (the Irish had tea), we rolled up our sleeping bags, packed our duffels and prepared to hoist our sore and chafed bottoms into the saddles. Fleece padding appeared to cushion two of the women.

Yesterday, we had complained that the ride was all uphill. Today, it was all downhill over steep slopes and rocky switchbacks.

The vertical ride rubbed fresh saddle sores and tortured different muscles. We rode silently, balancing ourselves as best we could, as our horses picked their way down the impossible trail overlooking a deep canyon.

In and out of north-slope forests of lodgepole pine and tamarack that shaded mosses, ferns and bouquets of foamflower, queen's cup and white bog orchids, we plodded, with now and then a blessedly level meadow brilliant with wild pink hollyhock, fireweed, golden arrow leaf, balsam root, gaillardia, yarrow. Even in our state of torpor, this over-abundance of beautiful sights and smells gladdened our hearts. The ugly reality of the burn of the 1988 forest-fire season ended the splendor. Instead of lush forest, the charred ghosts of trees hovered over us mile after mile. But it was interesting to see a new, young forest of lodgepole pine springing up to begin rejuvenation.

A downed tree blocked the trail and we dismounted, crawled under or climbed over and waited up the trail while Jack and Karen led the horses and eventually the pack mules around the high side. While eating our lunch as we waited, we saw a western tanager, Montana's most brilliantly colored bird.

On the trail again, we faced the steepest downhill yet to the canyon floor and the swift, knee-deep water of the South Fork of the Flathead River that had sculpted this gorge. Jack didn't even pause as his horse plunged into the stream, but I was breathless as Badger slipped and struggled for footing in the swift current. We were more than ready to camp in a grove of trees beside the river.

This was the favorite campsite of the fisherpeople. They whipped out their fly rods, donned their waders and scattered up and down the river. This barely fished river is famous for native cutthroat trout.

It had been another fourteen-mile day. Around the campfire that night, Jack told us how to ride a horse. It was about time. Don't just sit there, he said. When the horse takes a step, you take an imaginary step so that your weight in the stirrups coincides with the movement of the horse. Move the weight off your bottom and onto your feet and knees. Downhill, lean back in the saddle and point your toes out, putting your weight on your heels. Try to sit up straight and maintain a rocking motion with the horse's stride. For the rest of the trip, I concentrated on Jack's instructions. We rejoiced that tomorrow was to be a layover day.

The next morning, Jack led a nature hike through meadows and forests above camp showing us how to distinguish lodgepole from ponderosa pine, larch from fir and spruce; how to spot the slash on giant ponderosas where Indians had stripped inner layers for food in the last century; edible plants and berries; pitch blisters on pine and fir that will stanch a bleeding wound or help kindle a fire; where to find squirrel nests or plants for tinder—in short, how to survive in the wilderness.

During the long twilight that evening, the anglers again fanned out and in no time returned with breakfast trout. It was catch-and-release from then until dark. Even I caught a fish.

Rejuvenated by sleep, a rest day and a fine breakfast, I became aware for the first time of what was involved in packing up the camp kitchen: wood-burning tin stove, cabinets, picnic tables, folding stools, dishes, cutlery, pans, meat, produce, bread boxes. All had to be bundled into tarps and loaded onto the mules, together with the tents, duffel bags and other equipment. I had already noticed the simple but delicious food that Karen produced. It was the result of careful planning and packaging of first-class ingredients prepared without fuss by a great cook. During our ten days, the dinner menu varied to include Mexican, Italian, Chinese and American cuisine. We ate steak, ham, chicken, pork chops; salads and vegetables;

cheesecake, cobblers and brownies—everything but ice cream. (This was no weight-loss outing.) And coffee! Here's the recipe: Bring a two-gallon pot of spring water to a boil; add one-and-a-half cups of regular grind coffee. When the pot again boils, add a cup of cold water.

I hadn't hired out to be tough. My great-grandmother crossed the country in a covered wagon, but she was young and accustomed to hardship. As a twentieth-century octogenarian, I cherished comfort. But I was eager to tackle the next day's ride which would parallel the White River and bring us our first view of the storied Chinese Wall. Using my newly learned horsemanship, the morning went well, almost without pain. Riding was becoming fun!

We lunched on a bluff opposite Needle Falls, which spilled out from a pool behind a stone "eye" and sprayed into a reflecting pool below. Some horses were grazing with a herd of elk on the mountain above the falls. Whose horses? Jack opined that they belonged to an outfit camped on another drainage. It dawned on me that in four days we hadn't met or passed a soul since we entered the Bob.

I was unprepared for the feeling of isolation. I had never encountered it in my several busy lives—growing up in Montana, raising four children and leaving the West in middle age to live and work in Southeast Asia. We had returned to live and work on the East Coast before retiring in Montana.

I've seen the Great Wall in China. Montana's unstructured, asymmetrical, disorderly, savage, freeform wall has it all over the rigid, artificial, forbidding, manmade fence that snakes over the Asian horizon. There's no comparison.

We stayed for a day in a grassy meadow underneath the wall, sharing our camp with deer, marmots and Columbia ground squirrels. From this vantage point and as we rode underneath, over and around the great wall, changing light and imagination seemed to people the weathered stone with giant heads from the Easter Islands, saints from European cathedrals, Buddhas from the Orient. Here and there mountain goats jumped with aplomb along the stone face, grazing on unlikely green clumps. The wall in China didn't have mountain goats.

The other side of the wall seemed like an anticlimax as we dropped down into low country with well-maintained trails, flies and mosquitoes—and backpackers and other outfitters entering the Bob from the east. I felt surfeited by the scenery, the same as I did when I stayed too long and looked at too many paintings in an art museum. My eyeballs were tired. The last day's ride to Benchmark staging area was easy.

My husband, Winston, and some of our family members were waiting at our home on Flathead Lake. They seemed relieved and amazed that I'd survived the 140-mile, ten-day pack trip. They had, it seemed, worried about grizzly bears. Well, we saw bear scat and claw marks, but bears avoid noisy humans and strings of two dozen horses and mules. So what if I'd been felled by a grizzly in the Bob Marshall Wilderness of Montana at the age of eighty? What a punch line for my obituary—what a way to go!

Jean Gould

Aamaa Didi

A woman walks back and forth, up and down over rice, drying it with her feet. Thin and barefoot, she holds an infant. Together they cannot weigh more than eighty pounds. At the Bagmati River near a Hindu temple, two bodies burn, tended by low caste men in rags. On the other side, women wash clothes on rocks, two men bathe and a child drinks. Bagmati means "mouth of the tiger."

Elsewhere in Kathmandu, at Swayambhunath shrine, for example, Buddhists chant prayers to the motion of wheels while small monkeys chatter. A black goat wanders on the steep part of the domed *stupa*, or shrine, as a vendor plays a gentle melody on a wooden flute.

On unpaved streets, beggars with stumps for arms or legs sleep in dusty corners decorated with marigolds. Offering peanuts for sale in wicker baskets, women with gold teeth smoke cigarettes.

Before this month is out, this November, I will be the rice woman, the Hindu, the Buddhist, the monkey, that black goat. I will become the marigold, the river, the temple, and yes, even the wooden flute, the beggar. I will give myself over to flags of prayer called wind horses. And more. Much more.

Just now, of course, I do not know any of this. Just now, I am spending my first full day in Nepal, where I have come to celebrate my fiftieth birthday. Today, a witness, I am outside the high peaks and blue-purple skies enveloping this city. Predictably, societal contrasts energize me: whether you kill a man or a cow, you serve a jail sentence of eighteen years; there is no law regarding the murder of women.

Why have I come here? Why not? Although I feel somehow ageless, I am willing to acknowledge, indeed find it necessary to mark fifty years of living, to reward myself for having made it this far.

That night, I wake myself laughing, the taste of hot peppers and beer still on my tongue. Opening the French doors of my hotel room, I find the air heavy and fragrant in the walled-in courtyard. Bougainvillea, a lavender color only hours before, is now gray in the absence of light. Standing at the threshold, naked, I imagine rolling in the thick grass just beyond. The joy of all that has brought me to this place holds me as I dare to step outside.

At dawn the next morning, women and men huddle against the cold in doorways draped with flowers, as I leave Kathmandu for Pokara and the hills of Annapurna. The valley is fogged in. While the rusting van wobbles me over these ancient roadways, fruit bats large as opossums hang from pine trees. I am to spend ten days in the Annapurna range tuning up for two more weeks trekking in the Everest foothills.

I have joined a group of six others, mostly Americans, including one married couple. The others, two women and two men, have come alone, as I have. We are all white. As the sun rises and the day becomes warmer, we compare notes on training, expectations, nutrition, jobs. The woman who is to share my tent, Ellen from Missouri, is smaller, younger, knows more than I do, and for once, that doesn't rankle me, as I note that her self-sufficiency parallels mine.

The journey is slow with frequent stops in villages I am told have no names. Everywhere, children's noses run. And it is striking to realize just how equally fathers share the caretaking of young children with such obvious pleasure. One carries an infant under his arm, swirls it around, places it on a table and then kisses it with abandon. A child of three or four tries to split wood with an axe under a father's gentle supervision. Fathers, uncles, even teenage boys hold, rock or play with children as the treasures they are.

It is true that poverty, at least as it is defined by Westerners, is everywhere. Emaciated dogs roam the streets, their menacing ribs protruding such that it seems that the flesh must be inside and bones on the surface. If there are sewers at all, they run open in narrow ditches. In defense, some in our group speak about their possessions at home and their abundant lives. Some talk of "Saturday Night Live" and hairdryers and the Dallas Cowboys. When I sit on a dusty hillside and children cluster around me, I try out the hundred or so words of Nepali I have learned by tape. Ellen takes photographs of us playing tic-tac-toe. Later, a little girl with bright, almond eyes sits in my lap laughing when I ask her to sing, and I feel happier than I can remember, having abandoned myself to these moments. When the children ask for pens, for candy, for money, I ask them to draw in my journal while I sing "I'm a Little Teapot," and others touch my face and eyelashes and earrings and hair. My own nose runs. *Kitaab*, I say.

Book. *Kalaakaara,* I say. Artist. I cannot think of the word for writer. But they are more interested in my children. *Ek,* I say, holding up one finger.

When we set out from Pokara the next day for our first climb, we are all anxious and full of energy from months of physical training and healthy food. Our *sirdar,* or guide, is Gelbu, an optimistic Sherpa who will stay with us both here and at Everest. Leaving the town, we zig-zag past cows, goats and women with huge straw baskets full of sticks and grasses on their backs. Already, with the pink of dawn in the hills, it is warm, and my skin is moist with sweat.

We all sprint enthusiastically for the first hour of the climb, although we are going almost straight uphill at a sharp angle. I am ashamed to admit to myself that I am competitive, as if this were a race with a prize at the end, but as quickly, I give up the notion of being first when I see that others, at least on this first day, are fitter, stronger, taking less water. There is only one who is older than I: Hans, a German, who climbed Kilimanjaro for his fiftieth birthday.

When we reach our campsite, the Sherpas have tea ready, our tents up and warm water with which to wash. All day, walking on stones and rocks, one foot, then the next, there was little to see except the trunks of many tall trees. Here now, in this clearing at dusk, the terraced fields arrange themselves below us, geometrically perfect. The air is quiet and my body gives thanks for a day of strenuous activity as I stretch out my long legs, remove my boots and drop my pack. An inchworm floats on its invisible string just next to me with only the gigantic Annapurna behind it, and what is small and what is big seem not so easy to know as they did this morning.

The dinner of rice and lentils, *daal bhat,* takes no getting used to; it is splendid from this first day on the mountain. I have brought dried apricots and trail mix in my pack as a supplement, but I am almost never hungry, except at meals. All of us, as instructed, try to drink as much liquid as we can, although we are only at about 7,500 feet. Hans, an engineer, trained for Kilimanjaro by running up and down twenty flights of stairs during his lunch hour. Already certain of dysentery, he carries a roll of toilet paper around his neck on a string and has the huge, sweet face of a Saint Bernard. The married couple is so exhausted they skip dinner and disappear into their tent.

That night in our sleeping bags, Ellen and I giggle at ourselves. Just lying down is a major gift, we say.

"I'm glad you hate football," I say.

"I think this is probably the last excitement in my life for a while," she says. "When I get back to St. Louis, I'm going to try to get pregnant." Both of us left husbands at home. Mine, in fact, is an ex-husband, the second one. We decide to make predictions about the trip, but fall asleep in the middle of our sentences in what is to become a pattern for the time ahead.

That night, I begin the first of many odd dreams, odd in the sense that even for the otherworldliness of dreams, the people and events seem out of place. The colors are wrong. The time sequence is at once too slow, too fast. There are tangential people from my convent child-hood: a nun who let me play with her veil; a priest prying a commun-ion wafer from the roof of my mouth. And then, miraculously, I am in a place with huge plumed birds of gold and green and red, flying on their backs or under my own power. I wake replenished, as if I'd devoured an additional meal during the night.

During the next few days we slip into a routine that offers many comforts, beginning with tea before dawn and ending with dinner and sleep at dusk. In between, we climb and stumble and soar among the hills and other wild things: great plants with exotic flowers whose names I do not need to know; birds with large fringed wingspans not unlike those in my dreams.

Ellen, Hans and I join with Ann, a woman from Washington just out of college, to form an agreeable foursome. Ellen, thirty-two, and Ann, twenty-one, are tiny, no more than five feet tall; Hans and I are huge by comparison, as well as old enough to be their parents. All of us notice that our clothes seem to be more wrinkled than that of the other three, and as time passes, we speak less and less about home. Age and size and clothing are somehow irrelevant. Even the fact that Ellen is Jewish and Hans German appears to be of no consequence. Eventually, we will discover that allowing ourselves to be captured by this present experience is what connects us: the surges of energy and their counterparts; an awareness of the pulse of muscles. Breath. Air. Water. And mountain. Always the challenges of the mountain.

One afternoon, when I stop in the woods to watch a tiny lizard-like creature slither among begonia-shaped leaves, my heart pounds beyond its rib cage, and I realize I have lost track of time. Others have been tired, taken altitude medication or antibiotics, but I have maintained myself on eight to ten liters of water a day. Ellen has dubbed me "best sleeper." But now I am overwhelmed with fatigue, and we are spread out on this trail full of boulders and soft mud, so that I see no one. I hum Souza's "Washington Post March" and perch myself on a smooth, flat rock. The leaves are nothing like begonias, I realize; they are too red, too big. As the lizard stops just aside of my boot, I imagine that our eyes meet. But it's more of a snake than a lizard as its feet have vanished and its skin shows an intricate yellow design. The red tongue darts in and out, beautiful against the yellow-green, and my heart rests and my breath comes more evenly as I am honored by this interaction, which in another time might have been frightening. From my pack, I retrieve the iodized water I have come to crave and am able to rise after a long drink. But my feet, uncooperative, develop a will of their own, taking one tiny step, then another in such utter slow motion that I am exasperated.

Kami, a young Sherpa, arrives and takes my pack. *Pani?* Water? he asks. Too tired to make my jaw speak, I nod. As he holds my arm and walks with me to the campsite, I am sure I will not be able to continue; I might be having a heart attack.

"How old you are?" he says in English.

"*Pachaas,*" I say. Fifty.

"*Pachaas?* Fifty?" He is sixteen. Like the other Sherpas, he has called me *didi* or older sister; now he rolls his eyes and says, *aamaa didi,* mother/older sister. He never again lets me out of his sight. Strong and determined and oh-so independent in my real life, I love this kindness. My heart attack is gone.

When he deposits me at my tent with *chiya,* tea, the others are already at dinner, and I realize that it is nearly sunset as clouds gather over the greenness, over the heat of the day. Hot, thirsty, I sleep, wake up and know that this is, in fact, my real life, that whatever went on before is an island of some memory with only patches of truth in it.

Ruth Harriet Jacobs

Swimming Past Seventy

*A*t the end of August with fall breathing on summer, I am the first morning swimmer at Craigville Beach on a cool Massachusetts day. Because I am seventy-one and the wind is cold, the young lifeguard huddled in her sweatshirt says, "Good for you," as I head into the water. Her voice is patronizing, as if I were a child. She has no way of knowing I rarely miss my daily swim, whatever the weather, and that swimming is vital to this week's attendance at the Craigville Conference Center's Cape Cod Writers' Conference.

As the shivering lifeguard carefully watches her old-woman swimmer, I wonder what her attitude toward me would be if only she knew how tame this swim is. Unlike now when I am a registered guest at Craigville, I have taken many others where I am not entitled to swim.

I think back four months to early May when I swam without life-guard, illegally, at the Wellesley College lake, frigid in the cool New England spring. This was my first outdoor swim of the year, and I was exhilarated by the exercise, fresh air and leafing trees around Lake Waban. I was also feeling quite superior, because, seven decades old, I plunged right in, unlike the two young Wellesley students standing on the dock, seeking the courage to get wet. Perhaps they were afraid of campus police. I knew they would not put me in jail for swimming.

The students finally jumped in and screamed, "It's cold!" and in a minute they ran out to their towels and clothes. I continued to swim, warmed by swimmer's high. This was the beginning of my daily out-door regimen continuing until late October. Most of my swims are at the college's lake or the town pond, but now and then, I go to salt-water to commune with the ocean and ocean birds. On Cape Cod, many of my ocean swims are stolen. That only increases my enjoy-ment.

As I swim this August day at Craigville, I have an imaginary con-versation with the lifeguard that I know would shock her. I confess to her the high adventures I have finding and crashing choice swim-ming spots from a glitzy hotel in Bar Harbor, Maine, to the suppos-edly well-guarded Boca Raton Hotel and Country Club in Florida and the classy Biltmore Hotel in Phoenix, Arizona, with its gorgeous outdoor pool designed by architect Frank Lloyd Wright.

I imagine saying to the lifeguard that actually some of my special beaches on her Cape Cod in Massachusetts are restricted to residents or hotel guests or have very high parking fees. None of this inhibits me, as I swim early in the morning or early evening after the money collectors or the inspectors of car stickers leave. I park at the beach club of an expensive Cape Cod hotel as if I belonged there and use its beach house with hot showers after my swim, and this during peak summer months. Nobody suspects that a gray-haired septuagenarian is a beach crasher.

Mostly I cannot afford, when paying my own way, to stay at hotels with swimming pools, so I stay at a youth hostel or el cheapo motel and swim at the best hotel in town. It is easy to walk in at my age if you act as if you belong there. I've never been stopped. As I lift a swim, I can understand the thrill that kleptomaniacs must get. I feel self-righteous, because if I don't swim I get stiff and cranky and can't effectively give the workshops and talks I do around the country to help elders and elder service providers. Of course, when my way is paid, I stay at hotels with good swimming pools, so I figure it all evens out on the hotel swimming scale.

Probably I would shock the young lifeguard if I told her about my swimming-free escapades. Or she might think I was bragging if I told her how, on Anna Maria Island off Bradenton, Florida, all the timid people stayed in the warm motel pool while I alone swam in the coolish January ocean, sister to the fish.

I must add, so as not to alarm, that when I am the sole swimmer, I do not go out over my head in case I get the rare cramp. I do not take chances with my life. When I was ten, I almost drowned in an ocean swim. That near fatality did not stop me from swimming, but it made me cautious. I urge caution on others.

Another thing I am cautious about on my legal and illegal swims is always to have a notebook and pen handy on shore, so I can rush out of the water to write a title, line or even a whole poem given to me by the universe and the swimming process. I have stood on shore shivering with the excitement of creation and the cold, as I record these gifts of air and water, rocks, trees, sand, birds, waves.

For me, swimming is not a social event. Mostly I swim alone, reaching my soul as I stroke rhythmically and long. I don't get bored as I vary my strokes: Australian crawl, sidestroke, backstroke and breast-stroke. Mountain ponds are my favorite places to swim; they have transposed me from the mundane to the profound. I meditate, pray, recite others' loved poems, as well as compose my own poems while swimming.

One glorious June, when I was a resident of the Edna St. Vincent Millay artists' retreat, Steepletop, the swimming pool Millay originally created in the cellar hole of an old building was not filled, because the mountain-stream water used was too cold for most people. So I scoured the area and found other places to swim where I could have mountain views. My legacy to future residents was to leave directions for how to find these holy swimming holes. I like to think artists are looking at the mountains while stroking and are inspired by the views and water.

Now, as I swim at Craigville, I remember my long swimming history and all the tales I could tell that lifeguard, who thinks it cute and brave that an old lady can swim on a windy, cold day. For example, at midlife, when there was a terrible crisis in my life, I was unable to relax to sleep. A wise psychiatrist, who knew better than to prescribe pills readily, asked me what I did for exercise. I told her I loved to swim and did so in good months but couldn't in the winter. She pointed out that indoor swimming pools were better than not swimming at all.

Like many patients, I was a "yes but" person. I said, "Doctor, but I don't like chlorine and swimming between walls."

"The chlorine won't kill you and you need the exercise for your anxiety and tension," she said.

Her pushing me into being a pool user in bad weather was probably worth more than all our hours of talking. However, I can't blame her for my crashing of hotel swimming pools when I am out of town and unable to use the pools at the colleges where I am affiliated.

Had I not had the release of swimming, I do not know how I could have gotten through the death of a child, the death of a marriage and the death of some dreams. The physical act of swimming, especially of swimming in nature, mobilizes endorphins in the body that raise our spirits. True, other forms of exercise will also contribute to our mental as well as physical health. But there is, I believe, a spiritual quality to being immersed in the elements in a rhythmic way. To be swimming at sunrise or sunset, or with a mist over the waters, truly brings us in tune with the universe.

Oh, we who swim past the age of seventy are outrageous and courageous. Our limbs are flexible; our spirits soar. While the young sun on the beach, we know the ecstasy of water. When we have a bit of trouble walking, we can still feel powerful as we skim over the waters. We feel more complete than canoeists and other boaters who are only on top of the water, not in it. And, of course, we despise motorboaters who pollute with gasoline and noise.

A swimmer must also be an environmentalist. You cannot love to swim in lakes, rivers and oceans without working to end the pollution that drains into them. If I want future generations to enjoy swimming outdoors, I must support projects and causes that insure this, such as the Environmental Defense Fund and the North American Lake Management Society at a national level, and my local groups, such as the Charles River Watershed Association. There are local groups all over the country.

I have also worked to convert other people to swimming. It is a gentle exercise, safe for all and especially good for my age peers. It often dismays me how hard it is to get women to put on bathing suits. They often feel that it is disgraceful not to have a perfect size-six body or to have such marks of age as enlarged leg veins, wrinkles or brown spots. I am obese and spotted, but I get so much benefit and joy from swimming that I don't care who looks at me in a bathing suit. In fact, I often have to dress and undress at the shore. Though I am reasonably careful to cover myself with a large towel when changing, I am sure my abundance of flesh shows now and then.

But while swimming outdoors, I do cover my face with sun block to prevent skin cancer, and I swim early morning or late in the day as advised by my dermatologist. Actually, I worry about the young Cape lifeguard and others who fail to use and renew sun block in this age of diminishing ozone layers. In my imaginary conversation with the lifeguard, and in actuality afterwards, I remind her to use sun block. She makes a dubious face, probably thinking me a nagging old woman. Yet I thank her graciously for watching me swim and leave to go to my poetry-writing class.

Perhaps I will write a poem about beach crashing and shock the rest of the poets, or at least make them laugh. Maybe I will persuade some who have not yet come to swim at this beach by telling how swimming fosters creativity. I can be a nautical nag.

I plan to swim and crash past seventy, past eighty and however long I am here, before I swim in that great ocean in the heavens. Swimming is about the only place left where they can't reach you on the phone to interrupt your rhythmic, healing thoughts and dialogue with yourself and the universe. There are more species of fish than land creatures. Swimmers survive.

Acknowledgments

Gifts of the Wild was edited by Faith Conlon, Ingrid Emerick and Jennie Goode, staff members at Seal Press whose collective experience at the press spans two decades. They gratefully acknowledge the many people whose talents and support made the preparation of this book possible, especially the following individuals:

Holly Morris, former staff editor, whose groundbreaking anthology about fishing launched the Seal Press series on women's outdoor adventures. Holly was instrumental in shaping and developing this series; among her lasting contributions is the name by which the imprint is now known, Adventura Books.

Barbara Wilson, a founder of Seal Press and its co-publisher for many years, whose encouragement and editorial work on many Adventura titles were invaluable. Her discovery of the Canadian classic, *The Curve of Time*, paved the way for its U.S. publication.

Rachel da Silva, also a founder of Seal Press, who met the challenge of editing the first collection of women's climbing and mountaineering stories with finesse and enthusiasm. Her role as a leader and mentor for women in the outdoors is inspirational.

Susan Rogers, who edited two acclaimed collections of women's original writing in the Adventura series. Her fine talents as an editor and anthologist and her ability to discover and encourage new voices have been profoundly significant.

Barbara Weiser and Judith Niemi, whose rich collection of women's canoeing stories remains unrivaled. Barbara's devoted efforts to promote women's outdoor literature continue today in her role as manager of Amazon Bookstore in Minneapolis; Judith has been equally dedicated as the director of Women in the Wilderness in St. Paul.

Jean Gould, whose outstanding anthology of older women's outdoor experiences truly demonstrates that the spirit of adventure knows no age limits.

Linda Lewis, Gretchen Legler, Jessica Maxwell and Patricia McCairen, authors of four superb books that have enriched the Adventura series. Each of these writers has helped transform the canon of outdoor literature by placing women at the center of the action.

Clare Conrad, gifted book designer and artist, who designed this collection and many others in the Adventura series. Clare's exquisite illustrations grace the pages of this book.

Susan Zwinger, naturalist, activist and indefatigable writer on the environment, whose work includes the award-winning *Stalking the Ice Dragon*. Susan provided an eloquent foreword to this collection.

Lee Damsky, who in her role as Seal's production director steered the book on a steady course, through sometimes chaotic waters. Her attention to the details of production, patience with last-minute changes and thoughtful editorial advice were enormously helpful.

Rain Grimes, editorial assistant extraordinaire, who handled voluminous correspondence and endless research with aplomb and humor.

Stacy M. Lewis, whose creative input at the outset of this editorial adventure was vastly important and greatly appreciated.

Staff members Laura Gronewold, Lynn Siniscalchi and Ellen Carlin, whose efforts to increase the visibility of women writers are unfailingly energetic and itelligent.

Lastly, the editors wish to thank all of the writers who have contributed to the Adventura series, including those who could not be included in this collection. Their abundant love of wild places is inspiring and their extraordinary vision and literary talent are enduring achievements.

Contributors

DEBORAH ABBOTT works as a psychotherapist in Santa Cruz, California, and as a whitewater raft guide with Environmental Traveling Companions, an accessible wilderness program. Her poems and stories have been widely anthologized. She is coeditor of the book *From Wedded Wife to Lesbian Life: Stories of Transformation* (The Crossing Press, 1995).

BARBARA BECKWITH has written about her outdoor adventures for the *New York Times*, the *Washington Post, U.S. Air, Backpacker Footnotes* and *Adirondack Life*, and about women's issues for *Ms., Essence, Sojourner* and *Women and Health*. An outdoorsperson all her life, she has backpacked in almost every mountain range in the continental U.S. and spent time rock climbing, whitewater canoeing, winter camping and bicycle-camping in France.

M. WYLIE BLANCHET (1891–1961) was born and educated in Montreal. At eighteen she abandoned a promising academic career to marry Geoffrey Blanchet. In 1922 the family moved west and settled on Vancouver Island where they purchased the *Caprice* for six hundred dollars. Four years later Geoffrey Blanchet was presumed dead when he never returned from a day trip on the *Caprice*. But the boat was recovered, and two years after being widowed, Muriel Blanchet embarked on the first of her family's fifteen voyages along the coast. In the winters Blanchet lived on Vancouver Island, homeschooling her children and supporting them by writing for magazines such as *Rudder, Pacific Yachting, Blackwoods* and the *Atlantic Monthly*. Blanchet was in the process of writing a second book, this time about their Vancouver Island home, when she died at the age of seventy.

LUCY JANE BLEDSOE is the author of the novel *Working Parts* (Seal Press, 1997) and of *Sweat: Stories and a Novella* (Seal Press, 1995), which was a Lambda Literary Award Finalist, and of two novels for young people, *Tracks in the Snow* (Holiday House, 1997) and *The Big Bike Race* (Holiday House, 1995). She has edited several anthologies, including *Gay Travels: A Literary Companion* (Whereabouts Press, 1998) and the forthcoming *Lesbian Travels: A Literary Companion*.

GABRIELLE DANIELS was born in New Orleans in 1954 and has lived in primarily urban areas of northern California. She is an alumna of Hedgebrook Farm, a writing retreat for women, where the greater part of the essay was written. She is completing work on a novel about how religion and spirituality play a part in the lives of four black women during an eighty-year period.

CANDANCE DEMPSEY is an adventure travel writer whose assignments have taken her everywhere from the rose-colored city of Petra in Jordan to the Masai Mara in Kenya. She writes about nature and the outdoors for numerous newspapers and magazines. A regular contributor to *Seattle* magazine and Seattle Sidewalk, she lives in Seattle with her husband, Mark Rosenblum, and her son, Jacob.

MARY RELINDES ELLIS was born and raised in northern Wisconsin and received her B.A. in English from the University of Minnesota. Her work has appeared in such magazines and anthologies as *Glimmer Train*, the *Bellingham Review*, the *Milwaukee Journal's WISCONSIN* magazine, *Uncommon Waters: Women Write About Fishing*, and *Bless Me Father: Stories of Catholic Childhood*. She currently resides in Western Wisconsin.

ALICE EVANS is a mother, poet, journalist and fiction writer living in Eugene, Oregon. She grew up in Kentucky and knobs of southern Indiana. Her work has been published in many venues, including *Poets and Writers* magazine and the anthology *Solo: On Her Own Adventure*.

BETSY ALDRICH GARLAND completed the high-ropes course at United Methodist Camp Aldersgate in Rhode Island while serving as a "senior" counselor to high school age students. The Executive Director of the Volunteer Center for Rhode Island from 1975–1995, she consults and trains widely in the nonprofit sector on volunteer and board management. A 1990 master of divinity graduate from Harvard University, she also works with communities of faith and professional volunteer administrators on the empowerment of laity. But to Marina, Celia and Alden, she is simply Grandma Betsy.

KATHLEEN GASPERINI is the publisher and editor of *W.I.G.* magazine, an art/sports/culture zine for women in general (Generation F). She writes several women's snowboarding columns for various publications, as well as stories on skiing, mountain biking and surfing. She is the co-founder of Boarding for Breast Cancer, an annual fundraising event.

JEAN GOULD is the editor of *Season of Adventure: Traveling Tales and Outdoor Journeys of Women Over 50* (Seal Press, 1996) and the author of the novel *Divorcing Your Grandmother* (William Morrow & Company, 1985) as well as a number of short stories, reviews and personal essays. A book review editor at *Sojourner: The Women's Forum*, she lives in Natick, Massachusetts.

SUE HARRINGTON'S climbing career started on the side of a dormitory building while attending the University of Rochester School of Nursing in New York State. From there she progressed to climbing rock on the Niagara escarpment and mountains across the United States. Her love for the outdoors inspired adventures in Alaska, Mexico, Canada, Argentina and Nepal. Sue received her master's degree from the University of Washington and now works as a family nurse practitioner in Seattle, Washington. The neighboring Cascades are her favorite mountains to explore.

LORIAN HEMINGWAY, half Cherokee Indian, was raised in the Deep South. Her many fishing pieces have appeared in the *New York Times*, *Sports Afield*, *America*, *Ocean Fantasy*, *Pacific Northwest* and *Horizon* magazines. Her novel, *Walking into the River* (Simon and Schuster, 1993), was nominated for the Mississippi Institute of Arts and Letters Award for Fiction and has been published in nine countries. Her latest work, *Walk on Water* (Simon and Schuster, 1997), is a fishing memoir. Hemingway is director of the Lorian Hemingway Short Story Competition held each July in Key West, Florida.

PAM HOUSTON'S collection of short stories, *Cowboys Are My Weakness* (W.W. Norton, 1993), was the winner of the 1993 Western States Book Award. She is the editor of *Women on Hunting* (Ecco, 1994), has published fiction in *Mirabella*, *Mademoiselle*, the *Mississippi Review* and *Best American Short Stories*; and nonfiction in the *New York Times*, *Outside*, *House and Garden*, *Elle* and *Allure*. Houston is a licensed river guide and lives in Creed, Colorado. Her new book, *Waltzing the Cat*, will be published by W.W. Norton in 1998.

RUTH HARRIET JACOBS, Ph.D. is a sociologist and gerontologist at the Wellesley

College Center for Research on Women. Her eight books include *Be an Outrageous Older Woman* (HarperCollins, 1997), *Women Who Touched My Life* (Kit Press, 1996), *Button Button Who Has the Button?* (Kit Press, 1996) and *Older Women Surviving and Thriving: A Group Leader's Manual* (Families International, 1988).

GRETCHEN LEGLER is the author of *All the Powerful Invisible Things: A Sportswoman's Notebook* (Seal Press, 1995). Her short stories and essays have appeared in the *Indiana Review, Grain, Hurricane Alice, American Nature Writing 1997, Orion* magazine, *Uncommon Waters: Women Write About Fishing* and *A Different Angle: Fly Fishing Stories by Women.* She won a Pushcart Prize in 1992 for her essay "Border Water," and another in 1997 for her essay "Gooseberry Marsh." She recently received a National Science Foundation Artists and Writers fellowship to travel to Antarctica. She teaches creative writing, women's studies and English at the University of Alaska, Anchorage.

SUSANNA LEVIN grew up in Long Beach, New York, and graduated from Swarthmore College in 1985. She wouldn't have survived either without sports: softball, soccer and volleyball. She has worked as an editor at several magazines including *McCalls, Walking* and *Women's Sports and Fitness.* She lives in Portland, Oregon.

LINDA LEWIS is a writer and editor who "got the religion of rowing at age forty." She has worked as a journalist, a book sales representative and a public relations specialist. She is the author of *Water's Edge: Women Who Push the Limits in Rowing, Kayaking and Canoeing* (Seal Press, 1992). She lives in Seattle.

ANN LINNEA is the author of *Deep Water Passage: A Spiritual Journey at Midlife* (Little, Brown & Company, 1995), a book that recounts her circumnavigation of Lake Superior, and is co-author of the award-winning *Teaching Kids to Love the Earth* (Pfeifer-Hamilton, 1990). She now lives with her school-aged children on an island in Puget Sound, where as co-founder of PeerSpirit she offers classes, seminars and consultations to people ready to make spirit-based change.

JESSICA MAXWELL, formerly a columnist for *Audubon* magazine, writes regularly for *Esquire* and *Forbes.* She is a contributor to *A Different Angle: Fly Fishing*

Stories by Women and is the author of *I Don't Know Why I Swallowed the Fly: My Fly Fishing Rookie Season* (Sasquatch Books, 1997) and *Femme d'Adventure: Travel Tales from Inner Montana to Outer Mongolia* (Seal Press, 1997). She lives on Oregon's McKenzie River.

PATRICIA C. MCCAIREN left her native New York City when she discovered whitewater rafting on a trip down the Colorado River through Grand Canyon. She has been rafting for more than twenty years, and worked as a guide for five years. She is the author of *Canyon Solitude: A Woman's Solo River Journey Through Grand Canyon* (Seal Press, 1998) and *River Runners' Recipes* (Menasha Ridge Press, 1994). She takes time to be in the wilderness as often as possible. She currently lives and works on McMurdo Base in Antarctica.

JUDITH MCDANIEL is a writer and activist who lives in Tucson, Arizona. Her most recent books are *The Lesbian Couples Guide* (HarperCollins, 1995) and a novel, *Yes I Said Yes I Will* (Naiad, 1996). Although the southwest desert and canyons have become home in a spiritual as well as physical sense, her canoe trips in the Saranacs were an early foundation for a deep and continuing connection with the out-of-doors.

KAREN A. MONK is a United Methodist clergywoman living in the Catskill Mountains of New York. She is co-pastor of parish in the city of Kingston, and is a spiritual director and child psychotherapist working with urban children. Abbey and Callie are currently unemployed, and keep her awake to the constant need for play in our lives.

HOLLY MORRIS is the editor of *Uncommon Waters: Women Write About Fishing* (Seal Press, 1991, 1998) and *A Different Angle: Fly Fishing Stories by Women* (Seal Press, 1995). Her writing has appeared in several anthologies and she is a columnist for ABCNEWS.com. Morris is the creator and host of the travel docu-biography television series, *Adventure Divas*. She lives in Seattle.

P. K. PRICE writes non-fiction, poetry and fiction. She has completed two novels, both set in the high desert of the Southwest. An attorney by training, she specializes in international law, acquistions and secured transactions. This allows her to support five horses, her gypsy nature and her love of the Colorado Plateau. She lives at her farm, Tortuga Cay, La Quita

Paloma in Mission, Texas.

HEATHER TREXLER REMOFF is a freelance writer and amateur naturalist who lives in Eagles Mere, Pennsylvania. Her published work has been featured in periodicals in the United States and Canada. She is also the author of *Sexual Choice* (E.P. Dutton, 1985) and *February Light: A Love Letter to the Seasons During a Year of Cancer and Recovery* (St. Martin's Press, 1997).

JANET RODDAN lives in Vancouver, British Columbia. She teaches high school students video production and languages and works as a rock guide in the summertime. She successfully survived turning forty and continues to play and explore in the mountains of British Columbia and Alberta.

SUSAN FOX ROGERS is the editor of *Another Wilderness: Notes From The New Outdoorswoman* (Seal Press, 1994, 1997), *Solo: On Her Own Adventure* (Seal Press, 1996), and *Alaska Passages: 20 Voices from Above the 54th Parallel* (Sasquatch Books, 1996). "One of the Boys" was the starting point for her young adult novel, *White Lies* (Alyson Books, 1998).

SHERRY SIMPSON earned an M.F.A. in creative nonfiction from the University of Alaska Fairbanks and now teaches journalism at UAF. Sasquatch Books will publish a collection of her essays, *The Way Winter Comes* in 1998 as part of the first annual Chinook Prize. She grew up in Juneau and lives in Fairbanks with her husband.

LIN SUTHERLAND is a freelance writer of twenty years, specializing in humor, travel and people. She has been published in numerous magazines, including *Field and Stream, International Living, Woman's Day* and *Outdoor Photographer*. She teaches travel writing at the University of Texas and horsemanship and riding at her family ranch in Austin, Texas.

WUANDA M.T. WALLS, an eighth-generation Pennsylvanian, has traveled extensively throughout the world. She has contributed articles to numerous publications, including *Essence, The Boston Globe, The Baltimore Sun Magainze, The Denver Post, Salt Lake City Tribune, Bon Appetit, Modern Maturity* and *Emerge*. She is a contributor to the anthologies *Season of Adventure: Traveling Tales and Outdoor Journeys of Women Over 50* and *Go Girl: The Black Woman's Book of Travel and Adventure*. She is currently writing a novel and a collection of inspirational essays.

LAURA WATERMAN is a New England climber. With her husband Guy Waterman she has co-authored *Forest and Crag: A History of Hiking, Trail Blazing, and Adventure in the Northeast Mountains* (Appalachian Mountain Club, 1989), *Yankee Rock and Ice: A History of Climbing in the Northeastern United States* (Stackpole Books, 1993) and the companion volumes, *Wilderness Ethics: Preserving the Spirit of Wilderness* (Countryman Press, 1993) and *Backwoods Ethics: Environmental Issues for Hikers and Campers* (Countryman Press, 1993). Her fiction has appeared in such literary magazines as *The American Literary Review*, *Folio*, *Blueline*, and is forthcoming in the *Eureka Literary Magazine*.

NAN WATKINS was born in Bucks County, Pennsylvania, of Welsh-American descent, studied music and German literature at the University of Munich and the Academy of Music in Vienna and has degrees in those subjects from Oberlin College and Johns Hopkins Univeristy. As a translator over the past twenty-five years, she has published various works in *Dimension*, *Asheville Poetry Review*, *Nexus* and *Oxygen*. As a musician and a composer, she is an active electronic-keyboard performer and organist, and has appeared on four recordings, the most recent of which is her first solo album of original compositions, *The Laugharne Poems*, released by Fern Hill Records in 1995. She has lived in the Great Smoky Mountains of North Carolina for the past twenty years, currently residing in Cullowhee, North Carolina, where she works as a reference librarian at Western Carolina Univeristy.

BETTY WETZEL grew up working on her father's weekly newspaper in Roundup, Montana, and graduated from the University of Montana School of Journalism. While rearing four children—three (liberated) daughters and a (liberated) son—she worked as a newspaper correspondent and freelance writer, which she continues today. While living in the East, she was the first publicity director of Oxfam-America in Boston. When her husband (of fifty-five years) was assigned to an education project in Bangladesh (then East Pakistan), she worked at the Southeast Asia Cholera Research Laboratory. Since returning to Montana, she has been a regular writer for *Montana Magazine* and is the author of *After You, Mark Twain* (Fulcrum Press, 1990). "Near Eighty—and Tall in the Saddle" was originally featured in the travel section of the *New York Times*.

Credits

"Spirit Walk" by Karen Monk first appeared in *Another Wilderness: Notes from the New Outdoorswoman*, edited by Susan Fox Rogers. Copyright © 1994, 1997 by Susan Fox Rogers. Reprinted with permission of the author.

"Walk on Water for Me" by Lorian Hemingway first appeared in *A Different Angle: Fly Fishing Stories By Women*, edited by Holly Morris. Copyright © 1995 by Holly Morris. Reprinted with permission of the author.

"Mike's Credo" by M. Wylie Blanchet is excerpted from *The Curve of Time*, by M. Wylie Blanchet. Copyright © 1968, 1993 by the estate for the late Muriel Wylie Blanchet. Reprinted with permission of Whitecap Books.

"Night Skates" by Susanna Levin first appeared in *Another Wilderness: Notes from the New Outdoorswoman*, edited by Susan Fox Rogers. Copyright © 1994, 1997 by Susan Fox Rogers. Reprinted with permission of the author.

"Mushrooms" by Gretchen Legler first appeared in *All the Powerful Invisible Things: A Sportswoman's Notebook*, by Gretchen Legler. Copyright © 1995 by Gretchen Legler. Reprinted with permission of the author.

"What Makes Grace Run" by Heather Trexler Remoff first appeared in *Season of Adventure: Traveling Tales and Outdoor Journeys of Women Over Fifty*, edited by Jean Gould. Copyright © 1996 by Jean Gould. Reprinted with permission of the author.

"April Fools on Polar Circus" by Janet Roddan first appeared in *Leading Out: Women Climbers Reaching for the Top*, edited by Rachel da Silva. Copyright © 1992 by Rachel da Silva. Reprinted with permission of the author.

"Superior Spirit" by Ann Linnea first appeared in *Another Wilderness: Notes from the New Outdoorswoman*, edited by Susan Fox Rogers. Copyright © 1994, 1997 by Susan Fox Rogers. Reprinted with permission of the author.

"Learning the Ropes" by Betsy Aldrich Garland first appeared in *Season of Adventure: Traveling Tales and Outdoor Journeys of Women Over Fifty*, edited by Jean Gould. Copyright © 1996 by Jean Gould. Reprinted with permission of the author.

"Monarchs and Manatees" by Jessica Maxwell is excerpted from "Day of the

BOOKS

ADVENTURA BOOKS is a popular series from Seal Press that celebrates the achievements and experiences of women adventurers, athletes, travelers and naturalists. Browse the list below—and discover the spirit of adventure through the female gaze.

CANYON SOLITUDE: *A Woman's Solo River Journey Through Grand Canyon*, by Patricia C. McCairen. $14.95, 1-58005-007-7.

ANOTHER WILDERNESS: *Notes from the New Outdoorswoman*, edited by Susan Fox Rogers. $16.00, 1-878067-30-3.

SOLO: *On Her Own Adventure*, edited by Susan Fox Rogers. $12.95, 1-878067-74-5.

SEASON OF ADVENTURE: *Traveling Tales and Outdoor Journeys of Women Over 50*, edited by Jean Gould. $15.95, 1-878067-81-8.

UNCOMMON WATERS: *Women Write About Fishing*, edited by Holly Morris. $16.95, 1-878067-76-1.

A DIFFERENT ANGLE: *Fly Fishing Stories by Women*, edited by Holly Morris. $22.95, cloth, 1-878067-63-X.

FEMME D'ADVENTURE: *Travel Tales from Inner Montana to Outer Mongolia*, by Jessica Maxwell. $14.00, 1-878067-98-2.

LEADING OUT: *Women Climbers Reaching for the Top*, edited by Rachel da Silva. $16.95, 1-878067-20-6.

RIVERS RUNNING FREE: *A Century of Women's Canoeing Adventures*, edited by Judith Niemi and Barbara Wieser. $16.95, 1-878067-90-7.

WATER'S EDGE: *Women Who Push the Limits in Rowing, Kayaking and Canoeing* by Linda Lewis. $14.95, 1-878067-18-4.

ALL THE POWERFUL INVISIBLE THINGS: *A Sportswoman's Notebook*, by Gretchen Legler. $12.95, paper, 1-878067-69-9.

THE CURVE OF TIME: *The Classic Memoir of a Woman and her Children who Explored the Coastal Waters of the Pacific Northwest*, by M. Wylie Blanchet. $14.95, 1-878067-27-3.

If you are unable to obtain a Seal Press title from a bookstore, or would like a free catalog of our books, please order from us directly by calling 1-800-754-0271. Visit our website at <www.sealpress.com>.